THE MUTOPIANS

BOOK ONE: IMPOSTER SYNDROME

SJ WHITBY

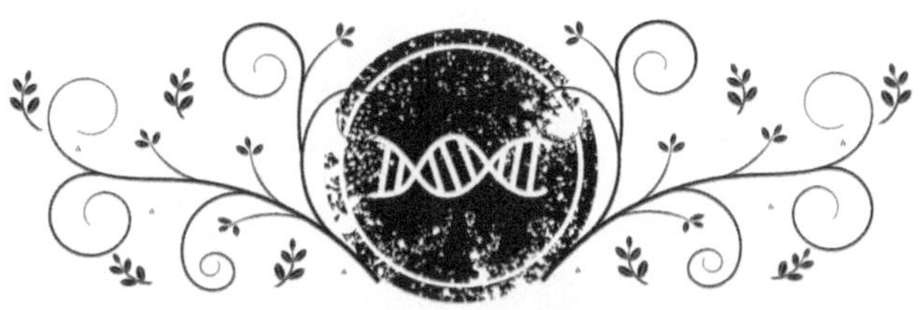

THE CUTE MUTANTS UNIVERSE

Cute Mutants Vol 1: Mutant Pride

Cute Mutants Vol 2: Young, Gifted and Queer

Cute Mutants Vol 3: The Demon Queer Saga

Cute Mutants Vol 4: The Sisterhood of Evil Mutants

Weapon UwU Vol 1: Godkillers

Cute Mutants Vol 5: Galaxy Brain

Shitty Mutants (Patreon Exclusive)

Project Himbo

Awakenings: A Cute Mutants Anthology

The Mutantsitters Club

CONTENT WARNINGS

This book contains subject matter that some readers may find distressing. Please be aware that The Mutopians Book 1: Imposter Syndrome contains on-page murder, warfare, blood, gore, bombings, poison, guns, and recreational use of alcohol. It also contains scenes of alien entities, body horror (including tentacles), hate groups (against mutants), conversion therapy (for mutant children), mind control, historical xenocide, psychological manipulation, an incident of suicide bombing, and hostage taking. There is significant discussion around depression and grief, including loss of partner, loss of parental figure, and loss of friends.

PREVIOUSLY...

This book takes place after the Cute Mutants series, and this section contains spoilers about those events. For more context and the full story, you can read the original series.

Once upon a time there was a girl named Emma Hall who gave her friends superpowers. This was entirely by accident and the source of these new abilities was a mystery. They joined together as a group called the Cute Mutants. The original team was:

Dylan aka Chatterbox, who could talk with objects

Alyse (Moodring) who could change shape with her moods

Bianca (Wraith), with strange creatures living in her chest

Lou (Glowstick), who glowed when turned on

Emma (Goddess), whose powers were unclear

Dani (Marvellous), who could use telekinesis when in pain

In the beginning, they wanted to help people and change the world, but they suffered attacks from those who wanted to use them. In one of these encounters, Wraith died at the hands of corporate security, which showed Dylan in particular what the stakes could be.

Later, they fought a mind-controlling preacher, whose daughter Violet (Penance) was also a mutant, capable of moving through secret passages in the world and turning herself into a bladed form. They saved Violet from her father, and she joined the team. They also fought a religious paramilitary organisation called Quietus, dedicated to wiping out mutants.

In time, they learned the truth of Emma's powers. She was the child of two incredibly powerful mutants: a telepath called Teen Spirit, and a reality warper called Heart of a Flower. In a last ditch effort to save mutants from extinction, Emma's mother had erased all knowledge of mutants from history. Heart of a Flower had twisted this act to also affect Emma's mother, and had been working in secret to build Emma and her friends up into a powerful force able to defeat humanity.

Once the Cute Mutants avoided Heart's plan, they found themselves in a desperate fight for survival against humanity. With many forces arrayed against them, they were desperate to find a place where mutants could be safe.

During this, Dylan began hearing a strange voice unlike that of the objects they usually spoke to. This voice led them to a cliffside where they learned it was an energy network named Cybele that lived within the planet. With the current state of the Earth, Cybele was very weak and the two mutants were presented with a chance to be reborn as a last ditch effort to save everything.

Both Dylan and Dani accepted, and were regenerated in a new plant form with new powers. They also learned of the ancient history of mutantkind, that the mutant species was born many years ago as defense against an alien race who preyed on humanity.

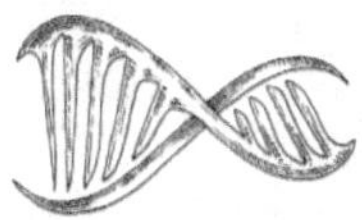

When they returned from their transformation, they found that a year had passed. Goddess was in an exhausting stalemate with a religious AI known as Michael. Many parts of the world had changed drastically in that time, with huge new cities built and many under the AI's sway. By this stage, due to how dangerous the world was for them, most mutants had been put into a form of cryosleep as protection. Emma had taken on all their powers, becoming the most powerful mutant in a long, long time.

The reunited Cute Mutants managed to defeat Michael, but Emma could not sustain her vast levels of power. The awful truth was that she would either destroy the earth in overload, or she could die and release all her power back to Cybele.

Emma chose to pass on, leaving the Cute Mutants in grief and disarray. However, Cybele used Emma's power to build an island for mutants to live on safely. It has been called Mutopia, and mutants from all around the world flock to it. In the aftermath of Emma's death, more and more mutants were awakened around the world with the power returning to the earth.

A year later, Cybele presented the group with a shocking surprise. She'd grown two children, plant-creatures who were part Cybele and partly created from Dylan and Dani's DNA. They were given to Dylan and Dani to raise.

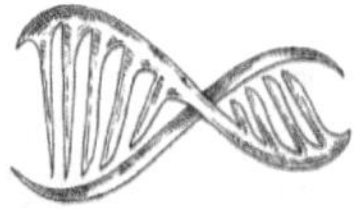

More recently, Violet aka Penance was stuck in a time loop, where she confronted the ghosts of her past, and came to a decision about her romantic feelings. On returning to Mutopia, she confessed her love for both Dylan and Dani, and they all entered into a relationship together.

During the same incident, a mysterious entity also came to Mutopia—the last surviving alien from the long-dead species that fought with Cybele. Xe is known as Tentacle Princess, and is now an ally of the mutants.

The world is still in a fragile state. The memory of the Dark Year is fresh in many people's minds, and the reality of a mutant nation is too much for some groups to ignore.

And the mutants are always waiting for the next threat to arrive...

CHAPTER 1
BACK ON MY BULLSHIT

SO THIS IS MY LIFE: it's two in the morning, and I'm hunched over my laptop like a gremlin, reading fanfic of myself. I actually like this time of day best because everything tends to shut the fuck up for a bit. Mutopia is great—having our own island home that's a proper mutant nation and everything—but it takes an awful lot of work to keep it running. I have to sit in meetings now. I've got my own team who goes around the world, doing covert shit. Ya boy has grown up and doesn't particularly fucking like it, to be quite honest.

There are too many problems to solve for one thing. Like an area of the English countryside which appears to be hallucinating, and people keep going in there and disappearing. Of course when any weird shit happens, people blame mutants, but this seems different. And yet it's still my problem, somehow.

So this is what counts as me time. When I can perch on the

end of the bed, read some ridiculous shit, and get pissed off at how inaccurate it is. I don't know who's writing this fic, but @shatterbox is either brilliant or an asshole. Maybe both, because those are two great tastes that taste great together. That's a joke directly from the fanfic, which is hella dirty. The writer seems to think I'm in a very different relationship than I am, although somehow they've figured out my whole OT3 thing with Dani and Violet. It's not something I was looking for, but at a certain point you can't deny chemistry, especially when it's fizzing between the three of you in an uncontrolled reaction.

I get why the author is obsessed with us. Take me, Dylan Taylor, aka Chatterbox, one genderfluid trashfire with powers of talking to objects. Connect me to Dani, aka Marvellous, one telekinetic lesbian ice queen. That's already instant drama, proper rivals-to-lovers shit. Put them through a bunch of near-death experiences—and actual death, just for kicks—have them almost fall apart and get back together in a romantic clifftop confession. Then you have Violet, aka Penance, the quiet, dark-haired woman with a shit-ton of religious angst, along with powers of teleportation and stabbing. She had a crush on me since we first met, while she was mind-controlled and trying to kill me. I mean seriously, the fanfic almost writes itself! After Dani and I died and came back, Violet's feelings for both of us got super intense. Right up until she had her own near-death experience and decided it was time to confess.

Now we're together in a relationship we're still finding the edges of. And despite being terrified of fucking it all up, I'm happy. There's still plenty of shit to deal with, and grief surging underneath it all like the tide, but Dani and Violet are my twin tethers. So, it makes sense the fanfic keeps going back to this. In the fic, everyone is very magically sexy, but in real life it was much more hesitant. Violet stumbling around her confession of love, me feeling so awkward that I leaned in and kissed her because it was easier than listening. It helped that my connection with Dani told me she was into it.

Then it was happening, and it was sweet and dizzying making out with two people at once. As a demisexual, I didn't expect that to ever happen but maybe this is cosmic balancing of the scales to make up for all the mad shit in my life.

Oh yeah, Dani's and my *connection.* One thing the fanfic has completely missed—in the whole million-plus words of it—is the alien makeover. I get it, it's probably too weird. They like to focus on the big dramatic fight scenes, all the angst, and so much sex it makes me exhausted just to read about. If I hadn't died and met Cybele, the alien energy being living in the centre of the world, and then got myself rebuilt with cool new plant powers, I might've called bullshit on it too.

It's not like we've been subtle since we got changed. First off, we destroyed some evil AI that was fucking with everyone's brains, then we bowled into the UN and did our *we speak for the trees* bit. If you've opened a news website at all in the last year or been on any social media, you've seen us. The mean, green half-mutant half-alien superhero machines. I guess it's a bit of a mouthful, and doesn't fit with the whole plot from the fic, which is actually pretty cool and involves us fighting an other-worldly menace—at least when we're not having epic arguments or fucking like it's our last night on earth. I page through the sex scenes because it's uncomfortable to read, especially since I finished a much tamer version a couple of hours ago.

The last part is where I lose it.

I lie back on the bed, looking at Dani's sleek head resting atop my chest. Violet is sprawled on my other side, pale limbs akimbo.

"What the fuck does akimbo mean?" I grumble.

It may seem greedy to some, to take these two beautiful women to my side and then into my bed. But I'm Chatterbox. I deserve it.

"The fuck is this shit? I don't deserve anything." I gnaw furiously on my thumbnail. Would you like a tour inside my brain, you fuck? Would you like to have all my insecurities shoved down your fucking throat? How does one person even love me, let alone two? What are the odds they're both going to end up with each other and cut me out of it, because god knows I can't even stomach myself so how do two brilliant, wonderful people end up—

"Hush." A soft voice murmurs in my ear and a hand trails down my spine, flattening all the tiny thorns that have sprung up and poked holes in my hoodie. "We both think you're amazing." Dani has always been gorgeous, distractingly so, with hazel eyes and perfect features and one of those pouting kiss-mouths authors are in love with. Since the alien makeover, she's developed a green tint to her tan skin, and is studded all over with tiny flowers that bloom with the seasons of her mood. They're sprouting from the collar of her long t-shirt even now.

"Sorry." I turn my head so Dani can kiss my offered cheek. "Did my stormy emotions wake you?"

"You're supposed to feel *love* down this connection." She nudges me. Our connection allows us to share certain images and thoughts and feelings. It's not a *direct* pipeline and we're not in any spooky mind-meld, but it has definitely brought us closer.

"I'm a bad learner. You know that." I run my fingers through her hair. "Takes me a long time to get certain things into my head."

"Yes, like I've told you so many damn times not to read that stupid fic." Dani reaches out and snaps the laptop closed. "It always makes you mad."

"Are you reading Shatterbox again?" Violet nestles in on my other side. She's not much over five foot tall, with a storm of dark curls that she sometimes tames. Her arms are warm from sleep and tiny golden blossoms spring up from my skin where she touches me. "I don't know why you do it."

"Because she's stubborn and a glutton for punishment." Dani tugs on my messy hair.

I run my fingers across the laptop. "It's weird reading about another me. I can't decide if they're more or less of an asshole."

"This is why you end up screaming when you should be sleeping," Violet says, mock-stern.

"It's hard enough to sleep at the best of times." The three of us turn at the voice from the doorway, although we know exactly who it is. "Even when you three aren't having loud conversations."

"Lys." I hold out my arms. She drifts towards us, losing coherence as she comes until she's little more than tears and dusk in the shape of a woman. "It's okay, it's okay."

The three of us get to our feet and surround the melancholy cloud, holding hands so we make a ring. Alyse has the power of physical transformation. While she's normally a tall, gorgeous Samoan woman, dark hair highlighted with honey, she can change to appear as anything she wants. Her default setting is to change based on mood, and since the woman she loved died saving the world, it's been... rough, to say the least. We all miss Emma. There isn't a day that goes past without it sinking its claws into me, shredding the emotional scars.

What would Emma do? How would she handle this situation? I should send her this meme, she'd think it's hilarious. What would Ems say about Dani and Violet, when she'd curl up on the couch with me to trade gossip.

"I can do the days," Alyse whispers. "Mostly, at least. But the nights are so fucking long."

"Come on, then." I reach my hand into the swirling cloud of her. "Let's find something to watch."

Our little house was grown from the island by Cybele. It's like a very large hollow tree trunk with interlocking branches and leaves as the ceiling. Flowers bloom on the inside, running along the walls. There's no glass in the windows, but if we're ever cold, leaves grow over seamlessly to shelter us. It's very beautiful, and Dani says it reminds her of the fairy stories she read growing up.

The last of our housemates stands yawning in the doorway to her bedroom, tail twitching around her shoulders. Marisol, aka Feral, is tall and lanky, with pricked up ears like a cat, and very sharp teeth and claws. She's very good at tearing out throats, but also at hugs.

"Y'all are very fucking loud," she observes, but with no malice at all. She links her arm through Dani's and joins us. This isn't what we do every night, but it's often enough. And this life might still be hard, but it's peaceful, and it's *ours*. We spent a long time running, hiding, and fighting with our backs up against the wall. Now we've got a place of our own, bought with our blood, Emma's sacrifice, and Cybele's power. The planet is awake again, and she's pissed, and we're her chosen defenders.

Except right now, we're a bunch of tired and sad people, all curled up together on a king-size bed and watching *Ted Lasso* on an oversized TV. It'd be cool to have someone like him helping out—unfailingly positive, my own personal cheerleader. Ray, the President of Mutopia, is wicked smart and surprisingly kind, but they're run ragged and are neck-deep in political bullshit. I'm technically part of the so-called government, but the only title I've ever been granted was Feral calling me the Minster of Fucking Around and Finding Out. We've got our own nation, but there are still enemies out there, and humanity's still pretty focused on watching the planet go down in flames. It'd be nice to have some dude turn up offering biscuits, and telling us we're doing great.

Although I don't think even Ted could stay cheerful in the face of my death toll. There are so many names it's hard to keep track. So I run through them in my head, some horrible rosary of the people I've failed. Batty, Wraith, Reverie, Leapfrog, Skye Eight, Skye Nine, Necrothoticon, Abby, Goddess. Those are just the ones I was *close* to. My teammates. If I widen the list to include every mutant who died on my watch, it becomes a parade of ghosts, unstoppable and unending. That's the worst joke about the fanfic. I'm not a superhero. I'm a chaotic idiot with superpowers, who's desperate and keeps fighting because the alternative is worse.

"Shh." Dani rubs my back in slow, rhythmic strokes while Violet presses a kiss to my forehead. Great. I'm so broken and greedy I need two people to comfort me in stereo. "None of that. You're not responsible for the entire world. You can't stop all the bad things."

"I want to, though," I mutter.

"We know." Violet curls her fingers around the back of my neck and rests her forehead against my cheek. "But it's literally impossible, so try and be proud of saving the world, huh?"

"Half-ass job of saving." Except I'm smiling, just a little, and I decide to soak up the comfort instead of pushing it away. I relax back onto the bed, only half-watching the TV, where I get four minutes of zoned-out cat in a sunbeam bliss before the kids start crying.

Oh, yeah. The fanfic misses that one too. Probably because

the baby twist is gross. Although they're not exactly babies, but alien creatures built from Dani's and my DNA and given to us as…

Well, Cybele is cryptic about that. I have guesses, but she won't even confirm if I'm right. They're definitely not like human kids. Both Pear and Mrs. Kim agree on that, but they've also thrown themselves into the grandparent thing, which is pretty cool. Less cool is the kids waking in the night, upset because they're hyperaware to the suffering of the planet.

"I'll do it," Dani murmurs against my cheek.

"No, I can." This is mostly said with the assumption that Dani will insist on doing it herself. Which she does, but the emotional tether between us pulses with amusement as she picks up my vibes.

"You look after Lys." She plants a final kiss on my head and disappears.

She isn't gone long, but comes back with the twins, Willow and Soo-yeon. Again, they're not *precisely* human, but the genetics thing really came through. They look mostly like Dani, which is lucky for them.

"You're sad again, Aunty Lys." They bounce into her lap and entwine their arms around her. Like Dani and I, they've got plant powers, so entwine is fairly literal. Alyse ends up in a cocoon of vines and sweet-smelling flowers. "We could tell. It's all through the network. But it's okay. Sometimes you need to be sad, because sad things happen."

Wow, these precocious children are already better at comforting than me.

At some point, Dani takes them back to bed, but I'm already drifting off. When she returns, I pop open one eye as she collapses down beside me. I hold out one arm and she nestles into me, Violet curled against my back.

Alyse is finally asleep too, with Feral half-draped over her, purring very faintly as she slumbers. The TV is still playing softly, some loop of late-night ambient music that's supposed to help with vibes. I don't know if anything can truly soothe my racing brain, but the four people around me definitely help. Our team is large and sprawling now, but this little group is my lifeline. Which means I need to protect them. So this is me, Dylan Taylor, human incarnation of a hungry forest. And if you fuck with the people I love, I'll end your life.

BEING LATE to sleep means I'm the last to wake the next morning. The others are already up, sitting on the edge of the bed, staring transfixed at the television.

"What's happening?" I yawn and stretch and read for Dani.

"Dills..." The tone in her voice is enough to alarm me, even without the pulsing dread through our emotional connection.

I'm immediately alert, my body humming. "Fuck. Who's in danger?"

"It's something else."

I slide off the bed and walk around to see the TV properly. A news report is playing, showing a fancy apartment building in a city I don't recognise. Police cars are parked outside, along with vans with the GIC logo on the side. This is the Global Intelligence Committee, which sounds boring as fuck, but is the new human organisation responsible for monitoring us. Which means this story is mutant-related.

"...CCTV footage confirms the suspect to be Dylan Jean Taylor, also known as the mutant Chatterbox, founder of

Mutopia and who some consider to be the most dangerous entity on the planet."

Fucking flatterers. The screen changes to show me. It's not great quality, and I'm obviously being suspicious as fuck, sneaking down the hallway of the building with my hood up. I've got my sword strapped to my back, which I don't usually do, but the real problem is—

"That's not me," I say. "I was never there."

"Obviously not." Dani frowns at me. The connection between us is flooded with anxiety, which makes my skin prickle. She's picking at the nails on her left hand. Whatever this is, it's serious.

"A GIC spokesperson confirmed they would reach out to Mutopia for questioning, although the ongoing political situation makes it fraught. However, given a crime of this nature and magnitude, it cannot go unchallenged."

"What crime? The fuck did I do?" I stare at the others.

It's the TV that answers first. "To recap our top story, wealthy philanthropist Derek Lancelot was murdered last night in his high-security apartment by someone who investigators believe to be—"

Oh shit. *Did* I do that?

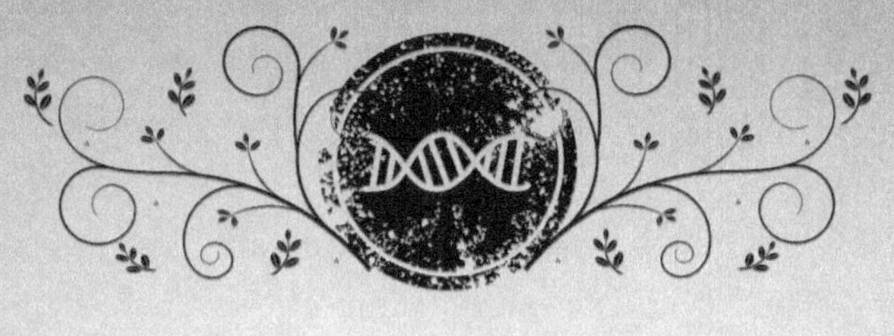

CHAPTER 2

1312 REASONS TO AVOID TALKING TO LAW ENFORCEMENT

I'M STARING at the image of a dead man on screen. Someone I apparently killed. I have no memory of it, but it would definitely be on brand. They call Lancelot a philanthropist, but his causes are virulently anti-mutant. I can't pretend I'm sad about his death, but I'd be happier if I remembered it.

"It wasn't you." Dani's voice is calm. "I'd know if you left in the night." The connection between us swirls with fragments of doubt, which makes me flush.

"Lancelot's a prick," Feral's claws *snick* out and retract again.

"I don't think I killed him." Please don't let murdery memory loss be a fun new problem.

"Not saying you did." Her eyes meet mine. "But my thanks go to our anonymous benefactor."

"Dani, are you sure it wasn't me?" I sit beside her on the bed, taking her hands.

"I would have felt you leave." Her eyes and our connection tell a slightly different story. "But it's the sort of thing you might do. The shit he's done…"

"I'm not playing the loose cannon card anymore." Although I did say I wanted Lancelot dead at our last council meeting. Except with more swearing. "We would have agreed on it."

"And Dilly wouldn't have done it himself." Violet pats Dani's shoulder. "She would've sent someone far more stealthy. I could've cut his throat without anyone knowing a thing. One blade extended in the dark."

We're watching the footage again. Me, creeping. Even in the low-quality camera you can see the green of my skin, and the faded blue of my hoodie.

"I'm not going to be caught on CCTV. Not when Keepaway can teleport me into the fucking room." It's hard not to sneer, but the lid I usually keep on my rage is rattling. "Someone's *framing* me. I don't know how, but some clone of me with a shitty Gamora paint job wants me to go down."

"It really does look like you." Dani's in analysis mode. "They even walk the same way."

"No flowers. No thorns."

"You don't always have those visible. Dylan, people are going to believe this. One of the world's most famous mutants committing murder on camera."

"I know." My hands make fists involuntarily. Sadly, this isn't a problem I can punch. Or stab. Lancelot is a problem *someone* stabbed, and they did us a favour honestly. That prick has too much money, and a hard-on for mutant extinction. *AI won't get the chance to kill us, because mutants will do it first.* That's his most famous quote. Even though a fucking AI called Michael almost got there first, and mutants saved the day.

"Still not sad about it," Feral says. "Lancelot's dead, and Dylan wasn't involved. One less problem in the world."

"Except there's someone out there with Dylan's face." Alyse pats my cheek. "Which is a very good face, but not for being public enemy number one."

"You need to talk to Ray," Dani says. "If they haven't already heard."

As if she jinxed it, my phone buzzes. Time to meet the boss.

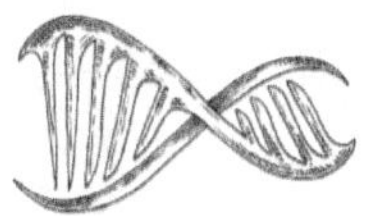

"DYLAN, please tell me you didn't do this."

Ray's office should be lovely and spacious, with a beautiful view of the sea and the sky. Except it's full of books and papers, so many you feel assaulted by information. Ray themself stands by the window, hands in the pockets of their impeccably tailored suit. They look disapproving, which I completely understand. Being the Black nonbinary president of one of the most analysed and fought-over nations on the planet is a difficult job at the best of times. And having one of your most notorious citizens as a murder suspect is not making their life easier.

"Of course I didn't." I'm trying to downshift my frustration.

"No, you'd send one of your assassin types. Penance is the most obvious choice, but you're dating her now, so maybe you'd send the alien one with all the arms."

The alien Ray's referring to is called Tentacle Princess, and xe is another one of my problems. Everyone thinks xe's very sweet, and xe *seems* eager to please, but at the same time xe's literally the last descendent of a species who almost wiped out humanity. The alien part of *me* keeps getting this low-level threat response every time I look at xer.

"Or I could talk an object into doing it." My mouth twitches. My original power was speaking with objects, but since the whole alien rebirth, things don't work like they used to. I've still got connections to my old objects, but everything else is glitchy. "And, fuck, I'd make it look like an accident at least. I wouldn't waltz in the front door with a sword."

"The weapon you have been watching so repetitively is also an imposter." My own blade, Onimaru Kunitsuna, floats into the room. He's a badass samurai sword who's been with me for most of my drama. "I would not consent to being strapped on in such a fashion, and the markings on the hilt are wrong."

"Fake me, fake sword," I tell Ray, as Oni circles around to hover behind me. "Someone wants us to look bad."

"That's always the case. This feels more subtle." They frown. "I don't like it."

"I was going to run off half-cocked and start investigating on my own, like a himbo Nancy Drew," I admit. "But Dani and Violet convinced me to talk to you first."

"This is why you need two of them." Finally, I get a smile out of Ray. "One person isn't enough to talk you down."

"I am very fucking high-maintenance." I laugh despite everything.

"And we're in a very fucking difficult situation," they respond, back to deadpan.

"Dani thinks I should front-foot it. Pop into the GIC, plead my case."

"And if they try to detain you?"

"We shall not stand for such things," Oni tells me.

I flex my fingers, willing my thorns to die back down. "I'll be my sweetest and most charming self. Which I can be, Ray, you've seen it. Occasionally."

"Not so much with authority figures. You've got a bit of a

history there." They take their seat, and I collapse awkwardly into another, one leg up over the side.

"Okay, fair. But you know how I feel about Mutopia. I don't want to get all fucking American about it and start chanting MU! ESS! AY! at every goddamn opportunity, but mutants need this place. I'm not going to burn that all down."

"I'm worried this is the first shot in a new, subtle war." Ray steeples their fingertips together and regards me over them, giving me such school principal vibes I want to slump even lower in my chair. "They're discrediting you for a reason."

"Yeah, I'm the most likely to pop off and fucking stab a prick."

They shake their head with the world's tiniest smile. "You're a powerful and charismatic leader. People know you. People follow you. They come to Mutopia because of you. If our enemies can smear you and tear you down, it will—"

I pretend to dramatically fall out of my chair. "Ray, are you complimenting me?"

"I'm attempting to explain my thought process." They're genuinely smiling now, wide and bright and very unlike them. It makes me nervous. "So I'll say yes to the GIC visit. We need a glimpse into what they're thinking. I'll send Fadilah with you. She's a lawyer by trade, powers of mood stabilisation via Cybele. I'm sending her for legal reasons, not to take the edges off you. For that, take Dani and Violet. They're the only ones who can keep you in line."

"And if it all goes to shit?" I ask.

Oni hums contentedly, because this is his happy place. We don't go into the field much anymore, and he's antsy. It's not like we ran out of villains. We're just supposed to deal with them differently now.

Ray fixes me with another stern look. "The three of you are

more than capable of handling anything the GIC can throw at you. Try not to attack anyone, but come home safely. Is that a line you can walk?"

"Yes, Ray." My knee jiggles restlessly. "I'm nervous now that I've got the go-ahead."

"Dylan, you're walking into the arms of one of our greatest enemies under suspicion of murder. You're *supposed* to be nervous."

"Don't like doing what I'm supposed to," I mutter, but Ray waves me out of their office. They've got a long to-do list and apparently don't have time to coddle me.

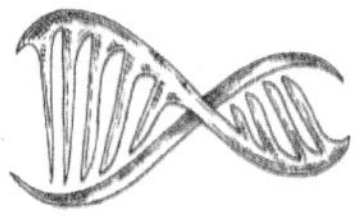

DANI'S already picked up on the outline of the plan over our connection, so she's waiting with Violet outside the government building.

"Ray says I'm amazing." I do jazz hands. "And that's why everyone's after me."

"Did Ray say those exact words?" Dani raises an eyebrow. "I mean, they're correct, but—"

"I'm paraphrasing, because they're very long-winded. But the important points are that they love me, and the mission's a go. We're supposed to take a lawyer to babysit us, while we figure out what the GIC knows, how serious they are, all that shit."

"I'm very much hoping you don't need a babysitter." I turn around to see a tall woman standing there, dressed in a suit as impeccable as Ray's. She's got dark skin, and a rich, warm voice. It would go over great in a courtroom. "I'm Fadilah, or Soother. Ray says I'm supposed to help you."

"That was quick." I narrow my eyes. "Wait, when did Ray organise this?"

"Before they met with you." Soother smiles wide.

"They *are* very sneaky." I nod. "So we're going straight in?"

"We need to make a good impression," Soother says. "Which means dressing the part."

"Really?" I complain.

Soother also has quite the line in stern looks. Maybe she takes lessons from Ray. "We want them to take us seriously. Wearing nothing but a hoodie is not the right move."

I sulk about it, but there are upsides to this plan. Once we're all dressed and ready, I get to see both Dani and Violet looking all spiffy. What is it with women and suits? There's something about it that short-circuits my brain a little bit. I can't look directly at them, like staring into the sun. Dani knows this of course, and she keeps standing there in ways that are distracting. I somehow manage to completely circumvent this rule, probably because I'm not a woman. I feel like I've been stuffed into a black cloth sack.

"You look hot," Dani tells me.

"I look fucking uncomfortable." My tone is far more savage than it has any right to be.

"It's actually adorable." Violet is taking far too much pleasure from this. In fact, both of them are, and it's downgrading their own hotness quite honestly.

"We don't have time for this." I fidget at the collar and Dani plucks my hand away. "Where the hell is Keepaway?"

"Here." They step out of thin air, a slim figure with close-cropped hair. They're our mutant teleporter, able to send anyone around the world with a touch. "Just admiring how good the four of you look. Especially you, Dilly."

"Oh hush." I give them a half-hearted scowl. "I preferred it when you were scared of me."

"It's okay to be nervous," Dani says quietly to me. "We're here for you."

Except she's not *exactly* here for me, because Keepaway has popped her off around the world.

"You do look cute." They wink at me, and tap my shoulder.

The world disappears around me, and for a brief moment I'm precisely nowhere. When it blinks back into existence, I'm in a plain white room with a table and two rows of chairs.

Along with my crew, who are sitting all demure, there are three other people in the room. There's a buff Indian woman in military gear who's obviously got the job of 'muscle,' and a slender Black guy with glasses and a fancy-looking tablet. Standing at the back, leaning against the wall as if she's trying to be innocuous, is a white woman with startling red hair and a slightly downturned mouth.

I'm the last to arrive, so I take my own seat with the others.

Fadilah is already mid-conversation. "—which is to say that Mx. Taylor's cooperation signals our desire to work together to resolve this unfortunate incident."

I lift my hand in the world's most awkward wave, twitch my fingers a couple of times and then drop it to my side. Fuck me. I hate this shit. I'm pretty sure the collar of the shirt got smaller during teleportation.

"A bold move to show up here," Buffy says. "We expected a proxy."

"Mx. Taylor has nothing to hide," Fadilah says. "There are a number of witnesses who can vouch for their presence on Mutopia during the time the crime was committed. Our island is not overrun with CCTV cameras—unlike yours—but people are willing to be deposed."

"All mutants, presumably?" Glasses blinks at us. "You can understand why we might be sceptical of said testimony, given Mx. Taylor's importance to mutantkind."

"If it wasn't you, who was it?" Buffy asks. "Do you have a clone running around?"

"There's no *clone*," Fadilah says.

Time for me to jump in. "Honestly, at this point, who fucking knows? I've been shot and stabbed enough times that maybe a mad scientist did clone me. Which I'd be extremely pissed off about, for the record, and I'd want to find them before you did."

"Or it could be another mutant," Glasses says. "You have a shapeshifter on the island, correct?"

I literally slap my forehead, which is not a good look. "Why would I send someone who looks like me to commit murder? There's no logic there. If we had a shapeshifter do it, why not make them look like a cop?"

"That's the assessment of our resident expert on you." Glasses taps away on his tablet. "They believe you'd have been more subtle and we'd never have known it was murder. They admit there's a small possibility that you knew that, and did it anyway because you wanted to—and I quote—fuck with everyone, but the risk seems too great."

"The risk is definitely too great." My voice is quiet, but everyone hears it. "Feels weird, there being an expert on *me* out there. Do I get to meet them and say hi?"

Glasses flinches, just a tiny bit, as if he was about to turn around and thought better of it. My gaze travels to the redhead against the wall, whose expression hasn't shifted.

"You have a name, expert?"

"Agent Decker." Her expression doesn't change. "But despite

my assessment, we have a problem that's difficult to explain away. Your DNA was found at the scene."

Dani's eyes narrow. "DNA in what form?"

"Skin cell fragments. Hair follicles."

"You realise Dylan's not even human anymore."

Glasses coughs apologetically. "Yet their DNA still sequences. This has been confirmed by our laboratories multiple times."

Violet literally growls, which takes me by surprise. She lunges forward, her hand unfolding until it's a ring of blades at the GIC man's neck. "When the *fuck* did you take Dylan's DNA?"

The buff woman goes for her gun, which is a terrible decision. A split-second later, Dani's at her throat, and the woman's gun hand is bleeding from a series of jagged thorn wounds.

Someone's banging at the door. This is about to turn into a clusterfuck.

"Everyone calm the fuck down," I shout. It's not like me to be the voice of reason. I'm still seated, cool as a fucking cucumber.

"Please." Soother looks taken aback by how fast this turned. "Lower your weapons. That includes mutants and humans. There's no need for this to escalate further. Obviously the GIC shouldn't have taken Dylan's DNA. Mistakes were made."

Everyone backs down and retreats to their side of the table. I'm kinda impressed when the buff woman wraps her jacket around her bloody hand instead of leaving the room.

Glasses dabs at his throat nervously, checking his fingertips for blood. "We exist to monitor global threats. Like it or not, you exist in that category. And if we had not previously acquired your DNA, we couldn't have identified the samples from the scene."

"You could have planted it yourself." Dani's still furious and it's pulsing down our connection like a fever. "You've got anti-mutant fanatics who'd love to smear us."

"We have *rigorous* internal processes," Glasses snaps. "No samples have been mislaid."

"It wasn't me." I put my hands flat on the table, and look the guy directly in the eye. "I can't fucking *prove it,* and I can't explain the DNA away, but I didn't do it."

Buffy's nursing her injured hand. "Would you allow yourself to be taken into custody while we confirm this?"

"That's fucking hilarious," Dani sneers.

Soother lifts her hands again. Her power must be working overtime. "Please don't waste our time. We came to you in good faith, but if you won't accept testimony from mutants on the island, we'll continue to investigate on our own."

"That's unacceptable," Glasses says. "You cannot be trusted to investigate a mutant."

"Fuck it, I'm done here." I get to my feet. "Keepaway, we're out."

They reappear in the room, right beside me. As they place their hand to my back, the pale redhead says my name, but I don't get to hear what bullshit this so-called expert comes out with next.

CHAPTER 3
THIS ISN'T HOW MURDER MYSTERIES ARE SUPPOSED TO WORK

"IT WAS a colossal fucking waste of time," I snap at Ray.

"Not entirely." Dani's much calmer now that we're back home. "We learned that whoever's pretending to be you has access to your DNA. That the GIC does too. I'd put money on some fucked up faction of theirs being responsible."

"Probably. They do hate me quite a lot." I pull a face. "And I'm apparently so charming!"

Ray's staring out the window, as if the answers float between sea and sky. "It's hard to imagine this is dealt with, isn't it?"

Dani nods. "I don't know if it's the GIC trying to frame him, or some mysterious creep. Either way, this is going to get worse before it gets better."

"Story of my life." I scowl.

I leave Dani and Ray to rehash all the damn possibilities,

while I swing by my parent's house to collect Willow and Soo-yeon. I doubt Pear was expecting grandkids in their future, especially not precocious little alien flower creatures, but they're loving it. The twins look mostly human, or at least the Dani-and-me equivalent, with greenish skin and flowers in their hair. They're the size of small toddlers, but they do not behave like that at all. It threw everyone when the kids showed up talking in complete sentences, not to mention the way they can shoot vines out of their hands, and how they've recently learned to vanish right in front of you.

I find everyone in the kitchen, where Mrs. Kim is doing 'baking' with them. The kids are obsessed with baking and seem to think it's the next best thing to actual magic, which they claim used to be 'a thing' but now it's not because 'the wrong people died.' Honestly, the shit they come out makes my head spin.

"Add more of the chocolate things, Halmeoni," Willow says importantly, balancing precariously on their stool.

"It should be more chocolate than cookie." Soo-yeon bends over the bowl. "Or biscuit?"

"We say biscuit, because we're from New Zealand," Mrs. Kim says.

Willow catches sight of me lurking in the doorway. "Pear, are we from New Zealand? Or are we from Mutopia? Do Mutopians say biscuit or cookie?"

"We say either." I grin at them. "The important thing is how they taste."

"Is that supposed to be profound?" Soo-yeon asks me.

"Fuck knows," I say, and get a stern look from Mrs. Kim about *language*. The thing is, these aren't ordinary kids, because as far as I'm aware, babies don't diss you about your lack of fucking profundity.

"Grandpear, why did you raise Pear to say language so much?" Willow asks.

"You can call me Ness, for the hundredth time." My parent joins me at the bench where we look over the chaos of ingredients. I get why they don't like the name Grandpear or even referencing the concept of grandparents. Being called Pear makes me feel old and withered like an ancient tree who's well past their fruit-bearing years. The twins have really latched onto the concept of family, and take great pleasure in detailing the numerous aunts they have, along with their Uncle Lou.

"Is everything okay?" Mrs. Kim asks me. "We saw the news."

"I didn't do it."

Pear gives me a slightly surprised look, which is fucking rude of them. I give them all my ancient wisdom and poke my tongue out.

Mrs. Kim looks up from the bowl. "I didn't think so. You're far too smart for that, Dylan. You would've done it quietly, in the night, and nobody would have known anything was wrong."

Pear's still frowning, and it makes me uneasy, and I end up talking much louder than I'd like.

"Everyone keeps being so shocked. Like I make a habit of sneaking around k-wording people in secret."

"What's k-wording?" Willow whispers loudly.

"There are lots of k-words." Soo-yeon's eyes flick in my direction. "But I think they mean kill, which we're apparently not allowed to do, even if it's people who are hurting Green Mum."

Green Mum is obviously Cybele, who I'm hesitant to take advice from. I give Pear a helpless look, because even if I read parenting books—which I don't do as much as I need to—

they've been no help with children who want to take bloody revenge for environmental catastrophes.

"The point is, none of us are k-wording anyone," I tell everyone. It's mostly true, at least in regards to the specific people in this specific room. There is a team of people who have definitely k-worded on my very clear instructions. It's not something I'm proud of, but my life has gotten very complicated and confusing, and sometimes k-wording solves certain intractable problems.

"What's going on then?" Pear asks. "On the news, they're saying—"

I'm still slightly annoyed by their reaction. There's been tension between us at times due to some of my more violent choices, but I'm trying to keep a handle on things. Even still, I bite off the first few words of my sentence a little too hard. "I know. Someone's trying to frame me. Now the GIC would like my head removed, just to make their damn lives easier."

"You know that won't kill you," Soo-yeon tells me. "The only way to kill you is—"

"Yes, Soo, but I don't want people to know that because it saves that little surprise for later. A trick up my sleeve. Or inside my hood."

Nobody appreciates my joke, especially not Pear. It's probably in bad taste, given that I've already died once and spent a whole year being regrown, during which time they mourned me.

"I don't like the idea of someone running around with your face." Pear frowns at me.

"It's not my fault! It's not like I entered some steal-my-face competition online."

"But what are they up to?"

I've got no idea how to answer that question, because my

only guesses are wild stabs in the ominous dark. I'm saved by Dani showing up.

"Hello, darlings." She kisses me first, and then plants a kiss on each twin's petal-strewn head. "How long until the biscuits are ready?"

"They're only just in the oven," Mrs. Kim said.

"Chocolate chip, right?" Dani scoops Willow up into her arms. "Like I asked for?"

"They're my favourite too," Violet says from the doorway.

"Bonus Mum!" Soo-yeon bounds across the room and hurls themself bodily at Violet, who catches them comfortably. It's what they started calling Violet the moment the three of us got together. Everyone except her thinks it's hilarious. She doesn't mind it when the twins do it. They have a way of getting into your heart.

"What have you two rascals been up to?" Violet asks.

"Baking and discussing the morality of killing people," Soo-yeon says.

"That seems very on brand." Violet winks at me. "You doing okay, Dills?"

"Fine." I shrug. "Waiting for everything to blow up. Feels like any other day really."

Dani is scraping the bowl of the dregs of cookie dough, although Willow steals a good portion of it. It's the domestic bliss portion of our lives, which makes me feel both sad and happy at the same time. I never imagined I could have all these mundane and beautiful things with me pasted clumsily into the middle. It's wonderful, but there's a hole where Emma should be. It'sJ not about losing the power source that enabled us all to be more. One of my best friends is gone. Someone I loved so fiercely it took my breath away. And we both fucked things up pretty good on our way towards cataclysm, and there's never going to be a chance to fix any of that. I'll never get to hug her again, never collapse into the seat beside her and see that look of delight in her eyes when she realises it's me. She's been gone over a year, and while time papers over the cracks in my heart, I still feel them when I breathe.

It seems like everyone picks up on my vibes, because I'm surrounded by the whole group and everyone's hugging me. It gives me a few moments to let the emotion pool in my heart and then ebb out. When we're done, I do feel better. Mostly. The rest of the evening is far more chill, but I still feel vaguely unsettled. This malevolent twin is haunting me. What the fuck are they up to?

I go to bed earlier than usual and drift off to sleep, alone in a bed that seems enormous without the other two.

I WAKE to panic surging down the connection between me and Dani. I'm still alone in the bed, which is odd because it's fucking—

Three in the morning?

"Keepaway!"

Seconds later, they're in the room with me. It's rude to constantly use them as my ride, but they do have objectively the most useful superpower. Sometimes we use it to go out for ice cream together, and sometimes we use it for shit like this.

"There's a problem." They're pale and dishevelled. "Down on the—"

"Isn't there always?" I hold out my hand. "Take me there."

I reappear on the beach on the east side of the island. It's raining, a mild but persistent drizzle. Pale globes of light float in the air. There's a girl on the island who blows them like bubbles. Right now, they're illuminating a body lying face down on the sand, waves tugging playfully at his ankles. There's three big white letters stencilled on the back of his body armour.

GIC.

"Never a shortage of assholes in the world, is there?" I crouch down and roll him over. His throat's been cut with immense enthusiasm. Probably Violet or Feral.

There's a flicker in my peripheral vision.

Oh look. Something to punch.

Since Dani and I got rebuilt, we've got new abilities—a whole *weapon of the world* thing. When I get to my feet and two guys are rushing at me with guns, I let them fire. Underneath what looks like human skin is a bunch of tightly-packed moss and soil, with little capillary-like things that flow water and sap around my body. Their bullets blow straight through me, and my body starts busily sealing itself back up, growing more of me to fill the holes.

Then I'm already upon them, a fast-moving storm front, leaves tossed by wild winds. When a tree like me falls on two GIC soldiers, it definitely makes a sound. I pull my punches— instead of turning my fists into tangles of thorns, they're solid wood. The men try to readjust to my speed, and the fact their body shots didn't take me out, but I catch them a couple of solid blows to the head, and they both go down.

They'll wake with concussions, but at least they'll be alive. I squirt out some Spider-Man style vines from my wrist to tie them up with. It's always gross doing this, but it's very useful. Once they're immobile, I get back to my feet and look around for the next problem.

"Dilly!" Violet unfolds herself out of the air. She's still

wearing the long t-shirts she wore to bed, and her three-heart silver pendant. "You're up."

"Hard to sleep through the ruckus." I give one of the guys on the ground a kick. "The fuck is this?"

"GIC surprise." She wiggles her fingers. "Guess they figured they had a shot at taking you into custody. Dan suggested giving them some rope and watching them hang themselves, so here we are."

"How many dead?"

"Only one, before I realised." She gestures at the guy drifting in the shallow waves. "I tend to react sharply when the ones I love are threatened. Sorry."

"I'm not mad." I pull her close and press my lips to the top of her head. Things are relatively new with Violet, but I still get those effervescent bursts of surprise that this amazing person *likes me this much*. She's so different from Dani, more tentative and guarded. Sometimes I feel she's a closely-held flame, but if I kiss her just right, she unfurls into all this kindled desire, like even her passions are carefully folded away. It shocked me when she confessed her love for me—a fact that never ceases to make Dani laugh—and even more so that Violet would choose me to nestle her heart alongside. I'm chaos and a brooding storm, but she feels safe in my harbour, berthed in the lee of my body. Every kiss from her feels like a small and precious gift, something that flutters into my heart to roost there.

She trails her fingertips along my cheek. "Once we realised it was a political invasion from the humans, we took it easy. Feral's got twelve others lined up down the beach. She wants to make a bonfire. Not to roast them, but maybe to scare them when they wake up? The plan is unclear."

"Right." I grab hold of my two and start dragging them through the sand. "Let's complete the collection. In the morning, we'll have to figure out what the fuck to do with fourteen assholes. Right now, it's too hard."

Feral already has the bonfire lit by the time we get there, and we line mine up with the others. Then Dani, Violet, Feral and I all snuggle up into a line near the fire and watch in dozy silence as the sky lightens fractionally towards day.

"Holy shit." Something streaks into the sky and pulses there like a low-hanging star.

"Flare," Dani says.

"Someone's out at sea." Feral's got the best eyesight of any of us. "Waving a white flag. Redhead, kinda cute in a sulky way. Do we kill her?"

"Tempting, but no. That's my creepy expert. Let's reel her in."

It's Decker alone, floating in a sleek little black boat. She's dressed in a GIC uniform and looking dejected. As soon as she gets close enough, she leaps out and sloshes through the water towards us. Her hands are held high.

"I'm sorry! I come in peace!"

"Yes, otherwise we'd be so terrified," Feral mutters with a smirk.

I stomp down the beach. "You fucking invaded us, Decker. Fifteen assholes showed up. You're lucky that fourteen get to leave with intact throats."

Her face twitches when she hears that news. Probably didn't expect to take so many colleagues back with her. "This was a clusterfuck."

"No shit. Whose idea was it? And put your goddamn hands down. You're not a fucking threat."

She lowers them slowly, still nervous. "There are factions within the GIC, and they disagree on the best way to handle the

Mutopia situation. Some favour non-intervention, others favour…"

"Extinction?" My voice is cold.

"Increased monitoring and potential incarceration. Then there are those like me, who argue for collaboration."

A frustrated noise escapes my throat, and Decker flinches.

"Did they have a reason for this nighttime surprise?" I ask.

"There's been a second murder. You were captured on tape again. Can I show you?"

This is the last thing I need after getting so little sleep. "Fucking brilliant."

"Here." Decker fumbles for her phone and holds it up. We all cluster around to watch a figure in a hoodie and black jeans striding down the corridor in an apartment building. They're wearing skate shoes with a luminous DNA pattern winding around the heel.

"They're so much like you," Dani says. "It's creepy."

"Who the fuck filmed this?" I frown at the screen. "It's not CCTV."

"We think it's a drone," Decker says. "The murderer wants people to see this."

The camera swings around to show the on-screen Dylan kicking the door down. It's the action of someone who's done it before. They're better at it than me, honestly. We get a wide shot of three people scrambling up from a large table. It's covered with guns along with a large, complicated electronic device. It looks half-disassembled, but it's got an all-too-familiar golden eye logo on it.

"Michael tech," Dani breathes.

It's fucking typical. Half our time is spent chasing down the remnants of that goddamn AI and the fanatical assholes who still believe in his anti-mutant agenda. Most of the tech doesn't work without him controlling it, but you find little groups of science douches trying to get it running again.

The on-screen Dylan makes short work of the people in the room, but there's something nagging at me about the footage. It takes three attempts before I put it together.

"Fuck." I stab my finger at the screen. "The sword."

"Exactly." Decker inches the footage back and we watch as Fake Dylan steps over a body and holds out their hand. The sword tugs itself out of the corpse and back into their grip, just in time to slice through the neck of the second victim.

"Holy shit." Dani stares. "They can talk to objects."

I gnaw on my thumb as we watch it again. "Or they're telekinetic, or doing it with fucking magnets, but it sure as fuck looks like a mutant."

"That was the conclusion of GIC analysts," Decker says. "And the reason they immediately greenlit an attempted rendition of you into custody. It wasn't until the plan was underway that someone—me—checked the timestamps of the footage and saw that it occurred while you were meeting with us."

"Left hand, meet right hand." Dani claps hers together. "You assholes should chat more. Were there any real clues?"

Decker nods. "More of Dylan's DNA. And also a flower petal."

"Shit." Dani inhales sharply. "They're really trying to pin this on you, Dills."

Decker fumbles in the pocket of her vest. "I brought you part of the petal. It's being analysed back at the GIC, but you might understand more given your... relationship with plants." She brings out a plastic bag with two glass slides inside, a fraction of a bright blue petal sandwiched between.

"What the fuck kind of flower is *that*?" I peer at it.

"I don't recognise it." Dani pockets it. "But thank you for bringing it here. Genuinely."

"You stole *evidence,* Deck." I clap her on the back. "Now that's what I call collaboration."

"Yes." She lets out a deep breath. "So let's hope I don't get caught."

"You're bringing back fourteen live GIC agents. Tell them you talked us down from murdering them all. That should get you brownie points."

Decker looks at me, a slight frown on her face. "This person's still out there, Dylan. With your face, killing people in your name. It's still a problem."

"Yes, friendly expert. I have many problems. We'll take care of it."

CHAPTER 4
ENTER THE WEIRDLANDS

ONCE DECKER IS off the island, Dani and I head straight into the forest with the petal. There's no point taking it to a lab when you've got part of an immense nature spirit slumbering in your backyard. Today, the trees are silent, the wind barely rustling the trees which tower above us.

"Green Mum's busy." Willow sidles out from behind the nearest aspen, looking like some tiny, bedraggled dryad. "Stopping disasters."

"Yes." Soo-yeon joins them, shaking their head. "You're supposed to solve your own problems. That's what you're *for*."

"Thank you, my darling babies, for the amazing pep talk." I hold out my arms, and despite their words, they come to me for a cuddle. Dani keeps trying to explain to me about the alien half and the human half, and how there's a tension between them sometimes, but I still feel that little sting of rejection when the kids act stand-offish. Even though I've got so much love in my life, a part of me still hides in the dark, waiting to pounce on any proof it's not true.

"Why did you want her anyway?" Willow winds a hand through my hair.

"Do you know what this is?" Dani fishes the fragment of petal out of her pocket and dangles it like a lure.

Soo-yeon wrinkles their nose. "Oh. That's from the Weirdlands. The English one."

"Really? How do you know?"

"Energy. It sort of vibrates differently. Makes no sense, like Willow when they're excited."

"Thank you *so much,* my darling sib." Willow puts their nose right up close to the bag and inhales. "Smells nice though. Can we come?"

We don't understand the Weirdlands, not a teensy tiny bit. There isn't only one, and most of them are very small—there's a hillside in eastern Argentina where the laws of reality cease to apply. The biggest is in Dorset in England, which has been completely barricaded off so that nobody can go in.

Mostly because very few people who do ever come back out.

Those people tell stories that sound like a bunch of hallucinogenic nonsense that's easy to write off as someone eating some bad mushrooms. Cybele doesn't like talking about them at all, like they're embarrassing scars received after a dodgy night out.

"Nope." Dani's very firm on this point. "That's not going to happen. You two are not to go into the Weirdlands for any reason."

"We've already been," Willow says, a tiny bit smug.

I click my tongue. "Then don't go *back.*"

"Fine, but how come you get to visit?"

Dani sighs. "Because we have to. And we want to worry about you two haring off into some bizarre sinkhole because you think it's interesting."

Soo-yeon scowls, but Willow leans in close. "It's a fair point, Soo."

The twins reach out with their vines and wrap them around both Dani and I, pulling us all together until we're tangled up in a very close and complicated knot.

"You need to be careful," Soo-yeon says. "We want you to come out in one piece."

Dani gives me a meaningful look, like *see, they do love us.*

And I hold them close, and that desperate urge to protect hums in my chest. To find a version of the world where my flower children can flourish.

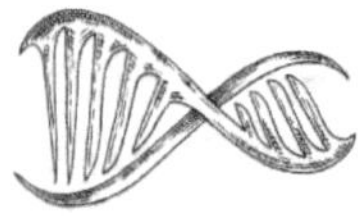

THE CONVERSATION with the rest of the gang is far less chill. Mostly because I propose that Dani and I go in alone.

"I'm not letting the two people I love go in there alone." Violet is actually shouting, which is rare for her. "There's no way."

"We'll be fine," I say for the fifth time.

"You know the silent passageways I move through when I'm teleporting? The ones around the Weirdness *bleed.* They're horrible slithering cuts where things come *alive.*"

"Y'all are simply not leaving me behind," Feral says, far more calm than Violet's trembling anger. "I won't stand for it. We're not a team, we're family."

"That too." Violet stabs her finger at me but thankfully not in blade-form.

"Fine." I hold my hands up in surrender. "The team rides again." I'm actually relieved. Going in with everyone makes me feel immediately more confident.

"I think I'll stay behind." Alyse is at the window, looking out at the darkening evening sky. "School is busy, you know. It's always busy. Probably better for me to focus on that rather than…" She waves one arm vaguely.

The rest of us exchange glances, a series of escalating shrugs and head jerks that ends with the others staring at me. Things since Emma have been hard for her, even now. Time heals, but it's not exactly quick about it. I do my best to be there, but I'm not the world's best at slow and subtle shit.

Feral makes an ushering motion with one claw. I roll my eyes so hard they might drop back into the mossy interior of my skull.

"Lys." I cross to the window beside her. She takes my arm gratefully.

"Be safe in the Weirdlands, Dilly."

"I think you should come with us." The words feel clumsy in my mouth. "I'm worried about you, being stuck back here on your own. And, fuck, I know there are *reasons*, and nothing's the same now that, you know…" I skirt this a lot. We all do. Saying the name feels like air being stolen from my lungs. We took a wrong turn somewhere and we're in this void where nothing makes sense.

Alyse makes a tiny, soft sound and leans her head on my shoulder.

"We're in a world where Ems is gone," I say. "And nothing can make that okay. But we're still here, and we can do things to make it better for everyone else."

There's a long silence, and all I can hear is the swishing hum of my body and the occasional stifled cry from Alyse's lips. Everyone else watches us while we watch the sky.

"It's what Emma always did." Her voice is steadier than I expected.

"Yeah. She fought, even when the world got way beyond fucked."

She makes a sound almost like a laugh. "I get your point, Dylan Jean. No need to rub it in."

"Does that mean you're coming?"

"Yes." She half-turns so she can wrap her arms around me, and I feel her skin transform into cool steel. "Let's do something dangerous and reckless again."

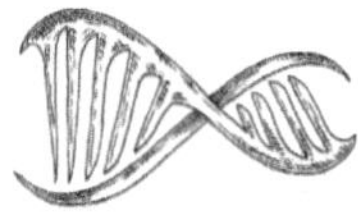

WE TRACK DOWN KEEPAWAY, who is also not a fan of the Weirdlands. "I don't really understand the limits of that place." They fidget, but at least meet my eyes. "It's like I'm dropping you into a bottomless pit."

"Just pop us in over the wall." I give my most encouraging smile. "We're tough."

"Fine." Keepaway's gaze travels over the group. "You're all on board?"

Feral fakes a yawn. "We see impossible shit everyday."

"I'm gathering this means you're not coming with us," Dani says.

"I'd rather not." Keepaway looks down. "The thought of being somewhere I can't escape from? I get all panicky. Even just thinking about it, I'm—"

I pat their shoulder. "We'll find our own way out. Get back

to the border wall, pretend we're one of the lost parties. Plus Vi can always cut her way out and raise the alarm."

Violet doesn't look entirely enthused about this plan, and I remember what she said about wounds in the world. Surely it can't be much worse than waking up after a year to find a religious AI had taken over half the world.

"No point standing around crying. Let's go investigate."

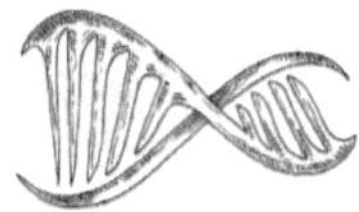

KEEPAWAY DROPS us right inside the border wall as promised. It looms over us, sleek and black and near featureless. I wonder if it was grown from the same nanotech the Michael AI used. I know there's some hotshot mutant scientist who's been retraining the nanomatter as part of some seawall project to help combat rising ocean levels. Way above, there's razor wire, and in the distance is the glint from a guard tower.

They're serious about keeping people out.

From our current vantage point, I don't see what the fuss is about. There's a thin strip of bare dirt where the grass deadends just before the wall, but aside from that the landscape is beautiful. We're on top of a rise, so we've got an amazing view. We're on the edge of a lush meadow, with green hillsides in the near distance, speckled with grass and purple heather. Just ahead is a small copse of trees with a ring of flowers surrounding it. It's hard to see a threat.

"Bucolic," Dani says. "Perfect day for a lovely hike."

"Probably means something's going to jump out and eat us." Feral's claws are out and her tail twitches behind her head, metal barb flashing in the sun.

"Pretty and dangerous." Alyse takes a few steps across the grass. "Kinda like us."

I squint up at the sky. It looks like it's bowing inwards, like something's on the other side of it, weighing it down. When I stare too long, little coloured dots float in front of my eyes like glitchy pixels dancing.

"Don't look at the sky." I drag my eyes away from it and back to the others. "It's..."

Of course Feral has her head tipped back. "What the fuck is up there?"

I grab her by the scruff of the neck and tip her head down to meet my eyes. "Something Weird with a capital W. Like the Lands. Let's not attract unnecessary attention."

"Fine." She scowls at me. "This place throws off my predator sense. I feel like *prey*."

"Please can nobody else make any more sinister fucking comments," I grumble. "It's making me feel—"

The world puckers and twists, and for a moment I'm staring into a hole drilled through the universe, stars and galaxies rippling inside luxurious folds. Then it all collapses down like a bubble being burst, and I'm staring at a small and wrinkled grey alien standing in the middle of the grassy landscape. Xe is mostly humanoid, but with baggy skin like one of those cute dogs and quite a few too many arms. It's pretty adorable. And yet I still have the awkward feeling every time I look at xer, like I'm waiting for xer to bite.

"Tentacle Princess." I smile awkwardly. "This is a nice, uh, surprise."

Part of my awkwardness is related to our tragic backstory. Way back at the dawn of time, when Cybele was an energy network happily subsisting alongside early humans, some alien monsters crash-landed on our planet. They were looking for food, and Cybele was a total snacc. They devoured her until she was a tiny husk and then these aliens set themselves up as gods. This mostly involved floating around in the ocean as giant flesh temples and eating people. And so it went, until the remnant sparks of Cybele flickered to life inside a pair of humans, changing them forever and creating the first mutants.

Lucifer and Lilith. You've probably heard the stories, but they're a little different to the ones we know. You can argue whichever religious corner you want, but there are exactly two entities still alive who were there at the time, and I've talked to both of them. Not bad for a chaos gremlin from New Zealand.

Tentacle Princess is the sole survivor of the flesh temple species—a baby god who hid under the ocean when mutants rose up and saved the humans. Possibly a mistake in hindsight, but their hearts were in the right place. After that, Tee Pee floated down in the dark until some mad scientist dug xer up. In the intervening time, xe had a change of heart and wanted to keep the mutant species alive as atonement.

"You have arrived," xe says, like xe was expecting us. "Welcome."

"The fuck are you doing here, TeePee?" Feral asks, draping one furry arm around the alien's shoulders. "It's not safe."

Alyse has drifted off, looking around at the landscape like she's a stunned tourist. I frown after her, even though she can technically take care of herself.

"I am fond of this little garden." The alien spreads all xer arms wide. "The sprouting of a long-buried seed."

"You know what this place is?" Dani asks.

"Of course. This is a flower of my long-past people. Buried deep in the soil of your Earth, unable to grow until recently— first the tampering performed by the entity known as Michael, then the outpouring of energy from Cybele. It has evolved somewhat, but it reminds me a little of what we could have been, if my people had been less brutal and ruthless."

"This place is terrifying," Violet says, eyes narrowing and fingers twitching like they want to burst into claws. "Not some holiday destination."

"It is fertile soil, and inevitable things will grow here," Tentacle Princess says, all dreamy like xe's basking in eldritch energy filtering up from the ground. "Some of them have minds of their own."

"Fuck's sake." I grit my teeth. "Did a version of me grow here?"

Tentacle Princess opens xer eyes very wide. "Whatever do you mean?"

"There's another me running around the world causing trouble. Did it come from this fertile soil or whatever?"

Tentacle Princess emits a series of noises. "You do not have a duplicate?"

I frown. "No. At least... God, no. Pear would've told me. Surely. Unless I ate my twin in the womb and the psychic projection of them finally found a body and—"

"This isn't the comics." Dani rubs my shoulder.

"Is there another me here or not?" I swallow my irritation.

Tentacle Princess tugs at xer face in a parody of thoughtfulness. "I have a small confession to make. Your physical exteriors are not something I perceive easily. I get a generalised impression, but the differences between you are difficult to identify. What I can confirm is there are no other plant-forms alive on this plane of existence aside from those in your family."

"They look *exactly* like me and they somehow have my DNA. And maybe they stole it, but there's something fucking weird going on. Like I know there's probably a more logical explanation, but my brain keeps screaming *clone*. And you can say that's a comic book answer all you want, but—"

Tentacle Princess tentatively extends one arm and pats at mine, as if xe's stroking the air around it. Xer dark eyes light up, tiny stars flaring in their depths. "There is nothing here that tastes like you. In fact, I am not even sure such a thing exists in this world. Or if there is, it is hidden from me."

"What could hide from you?" Dani asks.

"I can only speculate," Tentacle Princess says. "But the inevitable conclusion would be something both very powerful and extremely malicious."

"Of course." I throw up my arms and glare at the bulging sky. "So this is my *fucking* life."

CHAPTER 5
IMAGINE A COSMIC DONUT

TENTACLE PRINCESS DROOPS, like xer skeleton has fled and xe's collapsing in on xerself. "I am so dreadfully sorry I cannot assist you further."

"You're trying your best." Feral pats xer gently.

"That's what is so difficult." Tentacle Princess flails, looking so much like one of those floppy inflatable things outside car yards that I have to bite my lip. "My people were monstrous and incomprehensible predators, who took advantage of your entire species, and I only wish to provide certainty to help balance the cosmic scales."

Given that our 'people' killed xer people in self-defence, it's a complicated history, but let's not broach that topic. I scowl viciously at the beautiful landscape, in the hope I can intimidate it into sharing its own secrets.

"I have discovered one odd thing," Tentacle Princess says in a very small voice.

"Bet that's scary too," I mutter.

"There is something wrong with the world." Xer eyes have gone very big, taking up a disconcerting amount of xer face, and I'm pretty sure xe has more arms than before.

"Lots of things, yes," Feral says. "It's fucked up in ways beyond counting, with oppressive systems that serve to—"

"Not that." The alien shudders. "I mean, that too. You have explained it to me, and it is self-evidently true and horrifying, the way you have all constructed this societal prison that oppresses so many, yet it is allowed to remain in place. But that is not what I refer to. The entire world is *bent.*"

"Bent how?" I feel a pulse of frustration.

"The energy is wrong. *Frothing.* There is a pinhole, but the area around has been burned clean. We cannot trace the source."

"Do you understand this?" I ask the others, but get only blank looks in response. "Sorry, Teeps, but you're speaking in higher-dimensional concerns or whatever. Can you say it a different way?"

"The easiest language to explain it in is math, but I have noticed many of you tend to dislike it."

"I love math," Dani says. "But your math is... something else."

For a brief second, Tentacle Princess transforms into an oscillating swirl of cosmic dust and far-off stars. It's like being punched in the brain very hard, but then the alien snaps back into physical form. "Imagine the universe is a donut," xe says, and although my brain still hurts, this is definitely a thing I can picture, so I nod along with everyone else. "And something has stabbed the donut, just the tiniest pinprick, and injected a tiny amount of poison into it."

"That doesn't sound good," Feral stage-whispers.

"It is not," Tentacle Princess assures us, even though it's pretty fucking obvious from context. "It is cosmically terrible. And reality is bending at the impact site. Let me try to assess the true scope of the—"

The alien falls silent and collapses to the ground, a wrinkled grey ball of skin with a few trembling nubbins of flesh poking out.

"Fuck." Feral stares down at xer. "Was that us? Or the Weirdlands?"

I feel the overwhelming urge to scream. "I don't have time for cosmic fucking bullshit! I'm trying to stop a murderer with my face." There's a lot more I want to say, that I'm so fucking exhausted all the time being on this impossible treadmill and trying to keep a miracle running. I should collapse in a heap like the alien in front of me.

"One problem at a time," Dani says.

But we're not that lucky, so I crouch down next to the alien. "Is there anything we can do to help? We're pretty good at punching things."

There's no response, and I look up at the others helplessly.

"You don't think it's connected, do you?" Violet asks. "This donut hole and the clone?"

I shake my head firmly. "Maybe it's not a clone. Maybe I've just got a fucking double with a pocket full of DNA."

"Or maybe you have a clone," Dani admits, and I find it oddly sweet that she believes me. "So this poison thing happens, and reality bends and spits out a clone of you. It's possible, right? Maybe this is only the beginning of a cascade of weird shit."

I snort. "You are the most cheerful goddamn person sometimes."

And then Tentacle Princess starts emitting a series of splintered tones.

"Is that xer agreeing or disagreeing?" I ask, wide-eyed, and for some reason this strikes us all as hilarious.

The tones don't stop, rising in pitch like an alarm. They bounce around inside my head like an extra-special cosmic hangover.

"This can't mean anything good." Violet winces, massaging her temples.

Dani reaches out to Tentacle Princess but her skin splits, ruptures crackling along it like fault lines. Vines spring out, winding her back together, but a thin, translucent sap gushes from the cracks.

"Fuck's sake." I haul her backwards. Everyone else is in retreat, but Dani's whole body is hissing and humming, like whatever complex plant systems have been shoved inside us—that nobody in the entire fucking world understands—are in a state of meltdown.

I scream for Cybele, but there's no answer.

Dani's skin is slippery under my hand, the sap near-boiling as it spills from her body. The tones coming from Tentacle Princess have blurred together into a single, sustained note that goes through me like a blade.

I fall to my knees. My own sappy heart is spasming wildly inside my chest. What is this *sound?*

It cuts off abruptly, and I can breathe again. I roll over and find my face pressed up against cool green skin. Dani. Not overheating, not dying. Her body hums again, the reassuring sound of life moving through her.

Violet crouches with us, holding us both close.

"What," Dani croaks. "The fuck. Was that?"

"Reality with a hole in it." I run my hands all over her body, checking that she's in one piece. The cracks in her skin are mostly healed, only the thin threads of disappearing vines showing where they were. "And bad fucking shit all around."

"Where's Tee Pee?" Feral yelps.

"Fuck." There goes my heart, hissing and spluttering again. We all assemble in a rough circle, looking down at the ground. It would be nice to say xe'd vanished without a trace, but unfortunately there's a lot of evidence left behind. There's a purplish-blue substance that boils on the sand, and some long, wet tendrils of flesh that look like…

Alyse is noisily sick. "You had to insist on bringing me along."

I stare down at the remains. "We didn't expect this. What the *fuck* is going on here?"

And then, to make matters worse, my two children saunter out of thin air.

"Didn't I tell you to stay home?" I grumble.

"Yes, but then all the energy went floop," Willow says. "So we can't just *stay home*. Something's happened to Tentacle Princess. And we love xer! Not as much as we love you, but a lot. Do you want us to find xer?"

My head's spinning. "Can you do it without bouncing around the world?" I ask, because I've made this mistake before of agreeing to things that I didn't intend to.

"Oh my god, *fine*." Soo-yeon groans, as if we have somehow inherited an alien teenager. "We can do it from right here and…"

"That's strange." Willow pokes at the ground.

"There aren't words for how strange this is, Will." Soo-yeon leaps from my arms and buries their limbs in the soil. "I don't like it."

"Hello?" Dani joins Soo on the ground. "You feel like filling us in?"

"Xe's gone." Soo-yeon tugs their hands out of the ground in a shower of soil. "I don't think xe's dead, because xer energy is in some stasis state where it hasn't returned to the universe like it should."

"It's a closed system," Willow explains earnestly. "And xer energy isn't there."

Soo-yeon looks out at the horizon. "We think xe's hiding. Way out in space. Maybe in one of xer voids, but we sort of... know about those... even though we're not supposed to. We're interested in things, I'm *sorry*."

I close my eyes, wishing for something to go right. When I open them, nothing has changed."Right, so we've still got to find this flower, and hope it's a clue. And now figure out why Tentacle Princess is hiding."

"Can we—?" Willow begins, but Dani cuts her off.

"No. Pop yourselves back home please, and do something nice with your grandparents."

"But—"

"Bup-bup-bup," Dani says, which shouldn't work at all, but somehow does. Some parental magic that I don't have. The twins miraculously fall silent, before giving us identical glares and vanishing.

"Rather you than me." Feral claps me on the shoulder.

"Yes." I roll my eyes. "Violet, can you poke around? Safely, obviously."

"We've got a very fluid interpretation of safe." She extends one hand and rotates it. Her index finger unspools into a complex, folding blade. The tip of it pokes a ragged hole in the air. I've never seen her do this at a glacial speed, so I lean in, fascinated. I've asked her to take me on a date into the secret passageways of the world, but I don't have access.

Violet grimaces. "There's something… stuck. It's all gunged up." She tries to retract her finger, but it's wedged in. When she yanks it back, a whole chunk of reality comes with it. There's a hole in the world, big enough for me to shove my fist through.

Then something oozes out of it. It's like an elongated bee or a small, furry missile with teeth. A small cluster of stingers at one end rotates lazily, each trilling a different note. Feral swipes it from the air with one claw. A thick and meaty smell spills out, a noxious cloud that roars into my brainstem and turns my vision into blinding refractive tears.

I swipe at my face, dislodging a cascade of tiny gem-like crystals that have crusted around my eyes. Okay. Now we've really arrived.

"Feral," I growl. "No punching the Weirdlands. It makes everything worse."

My eyes are mostly clear, and I can see the others have got the same crystals forming over their faces, creating glittering masks. Through the hole Violet made, something glistens. A larval form, white and writhing, birthing its way through. Reality quivers around it, tiny cracks appearing in the scenery.

I wave my arm. "Everyone head for those flowers. I'll go last."

Feral bounds off with Alyse right behind her, then Violet and Dani.

I jog after them, but I can't help looking over my shoulder to see whether that goddamn thing has squirmed its way free yet. My brain supplies the helpful image of the sky overhead being full of billions of them, and when it finally fucking tears under the weight of them thrashing about and reproducing, we're going to drown in a flood of pale, writhing grub-like things.

I'm so busy looking back that I run smack into Dani, and we sprawl to the ground together. Everyone's stopped outside the ring of flowers, and now that I'm up close and personal with them, I can see why. While they're not any match for the flower we got from Decker, they're astonishingly beautiful. They're a mix of bluebells and snowdrops and fuchsias, delicate shapes forged from carefully folded metal, the same way you make swords. Each is stained with drops of pristine colour, but the edges are darkened and look rusty. I make the total noob mistake of leaning in even further, which is when three flowers lunge at me, petals reconfiguring into hook-shaped blades which bite into the meat of my shoulder.

I don't know what they'd do to humans, but my 'flesh' these days is a tangle of moss and ferns, with vines threaded between them that carry sap like blood. So all the flower attack does is spray a bunch of sap everywhere and send chunks of plant material flying.

"Ouch." I reach down and grab one by the root, yanking it out of the ground despite the way it chews at my flesh with its friends. "That'll do, you little fuck."

As soon as I've tugged it from the ground, the metal flower goes quiet in my hand. I give it a shake and it slowly extends until it's a gleaming blue-purple blade nearly as long as--

"Humph." Oni drifts down out of the sky. He doesn't quite look like himself, his usual pristine blade dripping with an iridescent sheen, but the disgruntled humph is enough to convince me that I'm definitely looking at my sword.

"You're supposed to stay where it's safe," I tell him.

"It is not in my nature to let you enter into danger without me by your side."

"Yes, sure, but this is Clusterfuck City so try not to get any weirder than you already are."

"And I see you have already replaced me with another blade."

My fingertips curl around Oni's hilt. "Two swords are better than one."

Dani's already reaching into the flower patch, ignoring her own cuts to retrieve a blade of her own. "What? I've always been jealous of this whole vibe. You know that."

Feral is eyeing up the flower patch, so I remind her that she has claws and doesn't need one.

"How about you, Lys?" I ask.

"No. I'll transform if I need anything." She's still melancholy and distant, like she's watching things I can't see. It unnerves me, but it helps to be holding two swords. Then the trees ahead start grumbling, and my good feeling evaporates *fast*. Their tones are low and urgent, but it's a language I don't recognise.

Then they all begin groaning in unison, their trunks melting like they're made of soft wax. A glowing figure strides between them, heat pouring off their body. A melody accompanies them, as if they're a villain with their own theme, a twisted series of notes that seems heat-blackened, as if they're about to crack open to reveal ash inside.

The new arrival looks almost like a person, although they have an enormously elongated head, one that seems to be paused mid-explosion with dizzying patterns of kaleidoscopic light shooting from the back of it. It's as if a cosmic projector is unspooling, playing the universe's jaunty procession towards heat death. Their smile is a stretched-lip gape showing off pale headstone teeth.

"All the better to eat you with," Alyse says with a shiver.

"You think we should stab this one?" Dani murmurs.

I grip both my swords tighter. "Give it a minute."

The figure comes to a halt in front of us. "Greetings." The word evaporates around him in bubbles of glowing light. "My name is Dr. Wolus. It's absolutely splendid to meet you."

"No way." Feral's hackles rise. "Pass me a sword, Dilly. It's stabbing time."

CHAPTER 6
IT'S JUST GOOD TIMES WITH THE SCIENCE BROS

"DON'T STAB ANYONE," I tell the group at large. "I doubt it'll help."

"Remarkably well reasoned," the apparition calling himself Dr. Wolus says. "How long have you been in the Weirdlands?"

"Long enough to know it's fucked."

He throws his head back and laughs, a huge booming sound that emits a greasy stream of light. It skids along the underside of the sky before plummeting back to earth, leaving a damp river that chuckles faintly.

"Did you see that?" Alyse is staring up into the sky.

"Yeah, babe." I try to take her hand. "A creepy giggling river."

"No, not that. *Emma* is up there."

This cryptic statement makes everyone gaze up into the sky,

including Dr. Wolus. I can't see anything, my eyes skidding over the placid blue like it's ice.

"I see nothing," Wolus says eventually. "Who is this Emma?"

Dani shakes her head. "We'll ask the questions. Starting with who the hell are you?"

The man bows. "My name is Dr. Bobosy Wolus, and I am a mutant who has made it my life's work to study this anomalous terrain, referred to colloquially as the Weirdlands. Right now, it is only my husband and I. We did have some graduate students assisting us but they were…"

He doesn't seem to notice that he never finished the sentence.

"Eaten?" I suggest pointedly. "Turned into weird light? Drowned by a rain of larvae?"

"No, I think they went home." He's still staring up into the sky. "Perhaps they never made it. Although this place is constrained geographically, it is infinitely deep and therefore easy to get lost in. Until you assimilate, of course." He beams at us again, and we all flinch away from the moonlight glow of his teeth.

"What does assimilate mean?" Violet asks with a shudder.

"It's the only way to truly understand this place." Bobosy hitches up the leg of his tattered khaki slacks, revealing a ragged cut on his ankle. It sings softly, an echo of his arrival theme, and then smirks at us with bloodied lips. "Yes, it's an infection, and yes, it hurts terribly. But then you're part of it. It no longer attempts to expel you."

"It can infect you?" Feral isn't the only one busily inspecting every inch of her skin for cuts that might let the Weirdlands in.

"That doesn't matter. We're here to find Emma." Alyse's

tone is dreamy, and she drifts past us. "Dr. Wolus, can you tell us more about this place?"

I look at Dani helplessly, but she only shrugs in response.

"What the fuck does that particular shrug mean?" I hiss.

"It means we're already *here*. If Alyse can get some…. I don't know, closure or something, isn't it worth it?"

"The only thing she's going to get here is a bad trip." I shove my hands into my hoodie pockets, and turn to Violet. "What's your vote?"

"I still hate this place." She wraps her arms around herself. "But we need to find answers, and we're all here to protect Alyse, right?"

Yes, sure, but I really don't like the look in my best friend's eyes. What Dr. Wolus said about *infinitely deep* makes me think of falling forever into the dark, like Keepaway said. Nothing about this place can be trusted.

"Goddess," Dr. Wolus is transfixed. "You saw Goddess *here*? Resurrected? Incarnate? Or transfigured in death?"

"I'm not sure," Alyse says. "But it was her, I swear. She's here somehow."

"The Weirdlands are both hungry and sensitive," Wolus says. "If some part of Goddess was to manifest beyond death, this place would be a logical choice. All manner of lost things end up here."

And I fucking hate this so much, because I would love nothing more than to sit down with Alyse in some grassy green field, and give her all the answers she needs. But there's no simple or beautiful picture I can show her. Some things just fucking suck, and I don't know what else to say about that.

"Told you we should have stabbed him." Feral punches me in the shoulder. "We can still change our minds. This feels like our version of a gingerbread house. Something fascinating, but it's going to eat us."

"Answers first," I tell her, and shoulder my way to the front of the group. Maybe I can distract Wolus from talking to Alyse. I fish the little blue petal out of my pocket, the one Decker retrieved from the crime scene. "Uh, Doctor? Have you seen a plant like this before?"

His eyes brighten as he looks at it—literally, until they're painful to look at. "Yes, I believe this is a plant that grows here. In the deepest parts."

"Can you lead us there?"

He hums, a deep thrumming in his chest. "Perhaps, perhaps. It is a strange and tortuous path to find anything in the interior. We shall ask our way and hope that we are guided."

I'm mostly tired of his ominous bullshit, but it's still a lead.

"The strangest things are buried," Dr. Wolus continues, waving a sparkling fingertip in the air like a firework. "The seeds of this place lie deep."

"Huh." I catch Dani's eye. We let the scientist go on ahead a little way, then each extend a delicate tendril into the ground. We've got some limited ability to jack into the entire Cybellian network, and—

Things are crawling, slimy things beneath the slimy ground, a thousand thousand mouths opening in supplication. And a *song* underneath it all, rising and falling, a call, an eternal shriek passed from thread to thread in the darkness, a feverish web of connections tangled until it collapses under its own weight and in the black hole heart of it, the song rises again and from that weighty singularity an inexorable feeding gravity pulls at me, dragging me under. I shall become a mouth, a note in the song, a node in the glorious, incandescent—

Something hard smacks right across my face, sending me

sprawling backwards. I'm uprooted, any connection with the soil lost. Dani's beside me, on hands and knees, retching up a thin yellowish slime that spits like hot oil when it spatters on the ground.

"No." Oni hovers above me, his blade spotted with ruin. "That shall not happen."

"Are you okay?" Violet sits between us, trying to soothe both at once. "I'm assuming Oni's on our side here, but..."

"Yeah, he's good."

Violet pushes damp curls off her face. "So how worried should I be?"

I watch Bobosy Wolus, still wandering ahead of us, pointing out something in the sky to Alyse, who turns in a slow circle. There's delight in her eyes, which I should like, but the antlers jutting from her forehead and the damp, twitching moth-wings on her back make incoherent fears churn in my gut. This place and its strangeness, beckoning her towards change.

"I don't know," I admit. "I'm worried about a thousand things at once."

"Sounds like a regular day for you." She strokes damp hair off my forehead. "We do what we always do. Keep an eye out and stab whatever needs stabbing."

"There's a reason we love you, Vi." Dani looks as shaky as me.

Up ahead, the doctor lets out a triumphant shout. "And here we are. Welcome, visitors, to our home."

I'm still feeling about fifty percent sure this is a trap, so we dash off towards Alyse before she springs it on herself. She's on the crest of a hill, looking down into a little valley. A stream of what looks like actual water burbles down the other side, pooling into a small lake. On the edge of it are a series of makeshift huts, sparkling slightly in the woozy blue glow of the afternoon sky.

"Looks normal enough," Feral says.

"Makes it trappier." I'm frowning down at the idyllic scene when a head pops out of a doorway. His long braids coil around his head in a slithering, nauseous motion, and he wears a lurid green t-shirt that flutters over his body.

"These fucking guys," Feral says under her breath.

"Bo," the man calls. "You found them! They're alive!"

There's an unmistakable fondness on the face of both men, and it's the first thing I've seen in this damn place that doesn't give me pause. These two assholes might be genuine about one thing at least.

Wolus draws himself up to his full, impressive, possibly eldritch height. "May I introduce you to my husband, Orrell Gawain Remus Burke. Or Rell, as I call him, because the rest is quite a mouthful. My love and my partner in this mad endeavour."

"Cool," I drawl. "I'm Chatterbox, and this is Marvellous, Penance, Moodring, and Feral."

Both men gape at me. I've gotten used to not needing to introduce myself.

"*The* Chatterbox?" Wolus asks.

Rell roars with laughter. "Typical Bo. Has the world's most famous mutants coming for supper, and doesn't even realise." He slings an arm around his husband's waist, and where the strange kaleidoscopic light from Wolus's head falls, Rell turns ghostly and insubstantial. It's a good reminder. We might not be dealing with a couple of enthusiastic science bros in nerdy research love, but a couple of vaguely human-shaped hallucinations that want to eat us and turn us into sparkly jam.

"You're an astonishing group." Wolus shakes my hand again. "Where are the children? I simply must meet them."

It's amazing how two sentences can change the mood so fast. Now they're face to face with a bunch of people who would quite cheerfully kill them.

"Nobody meets the kids," I say, in my best Wolverine voice. "And how do you even know they exist?"

"I thought…" Wolus trails off again.

"It seems…" Rell doesn't have any more luck in completing a sentence.

"Boo." A small figure pops out of thin air to perch on my shoulder.

"Willow, for *fuck's sake.*"

"Sorry." Soo-yeon sidles out of existence to take position curled up within Dani's left arm. "But it's way too interesting to stay home."

"Curiosity is a good thing," Willow informs me. "And we're not cats, so it's fine."

"Will, I don't think—"

"A joke." My uncanny alien child winks at me. "We've been practising human jokes."

"We're not very good at them yet," Soo-yeon sighs. "The point of all this is that we're not children. Not even close. We're new, that's all. It's different. And we can look after ourselves, so if these eager little…" Their head tilts. "…monsters? Decide to poke at us, we can k-word them ourselves, without our *parents* having to step in."

"Except we won't." Willow pats my head. "We'll zip ourselves away first."

"Okay, *fine.* But the children aren't part of your experiments," I inform the science husbands. "We're here to find this damn petal, and that's it." That's not remotely it, but I don't want to show our hand too much, and I definitely don't want to mention a possible clone of me to these two.

"Of course!" Wolus leans his head in towards his husband's. "They're looking for a flower."

"Theoretically a simple task, but the energy patterns here can be difficult to pin down." Burke tugs on one particularly eager braid. "We'll have to beg the algorithm."

The scientists stride off towards a different hut. Alyse follows, with Violet hurrying after as protection, but the rest of us hang back with the twins.

"Can you sense anything interesting in here?" I ask them.

"The men were right about the energy patterns." Soo-yeon gestures in odd shapes with their hands. "It's all…"

"Fucked," Willow suggests. "Sometimes it's the best word, no matter what Halmeoni says."

"It would be really great if the two of you went *back* to Halmeoni's," Dani says sternly. "One less thing to stress out about."

"Ugh, *fine*." Soo-yeon reaches out a hand to take Willow's. "You spoil all the fun."

"Don't get eaten." Willow plants a kiss on my cheek, and the two of them disappear. Their new teleportation habit is disturbing, but at least they can't take people with them yet. With the speed they're changing, it's probably only a matter of time.

Up ahead, Violet and Alyse follow the scientists into our destination. There's still a possibility the houses are carnivorous, so we hurry to catch up. The hut's definitely bigger on the inside, and the floor is spongy in an unpleasant way, but nobody's being eaten. In the middle of the room is was once a computer, although it's undergone some evolution since then. The glowing logo on the front has become a three-dimensional hologram that projects a series of twisted glyphs on the walls, and odd tentacle-like growths of cable spill from its guts, cycling through sickly neon shades.

"Oh wonderful algorithm," Wolus intones. "We are intending to find these flowers we have termed *eldritch horribilus.*"

"And also the mutant Goddess," Alyse blurts out. "Or some portion of her consciousness that may reside here."

I grit my teeth, ready for some dire consequence, but all that happens is the computer flashes and hums to itself.

"Alyse," I whisper, but she studiously ignores me.

"Excellent," the computer burbles in a lightly-accented voice. "I'll get right on that. Finding things is usually easy. It's always in the last place you look, right? So you make sure the first place you look is the last place. The only tricky bit is finding the last place, but I'm on it. You just wait."

We all stand awkwardly in the hut, watching neon flashes dart over the walls.

"It might take a while," Wolus says eventually. "And it grows late. Perhaps you wish to eat, or sleep."

"We're not eating anything here," Dani says, and Violet gives emphatic agreement. "And we'll sleep, but someone needs to keep watch."

"As you wish. Rell and I will retire for the night, and we shall see you again in the light of a new day, when answers aplenty lie in store for all of us." The scientist grins enormously, his pristine teeth looking candy-coloured in the light from the computer. Then he turns and trots out of the computer room, arm in arm with Burke.

When we exit, night has fallen, like it slammed into the day in a catastrophic accident. The sky is a deep, rippling black, like we're looking up at the underside of a vast lake. There's a complete absence of stars, only patterns of faint, wavy lines that oscillate in place.

We trek back up the hill away from the houses. The plants track us as we pass, flaring their fluorescent-bright petals like tiny faces of furious deities.

"I'll take the first watch," Feral says. "I'm all fidgety."

I stare at the ground doubtfully. "I don't think I'm going to sleep either. But I guess I'll try."

We all arrange ourselves in a row, a whole series of spoons side by side. Feral sits cross-legged on the end, claws out and tail twitching. I pull Dani's arm tighter around me and nestle into Alyse, stifling a sigh.

There's no way I can possibly sleep under this rippling sky. It'll probably fall on me the moment I close my eyes.

CHAPTER 7
DROWNING IN METAPHORS, AND OTHER WAYS TO SPEND YOUR VACATION DAYS

WHEN I WAKE, the deep black of the sky has slowly been encroached on by a spill the colour of sour milk. Even Oni lies asleep beside me, looking like nothing more than a sliver of rusted metal. When I brush my fingers along his steel, he murmurs something I can't translate. This fucking place. I'd say it's weird, but that seems redundant at this point.

Around me, dark shapes hurtle up from the ground. They disappear into the surface of the sky with barely audible splashes, sending woozy ripples out in blurry circles. My stomach lurches, and I drag myself away from the group and retch up something that flutters out of my throat and away.

We didn't eat anything, I'm sure of it. But we've been breathing the air of the Weirdlands and who knows what awful shit we've inhaled. I'm on the verge of ripping my chest open and airing the damn thing out, making sure there aren't any creepy spores or anything.

And then I spot Alyse.

She's supposed to be keeping watch, but she's standing about twenty metres away, wearing only a long t-shirt. Her head's tilted upwards, and her whole back is arched uncomfortably, like she wants to take in as much of the sky as she possibly can. I wonder what she sees there. The patterns are random and chaotic, signifying nothing. But then I'm not the one who's desperate for a sign of the impossible.

I pad over, the grass slick under my bare feet.

"Hey, Lys." I stand beside her, close enough that the back of my hand brushes hers.

"Dills. Pretty night, huh?"

"Odd, but yeah. Like standing on an alien world, a little bit, huh?"

"It's not so different." There's a smile on her face, but tears on her cheeks too. "It's a half-step away from our world, which is why she wound up here."

"Babe, I don't think—"

"It makes sense, Dylan. Think about it. Her consciousness wasn't just something that could vanish like that. It's not a wave returning to the ocean. She was always bigger than that. There's part of her here, I can feel it, and when that computer—"

Anger stirs in my chest. At this place, at these scientists for encouraging it, at Alyse for being so gullible. "If that computer does find Emma out here in the Weirdlands, it'll be some monster mimicking her face so it can feed on us. And I think you know that, but right now you'd rather have a lie than—"

"Stop it." For a moment, I think she'll hit me, but she's transforming into a shattered ruin of a statue, poison red light leaking out of the cracks. "It's just too hard, Dylan. I can't do this anymore. Can't get up each day and miss her. I have to find *something*, some version of her. Otherwise I'm me, alone, untethered."

There's that slight sting of rejection again—because what are we? Not good enough to be counterweights to hold her to this world? And beyond that, the exhaustion from always propping her up, from being so calm and soothing, day after day when we're all fucking hurting.

"So what?" I don't have the energy or the inclination to leak any of the venom out of my voice. "You're going to pour yourself into the fucking sky and become one with the Weirdlands?"

The Alyse statue is crumbling, the centre of it a howling inferno. "I don't know, Dylan. All I know is that this is something that finally feels real, you know? A glimpse of her in the middle of this—"

"No." I'm shaking all over, and all I can see in my mind is the place where Emma died, and Alyse sitting among it, covered in flowers "Fuck this. I'm not going to let you do this. You're not disappearing."

For a moment, the statue is gone, and it's only Alyse, my best friend, her eyes so sad there's no transformation necessary to show me the pain she's feeling. "It's not your choice." She looks upwards again, and her eyes reflect the pale glow from the sky. "I'm sorry."

I've never been the best at containing my feelings. Emotions are complicated, surging things that transform inside you without warning. The ones I have about Emma are the worst. There's an uncomfortable pit of guilt, because I've still got the two women I love in my life, and haven't had them snatched away in some noble sacrifice play. Even worse, the death of my lover was undone, a gift from the universe that Alyse has never received. There's grief of course, so much so that it's sometimes smothering, drowning out joy in the recognition of all the small things I can't share with my friend who's gone. Even a tiny thread of jealousy, that Emma doesn't have to fight anymore, doesn't have to square her shoulders and look towards the next enemy, wondering what the fucking cost will be this time.

And then there's so much anger. At myself, for not finding a way. At Emma, for being a super cosmic badass and still not finding her own goddamn loophole out of death. At everyone else, for standing by and letting it happen.

At Alyse, for not pulling herself out of this hole.

"You need to snap out of it." Thorns spring from my shoulders, long and wickedly sharp. "I've been tiptoeing around you, saying I can't possibly imagine how hard it is for you. Except I can, because I loved Emma too and I lost her as well. And then some days it feels like I lost my other best friend as well."

"Fuck you." She's thornier than I am, a twisted wooden shell for her to scream through. "Seriously, Dylan. Fuck's your favourite word. Maybe you'll listen to me now. I've been trying *every fucking day*. You think I like smiling for everyone? So they don't feel guilty, so they don't have to fucking coddle me. I know I'm a burden. Don't you get that? I fucking *know*."

I want to destroy everything. To pulp the world like rotten fruit, smashing down until I can find the hollow pit at its centre and obliterate myself inside it. How can I love this person so much and be so utterly useless at showing it?

"Godfuckingdamnit." I'm gasping, I can barely find the words, let alone force them out past my frustrated, furious tears. "I wish you'd fucking *let* me carry you. I know I'm a disaster and always have been, but I've got room for you in my arms, Alyse. No matter how many people I'm kissing, no matter how many goddamn alien kids I'm trying to raise—and fuck's sake, is there a person less suited for that job?—I want to be here for you. When I say you're my best friend, that's not just a thing I say. It's baseline me, a bedrock part of who I am." I slam my fist into my chest, sending chunks of moss flying. "I fucking need you in my heart."

She tries to talk, but no words come out around her harsh, hacking sobs.

I take her in my arms. "I cannot fucking lose you, Lys. The thought of it makes my brain run away. And I'm sorry for being an asshole, but it *terrifies* me to have you chasing into darkness, following a dream of Emma that's not real."

The ground underneath us crumbles and slips away, and the two of us are falling. There's a blizzard of tears swirling around us, and a vast dark ocean of grief below. When we hit it, still clinging to each other, there's no sensation of impact. It simply swallows us.

Salt stings my skin and we swirl together in infinite darkness, two specks holding fast.

"Is this really what you want?" I ask her. "To be gone like this."

There's a long pause. "No," she whispers. "I want you to come find me."

"I'm here. And we loved Emma too. We all did. I know it's not the same."

"I know, I know. And my grief fills up the room, and nobody else has room to breathe, and wouldn't it be easier if…"

"None of this is ever going to be easy." I kiss her forehead. "It's not, and it sucks, and I fucking hate it on a daily basis. But it's not something I can fight, it's something we have to walk through. And it'll be a hell of a lot easier together, so you need to understand that we're here, and I will come find you in the dark. Every time. No matter how many times it takes. And all I need from you is to be here when I come looking. Don't lose yourself."

"It's so big." She looks around at the void. "How can I ever get through?"

I pull her closer to me, so there's no way she can drift. "I don't know. It seems like there are no edges. But maybe we just can't see them yet. And they're creeping closer, a little bit at a time. And one day we'll wake up and there will be light outside."

"Yeah." She leans her head on my shoulder. "Thanks for coming to find me, Dilly."

"I'll always come for you. Like a fucking superhero. Always here to save your grief-stricken ass."

She laughs at this, but then she's crying again, because it's only one step away. "I'm sorry, I'm so useless."

"Nah. You've taken a pretty hard punch. You're lying down, wondering if you can get up. Just gotta catch your breath, realise the pain means you're alive. Then you stand up and keep moving."

"And you've got your hand outstretched, pulling me up."

"Of course. We're like best friends times ten thousand and then set on fire."

"Set on fire." She's finally smiling again.

"Yes. I'm eternally dramatic." I wrap my arms around her so she's crushed against me. "It must seem like terrible luck to be saddled with me as your platonic soulmate, but I do love you so fucking much."

We surface from the darkness with twin gasps, as if we've been holding our breath for hours. Somehow we're back on the hilltop underneath the curdled sky, as if we were never anywhere else at all.

"Were we just drowning in a metaphor?" Alyse asks me.

"It's the Weirdlands." I pull her down to the ground so we can sit, because it feels less likely to crumble away underneath us again. "So honestly, who fucking knows?"

"Thank you," she whispers to me, tucking her head back into my shoulder, among the night-flowers that bloom there, delicate twirling arrangements of moonflowers, primroses and lilies. "For always coming to save me."

"Gotta be the advantage of having a best friend who's a superhero."

"One little bright side, yeah."

We sit and look out at the slumbering landscape. Columns of bone-coloured smoke rise in the distance, swirling around vast skeletons of impossible creatures daubed with luminescent paint. Nearer to us, blue fire crackles between the tops of the trees, forming curlicues of half-letters as if they're trying to speak to us but can't find the words to say. Against the pall of the sky, fluttering silhouettes dance, smearing themselves mothlike over the glow.

"Dilly?"

"Yeah?"

"If that weird computer thing does find Emma, what do I do?"

"I think you'll know if it's real or not. You knew her better than anyone. And if it's not real, then it's easy."

"We fucking punch it." She pats my knee and then snorts with laughter.

"This is a joke now?"

"I don't know. It's funny and sad all at once. We come to this strange, magical place, and our first instinct when we see something we don't understand is to smack it in the face. But if we try to rise above and be better people, it'll probably eat us."

"Okay, fine." I place one hand over the hissing pump of my

heart. "I solemnly swear I will try to talk to the monster before hitting it, or even poking it with a sword."

"Good. Because monsters aren't all bad, you know?"

A smirk lifts one corner of my mouth. "Oh, believe me, I get it. Shit, I'm a monster myself. Both my girlfriends. Most of my friends, half the people they're dating too. Honestly, you might as well call us Monsterfuckers, Inc."

She giggles, an honest to god sound of delight, and I feel a punch of joy in my heart. One more step through the darkness.

The two of us sit together for the rest of the night, making stupid jokes, gossiping about our friends, and watching that strange sky rot into the sickening white of day.

CHAPTER 8
GRUESOME ENDINGS ARE THE BEST TIME FOR BUFFY REFERENCES

IN THE MORNING, everyone else seems remarkably well rested.

"I don't even remember my dreams," Dani says.

"Given that Lys and I had a very dramatic screaming match right beside you, I'm relieved."

Her eyes search my face, but whatever she finds there smooths the anxiety crease out of her forehead. "Ah. One of those. I'm glad." She takes hold of Alyse's hand impulsively and presses a kiss to the back of it.

Feral's back to her prowling, agitated state. Rest did nothing to take the edge off. "You might be feeling chill this morning, but all my predator senses are screaming at me."

"She's right." Violet looks pale and drawn, as if she didn't sleep at all. "This place is very wrong, and if you don't feel it, then I think it's dulling your threat response."

"Don't worry." I reach up to brush my fingers along Oni,

who buzzes around my head like an insect. "We'll be ready for shit."

Wolus and Burke stand at their front door, waving to us.

"Don't eat the food," Violet reminds us. "I know everyone's hungry but—"

"This isn't Fairyland," I say.

She shoots a glance at me. "Let's act like it is. No food, no drink, no bargains. Can we do that at least?"

"Hey." I step closer to her, and she flinches away at first, but then comes into my arms to bury her face in my chest. "Talk to me, Vi. What's wrong?"

"We're *inside* this place. I see blood when I close my eyes. I *feel* the infection slithering over my skin, looking for a way in. It's looking for hosts, Dylan. And we're so very, very appealing."

Violet's right about this place. It's lulling me. Which means I'm the prey.

"Let's get this over with." I coax my involuntary thorns back down.

We go single file back down the hillside to the houses, where the scientists wait. Wolus's giant head still pours coloured light, and Burke's braids twist in hypnotic patterns. They allowed themselves to get infected. The Weirdlands live in them. Feels like a good thing to avoid.

The computer room is bathed in a pale blue glow. The device itself looks as decrepit and encrusted as before, but a tree has grown around it. Its branches are twisted like a cypress, but luminous red fruit hangs from the lower ones, gleaming in the light. Apples lit like stars.

"The answers you seek." Dr. Wolus bows low. "About your Goddess."

"Don't eat the fruit," Violet hisses, but she may as well be speaking another language.

Alyse strides towards it. I don't think any one of us could stop her, but we all try.

I fling myself at the tree as it reaches out a single branch. A twisted limb catches Alyse by the hair. The ground turns liquid beneath her feet, as if she's stepped onto the surface of a filthy lake. She plunges downwards and is gone.

"How fascinating." Wolus's eyes flicker from within, as if all his rotted brains have been scooped out and a candle flickers there instead.

Fuck it. I'll deal with him later. I sprint after Alyse, diving into the murky depths myself. A lot like our metaphorical experience last night. Underneath, it's cool and green. I'm in a vast sea of something in-between water and glass. Far below, a trail of glistening bubbles is the only sign of Alyse.

This place doesn't want me. It constricts, throttling, solidifying around me to barricade me away. It's Alyse that it desires. Luring her in with promises of Emma. Perhaps if it assimilates her, the Weirdlands will be able to transform into even more monstrous things.

Then Violet churns past me, bladed hands hacking at the glutinous substance that surrounds us.

Clever. I make my own transformation, thorny claws ripping and tearing. Alongside me, Dani mimics my changes, and Feral has her own natural advantages. The four of us, digging through the guts of the Weirdlands to find our friend. Glowing fluid boils from the fissures we slash, curling ribbons of light dazzling me. I blink away lurid tears, following the stormy darkness of Violet's descent.

There's no further sign of Alyse. No bubbles, no glimmering wake.

All those promises I made to her last night. *I'm always coming to save you.*

Violet disappears abruptly ahead of me. I put on an extra burst of speed and crash through the floor directly after her. We come out in a wide cavern lit by the light spilling from the sea we've just come through. The floor is carpeted with thousands of miniature trees that bloom in neon shades of green and blue.

And in the middle, Alyse dangles from the horns of an enormous creature that looks like a gnarled twist of rock with an enormous ram-like skull sitting atop it. They haven't pierced her skin—she's transformed to have hoops jutting from her collarbones that slip easily over the jagged knobs of bone. Her eyes are closed and she's completely limp, as if she's sleeping.

The perspective of the room is all wrong—from this angle the hollow eyes of the skull look bigger than the room itself, and in the depths of them I can see the room again but from a different angle.

"Finally." Feral winks at me. "Something to punch."

"Stealing my lines." I leap forward with her, dwarfed by the size of the monster.

The creature howls and spits, trampling the tiny trees as it leaps towards us. They crack beneath like matchsticks, a pale fluid leaking out. I wreathe the bone-thing in vines, scrambling to slam my thorny fists into the fissures of its joints. It shrinks under the combined onslaught of the four of us, perspective downshifting it until it's the same size as we are. Dani grips tight onto one of the horns, shearing it clean off.

Alyse tumbles to the ground. Her eyelids flutter. "No Emma. Not even a whisper."

I pick up the severed horn and plunge it into the creature's chest. It quivers and slumps, revealing itself to be no more than a rickety collection of bones wrapped in an old blanket. The hell was this thing?

"You okay?" I crouch beside Alyse.

"You told me." She blinks tears away. "But I thought maybe…"

"It was worth a try." I wrap my arms around her. "And you're safe now."

"What's this?" Dani's found something among the slimy muck on the ground. She cradles it to her chest and wipes off all the gunk. It reveals a wooden box, ornately carved with symbols.

"Trap," I say succinctly. "Leave it. We need to get out of here."

"I'm not sure. This feels like Cybele?"

I brush my fingertips against the surface of the box, and there *is* a resonance that feels familiar. "Bring it with us to look at later. Right now, those fucking guys are going to give us some answers."

THE TRIP back to the surface is remarkably easy, like we've wounded it and it's spitting us back out in disgust. Except when we bob to the surface of the lake, we find the rest of the Weirdlands unchanged. The scientists stand in the middle of the room, watching eagerly.

"That thing tried to fucking eat Alyse," I growl, hauling myself onto solid ground.

"Assimilation is inevitable." Burke leans past his husband, braids twitching. "It's less than you imagine it to be, and also far more. Stubborn individuality is a curse much of humanity suffers under. You understand, Chatterbox and Marvellous. Cybele may be a more distributed hive, but a network all the same."

At the word *hive,* a rising hum becomes audible. I think it was there all along, but now it's definitely louder.

"I don't think you understand Cybele at *all,*" Dani says.

"What are you, if not nodes?" Wolus's eyes are almost as bright as his teeth. "Nodes that could be integrated into a far greater whole." Behind his teeth, in the dark cavern of his mouth, something glistens. Something *slithers.*

"Oh, hello there," Feral says, and buries her claw in his throat.

"Feral," I scream, but Oni's flying into the room, burying himself up to the hilt in Burke's stomach. Maybe they know something I don't.

"I'm proving a point." Feral yanks her hand out in a shower of blood and stringy tendrils of flesh. Inside the ruined flesh is a mass of tiny white grubs that pulse like a heart.

Oni wrenches himself backwards in an arc that disembowels Burke, like slicing open a sack. Except all that falls out is a series of tumorous lumps like a string of onions, mottled a sickly blue-green and steaming faintly.

Neither of the two seem inconvenienced at all.

"Assimilation into the hive is inevitable," Wolus says, almost tenderly. "It would have been simpler to take you into the heart and have you blessed, but once your physical shells are compromised, the process will—"

"You *used Emma.*" Something hurtles past me, a creature made of blackened chrome with a thousand sharp edges. From context, I can figure out it's Alyse, but by the time my brain has supplied that fact, she's already reduced Wolus to a pile of glowing meat and shattered pieces of gemlike teeth.

"Fuck." I feel oddly like the model of restraint

I'm not surprised when the fucking hut starts collapsing in on us though. The two scientists aren't the avatars of the

Weirdlands. They're a pair of indistinguishable nodes in the whole.

"Intrusion detected," the computer says. "Deploying countermeasures."

Shards of wood stab down from the hut roof, plunging into the ground and sending up scalding plumes of smoke. Alyse smashes through one of the walls to outside. I pull Violet into me, thorns up, and leap out after her, Feral and Dani hot on my heels.

"The fuck do we do now?" I shout. "Randomly stab things?"

"Run for the border wall." Feral points in a direction that I don't even think is right. "We need to get out of here."

Behind us, the computer drags itself from the wreckage, its cables sparking and bleeding light. It's alive too, like everything here. In the distance, enormous skeletons flail their way out of the soil they're half-buried in. I think we're about to fight this entire fucking place.

Feral's gone bounding up the hill to retrieve the flower swords, which don't seem to have activated any dark powers. Maybe we disconnected them when we pulled them from the earth. Either way, extra weapons are precisely what we need.

As soon as Dani gets hers, she strides over to the computer, hacking and slashing at the cables while it burbles a mix of threats and entreaties. Feral is dealing with a horde of tiny misshapen wooden figures that have spilled from the ruins of the hut, and Alyse is busy fighting a glistening white snake with Dr. Burke's head. Images I'm going to have to scrub from my mind, but—

Violet. Where's Violet?

I spot her at the foot of something grotesque. Wolus has returned as a tower of flesh. That same beaming smile is plastered on the outside, replicating as it rises until the vast structure grins down from a thousand mouths. Oni ascends him in a spiral, leaving huge rents in the tower's sides that gush luminous blood in arcing sprays. It doesn't stop him booming out more slogans. "Join the hive, submit to the glory of assimilation, become one entity."

Usually, I'd expect Violet to be in her element, but she's cringing away. I rush over to her, ignoring the thousand and one things I should be stabbing.

"Babe." I shelter her in my arms.

"Every time I try to use my hands as blades, they cut new horrible things into the world." She's agitated, almost panicking. "I hate being helpless."

"Take this." I shove the flower sword into her hands. "Poke anything that gets close and let me do the himbo thing."

The Wolus tower is collapsing, hitting the ground like a felled tree, but at the moment of impact it transforms. What lands on the ground is the man who greeted us. No wounds in his throat from where Feral tore into him, but the same glow pouring out of his skull.

His voice booms golden light. "We don't have to do this at all. This is so unutterably pointless. You fight an impossible battle, and one that shouldn't be fought at all. A merger between Cybele and the Weirdlands is of benefit to all. Don't you see that? Expanding the hive is beautiful and inevitable. The world will be at peace, at *one*."

"You can't trust him." Violet has a white-knuckle grip on the sword.

"The girl doesn't understand." Wolus spreads his arms wide. "Her perceptual mind is clouded and she misunderstands the nature of what we are. What she sees as an infection is simply a new mode of being. You're only frightened, dear Violet, because you're looking *up* the evolutionary scale. It's an infection, yes, and it hurts but—"

I have a flashback to him saying these exact words to us before. Showing us—

Oni senses what I'm going to do, and moves before I even pull my arm back. He slices through the air in one swift, sharp motion and severs Bobosy's leg just below the knee.

The transformation is instantaneous. The person who collapses to the ground is a fairly ordinary man, although he does have a particularly large head, one with a rough cloth bandage wrapped around it and blood seeping from the back. He's shivering violently and his leg pulses blood. On the bright side, a lot of the other activity around us has stopped.

"You're fine." I use some of my own vines to make a tourniquet for his leg. "Better than fine, probably, because I just unassimilated you rather violently."

"Thank you." His teeth chatter. "Oh god, it hurts. Everything hurts. It's like I'm being burned alive. Cut off from it... It's agony. But thank you. Sorry."

"Your husband." I grab at the man's collar. "Where's his infection?"

"His hand. Left." Wolus blanches. "Be gentle, please."

I don't even bother rolling my eyes. "Fuck that. Alyse! Cut off the asshole's left hand."

She pivots in one smooth movement, one hand transforming into a wicked silver blade which slices through Burke's arm just above the wrist. It has the same immediate effect, and now we're left with two injured scientists who rush to each other and cling pitifully. They still look mostly the same, aside from any glowing or twitching.

"We've bought ourselves some time," Dr. Wolus says faintly. "Although not much. We are very rich hosts, and so the Weirdlands exerted most of their control over this locus through us. But there are many other loci, and many other dangers. This place is truly alien, you see, and it works on principles we cannot understand."

"The hive will come here." Burke's braids hang limp over his shoulders. "Every part of it. You've proven yourselves a very grave threat, which will make you an even greater target for assimilation."

"I miss it," Wolus whispers. "I hate it, but I miss it too."

"I know." The two men embrace more tightly.

I give them about five seconds and then poke one of them unnecessarily hard. "So how the fuck do we get out of here? Is there some king shit larva monster we can kill? A shortcut to the wall through some geography accident?"

"Oh no." Wolus shakes his head. "We are quite, quite doomed."

"The price of freedom." Burke gives a hacking cough.

"There's got to be a way," Dani says. "We can't risk bringing the kids in here. Keepaway can't even *see* in here. Sorry, all I'm doing is ruling things out."

"I say we fight our way out," Feral says.

"I vote for that option." Alyse is still gleaming metal, a collection of blades hammered into the shape of a woman. "They used Emma to try and lure me, to make me one of them. I've got a lot of emotions to work through, and stabbing will definitely help."

"Might be the only chance we have." I look into the distance where the sky is darkening with the approach of *something*. "As long as we duck the giant skeletons and the worst of the other nightmares. It's going to be a hell of a fight. Lys, can you transform up and carry these two science idiots out?"

"There might be a quicker way," Violet says.

"Which is?"

"I cut my way out. Get back to Mutopia, find One Thorn and get them to open a door into here. If anyone can, it's them. If not, you'll have to fight your way to the wall."

"But cutting your way out..." I trail off, because I see the fear in Violet's face.

"Yes, it'll be disgusting, diving through a lake of blood and wallowing in infection with all the hideous things that crawl there. But I'm tougher than I look."

Dani takes her hand. "You don't need to do penance anymore. You know that, right?"

"Mostly." A tiny smile flickers across her lips. "But I'm the only one who can do this. The rest of you have the hard job of holding shit down. Because you better be here when I get back."

"I think you'll find we're pretty hard to kill," I say.

"Hey, I've died twice," Dani sings with a little flourish.

"I love you," I tell her, because who else will give me *Buffy* references when we're about to meet a gruesome end?

"They're coming." Feral stands perfectly still, looking into the distance.

Violet wraps her arms around my neck and pulls my head down to hers. "This isn't a goodbye kiss. It's a kiss that says don't get too stabbed, because I am going to do many, many things to you later on that will require you to be uninjured."

It's soft and tender, and it makes my stomach do a weird flip thing, or maybe that's the oncoming battle. But she gives me back my flower sword, and I've got Oni at my shoulder as Violet turns towards Dani, and lifts her face again. I always like seeing them kiss. I've got plenty of jealousy about various things, but not that. Moments of tenderness among the people I love keeps me going.

"I'll be back." Violet twists herself into some jagged,

complex shape. She's a bloody scrawl across the background of the world, and then she burrows inside. Reality bleeds around her. It gushes watery fluid, pus-yellow and smelling like decaying flowers. Sightless things spill from the hole, flailing their sharp-edged bodies and gnashing at the air. They scent us, and they want to feed.

More spill out in a rush, and the group of us stand together, blades drawn.

Now we have to fight, and hope Violet makes it through.

CHAPTER 9
THIS IS OUR FIGHT SONG

BATTLES AREN'T REALLY something you get used to. They're loud and overwhelming and you're so hypersaturated in emotion you can't find your footing. You're constantly scared you're going to die. That you'll fuck up and get killed, or worse, make a mistake that gets your friends killed. It helps slightly to be in here with this particular group, because we can handle ourselves better than most. Feral is the definition of an apex predator, and Alyse is transformed into a weapon of such grace and purity, it would make a thousand warriors weep. Then there's Dani and me, with thorned fists and vine whips. The rage of so many felled forests and destroyed habitats.

So yeah, we're pretty badass. We've walked away from some intense battles.

But this one's brutal. You punch a monster, and sometimes it cracks and hatches something worse. The blood *sings,* and drags you down into tangy iron puddles that coagulate around you. The sky opens and rains down fluttering terrors with mangled human voices and wings patterned with threats. Underneath, the ground is soft and treacherous, trying to steal away the bodies of the doctors that lie huddled at our feet. The entire world that surrounds us is dangerous, and there's no safe harbour except our friends. If I had any questions about whether this place was alien, they're all gone now. The only things left are the complicated *why* and *how* ones, and they'll have to fucking wait.

We end up fighting in a huddle, back to back and trading off against incoming enemies. Our communication is reduced to barked orders and warnings. I'm getting the sinking feeling that we're not going to make it. Feral is getting frantic, Alyse's movements are becoming mechanical, and Dani and I are like one entity all stitched together with vines.

The giant skeleton-beasts are almost upon us, tottering on twisted towers of knotted bone, their massive skulls slicing through the damp air like necromantic ships, the glowing sigils on their skulls lighting them up like some futuristic inner city. From the cavernous holes of their eyes pour flocks of things that might have been birds, but are now networked together with bloody twists of cable into a single entity borne on thousands of dark, rushing wings.

We're trying to retreat along the ridge-line but the sheer size of these creatures makes them gobble up the distance. We're going for the wall, but the whole place is *changing.* The ground becomes impassable, huge stretches of gurgling bog with clumps of mushrooms sprouting, huge growths that look like stout little people in trench coats and slouch hats. I'm sure I see the glints of eager eyes watching us. Much further, and we're going to be trapped between the goddamn fungus and the bone-ships.

"Feeling those last stand vibes real fucking hard." Feral's limping and there's a ragged cut down her left side. I've packed it with moss from my own shoulder in the hope it'll stave off the hive infection. If she gets assimilated, she's going to be very hard to stop. I imagine what it might look like, her face bathed in sickly rainbow light, claws elongating into endless razors, her beautiful face twisted into nothing but hunger.

When I see the door, I think I must be imagining it. It's a plain wooden door with a brass handle, so mundane it can't exist here.

Until it bangs open, and a blood-drenched figure stands on the doorstep. She's trembling, tears cutting tracks through the gore. Dani and I scream in unison, and go sprinting towards her. Alyse is smart enough to pick up the two scientists in giant hands and dive through the door to safety. Feral fights behind us, killing anything that tries to slow down our escape.

Dani and I hug Violet between us, her body trembling against ours.

"Have your reunion time *inside,* bitches." Feral gives me a violent shove from behind, and we all go tumbling through the doorway.

It slams behind us so hard that dust drifts down from the ceiling.

We're all in a painful, messy pile, but we're safe and Violet's in our arms.

"Are you okay?" I try to wipe some of Violet's face clear of blood so I can kiss her properly, but she's a complete mess. "Fuck, some of these cuts are *yours.*"

"Yes, and it hurts. No, that doesn't mean let go of me. I'd rather be squashed by you than not feel pain."

"Well, *that* is a terribly unpleasant place, isn't it?" The calm voice of One Thorn comes from the walls around us. "The nasty little creatures tried to infect me. Can you believe that?"

"Yeah, I bet it'd love you." I stroke Violet's matted hair. "A pipeline to the rest of the world."

One Thorn is a mutant who takes the form of a house that's capable of extending a door into any location in the world. Once upon a time, when there were twins in charge of the house, their reach extended into the universe and *beyond,* whatever that means. Since the violent disagreement that ended their partnership and truncated their powers severely, One Thorn has been building up their strength again. Strength that we can't let fall into the hands of some predatory hive mind lurking in the Dorset countryside.

"Let's not go back there again," Dani says.

"Maybe make those damn walls bigger." Alyse is slumped in what looks like a very comfortable armchair that One Thorn has materialised for us. There's enough for all of us, but right now lying on the floor is the extent of my abilities.

"I've disconnected from the Weirdlands, and am currently reconfiguring myself so this room leads directly to Mutopia," the house says. "Given that you all seem rather the worse for wear."

"Next time I tell you I'm spoiling for a fight, you can slap me." Feral blinks at me, the pupils in her large golden eyes enormous. Her fur is crusted with a mixture of slime and blood, and her ears are still flat against her head. "Think I've had enough."

"Are the science bros okay?" I ask Alyse.

She nudges Wolus with one foot. "Breathing, sure. Conscious, no. The shock of being disconnected, probably.

These two assholes, poking around in that place and getting themselves half-eaten."

I manage to pull myself up to my feet, using a whole bunch of vines to anchor me, and stand there with Violet cradled in my arms. She's nestled in against my chest, and now I can see the thousands of tiny cuts all over her skin.

"You did it," I whisper.

"Told you." She forces a smile, but more tears spill down her cheeks. "Had to get you back."

"What was in there?" Feral asks.

"The hive." Violet's voice is quiet. "That's where it lives. In the passageways behind the world. It's sprouted, and there are tendrils everywhere. The Weirdlands is the place where it's infected and can poke out into… realspace, you could call it. So to get out, I had to go through and find a clear path so I could reach One Thorn."

I can tell Feral has a lot more questions, and honestly, I want to know as well, but Violet's so bashed up and bleeding that I shake my head and we all fall silent.

"Done," One Thorn says, moments later. "This exit now leads to Doc's office. No need to thank me, it's all part of the service."

EVERYTHING HURTS as we go limping out of the door that not so long ago was our exit from the Weirdlands. Doc isn't too surprised to see us, although she is at the extent of Violet's injuries. The little cuts cover her entire body, some of them neat incisions and others twisted symbol shapes. Even worse, the top part of her left arm has been completely skinned, and the knots of her spine jut through the broken skin of her back, the ends split as if they're about to blossom like flowers.

"How are you even alive?" Doc glares down as if Violet did all this on purpose.

"I'm tougher than I look." She grins despite everything. "I keep telling Dilly this."

"Well you're a very lucky, very reckless girl."

Violet blinks up, tears in her eyes. "Sorry, Doc."

Doc shakes her head and her short locs bounce. "Oh, don't give me those eyes. Lie back and let me do my thing."

Just like the rest of us, our mutant healer is a lot less powerful now that Goddess isn't around to boost her. Fixing up Violet exhausts her so much she has to rest before we take our turn. I would describe having my girlfriend all healed as the best medicine, but I'm too sore to be anything less than irritable. Especially when we discover that Tentacle Princess is still mysteriously gone. No clues as to where she might be. No messages about what exactly she's hiding *from*.

Violet, now all smooth and pristine, cheers me up by telling me horror stories about the hive.

"I guess the closest description I can give you is psychic bugs."

Feral and I compete to give the biggest gross-out face.

"They're a seed that was planted a really, really long time ago, blooming underground and unseen. That cave where Alyse was—where we fought that bone-thing—it was very, very old. But Cybele's energy overload worked on it the same way it did to some mutants, and now it's all grown up to the surface."

"The visions of Emma," Alyse says. "They weren't true, were they?"

"I don't think so." Violet hugs her knees. "I'm sorry, Lys. I know that was hard. The hive wants to grow. It wants to *under-*

stand. A lot of this… damage was the hive trying to eat me." She runs her fingertips over her arm, and I mirror the movement across her skin. "It wanted to learn what I am so it could assimilate me."

"It sounds like you're apologising for it." Dani's perched on another chair, frowning.

"It hurt like hell, and I was sure I was going to die…" She prods at her spine. "But I think the two scientists gave it their own desire. They're the ones fascinated with Cybele and understanding the world, so the hive copied it. Once the scientists were disconnected, it was starting again, trying to understand *me.* I think that's part of how I got out. I made it clear I didn't want to be part of it. I tore myself free, no matter how much it hurt."

"That's my girl." I run my fingers through her newly clean hair.

"Understanding the world is a good instinct, but less so when you feed it to a hive mind. It's just like any other mutant. Lots of power and potential, but you have to be careful what you use it for." She gives us a big grin. "Thus endeth the lesson. Sorry, sometimes the preacher's daughter still comes out, doesn't it? Gross."

I can't help but laugh. "No, it's a good lesson. It's always been the way. Think of how many mutants we thought were our enemies, but we've brought into the family. We're better off together."

"We are *not* going back and adopting that hive mind," Feral says. "At least not before dinner."

"I'm not suggesting that, but I don't think we should kill it either. It's something to learn about, be gentle with. Maybe it can help fix the world."

"You didn't happen to find any clues while you were in there?" I ask.

Violet shakes her head. "There were lots of flowers like ours, but it's not a straightforward question and answer type deal when you're talking to a hive mind."

"Back to square one." I scowl around the room, but by this point, Doc's finally recovered, and she takes a look at our two doctors. Feral's got a pretty solid healing factor and Alyse can transform most wounds away without any trouble. Dani and I will heal on our own, given time to bloom overnight.

"This thing is intriguing." Dani frowns at the wooden box in her lap. "It's like an old fashioned puzzle box, but I can't figure out the steps to open it. It's definitely made from Cybele's wood though."

I lean in to run my fingers over the surface. The grooved pattern is complex, forming a garden pattern on each side. "So why was it sitting in some ancient cave, guarded by a skull monster?"

"No idea, but look. You can press in the flowers." Dani splays her fingers and there's a tiny click sound with each one. "There will be a combination that'll unlock the next layer."

"Or just smash it," I say with a shrug.

"You can't do that!" Dani looks horrified. "You have to solve the puzzle. Forcing it might destroy whatever's inside."

"It's probably something terrible." I nudge her shoulder with mine. "But you're cute when you get all nerdy and obsessive."

She shakes her head, but she's smiling. "I just like to figure things out."

"Better you than me." I lean back against her, my brain chewing on its own puzzle box. The pieces of our situation are swirling in my head and won't fit together: a mysterious possible-clone of me, an alien environment sprouting in England, the disappearance of Tentacle Princess, and some *threat* from outside.

My moody thoughts are interrupted by a knock at the door.

"Lucifer!" I'm still shaky, but I stagger over to greet him. "Where have you been?"

"Missions." He grins at me. "On your orders, general."

My ex-boyfriend—whose name is actually Lou—used to be part of our original superhero team called the Cute Mutants. At some point along the way, half split off to become the black-ops paranormal investigation team known as Weapon UwU. It means we don't see each other as much as we used to, but we're still close. And he always smells ridiculously good, like he thinks he's a fucking love interest or something.

"You here to welcome us home or—"

He grimaces. "Shit's hit the news again."

"It's bad, isn't it?" I glance over my shoulder at the others. "Every time."

"There's been another murder." Dani's gaze is steady.

"Bingo." Lou gives finger guns. "Some GIC agent called me directly with a phone that Violet apparently gave her?"

"I did that." Violet shrugs as we all stare at her. "What? She said she wanted to help, and she's been decent so far."

"They're trying to keep this one under wraps," Lou says. "The media haven't started shitstorming. Decker said you can look around if you're quick."

"A trap?" Dani scowls. "The GIC are gunning for you, Dylan."

This kicks off an argument back and forth, which is wasting time when we could be actually taking action. One of my least favourite things.

"Fuck it," I say, loud enough to shut everyone up. "We'll go in. If it's a trap, I'll punch someone. But we've got to solve this goddamn mystery before it spins out of control, so we can't turn up our noses at clues."

Dani purses her lips and then nods. "Fine. But I'm going to break that woman's face if she's fucking with us."

"I'll cheer you on, love." I wink at her and then call for transportation.

CHAPTER 10
CRIME SCENE INSTIGATORS

WE USE One Thorn to reach the crime scene. Keepaway's technically faster, but they're exhausted after a mass rescue event in Johannesburg. The house creates an extra door right outside the apartment of the victim. We don't even know who's dead yet, because the only information Decker gave Lou is an address. It makes me edgy, but my motto—if I bothered to have one—would be that action is better than inaction. Even sticking my head into a terrible situation. Being this close to our *last* disastrous outing into the Weirdlands should make me gun-shy, but apparently not shy enough.

The hallway looks entirely ordinary, relatively clean, with all the doors firmly closed. Muffled television sounds come from somewhere, and there's the faint smell of takeaways.

I rap on the apartment door and then stand back and wait, flanked by Dani and Alyse. Violet's asleep, and I used my best bossy partner voice to make her stay that way. We're dressed in what Dani calls our Grant Morrison outfits, after an early 00s era of the X-Men when they got edgy and hip. There's a lot of leather, but we really do look like we're prepped for kicking ass. Some might consider that the look is slightly spoiled by the delicate flowers running along the lines of our collarbones but we contain fucking multitudes. Oh god, listen to me, I really am on edge. Just answer the goddamn door, you fucking—

It swings open to reveal Decker. Her red hair is shorter than last time, and her freckle-dusted cheeks look pale. She's wearing a grey suit and thin-framed glasses. Behind her is an apartment so bland it looks like a crappy motel room. Threadbare two-seater couch. Plain formica dining table with two chairs.

"I wasn't sure you'd come." Her voice has a slight nasal twang. "Thought Marvellous here might talk you out of it."

Dani is very unimpressed with this show of Decker deduction, and steps around the agent and into the room. "We're not here so you can show off how well you know us, spy girl. Who's the corpse?"

"Anastasia Beregova. Who you might know better as—"

"Anna Hume." My jaw clenches. "Another good choice, fake me."

"Through here." Decker stalks across the living room and pushes open the door revealing a tiled bathroom. "Throat slit in the bathtub. No sign of forced entry. This isn't Beregova's apartment, obviously. Her real place is much swankier. This place is owned by some religious organisation as a halfway house. I'll follow up on that lead."

I follow the agent into the bathroom and look down at the frothy pink water surrounding the fully clothed body of a woman. The wound in her throat is so deep that her head is almost severed. Her t-shirt says *Chatterbox Was Right*. I've seen a bunch of knockoffs, but this looks like an original. Another weird flex on the part of the killer to dress her like this.

"Odds a sword did this?" I ask.

"High."

"Fuck." Anna Hume's face looks waxy and bloated, far different from her numerous videos. She's made a name for herself as a pro-human activist who deliberately targets kids, feeding them disinformation about mutants. It's bad enough when she makes human teenagers even more hateful, but when you meet a mutant kid who's internalised everything she says, it's a whole other story. And then there are the ones you don't meet.

"I'm glad she's dead," Alyse says. "I'm sorry, but I am. She was evil. There's no other word for it. The Weirdlands is a fucking paradise compared to her."

I completely agree, but I'm also worried about the rain of shit when this news breaks. Anne Hume, killed by Chatterbox. Silenced for speaking the truth. The mutant threat proved real.

"How do we cover this up, Agent Decker?" I ask. "I'm assuming that's why we're alone."

It's very quiet in the apartment. Decker's framed in the doorway. I can see the outline of the gun in her jacket. There's no way she's fast enough to beat Dani, who's a few paces closer than me.

"That's a very large reach, Mx. Taylor."

"No, I don't think so." Dani steps even closer, and the agent flinches very slightly. "There's something off about the whole situation. Even if you're the GIC expert on us, you're acting suspicious as hell. Giving a phone to Violet so you could contact us. Warning her about the GIC coming for us. Letting us tramp through a crime scene before your asshole goons. You're obviously up to something. I can only hope it's helping us." She lets the pause drift on long enough to get some teeth. "You know, for your sake."

It's unpleasantly warm in the bathroom, as if the heat from the water has soaked into the walls, almost like a sauna. The tap still drips with a desultory plink into the tub, spreading pink ripples that stop at the body.

Decker's eyes move to the corpse, back to Dani, and then to me. She finally nods. "Okay, here's the deal. Hume was in a tumultuous relationship with an ex-Quietus piece of shit called Harmon Faustus."

"We know Faustus," I say. "Feral wants to kill him."

"Feral wants to kill a lot of people," Alyse points out.

Decker only looks slightly bothered by this fact. "It suits me to pin this on him. For… reasons. Especially if we have mutants to stage the scene."

"That's a quick turnaround in attitude," Dani says.

Decker gives her an amused look. "I've been obstructing justice for a long time in the name of you and your friends, Ms. Kim. This is only the latest chapter."

I raise one eyebrow. "This seems like a story I want to hear more of."

"And yet framing someone for murder takes priority." Decker adjusts her collar. "I'll take suggestions for which mutants you think would be useful here. I assume your teleporting friend can move the body."

"We've got a couple of waterbenders to wring out the corpse," Dani says. "I think Katara's the most likely to keep her mouth shut. The Undertaker can transform flesh, so we can heal the cut."

"My bigger concern is Faustus," Decker says. "We need a drug that can scramble him enough that he won't remember anything that happened. There's stuff in the GIC system but I can't walk in and take it without raising alarms."

"Or a mutant who does the same." I snap my fingers. "Lys, who's that friend of Sluggo's? Lives in that old mutant house in New York?"

"Confusio," Alyse says. "Yeah, that'll work. He'll be scrambled like an egg."

"Your metaphors." I kiss my fingers. "So beautiful."

The actual business of covering up a murder isn't hard. Our plan works flawlessly and before long we have Faustus locked his own apartment, lying next to the body of his girlfriend. Given the police history that Decker showed us, he'll be the prime suspect, and given the things he's done in the past—forgiven under the same post-Michael 'amnesty' that let mutants walk free of alleged crimes, he deserves any punishment coming his way.

We're really good at this shit. Humans should be grateful that we're the good guys.

ONCE WE'RE DONE with the frame job, Dani's still suspicious. "Convince me this isn't a long con, Agent."

"Despite me trashing one crime scene, faking another, allowing a mutant to mould a corpse like it's plastic, and framing a man for a crime he didn't commit? You've confirmed there are no signals going in and out of this place, so I'm not surreptitiously recording."

"I have very little faith in humanity, and especially that of the intelligence agencies." Dani's eyes are far colder than I'm used to seeing them, leaves frozen under ice. "The GIC would do anything to take us down."

Decker nods. "You're right. Their fear drives them to abominable things. And that's exactly why I've stayed in there, to stop the worst from happening." A flush creeps up her cheeks. "Not that I've always succeeded, but I've done my damn best."

"The evidence is destroyed anyway, Dan." I keep my voice soft. "If they figure out something's wrong, they can't pin this on me. I suppose there's Decker's testimony, but I'm sure a little brain-scrambling can take care of that."

Decker's eyes widen. "I swear to you, Chatterbox. You can trust me."

"Too risky." Dani's voice is flat, her eyes flatter.

Decker's scrambling, talking a mile a minute. "Wait, I need to remember this. It's how I can help you best. If there are gaps in things they'll be suspicious. Dylan, please. I've been watching you since high school. I was living in the house across the street from you, working for EMID. It was me who intervened when Quietus tried to take you after the Firestone incident. I killed all of the agents who worked with me. They were double agents for Quietus, except for my undercover mother, who caught me and was going to turn me in. I'm—"

"She's telling the truth." Fetch steps out of the adjoining room. She's another member of Weapon UwU. Her power is to see what other people are scared of, and read the truth in what they reveal. If Decker really is on our side, she's an advantage that's far too good to ruin by scrambling her brain. "So many fears it's like a web. Always trying to keep ten steps ahead of so many people, balancing allegiances, keeping such an astonishing array of secrets."

"Awww." I find myself smiling enormously. "You almost restore my faith in humanity, Decker."

"Almost." Dani winks. "Sorry for messing with you, but we had to be sure."

Decker's nostrils flare. "I understand. It's a lot to ask of you."

"You get to live, Decker." Alyse slaps her on the back. "You should look happier."

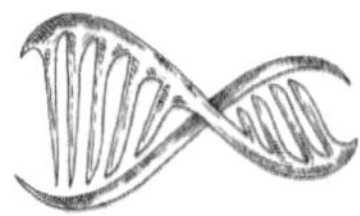

NEXT, Keepaway bounces us back to the original crime scene to scour it for clues. The apartment is already near-obsessively clean and the only thing we find in it is a single tarot card, tucked under the couch.

"The Hierophant." I hold it gingerly between my thumb and forefinger. "Can you run prints on this, Decker? Without anybody else knowing."

"Sure." Decker pulls out her phone, which makes us all tense up. Even if we trust the agent, there's no way we trust her bosses or her fancy GIC phone. Alyse reaches into her pocket and pulls out a little electronic widget that runs a very basic AI derived from Emma. She attaches it to the phone so it'll nerf any signals, and probably keep track of a thousand other things too, knowing Ems.

Decker doesn't argue with any of this, and taps away at the app. "No prints aside from the tiny partials you just left. Which by my reckoning makes this a message from our suspect."

"These types of assholes always love their messages." I drop the card onto the tiny formica table and we all cluster around it. "But what the fuck is a hierophant?"

"Some sort of priest, I think," Dani says, but then she has to double-check she's right on Google. Then she tumbles down a rabbit hole about ancient Greek mysteries and into a full nerdy meltdown. "They're involved with Demeter, who's analogous to Cybele. And her daughter Persephone, who was stolen away by Hades and then returned. The interesting point is it's all metaphorical shit to do with the rebirth of plant life."

"You lost me way back." I'm looking up the tarot card itself. Mostly, the image search results for Hierophant depict a boring Pope-type character. Ours is a rough black and white drawing, a figure with an animal skull draped in a cloak, surrounded by moons and carrying a weird cross with multiple bars on it. I don't find it until the fifth page of the image search, which is real dedication on my part.

"It's called the Outer Darkness tarot." I flick through some of the other cards, which feature the same scratched-out line drawings with skulls and cryptic symbols. There's something oddly compelling about them.

"That's who this place is registered to," Decker says. "The Church of the Outer Darkness."

"Cult," Alyse says.

"Definite cult," Dani agrees. "It's a bible thing, I think." She taps more into her phone. "Yeah, look. *The children of the kingdom shall be cast out into the exterior darkness where there shall be weeping and gnashing of teeth.*"

Alyse grimaces. "Always so cheerful, the Bible."

"I hate this shit." I stare down at the card. "Is it one of those old-fashioned calling cards, like they're trying to introduce themself? Or a weird threat? Or are they flirting with us in the weirdest possible way?"

Decker taps her fingernail on the formica. "Here's my reasoning: these murders are high-profile targets to make mutants look bad. This means our unsub knows your people of interest, and they want the consequences to fall on you. But it's complicated, because they're taking out people who are anti-mutant, which leads me to the conclusion that we're dealing with a destabilising third party."

"Someone who's not human or mutant?" Dani asks with a frown.

Decker shakes her head. "Unlikely. Someone whose agenda is served by the conflict. Like how weapons manufacturers want regional instability so they can continue profiting off it."

I let out a plaintive groan. "You're making me feel even worse."

"Sorry, I'm simply following threads. In these situations, we ask cui bono i.e. who benefits? That's who we need to find. In the meantime, I suggest we investigate this Church of Outer Darkness. I'll pull my threads, you pull yours, and we'll continue to share information." She flushes again. "If that's acceptable to you all, of course."

Dani scoops the tarot card off the table and slides it into her jacket pocket. "Agent Decker, I think you might have won me over, despite the odds." She favours the agent with one of her dazzling smiles. "Let's dig into cults together, shall we?"

CHAPTER 11
WAILING AND GNASHING OF TEETH

BACK ON MUTOPIA, Dani and I stop in with Weapon UwU. They live not too far away from our little cluster of houses, a short distance along the headland towards Emmaline City. We find Lou and Katie playing a card game and accusing each other of cheating.

"Chatty." Katie springs up from the table, conveniently scattering cards everywhere, which probably means she was the one up to no good. She's short and muscly, with a shaved head and flame tattoos all up and down her arms and neck like a sports car. Her mutant name is Dragon for a very obvious reason. "It seems like it's been ages."

"That's because it has, brat." I run my hand across her prickly scalp. "And we're here on business. We seem to have run ourselves into a cult."

"Oh my god, I'm so tired of them," Katie groans. "Is this

another Michael one? They're the worst. All these sad people trying to upgrade themselves with chips in their heads."

"Not sure yet." Dani joins Lou at the table. "They call themselves the Church of the Outer Darkness." She fishes the card from her pocket and slides it across the table to him.

He frowns. "That looks oddly familiar. Let me look around." He pushes his chair back and then pauses. "Is this to do with the piece of news I dropped on your doorstep earlier?"

"Yeah." I sigh theatrically. "It's all annoyingly vague."

"Just give you something to punch, right?" He grins at me.

"That's one thing cults are good for," Katie tells me. "Punch the leaders and the true believers, set the rest of the people free."

"Amen." Lou disappears into the other room and returns with a tattered old ring binder, the kind we used to have at school. He splays it on the table and starts flipping through it. "It's my weird shit file."

"You're such a nerd. Maybe I do have a type." I peer over his shoulder. Mostly it's a lot of confusing pamphlets, with the occasional drawing and scrawled manifesto. "This is not a fun hobby."

"No, it's weird and gross, but look." He's stopped on a page with another of the tarot cards in it. I reach down to snatch at it, but he knocks my hand away lightly. "Look with your eyes, Dilly."

This particular card is called The Magician. It has another skull-headed figure, this time without a cloak and with the infinity symbol carved into the white bone. Surrounding the figure is a wild abundance of flowers. I check online, and once again it's a creepy and stark interpretation of the standard card.

"Flowers," Dani says. "Like Persephone."

"Like us." I put the Hierophant beside it. They're definitely from the same deck. "Where the fuck did you find this thing?"

"Luckily, I keep meticulous notes." He nudges me. "Because I'm a terrible nerd. This happened just over three weeks ago. We went in to investigate reports of some cult abducting mutant kids for conversion therapy. The cult had mysteriously vanished, and there were no missing kids. Only this single card."

"Three weeks ago?"

"Yeah. And when I say vanished, I mean like fucking raptured. Gone in the middle of the night. Things were still laid out for breakfast. We did a brief forensic sweep and didn't find any blood or anything. Our working theory was that they'd figured out they were being raided, and bailed at the last minute. The card seemed a very odd thing to leave behind, that's all."

"Well this breaks my fucking brain." I slam my hands onto the table. "How does this random cult link to anything?"

"It doesn't," Dani agrees. "Which means something else is going on."

"This cult that vanished wasn't called anything to do with Outer Darkness was it?" I ask.

"No. It was something about Free The Human Within. There's a Bible verse about outer darkness, something about--"

"Gnashing of teeth, yeah. We got that." I trace my fingertips over the surfaces over the cards. They have a silky finish, but are slightly embossed. They feel expensive. Collector's editions. More than ever, I've got the sense that someone's fucking with us.

Which makes my decision easy. "Let's go find these assholes. It's time to fuck back."

Dani gives a gurgle of laughter. "I'd fall in love with you on catchphrases alone."

SADLY, it takes actual research before I can get to unleashing my frustration. Dani and Violet are actually good at it, whereas my skills are mostly limited to finding memes and asking irritating questions. Sometimes my questions are so annoying, it shakes loose a whole new avenue of investigation, so I gamely keep it up. This time, I'm oddly quiet because I'm diving into the full Outer Darkness tarot deck and it's freaking me out. First off, the Fool card is slightly reminiscent of me, even with the whole skull-head thing. Something about the slouched way they're standing, the frayed cuffs of the hoodie-like outfit. I figure it's my brain playing tricks on me until I get to the Empress card, which has such Dani vibes I nearly drop my laptop. It's her in ice queen mode, all power, confidence, and sneering hotness. And then I find The Lovers, which has two feminine figures and one androgynous one bridging the gap between them. It doesn't stop there—the Hanged Man has my face behind the skull, Death is patterned on Emma, and the Devil is clearly Cybele.

"Fuck me." My voice is hoarse. "Does anyone else see our faces in here?"

"Holy shit," Dani grips my shoulder hard. "That's *me*. They're creepy."

"Which one's mine?" Feral leans over my shoulder and starts swiping. We eventually find that she's the Chariot, and Alyse is the Star. None of the others are people we recognise, but I can't figure out if that's a hint in itself.

We end on the Tower, staring at the two plummeting figures.

They look devoid of expression, resigned to their fate. The bolt of lightning striking the top looks alive, like an arm reaching.

"There's writing, too." Alyse stabs a finger at the screen, where the scratchy pattern at the Tower's base forms a series of elongated letters.

"It's like some escape room shit." Dani squints and takes a step back. "I think it's an address. 205 Darnton Road."

A quick search shows a bunch of places around the world with that address. Only one's in the middle of some decrepit, foundering suburb of Manchester that's still abandoned after the Dark Year.

"Obvious choice," Alyse says. "And an obvious trap."

"We have to go." I look around at the others. "Trap or not, but this is getting increasingly fucked, and ignoring it won't make it go away. We'll take Keepaway, bounce in and out."

"Can you actually heal up before we go?" Dani pokes at the ruin of my right shoulder. "Everyone else is smart and has taken care of themselves. Even Feral."

"Fine." I sigh in frustration.

The good news is the kids are happy with their grandparents, and Violet's still slumbering peacefully. It'd be nice to curl up in bed with her, but we heal a lot faster in the forest, so we head to the top of the island. There are a few thousand humans and mutants living on Mutopia, but it's mostly one giant nature preserve and the forest runs everywhere through it. Even through the town, where half the buildings are hollowed out trees.

The Crown is where Cybele's power is strongest. If you want to meet her physical avatar, that's where you'll find her. Right now, I need the wellspring of energy that surges here. I feel calm the moment we enter the forest. Calm*er*. I haven't truly felt calm in a long time. I don't know how I'm supposed to.

"Hey." Dani takes hold of my hand and pulls me towards her. "You want to talk?"

"Brain is racing. Too many scenarios."

She plunges her feet into the soil, extending vines down deep and then wraps her arms around me, pulling me close until I can feel the thrum of her heart. "I'm sorry. I feel like I've infected you with this catastrophising shit."

"Dan, I'm perfectly capable of thinking terrible things."

"Yeah, but you used to think them about yourself. Now it's the whole world."

I frown. "This is actually a little bit true. Wow, thank you so much, love of my life. It's really all your fault."

She laughs, and I feel the vibrations of it move through me. I allow my physical form to cave inwards, so she's properly nestled inside me, the two of us a tangled mess of branches and ferns, our internal vines twisting together so we can share the sustenance from the island. We're like two trees that have collapsed in on each other, ancient and gnarled and impossible to separate.

"I'm so fucking *exhausted*," I murmur. "But we can't stop, because everything's always on the verge of disaster. Sometimes Mutopia is like having a flame cupped in your hand in the middle of a fucking gale-force rainstorm."

"I know. It feels like we're in one of those roguelike games, you know, like the world keeps generating new enemies for us, but we can barely level up and the loot that gets dropped is so shitty."

"Are you calling me shitty loot?" I ask in tones of great offence, which means she can't stop laughing. And *there's* the energy, surging up through us. We're only two small twigs in the middle of the forest sprawling around us, but oh, how we bloom. The two of us are titanic, looming up over the island so we can see it all, our tousled, waving heads spilling blossoms on the breeze. And it doesn't feel like a burden to protect anymore, it feels like a privilege to have it lying beneath our outstretched arms, a near-extinguished species having a safe harbour for the first time in so long.

I am worried, Cybele says, a murmur on the breeze.

And here I was, feeling cheerful for a moment.

Hush, complaining child. You must understand both the joy and the fear. Something is coming. Stirring at the edges of my web. Not prey dancing on the strings, but a predator.

Please tell me I'm misunderstanding you.

Perhaps I am over-sensitive and reacting to threats that are not truly there.

Or we're really fucking up against it this time. Dan, are you hearing this?

Yes, but I'm trying to ignore it and soak up all this beautiful energy.

That is good. Cybele's voice hums against my skin. *Let us not worry before it is time. Grow and bloom, my sweet protectors. Whatever comes, you will need strength, whether it is to be shepherds or warriors.*

I try to glory in my strength and power. To defy the future with my arms around my love. To see myself as a shield against the dark. That stupid goddamn fanfic thinks I'm flushed with my success, a powerful warrior blessed by fate and circumstance. Except I know the truth. I've seen the fallen. I know how fucking close it comes, time and again, to going the other way. How lucky I am to be alive, to be here and feel this fear.

Love from Dani surges through me, but not only her. The children are there too, twin green suns that burn with so much energy from this perspective that they're blinding. And Dani's extended tendrils out through the island to anchor them beneath all the people who love me. Starting with Violet, turning over in our bed and Alyse sprawled restless beside her.

Moving on to all the others who fight with me, then to Ray in their office, to Pear and their girlfriend in the cute little cottage they share, to everyone who's come to this island to find solace and strength. My own forest, all those who grow up around me.

"See?" Her voice is a glade to bask in, shaded and sweet on a sweltering day. "This is what we have. This is our family."

When I open my eyes, I'm back within myself, standing with my arms around Dani in the middle of the forest. The connections still hum within me, the knowledge of what I am.

Dani's beaming at me.

"Show-off," I say, but I kiss her for a long time.

When we come out of the forest, the rest of the team is waiting.

"Bloody hell. Do you bring more bad news?" I ask.

"No." Violet shakes her head. "We all felt those dreams of yours. Whatever's coming, we're ready to fight."

"Jesus." I wish I'd grow out of tearing up at these sappy moments, but apparently age and alien resurrection isn't enough. "You fucking assholes."

We used to do group hugs all the time, but they've felt incomplete since Emma died. They still happen, but there's a hole of grief we stumble into. This time, we cling just as tight, but nobody cries. I don't think it's because we're over her, or anything like that. Right now, the fight comes first.

In the moment we break, I get a brief vision, something spilling over from the dregs of my connection with Cybele. It shows me her energy network as a bright tangle encircling the globe.

And something picking its way through the shadows, plucking the end of a strand very deliberately.

CHAPTER 12

MAJORLY FUCKED ARCANA

I'M EDGY ABOUT EVERYTHING, so Dani insists I need to sleep like a normal human being before we go on our mission. No matter how many times I insist I'm neither normal nor human, she doesn't listen. She does rub my back though, which I like.

I drift into a fitful sleep—no dreams that make sense but scattered images like a photo album on shuffle. When I do wake, it's to kissing sounds, and breathless noises coming from Violet's throat. It's far from the first time this has happened. There are sometimes awkward moments when it comes to three people sharing a bed and a relationship, but mostly everyone's chill and so it all works out. I try not to feel any obligation to join in, or any sting of rejection for missing out, even though my mind likes to snatch at any thread that will lead down this path.

So I lie there and pretend to sleep, my half-closed eyes

watching the shapes they make as they taste and touch each other. It's the soft little lustful things they whisper that push me over the edge. I can't resist pressing my own hand between my legs.

"Told you they were listening," Dani murmurs.

Violet laughs, deep in her throat, and rolls over. She throws one leg over me, kissing my throat. Her body is warm and soft, and my hand drifts up her thigh as she pulls herself up to straddle me. Dani nestles in, the length of her body pressed to mine as if she wishes to melt herself into me in delicious fusion. Her teeth graze my flesh, her mouth imprinting a series of promises into my skin.

"I love you," I tell them.

They give their own declarations back to me, whispered into my mouth in turn. They touch me, and they kiss me, and they rouse me to fervour. I arch my back and I fist my hand in the tangled storm of Violet's hair. Her cheeks are flushed and her skin is faintly damp from Dani's kisses.

Dani grinds against me, petals blooming along the lines of her collarbone. They open to my touch, and I taste them along with her skin, the dewy bloom of her. I want to drown in them, the deep lake of their desire. To be both object and subject, to feel their responses, their quickening pulses, the sounds as we trade touches. I spent so long trying to feel at home in the shell of my physical existence. Whether it is human or mutant or plant, I am still a mind shackled to a form. And yet these two lovers of mine take me apart down to my foundations and let me build myself up again. This body is a link that connects us together, like the three-heart pendant that Violet wears around her neck, swinging above my lips as she rocks atop me.

Dani's fingers circle me, and sensation blots my worries

from my mind. All I am aware of is three bodies twined together in the silken dark.

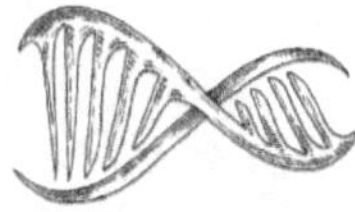

ASHTON-UNDER-LYNE MIGHT HAVE BEEN beautiful once. I don't fucking know England at all. But Manchester was one of the nexus points that Michael built his cities on, and so anything around it became fuel for the nanobots. Most of those places are nothing but ruined earth, scoured flat, but this particular suburb ia mostly rubble. The stubs of buildings jut from the ground, and a few scrappy trees poke up from ash-heaps. Darnton Road has a mostly intact pub called The Miners Arms at the end of it, along with a pile of hollowed-out servitors. I'm not sure if it's a gruesome golden reminder of Michael's power, or street art I don't understand. The houses are mostly knocked flat, but three stand intact in a row partway down.

Sure enough, one of those is 205. My mysterious doppelgänger—if that's really who's sending me these lovely notes—definitely likes this ominous vibe.

"I'd say I've got a bad feeling about this," Alyse says. "But that seems like a cliche."

"Cliche won't stop something jumping out at us." Feral nudges at the front door with one foot. The paint is peeling off in strips and a white fungus spots the wood underneath. The slot of the letterbox has some dark fluid spilling from it, long-dried. The door swings inwards with an exhausted creak.

I cross the threshold with an internal wince, but nothing terrible happens. Inside, the hallway is filthy. The walls are coated with something greasy and dripping and the long rug that runs down the floor is half-rotted away. There's a small table with a lamp sitting on top that's exploded, leaving a huge scorch mark on the opposite wall in the shape of a person.

"Lovely," Violet murmurs. "I respect their commitment to the aesthetic."

Keepaway hovers at the end of the path, as if they want to bail. I give them an overenthusiastic thumbs up and they nod. They'll stick with us. They're my escape plan if this is a trap we're not ready for.

"I fucking hate waiting," I growl, and stomp further down the hall. The roof has been torn away to show the heavy grey of the overcast sky. It's drizzling very faintly, but none of the water seems to make it inside.

At the end of the hallway a hole leads down into pitch-black darkness.

"Torch." I hold out my hand and someone passes it to me. It's a military-grade one we stole from some Quietus offshoot, but even that dazzling brightness barely pierces the murk. There are steps, roughly carved from stone pale enough to have a vague suggestion of bone. "And look, the creepiness continues."

Feral's fur is all fluffed."I hope everyone's ready to punch shit."

"Down we go." I step gingerly onto the first step.

The steps are wide but go down steeply, curving around as we descend until the light from above is lost. Everyone's got torches now, waving them around to try and spot something useful, but it's nothing but a shaft descending into the earth. There's a moment where I think we're stuck in an endless nightmare spiral, but around the very next bend my torchlight reflects off dark water.

"Flooding," I call back. "Let's see how deep it is."

Luckily, the water only comes up to my shins. It's bitterly

cold, and the whole place smells of old stone and something sweetly floral. Ahead, a narrow tunnel leads into the darkness. I slosh forward and hold my torch up. It gleams off something metallic and when I move closer, I find another tunnel heading off into the dark. Not one, but a whole series. Each has a small metal disc set into the rock above it, marked with an incomprehensible symbol.

"This better not be a maze." Feral peers into the mouth of one tunnel, flashing her torch in. It reflects off something moving in the water, and at least one person screams. Maybe one of them was me. "Stop it, you babies. It's only flowers."

She's right. It's a mass of vegetation, floating in the water, roots and leaves sprouting strange flowers I don't recognise. Their petals are a deep purple, multiple layers of them spotted with the same white fungus from the door.

"I think those flowers…" Dani trails away. "I don't recognise them."

"They're in all the tunnels." Alyse calls from the darkness ahead. "There are six. Each with a different symbol, but all the flowers look the same."

I wave my torch at the first one. "Let's do one at a time. And no splitting up, for fuck's sake. We're not in a rush, so let's map this place properly and not write ourselves into a horror movie."

The first tunnel dead-ends quickly, although someone has scratched a bizarre rendition of The Tower tarot card into the wall. In this version the tower has been reduced to rubble, and the people lie shattered on the ground.

"Annoying ominous fuck," I grumble. "Just fight us and be done with it."

Dani shakes her head. "They want us off balance. I just don't know *why*."

"Distraction?" Violet asks. "Keep us away from Mutopia so they can launch an attack?"

I frown. "Maybe, but we can get back in seconds. Besides, we're far from the only defence the island has. The first asshole who tries is going to get one hell of a shock. I hate this shit. It's so goddamn elaborate."

"Psychological games," Dani agrees.

In the second corridor, the flowers are larger, growing in wild and unrestrained tangles to climb up the damp walls like ivy. We have to push our way through, and it's me who has the joy of discovering what nourishment they're using.

A corpse bobs in the water, pale gaze directed at the ceiling. The mouth is forced wide open, blooms spilling from it. There are huge gashes slashed into the torso to allow the flowers to twine their way out. It looks like someone left this person here to be a garden. And it's not only one. By the time we reach the end of the corridor, we count twenty-two bodies.

"One for each of the Major Arcana in the tarot," Dani mutters.

"Or for the Taylor Swift song." I nudge her. "Let's not get superstitious just yet."

"Hard not to." She flicks her torch up to reveal a representation of the Death card drawn on the end wall. This is less abstracted than the real cards, the face painted in loving detail. It's vividly like Emma, almost as if she modelled for the card sometime before she passed.

"I'm going to take great pleasure in punching this prick," Alyse says conversationally.

"Would it help to hit me since we share the same face?" I ask.

"No. It's very specifically the mind that's doing this."

I put my arm around her. "I know it sucks, babe, but we're

going to find whatever the hell is doing this. Then we can do the stabby thing."

The third tunnel is narrower, and far longer. Instead of running straight, it twists around so much I can't actually figure out the geography of it. It feels like we've spiralled inwards so far we'd run into ourselves. There are fewer flowers here, and no corpses at all. The water grows slightly deeper as the floor slopes downwards.

When we reach the end, we find another tarot drawing on the wall. This one is Judgement. In the card we saw online, the angelic creature blowing the trumpet had no face—only a blank golden mask. In this version, my own face stares back. The eyes are blank holes in the face, opening onto nothing. The mouth pressed to the lips of the trumpet has what look like fangs, and the creature's heart is drawn as another gnashing mouth in the middle of its chest.

Flowers bob in the water, nudging up against the painting lovingly, as if they long to climb it and brush their damp petals over it like delicate brushes.

"This is definitely my least favourite picture of you," Violet says.

"It's not them." Dani tilts her head back, eyes narrowed. "Hello, fake Dylan."

"Nice to know your creepy copycat is so committed to the bit," Feral says.

"Next tunnel." I turn to leave. I don't want to see more of this. It makes me feel like the walls are pressing in on me. Flowers swirl at my thighs, petals clinging to my trousers. I brush them away absently.

"Wait." Dani's standing very close to the wall. "There might be clues in here. Judgement implies moral disapproval. And wait, there's something on here." Dani reaches out to touch the drawing.

"Don't—"

I've seen many impossible things since I became a mutant, but nothing as disturbing as watching that goddamn tunnel drawing blow its trumpet. The sound is hollow and reverberates through me so hard, I feel the wooden scaffold of my skeleton tremble. The image warps and blurs, as if my eyes are full of tears, and when it clears Dani is gone.

The angel with my face has discarded the trumpet and its mouth gapes into a hole ringed with teeth. Worse, there's a new figure standing below, gazing up in awe and supplication. Her hair hangs down long, and flowers are braided into it.

I think I'm screaming. Someone is. I slam my hands into the rock over and over, until they split and smear sap over the surface. Violet takes hold of me, pulling me back.

"Take me, you fucking asshole," I scream at the wall.

"Jesus." Alyse spins me around and takes hold of my face. "This is a *trick*, Dylan. The wall didn't eat Dani. She went through it. She'll be on the other side." She snaps her fingers. "Keepaway, can you get in there?"

"There's nothing." They cringe inwards, as if they fear letting me down. "It's solid rock."

"Trap, trap, trap." Feral paces with claws out.

Violet steps forward, her face pale and her lips set. She extends her left hand into blades and pries at the edges of the painting. Rock chips cascade down, but the more she scrabbles, the more desperate her expression becomes. "Keepaway's right. There's nothing behind here."

CHAPTER 13

WEIRD FLOWER LUST MAGIC

I'M PARALYSED WITH INDECISION, chilled by the water soaking into my body. "Think, Dylan, for fuck's sake." Flowers ripple around me and I shove them away, ripping at the root system that trails down through the water and away down the tunnel. Root systems. Dani and me, we're connected. Except in a place like this, so deep, surrounded by so much *stone*, it's the faintest whisper. Enough to give me some tiny dribble of consolation.

"She's not dead. I can't pick up anything solid, but her signal is around here *somewhere*."

"We'll find her," Feral says. "Everyone grab a radio, and don't touch any creepy drawings."

"Wait," I croak.

"Nope, this is how it has to be. I'm taking over, because you're all fucked up. You follow your connection and try to find Dani that way. The rest of us will do a basic physical sweep.

Violet, keep Dills from bad decisions. Like touching that fucking drawing."

"I won't." My hands are trembling and I can't make them stop. I stand and shiver as the rest of the team check their radios and wade swiftly back down the tunnel. The drawing looms over me, the image of my nightmare self and their gaping eyes, their hungry mouth. Dani bowing in supplication. No, that's not right. She would never bend.

"We'll get her back." Violet's voice is firm, despite the evidence. "She's out there."

"Trapped. Caught. At the mercy of something with my face."

"It's definitely fucked. No argument from me there." She kisses my damp cheek. "But she's alive, and that means we've got options."

"What if the other me hurts her?" Tears streak through my voice.

"No, sorry. We're not catastrophising right now. When shit comes true, we'll deal with it. Until then, you're going to use that spooky connection—the one I get so jealous of—and you'll find her with it. Okay?"

I'm miserable and rootless, my connection to Dani nothing more than a flicker. It makes me hungry for a spark, and I tilt Violet's face up to mine. I press my lips hard against hers. We're both cold, we're both scared, but we're *together* and that's something to drown out the despair, to fumble for a shred of certainty.

The flowers swirl around us, nudging themselves against my skin. As if they want connection too, as insistent for me as I am for Dani. Vines sprout from my fingertips and twine with the waterlogged tendrils. Nearly everything that grows on the planet is networked with Cybele. So despite the strangeness of this place, these will help me—

What the fuck? These flowers sting and bite, releasing a nauseous tide that curdles inside me. My instinct is to retract my vines, to snatch myself away from the acrid, bitter taste that's like sucking acid into my system.

"Hush," Violet whispers. "It's okay. We'll find her. I've got you. Connect to me and reach for her. The three of us together, always linked."

She places one hand to the back of my neck, and pulls me down so she can kiss me. Her mouth on mine, her teeth nipping at my bottom lip. The surge of our connection seeking that third point that completes us. It's enough to replenish the brackish foulness in my heart with something cool and clean. The sputtering clusters of my nerves restart, rippling a wave of feeling outwards. The flowers around us bloom, spreading their petals wide and sending up a cloud of luminous pollen that drifts down to settle on the surface of the water. Making a clear thread that leads back the way we came.

"Did we do that?" Violet murmurs, lips still close.

"Yeah. Weird flower lust magic. Flowers are super into reproduction and shit."

"Please don't say weird flower lust magic. It totally ruins the mood."

I keep one hand entwined with Violet, and the other with the flowers. What happened with them is something I've never experienced. My closest analogy is that they were part of another network—connected to a different power source—and now I've brought them into mine. They're plugged into me now. The flowers swirl around both of us, clinging to our thighs and dusting our skin with pollen so our arms and the hollows of our throats and our cheekbones glow. Their trail leads us out into the main tunnel, back towards the entrance, and then into the first one we went down.

"Anyone in there?" I call, but there's no answer.

Violet lifts the radio to her lips. "We're checking the first tunnel. Following a lead."

There's a flurry of acknowledgements—everyone else is alive but haven't found anything. Let's hope these flowers are legit, not some other layer to this nightmare hunt. The line of pollen extends all the way down the tunnel, dead-ending at the scratched-out drawing of The Tower.

"Come on. Show us the way." I'm confused by the sensations coming from the plants. They're eager, almost excited. I'm still not entirely sure I can trust them, so I send a bunch of vague query vibes through the network. There's no painful backwash this time, but a thrumming eagerness to please. We're still stuck staring at the wall though.

Violet clicks her tongue and extends her hands. They pass straight through the rock in front of us. "Okay, that was easier than I thought. Not even a real wall."

I still flinch as we walk through, but we find a small flight of stone steps leading upwards. The sensation of Dani's closeness floods back to me, but all the sensations are numbed.

Violet scrambles up after me as we race up the stairs and into a small square chamber. There are lights inset into the walls and ceiling. They flicker with a golden light that makes the stone appear buttery. Lying on a raised slab in the middle of room, bedecked with an enormous pile of flowers is—

"Dani!" I throw myself down beside her. "Wake up, please."

The connection between us is soporific, a thread hanging slack. Any emotion I push down it hits dead ends. Violet's across from me, stroking Dani's face and calling her name.

The pollen dusts everything, highlighting Dani's features in ribbons of gold.

The torrent of flowers spilling over her aren't connected to those from the tunnels. This chamber is another separate network, and that's what Dani's been connected to. Maybe to wake her up, I need to plug myself in. I bury my hands in the mass of flowers burying her, ignoring the thorns and icy venom.

I get an even stronger sensation of *wrongness*. These flowers are cuttings from a forest that grows outside of Cybele's shade, but it's also nothing like the Weirdlands. They don't like the warmth that pours from me, preferring icy slopes and frigid air. I try to rouse them like the others, but there are so many *more* and their poisonous touch resists me. My fingers are clumsy, but I follow the root systems down until I find the place they enter Dani. She's been pierced over and over, the flowers using her sap to flourish in this place they despise.

I'm going to need *more*.

"Watch her," I tell Violet, and jog back down to the watery passageway when I grab as many of the connected flowers as I can. They drape over my limbs and take eager root in the soil of my flesh. It's dizzying, being the heart of these strange blooms. They thrive on the taste of me, and their petals flutter wide.

When I re-enter Dani's chamber, I'm a floral monster, trailing thick ropy tendrils of plant matter behind me.

"Charge me up." I pull Violet in for another kiss. Weird flower lust magic.

When we separate, I'm gushing purple light from every incision the flowers have made in me. I open my mouth, and an incandescent beam pours out, making Violet flinch away. My vision blurs and I close my eyes against a rush of stinging tears. In the darkness behind my eyelids, visions unfold like they're played on a private movie screen.

Tiny blooms stud the side of an icy slope. It runs down to an enormous expanse of rippling dark water. It's night time and the stars are vivid points of light, some so big they look fist-sized. Ships float on this strange sea, vast and bulbous, moored beside docks which grow thick with flowers. Everything is silent aside from the lapping of waves and the only light aside from the stars are flickering purple buoys out in the deeps. I've never seen any place like this, but I immediately know the flowers are *from there*. That's their environment, the soil they thrive in. This place feels fever-bright and high-pitched.

"Dylan?" Violet's voice is high and nervous. It shatters the visions and brings me back to the chamber..

"Got to get the poison out." I collapse down onto Dani, draping myself over the blooms trying to colonise her. Together with the tunnel flowers, we can fight the massive overload flooding her system. Under my instruction, my flowers thread themselves through Dani's body, sapping the intruders of their venom and bringing it all into me. It's a very involved and flowery version of trying to suck the poison out of a snakebite.

The connection between Dani and I shifts from a dying trickle to a stream to a torrent. It becomes too much to process and we finally explode apart from each other in a shower of petals. I slump to the ground, far less vibrant, but still outlined in ghostly purple. The flowers connected to me are shrivelling, their petals crisping at the edges, and I'm vomiting up thick black goo like I'm possessed.

Dani sits up on the stone slab, pale and shivering. "Persephone," she whispers.

I spit up more poisonous slime into my lap. "Hello to you too, my darling."

"That's what this is all about." She makes a move to get down, but her body's still not working right. "Why are you purple and glowing?"

My answer turns into violent coughing, so Violet has to explain everything. By this time, the rest of the team has joined us and the story's being told yet again while I periodically puke up some foul-smelling substance that's getting increasingly green.

"I think that's a good sign," Alyse says encouragingly.

"Thank you," I croak.

Dani trembles in Violet's arms. "I think your duplicate is trying to replicate the Hades and Persephone myth. That's what the Hierophant refers to. They're stealing the plant goddess away to the underworld and killing her."

"Splendid." I wipe my numb lips. "Why exactly?"

"Hades wants Persephone to be his queen in the underworld. Demeter aka Cybele wouldn't allow it, so Hades kidnaps her instead. Zeus tacitly approves, but we have no Zeus equivalent, because who fucking needs that shit. Persephone was picking flowers, and Hades swooped her up and dragged her into the earth before anyone noticed." She looks around at us all. "It kinda fits right?"

Everyone else nods along, but I've got questions once I finish hacking up gross shit. "Okay, so that's mythology, which is all fucking whatever as far as I'm concerned. But why does my asshole clone want to be Hades?"

It takes Dani a few attempts to get her words out. "Okay, so it doesn't track exactly, but they're stealing me from Cybele. Or possibly from you. They're taking your bride—me, sorry—and spiriting her away to the underworld. They're your dark reflection, possibly wanting to unleash hell on earth."

"You would have literally died down here, Dan, not become a goddamn metaphor for harvest season."

"Perhaps I would have been reborn somewhere. Making a dark copy of me." Her movements are slow, like she's floating underwater. When she blinks, it's like the light in her eyes is shuttered.

I'm worried, but the only coherent thing I can find is rage. "I am going to stab this fucking version of me in the fucking face the first chance I get. Nobody's turning my girlfriend into a dark bride."

"I like this plan." Feral yawns. "I want a turn stabbing too."

"It didn't work though." Alyse helps Dani to her feet. "This whole Persephone thing. The murder, the tarot cards, and *this* place with the poisonous flowers. It failed. You're not dead, so Hadylan—you're welcome, by the way—doesn't have their undead flower bride as the Queen of the Underworld."

"Hadylan just sounds like *hey, Dylan*." I roll my eyes.

"Hades Dylan!" Alyse spreads her arms. "It's perfect."

My throat feels scalded, and all my limbs—do I really only have four?—feel limp and shaky. Every time I close my eyes, I see a flash of that other place, the soft hushing of the wine-dark sea as it rolls beneath the glowing furnaces of the stars. I try to knuckle them away. "You're right about one thing, Lys. Hadylan's big plan failed. So what the fuck are they going to try next?"

CHAPTER 14
EXQUISITE BY SEPTEMBER

"YOU'RE LIKE A CREATURE IN A CAGE." Pear sits in the window seat of their little cottage, watching me as I trudge my loop from the kitchen to the couch to the window and around again. "It's exhausting just watching you."

"It's been four days." I open and close my hand, stop-motion blooming a tiny daffodil in my palm. "Absolutely nothing has happened. Dani's still sick and nobody can figure out what's wrong with her. She's bloomed in Cybele's garden for fuck's sake, and she's still weak and woozy." I'm frustrated that with all the genius and powers at our disposal, my girlfriend is still sick from some poison flowers. I feel mostly fine, if you don't count dreaming about that flower place, wherever the fuck it is. It can't possibly be real, so maybe it's a metaphor for something.

"She says she feels fine," Pear points out.

"Yes, but she can't be trusted to look after herself." I let out an inarticulate groan. Dani's been in full research mode, which makes her a teensy bit boring. I love how smart she is, but her obsessions make her distracted. All her energy is focused on the chamber flowers, as well as that puzzle box we found in the Weirdlands. Apparently she's three layers in but it gets more cryptic as you go down.

"You'll find a way," Pear says. "You always do."

"There's no proof of that." I crash about in the kitchen, looking for something to eat. "And I'm so fucking tired of waiting for the next terrible catastrophe."

"The sword of Damocles."

"Well, I've got the sword of Dylan." I pat Oni, who's been very protective since the chamber disaster. "So Damocles can fuck right off."

"It's an allegory." Pear looks over their glasses at me. "For what you're going through right now, waiting for your doom to fall. In the story, it's about a corrupt king, but the principle is the same. You're a target because of who you are, and so you can never truly rest."

I throw myself into the couch. "You're very annoying, you know that?"

"Only trying to be helpful."

"Yes, you're a peach."

They smirk at me, even though I've made that joke a thousand times.

"And no, you're not annoying. Dan and I both appreciate you looking after the twins. Like, a whole fucking lot. I know it's not what you signed up for, but—" I finish with a cartoonish shrug, because I have no words.

Pear grabs a couple of beers from the fridge, and settles into the couch beside me. I immediately swing my legs up over theirs.

"The twins are delightful," they tell me. "It's surprising how much they remind me of you, given they're only slightly related."

"God, was I a nightmare?"

"You were adorable. Hideously fucking stubborn, of course. Your father said you inherited that from me, which I always thought was rude."

"Fuck him. What does he know?" I hold out my beer for them to clink.

"Look." Pear fumbles with their phone. "Here's a photo of you when you were about their size." On the screen is a little kid in denim overalls, dark hair in messy bunches. I recognise the scowl immediately.

I can't help but laugh. "I look like an asshole."

"Well, you sometimes were. Most people are at that age."

"All ages."

They clink their beer against mine. "Truer words, child of mine. It's a hard phase to grow out of." They stare at the bottle as if there's immense wisdom written on the label rather than various warnings. "I am proud of you, Dilly. I hope you know that."

"Jesus, Pear. We don't need to do this."

"We do, actually." They glance at me, and then back to the bottle, which is far safer. "I avoid painful conversations a lot of the time. Easier to—I don't know—hope they go away. And, shit, sometimes they do, so it's an intermittent schedule of rein-forcement."

I cover my face. "Is this a fucking psychology lesson?"

"Sorry, even now I'm talking around it. My point is that we both avoid these conversations. You've got a girlfriend who doesn't always let you, but you and I are very good at changing the subject."

"So how about those pesky humans, huh?" I give them a thumbs-up.

"Dylan, please."

I lean my head back so I can stare at the ceiling. "Fine."

"We haven't seen eye to eye about everything all the way along."

"Oh, you mean about the murdering?" My voice is too dry. "Or the other murdering? The bank robbing or starting a war? The dying without permission? Coming back as an alien? Starting a new country? The way I piss you off by singing that 'young nation' song from *Hamilton* to the kids over and over again?"

"You make your history sound ridiculous." Pear shakes their head.

"It kinda is. But I'm not denying I've made mistakes. Fuck's sake, I'm still going to. Sometimes I make a decision right in front of me and it'll be wrong. It's what—"

"Jesus fucking Christ, Dylan. I'm trying to say I'm proud of you, okay?"

We stare at each other for a moment. My mouth twitches. God, sometimes it's like looking in a fucking mirror. I can't help but burst out laughing, and a second later they do too.

"Sometimes you are very hard to compliment." Pear ruffles my hair, like they used to when I was a kid, scruffy and scowling.

I go back to looking at the ceiling. "It's hard for me." There's a lump in my throat from somewhere. "Because I owe you everything. You were the centre of my world for so long, and you got me through. So when I feel like I've fucked up, I'd rather shout at you or pretend it didn't happen than say sorry."

I tilt my head slightly so I can see them, and the tears in their eyes. "But I am sorry, for making you feel scared and shitty. I was shooting myself towards the future like a bullet, so focused on the battles I had to win that I forgot who taught me to fight." I wipe my eyes angrily. "Fuck, I hate it when I start giving speeches."

Pear leans across and hugs me so hard that some of my wooden internal framing creaks.

"God, I made so many mistakes, Dylan. So fucking many. I know you remember."

Of course I do. Not in great detail, but flashes of it. How the house was always too hot, the curtains always drawn. Learning how to budget, and knowing what everything in the super-market cost. Eating mostly noodles and cereal because that's all we had. The way Pear used to stare at me as if I was a ghost, as if I startled them every time I walked into their bedroom. And their goddamn songs they'd play on repeat, dirgy things with guitars and men with hollow voices. I used to hold my pillow over my ears, trying to block it out but they'd play them over and over until those sepulchral voices haunted my dreams. I think that's why I gravitated to K-pop much later—all that candied brightness and melodic energy was the furthest from Pear's songs of grief.

I used to shove a thin foam mattress under my bed and sleep there. It was the only place I could escape. I'd make tally marks on the wall in red and green crayon. The days Pear smiled, the days they didn't. Add them together, and it was the days they made it through.

I also remember them getting out of it. The way we'd walk around the block three times a day because it was exercise, and it was getting out of the house. Sitting on their double bed and reading comics together, talking about who our favourite mutants were. Getting excited about stories, about justice, about standing up and fighting for people who needed it. The day they called the lady from the food bank and we started getting fresh fruit delivered. The first time we cooked something together that wasn't a microwavable ready-meal.

We never got that fucking good at cooking, even now.

I try to forget the dark days. There were a lot of them, but we did get out. And even if there's a shadow, a lot of times we can't even feel it, even when things turn shitty between us. It's like something buried really deep, this little lub-dub heartbeat under the ground reminding me of the grave we clawed our way out of

"You're a person." I reach out and take their hand. "That's what unites humans and mutants, if you boil it down. We all fuck up, we all get lost. We all need friends to take us through the bad times. Sometimes that friend is your child. It wasn't your fault. Everyone else around you failed. But you succeeded. *We* succeeded. And that's what still gets me through."

"God, you're a fucking good kid, you know that?" They're openly sobbing now, and I am the worst fucking sympathetic crier in the world, which I absolutely fucking *hate*.

"Well, you're an asshole, so it's a miracle I turned out that way." I lean in to rest my head on their shoulder and we sit like that for a long time, until we hear the rustle of leaves and two small green figures leap over the back of the couch to land on us.

"You've been emotional," Willow says. "I can smell it. Or taste it? Senses are confusing."

"That's not polite." Soo-yeon nudges their sibling. "Humans are odd about their emotions and don't like you drawing attention."

"But they're family." Willow sprawls in my lap, looking up

at my face intently. "So we love their emotions because they're all part of the weirdness of them."

"Yes." Soo-yeon cuddles close to Pear. "I suppose we do. It's one of those odd things I think Green Mum wanted us to understand, and that's why we're in this shape."

"Tiresome," Willow sighs. "But it's sometimes fun."

"Come on then." Pear gets to their feet. "Let's do something more interesting than sitting around being all maudlin. I'm old and I've cried enough for one day."

We go into the kitchen and tell the kids they can make any kind of pizza they want. They immediately go overboard and scavenge ingredients out in the wild vegetable gardens near our little cluster of cottages. They're sprawling, with rambling hedges and tiny garden nooks. We end up playing hide and seek, before returning home with a whole sack full of vegetables to make pizza with.

It's one of those soft-focus afternoons, with the light all hazy and gold like someone's filming it for a happy family montage. For a moment, I don't feel that sword hanging over my head. I'm not a monster pacing in a cage, but someone safe with family. Over my connection with Dani, I feel the same reassuring pulse. Long-distance soothing me while she works with the others on tracking down this mystery figure. I'm almost relaxed, caught up in the moment and forgetting what else is happening in the world.

Then I hear a faint tapping sound at the door and my head snaps up immediately.

Violet's there, and I know immediately from the look on her face that something's up.

"They're back." I take a single step toward her, and Oni's already nestled into my palm.

"Yeah. It's Hadylan. And it's bad."

CHAPTER 15

CATASTROPHE, DESTRUCTION, UNEXPECTED CHANGE

VIOLET HANDS me the phone as we walk down the path away from Pear's house.

"Agent Decker."

Her voice sounds faint and wind-whipped. "Chatterbox. We've got another situation."

"I figured. You never call just to say hi." I ignore Violet's eye roll. "Tell me what's happening."

"We've got an incident in Sweden. Tiny little coastal village, miles from anywhere. Its claim to fame is this big stone tower, remarkably like the one on the tarot card. A sect of monks built it in the sixteenth century."

"So far it sounds fucking idyllic."

"Not so much. There's a tourist party trapped inside. Tour company records say sixty-five people including drivers and guides. Well, now there are sixty-three. Two have been thrown from the top of the tower. The person responsible is wearing a mask, but they say they'll keep killing someone every hour until Chatterbox shows up."

"Hadylan, you asshole," I mutter. "What the fuck are you up to now?"

"What was that?"

"Nothing, Decker. Do we have any more information to go on?"

"No. The only approach to the tower is across a stone bridge. Our friend says that if anyone crosses aside from you, they'll start killing way faster."

I shrug. "That's easy. I'm happy to go in alone."

Violet shakes her head furiously.

"Me and Oni can take care of ourselves, Vi. If it doesn't work, we'll send in the brute squad."

"I am the brute squad," she tells me. "Why not let me sneak in?"

I shake my head. "We don't know what Hadylan is capable of. Maybe they can detect you. I'll go bumbling in first and we'll see how that plays out. I promise, I'll be sensible. First sign of trouble, I'll set off every goddamn alarm."

"It's risky," Decker's voice says.

"It's always fucking risky. Text us the coordinates and we'll be there before you know it."

"I've always been so jealous of teleportation," she says. "It seems—"

I end the call and turn to Violet. "Where's everyone else?"

"Assembled." She gives me a tiny shrug. "Dani said you were having a nice moment for once, so we should leave you until the last possible second, but it got dark real quick."

I get about five seconds into telling the rest of the group my so-called plan before they're all yelling at me. It's exasperating because we don't have time for this, but I try to answer their questions.

"Yes, I know Dani got taken in the tunnels. But we're ready this time, and I'll have Oni. And you'll all be *right there* ready to follow me. This person is literally committing murder as we speak, and they're asking for me. If we try to pull something clever and a bunch of people wind up dead because of it..."

"I hate this," Dani says bitterly. She's still too pale. If I get my hands on Hadylan, I'm going to find out what the fuck is up with these poison flowers. Dani's been researching them incessantly but the only conclusions she's got are so full of scientific jargon they make no sense to me.

"Look on the bright side," I tell her. "Maybe you get to do the dashing rescue."

Feral drapes her tail across my shoulders. "Your dashing rescue involved poisoning yourself and vomiting a lot."

"Fuck you, hairball." I give the end of her tail a yank. "Let's go."

Keepaway teleports us in one after the other. A tent is set up on a grass verge at the mainland end of the bridge. Decker's there, with a whole bunch of Swedish cop-types and some GIC agents. Nobody seems super pleased to see us, even though I'm practically the guest of honour.

"It's been hard to swing approval for this plan." Decker looks exhausted. "But another person died two minutes ago, so..."

I stride out of the tent and stand at the end of the bridge, waving my arms furiously over my head. Here I am, you cryptic, sneering asshole. You've got what you wanted. Let's see what's next.

Decker's radio crackles, and then my voice comes out of the speaker.

"Good. Isn't reason so… reasonable? You've just bought the lives of sixty-two people if Chatterbox starts walking across that bridge right now."

I really want to make some snarky threat, but I manage to control myself. What if I say some devastating one-liner and some poor tourist gets hurled to their death? So I start walking down the bridge. No time for goodbye kisses or telling my friends I love them. They ought to know this shit anyway, and besides, I'm not going to fucking die.

The bridge seems awfully long. It's made of white stone, carefully carved blocks fitted together perfectly. Underneath, the grey ocean surges, cold and angry. And ahead, the tower. It's obviously designed to mimic the vibes of the tarot card. Rough stone at its bottom turning to smooth walls. A handful of little arched windows and a golden dome at the top, reflecting the feeble sun. This must be why Hadylan chose it. Some other message I don't understand.

There's faint movement at one of the windows. I'm assuming it's a hostage, not the suspect, because otherwise they'd be dead by sniper fire already.

"Shall I reconnoitre ahead?" Oni asks.

"No, Hadylan might take that as a threat. Don't worry, you'll get your moment." I'm thinking about how my evil nemesis summoned their own sword from the body of a dead man. We've still got no idea of their true powers, but if they've got telekinesis, can do shit with flowers, plus teleporting Dani through a rock wall… this could get interesting. And not in a fun way.

There's a small wooden door at the base of the tower, set into an archway of stone. I stand at it and knock.

Half a minute later, it opens. A woman with short dark hair stands there. She's dressed in a windbreaker and yoga pants, and her lips are pale. Nobody else is around. There's a passageway leading ahead, and a staircase spiralling upwards.

"Up." She raises one trembling hand, eyes averted.

"You okay?"

The woman closes the door slowly, teeth chattering. "If I leave, they'll kill the others."

"Okay." I take a deep breath. "If all this goes well, everyone's getting out of here, so hold on. We're going to fix this."

"My partner's up there." The woman clutches at my arm. "They need medication and they're scared. *I'm* scared. That person… there's something wrong with them. They're not scared or angry or anything. It's like it's a game and they're *bored*. They throw people out the window like it's nothing, like they're garbage or—"

"Don't worry. I'll stop this asshole." I don't have a noble speech about heroism and sacrifice. I'm going to punch shit, like I do best. I start jogging up the staircase. The tower is tall, so it's a long way up and I have to pace myself. I keep shooting glances up the open central shaft, but there's no sign of anything at the top. Before too long, I reach the first platform. There are four windows, one facing each direction. There's nobody here, so I don't stop and admire the view.

A few more turns of the stairs later, motion above me catches my eye. Oni tugs himself free of my grip.

"Wait, Oni. It could—"

A sharp sound above, then sparks fly. There's a flurry of movement, and an insanely fast rhythm of clashing swords. This worries me on a deep-down level, because Hadylan can control their sword well enough that Oni hasn't cut the other blade into tiny metal shavings.

And that's really fucking *bad*.

"Oni, please talk to me," I shout, but he's too busy saying something in Japanese. I've not heard him like this before. He sounds urgent, he sounds *scared*. I take the steps two at a time, using vines to get handholds so I can propel myself faster. I'm basically swinging my way up the tower, but I'm still not fast enough to catch the ascending swords.

I hope this means Oni is winning.

After a final flurry, the other blade beats a hasty retreat. Instead of darting after it, Oni zips back towards me.

"I am distressed, Dylan. Deeply and fundamentally."

"Talk to me, buddy. Tell me what's wrong."

"That blade is me."

Turns out my plant-form can still get chills. Like horror-movie oh-shit chills. "What the fuck are you talking about?"

"I would swear on my life this blade was forged by my maker and its form is the same as mine. It *speaks*, Dylan. It *lives* as I do. The only differences are the scars we bear."

"How is that possible?"

"I cannot say."

"You don't have a fucking long-lost sibling you never mentioned?"

Oni hangs in the air, rotating slowly. He seems dazed. "It is not another sword from the same master. That blade is me. I cannot explain it to you any clearer, Dylan."

"Then this other Dylan is probably me as well. Genetically, I mean. Maybe from before I died, but still. It's me, and they've got my powers, too. I was fucking right about a clone of some kind. Suck on that, Danielle. Comic books win again. But how the fuck does this make sense? How do you clone a sentient *sword*? God, I wish Dani was here. She'd understand a lot more of this than me. What I really want to know is—"

I'm cut off by Dark Oni's reappearance, slicing through the air towards me. My Oni intercepts, and then the two swords are off again. Let those two fight it out. It's time for me to face my own fucking monster. I start leaping up the stairs again, passing the second lookout platform. I try not to think of all the terrible possibilities stepping out of the future one by one to greet me. The hostages dead, my friends dead, me lying on a bier of poison flowers with Dani trying to save me.

At the third platform, I can tell something is wrong. The air blurs overhead so the rest of the staircase warps and bubbles. The same effect can be seen around the platform, extending almost to the walls of the tower. I shoot out some vines and prod the air around me. It's blisteringly hot and slightly rubbery to the touch. I hit it with a little more force, crisping the ends of my vines, but it repels me with equal force.

A barrier above and around me, like I've been trapped inside an invisible glass jar. Walling me off from the people I need to rescue.

"I want to talk." It's my voice. Not the one I hear in my head, but the annoying, nasal one I hear on videos. "Before we get to the heroic punching thing."

"Let the hostages go." I can't see where the hell they're hiding.

"Why would I do that?"

I shrug. "I won't talk to you if you're threatening to kill randos."

"You *will* talk." They appear on the other side of the barrier, dressed in a pale green bodysuit. It gleams wetly in the light streaming in from the tall arched window behind him. They leave damp footprints across the wooden floor as they walk towards me. The visor of the helmet is completely opaque, and I see my own face reflected in it, an irony that's not lost on me. "Or this could go horribly, horribly wrong."

"It's already fucked up." I step closer to the barrier myself, so we're only separated by a thin layer of forcefield. "You're making it worse. But you obviously want something, so let's skip the bullshit."

Their head tilts slightly. "You're direct. I like that."

"What I am is losing my fucking patience. Let the hostages go, and we can get to the fighting."

"As soon as the hostages are out, all your little friends will start bouncing in, and then there are so many *variables* to keep track of. I'd rather keep it between you and me."

I've got very few cards to play here. If I turn and walk out of the building, Hadylan will throw someone for sure. To make me suffer, to make a point, it doesn't matter. I can act tough all I want, but we both know I need to play along.

"Okay, let's talk." I coax the thorns down from my shoulders, let flowers bloom in their place. "I want to see your face."

Hadylan takes a step back. "I suppose it's only fair. I do find you inordinately fascinating."

I almost laugh at that. "Guess we're not so identical after all. You'd never hear me use that fucking word. Mostly because I don't know what it means."

"Oh, there's a difference or two." They reach up and depress a pair of studs on the bottom of their helmet. There's a hiss of air as it's released. It's all very fucking dramatic, and I can't help but roll my eyes as they slowly reveal themselves.

It's weird, looking at a face I recognise so well. Back when I hated myself, when I was trying to figure out what gender meant, I used to stare at my reflection and make sense of it. And it's that same face I'm looking into right now. The way Hadylan's hair curls around the nape of their neck, one lazy strand falling in their big brown eyes. It's familiar and impossible all at once, my reflection staring back at me with a smirk.

"Hello, you handsome devil." They smile at me, and that's an expression I *don't* often see. I realise why Dani and Violet always insist they love my smile so much. Even though it's on the face of a fucking monster, it looks charming.

I smile back, although mine feels forced. "Hello, Dylan."

CHAPTER 16
VS.

"IT'S FUCKING WEIRD, isn't it?" They're grinning, looking cocky as fuck. "Face to face with your almost-self."

"I'm mostly disappointed that you're such a prick."

"Yeah, I do feel kinda bad about that. Honestly. You probably don't believe me, but—"

"Who fucking cloned me?" I lean forward. "And what do you *want*?"

They laugh, delighted. "It's so much more interesting than that. And what we want is quite simple. We're going to end your line."

"The fuck does that mean?" I've got an awful, sinking feeling.

"Your new genetic line, I mean." Hadylan's lip curls into a sneer. "The planetary infection you call Cybele. You and your pretty Persephone. And most importantly, those two feral hybrid monsters you've got tucked under your wings."

I'm so angry I can't even talk. It's not only my own personal fury, it's leaching into me from Cybele. Whoever the fuck made this monster, it's an attack on us. They want to dig up the roots of Mutopia so that next time they try and eradicate mutantkind it's going to be permanent.

"You're a plague," Hadylan says. "It's not personal."

"But you have powers too." I slam one thorned fist into the barrier wall.

"Of course I have powers. This isn't about *powers,* Dylan. It's about Cybele. In my world, this is all vastly different. Powers are a gift given to the deserving, those with potential. Your monstrous progenitor was strangled in the cradle."

"Hold up." I'm still trying to parse that little speech. "In your world what?"

"Pay attention, Dylan. You're from the Age of Apocalypse." Hadylan drops the barrier in an instant, then hits me in the face really hard. Luckily, I can take a punch, especially in plant form. Everything sort of smooshes inwards, and I go flying halfway across the room to smash into the wall on the far side. I bounce off and crash onto the floor.

I push the panic alarm through my connection with Dani. Time to come in and rescue the hostages. I'm very, very happy to keep Hadylan busy while that happens. Mostly by hitting back. They're sprinting towards me, so I shoot out vines to pull them closer, then swing my left arm back, laden with thorns. I slam my forearm into their throat, and feel the spikes bite deep. When I tear myself clear, black fluid sprays from four different puncture wounds.

Hadylan staggers, hands to their throat.

I'm staring, half-shocked, half-triumphant. This seems way

too easy. Via my Dani connection, I know that Keepaway's upstairs, bouncing out the hostages one at a time, but it looks like—

"Oops." Hadylan drops their hands. The gashes in their flesh are little more than puckered holes which close up as I watch. "Aren't healing powers cool? I know you've got one too. Good enough to pull sweet Persephone back from the darkness. That pissed me off a little."

"What the fuck *are you?*" I growl.

"Put the pieces together, dear sibling. You already know." They give me that smile again, and draw two guns from inside their suit in one fluid motion.

I immediately start firing back. One of our handy plant-alien upgrades is being able to shoot tiny fast-growing seeds from my fingertips. It also means I can say *my hands are weapons* like a badass.

Unfortunately, Hadylan's suit absorbs my bullets and spits them out the other side. The floor behind them sprouts with an array of wild blossoms.

"Sorry." Hadylan tracks me with their guns. "We're a little more advanced."

Their gun fires flowers too. The floral bullets stitch a neat line across my chest, and I stagger backwards. My limbs won't respond properly, and I collapse onto the floor. Someone's scooping parts of me out with a spoon. Whatever's inside me is burrowing, unstitching, dissolving essential parts of me. This asshole's built a weapon to take me down.

Hadylan stands over me, looking down with a rueful expression on their face. "There's no point fighting. I'm relentless. I'm unstoppable. Imagine you, but with a real mission. Something far bigger than clinging to a tiny scrap of planet."

"Fuck off. You're such a dick." I'm focused on the disaster

inside me. It's a reverse of the trick I did in the tunnels. These flowers are spreading, trying to replace my internal systems with their own. It's about as much fun as you'd expect from that description. My body's being taken over, strand by strand, and I can't find a way to fight it.

Hadylan crouches down and tenderly strokes a lock of hair off my face. "You're so much weaker than I expected. But don't worry. This will all be over soon."

Dani shoves images down the connection between us. Nothing romantic or inspiring, but a diagram of a hybrid flower —a blend of what grows in Cybele's forests, and the ones we found in the chamber. Step by step instructions, animated like a flip book. Oh shit, so *that's* what you've been doing in your little nerd-cave. Figuring out the connections, and building something new. Thankfully, she's made it simple enough for me, even twitching painfully on the floor.

It takes a little encouragement to get my internal flowers to do anything but wilt. I flop about on the floor the whole time, drooling sap while Hadylan stands over me, dispassionately looking on.

Dani's plan did not account for how much this *hurts*. It's like having two different skeletons being built inside me in real time, except more painful. I think maybe I'm winning, but I'm a battleground. A thousand skirmishes fought all through my tangled root systems. Grit my teeth through the fucking pain. Follow my genius girlfriend's plan.

Piece by piece, drag myself back to life.

Hadylan is bored, whistling tunelessly through their teeth like faintly howling wind.

Okay, I'm feeling a *lot* better now.

I sit up in one swift movement, spinning the top half of my body, using my thorns to pierce Hadylan's skin. I'm wrenching at their body, burrowing talons into their neck while vines writhe under their skin. With one furious, breathless twist, their whole head comes off. Holy fucking shit. Did I do that?

I'm staring at the two parts of them lying on the ground, spilling dark blood and an oily, yellow fluid. I thought that shit was supposed to be impossible, but I guess I don't know my own strength. Isn't hybrid vigour a thing?

"Heal from that, asshole." I kick the head across the floor.

I tell Dani I'm fine, and she confirms the hostages are safe. Everyone else is out of the tower. The relief almost knocks me down all over again. We've defeated the villain and saved the day. I think you can call this proper superhero shit, rather than our classic morally grey vibes.

The barriers are all down with Hadylan dead, so I limp to the window and look out. My chest still hurts, but it's healing. I'm going to be okay.

There's just one loose end. One shiny silver fly in the ointment.

"Oni?" I call. "Is everything—?"

And that's when the tower explodes. The entire structure shakes, as if it's about to fall into the ocean. Heat washes over me like a wave, pressure sending me out the window and into the air.

I fall, spinning through the air like a sycamore seed. Above me, the golden dome atop the tower has split clean in half, and huge cracks run down the walls. Flames leap from each window.

There's someone else here. Not only Hadylan. There's a partner in crime, because someone fucking nuked the tower to re-enact a tarot card. As I drift down towards the bridge, I can see the greasy shimmer of another barrier blocking my way.

This one is a giant dome that encompasses the entire bridge and the tower, while leaving the rescue tent outside.

A figure stands at the base of the tower. They're wearing a pale green suit with a bulbous helmet on top.

No fucking way.

I shift my mass around to be less of a seed and more of a plummeting stone, crashing down into the other end of the bridge. When I land, little chips of stone fly all around me. I'm standing at one end, and the suit is at the other. Their posture is familiar, right down to the way they're tilting their head.

They grew their head back? What the fuck is going on?

There's nothing to do but run towards them. Find some other way. Maybe tearing out their heart will work. They charge at me as well, like we're in some ridiculous anime battle. Halfway there, they reach up and touch the studs that remove the helmet. It flies off their head and spirals off towards the sea below. Underneath...

Underneath the helmet is something like my face, except it's been split apart down the middle, and a mass of roiling tentacles writhes through the bloody gap. An alien, wearing my face. Or a version of me who's an alien, or host to an alien.

In my world...

The tentacles lash towards me and I send vines jetting from my fingers to meet them. We're still ten metres apart, but we're already trading blows. My vines don't have the sensitivity of my plant-sheath—which has as many nerve endings as my human skin—but I can feel the slickness of the tentacles underneath my grip, and the chill that pulses through them. They're thrashing about, trying to get a grip on me, but my vines are more nimble, twisting tight and tearing. The first tentacle comes free with a wet ripping sound, like bloated corpseflesh splitting under the ocean. A gush of blue fluid spurts out, loaded with ice crystals, smelling of salt and ammonia.

"You think you can kill me this way?" Hadylan calls. They've still got my voice, even among that ruined tentacle face. "In the shadow of the Holy Tower? I am Hierophant, Magician, and Fool. The trinity born to bring your world to the gallows tree."

"What the fuck are you *talking* about?" I slam my fist into them again with a satisfying squelch.

"You apostate monster. There's only one way I can die, and brute force is not the answer."

I thread my vines into the stump where one tentacle was, shredding more flesh, trying to follow it down to find whatever passes for a heart in this version of me. "Too bad. I'll try not to enjoy figuring it out."

We're completely tangled together, except I'm throttled by tentacles and they're choking on vines. I manifest as many thorns as possible, in the hope they won't like squeezing me so tight, but I only end up covered in gross icy blood.

There's no sense of Dani down the connection between us. That can't be a good sign.

"My gods are bigger than your god," Hadylan snarls, one dark eye weeping goo.

"Cybele isn't my god, you insufferable dick."

"Then what is she? The being who created you, the one who sustains your miserable species. You are insects who somehow slew a race of gods and so never understand your true place in the universe. Your extinction is inevitable."

I slam a thorny finger into the slick blackness of Hadylan's eye. "You know what's really depressing? Finding a version of me who's into bending the knee and saying hallelujah to a bunch of tentacle-faced assholes."

The pressure around my torso gets tighter and I hear a series of sharp snapping sounds, barbs of wood protruding out of my chest.

"Imagine how I feel finding a rootless, shiftless nihilist who fights for nothing more than bare survival, with no conception of their true place in the universe."

I tear another tentacle free from the squirming mass. "Guess we're both disappointed. Tell me how to kill you, and I'll put you out of your misery."

"You'll never succeed." Hadylan's split face writhes. "It's over now, anyway."

There's a howling sound from behind me, a rising lament.

"Oni, what the—?"

Something hits me from behind. It severs one of those fundamental connections that runs from my plant brain to the hissing pump of my heart. I urgently try to reroute things, but my body's seizing up on me.

Dark Oni bursts out of my chest, the blackened point of him carving a line down my belly.

Fuck me, not again.

How many times can one person come so close to dying?

I fall backwards again, and the last thing I see before I close my eyes is a silver blade, screaming down out of the sky.

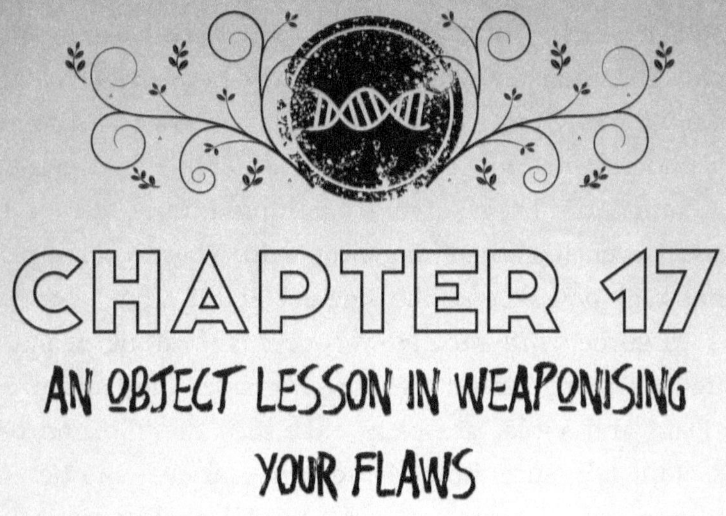

CHAPTER 17
AN OBJECT LESSON IN WEAPONISING YOUR FLAWS

THE NEXT FEW images come in fragments. My eyes aren't really working, and my body is frantically knitting itself together to get basic functionality going.

A sword, dripping sap with damp petals clinging to his blade. My blood, my flowers. Me, eviscerated in a pile of damp moss. Flailing like a drunk girl on an ice rink, except all the signals dead-end in severed vines. A felled tree, an uprooted stump, a bloom dying in poisoned soil. I should belong in a huge forest, sun filtering down through the leaves, warming us all as we cling together, a vast green network. Instead, I'm a tiny sapling, transplanted into a world that's stifling and cold.

Above me, Oni's elegant shape, no longer perfectly smooth but with a series of jagged nicks running along the length of him. The sounds coming from him are breathless cries. My sweet boy, so wounded, so battered. I cannot even help him. I'm in a dark well and my arms cannot reach the sky. So strong and broken. We're the same, and we're both failing.

But he will not fall. He flashes through the air, light glinting off him.

Hadylan reaches out, snatching their dark weapon in one tentacle. The monster who is me. They have my fervour, my smile, my ferocity but they wield it in the service of something I can't understand. How can that one difference between us be so fundamental? They serve something utterly, giving their entire self over. It's something I can't do. There's some part of me that will never bend the knee. I stand alone, and I ask others to come with me. Now here I am, alone again, and although so many would fight by my side, they're cut off. I hope Dani and Violet are okay, that they don't blame themselves. I'm not sure how Alyse will survive another loss. They'll need to be there for her. I wish I could write all this down.

I get blurry glimpses of a sword fight. It's too fast to know who's winning. My melting brain sends alert signals my body can't respond to. I must look like an ancient ruin in an old forest, grasses and flowers growing up around the stones, trees pushing up through the centre. My skeleton is shattered, and all the wild life in me springs up from it, unable to find the pattern that weaves me into a whole.

Oni hits the ground beside me. Hilt half broken, an enormous chunk taken out of him. My friend turned into a ruin too. Both of us severed and useless.

My fingers twitch again, reaching. Trying to wield him one last time.

Hadylan limps towards me through a spreading pool of blue blood. Tentacle limbs lie discarded, suckers flexing and falling still. Oni fought until the end, because of course he did. Not quite enough. This goddamn unkillable version of me. I was like that once. Indestructible.

I wonder if Hadylan feels pain, or if there's only the monster in their heart.

Dark Oni hangs over my head, like the goddamn fucking sword of whoever the fuck. The barrier stretches over the sky to make an impenetrable bubble encasing us.

My eyes droop closed.

There's no rescue for me. No miracle waiting. No Goddess to reach down and save me, no Cybele to grow me fresh. We've run out of chances, my sword and me. Two broken things, waiting for it to all be over.

Death is coming. I've brought my own share, been a dark shadow falling over people's lives. This is a turning of the wheel, and it's my turn to be crushed beneath.

I wonder if it'll be a relief, for it all to be over. Maybe Emma felt this way too.

No. Fuck that.

I force my eyes to open again. Push through this goddamn pain, saturated in whatever toxic blood Hadylan's fed my system with. Oni doesn't give up, and I won't either. We might be beaten to shit, trapped in a forcefield with a monster who wears my face. Maybe one or both of us is cut in half. That's not a reason to fucking stop. I fumble for something within the wreckage of my body. There. One jagged wooden rib snapped off by a tentacle. It feels like a weapon in my hands.

"Let me, my friend." Oni rises up from the ground. He whips through the air and the half-broken shard of him draws a single line along the length of his dark twin's blade. When he reaches the end, he twists in a tight circle, a final twist of the knife. The other blade shatters, pieces of metal flying like shrapnel. "I know my own flaws, you see, better than anyone."

Hadylan screams in response, furious at the destruction of their companion. I almost feel sorry for them, because maybe they're bonded just as closely as I am with Oni. If that's true, I feel some echo of their loss. Then again, maybe they should've thought twice before coming into my goddamn world to fuck with me.

Oni slashes through tentacles, a flurry of savage cuts. There's blood everywhere, painting the white stone in gritty cobalt streaks. Hadylan stumbles backwards. Every time they lash out with their tentacles, Oni is there to meet them, pressing his advantage. They stumble again, and further back, until they're pressed up against the edge of the bridge.

Oni arrows for their throat, and Hadylan tips backwards, vanishing from view. From my sprawled position, I can't see how they fall, but I'm hoping they're plummeting towards the ocean below. Maybe they're screaming. I think I'd like that. I remember how the rocks looked below, grey and jagged among the surf.

Another blink, and the sky is clear again.

Oni's quiet song comes from beside me. He's very faint.

Darkness floods my vision again, and this time it's welcome.

NEXT TIME I open my eyes, I'm looking at a lot of familiar faces. My body's found some shape again. I probably look like some decrepit wood troll, but it's better than being dead.

"They're alive," Dani shouts at someone I can't see, and then she and Violet both have their faces pressed in against me. I think they're kissing me, but half my nerves haven't grown back yet, so I can't really tell.

"Course I'm alive. I fucking *told* you." It's lucky I can't cry again yet, or I'd be blubbering.

"Yes, that wasn't nerve-wracking at all to watch." Dani kisses all over my face, which is probably gross since I think I'm just a grassy pile of moss with eyes sticking out. "Dylan, that was awful. What the hell is that thing?"

"Talk later. First show me Oni? I need to see him."

Dani and Violet help me sit up, so I can see where Feral's standing with the blade cradled in her arms. His perfect edges are battered with hundreds of fine chips, and there's one wicked looking gash taken out of him.

"You poor brave bastard. Look at you."

"I wear my wounds proudly," he grumbles. "I faced a worthy foe and overcame them. These are the marks of my victory. And you should not fuss over me while you are in such a grievously wounded state."

"Does it hurt, you big drama queen?"

"Very much." He hovers out of Feral's arms and comes down to nestle alongside me. "I have never taken such a terrible beating in my life. On the bright side, I have a new appreciation for my own talents. Only I could have made such a worthy adversary."

"I wish I felt that way." I get very clumsily to my feet and drag myself over to the edge of the bridge. Obviously nobody wanted to drag my carcass home in case I disintegrated. My limbs still aren't working properly, although they're stitched together roughly enough to get me some mobility. Below, the ocean is tempestuous and wild, a rumpled grey surge that thrashes against the rocks. There's no sign of Hadylan's body.

"You think they're dead?" Dani asks.

"We're not that lucky. They said there's only one way to kill them, and it's not brute force."

"Research time." She nudges me. "Won't that be fun? Starting with what the fuck that thing was. We couldn't see properly through the forcefield, but it looked like some kind of…"

"Tentacle monster." I don't think I'll ever be able to get rid of the sight of my ruptured face and those slender limbs spilling out from inside it. "Like if Tentacle Princess got inside me and puppeted my body around like a flesh suit."

"Jesus." Alyse shudders. "That's a little too vivid, Dills."

"I had to fight the damn thing. And they had my face! My voice! My goddamn smile!"

"Who the hell made it?" Violet asks.

"Okay, here's the headfuck part. Hadylan is me from a parallel universe. One like ours, except where the tentacle monsters won. Cybele died and those creepy god ancestors of Tee Pee's fed on humanity from then until now."

Everyone's staring at me without saying a word, so I start blathering on about the visions I saw when I communed with the flowers in that underground place—images I'm convinced were of Hadylan's version of our planet. The impenetrable dark water, the icy slopes, the fiercely burning stars. "They said we're from the Age of Apocalypse. Like this is a timeline that isn't right. They talked about their gods and killing Cybele."

"Are you sure this isn't from hitting your head too many times?" Alyse asks me. "Because you expect us to believe that in this parallel universe which is all tentacles and stuff, there's still a Dylan who has an Oni."

"Infinity is weird." Dani is pensive, staring down at the shattered pieces of Dark Oni. "By definition it includes a world like that, and every variation on it. It's hard to get your head around. That's if you believe classic multiverse theory. Fetch and I have talked about this a bunch. The part that convinces me is what Tentacle Princess said before xe disappeared. Remember, Dilly? Xe said that something *stabbed the donut*—which is presumably our world—and injected poison into it. Poison in the form of a god-host from the universe next door. It'd explain why xe was so frightened. Knowing your ancient, evil ancestors are coming back would scare anyone."

"I hate this," Feral complains. "It's bad enough having an evil Dylan, but this is all so much worse. What does the damn thing *want*?"

"They want us dead." Even though everyone's near me to offer comfort, I still don't feel warm. "Cybele, Dani, me, the twins. Our *line*, as Hadylan called it. Ended. I doubt that'll be good for mutants when Cybele's power is gone from the world. I'm pretty sure their plans for humanity involve snacking, but we're the primary targets."

"I'm still stuck on parallel universes being real," Alyse says.

"We've been to one," I remind her. "Some of us at least. Fetch and the gang killed Heart in one."

Alyse turns slightly pale, trembling a little. That battle wasn't a good one. "That was, like, a dead world. I hate the idea of there being a creepy Dylan in another world. Because that means there's other versions of me. Ones where I'm evil, or have no powers, or I'm the one who can talk to objects. I guess there are ones where Emma didn't die, too, aren't there? Ones where we're together and happy." It's her turn to hug herself. "I think I hate parallel me."

"I'm willing to believe in parallel universes," Violet says. "But we've got to deal with this one. You really don't think Hadylan's dead?"

I shake my head. "We're not that lucky. They're on a mission and they won't stop until it's done. Or until they're dead, I guess. And they're goddamn powerful, with all the things they can do."

Nobody looks happy. I prefer the speeches where everyone feels inspired at the end. But I'm cold and tired and barely have a body. I've got nothing else to give.

"The flower thing worked, huh?" Dani's proud of herself, and so she should be.

"Painful, but yeah. Never been so proud to have a genius by my side."

"It wasn't only me. That puzzle box gave me the idea. You know how I've been fiddling it with it—"

"Fucking constantly, yes. I keep waking in the night to you click-clacking with it. It's very annoying, but now I suppose I have to forgive it."

"But it's fascinating, look." She fishes it out of an inner pocket and brandishes it at me. "At first I thought it was a good distraction while I was convalescing, but it means things." She depresses certain flowers on the outer layer with deft movements of her fingers. Two sides spring open with a click, revealing new carvings underneath. These depict the structure of different flowers, and have intricate sliding panels that can move around.

"That's convenient." I frown at it.

Dani tilts her head from side to side, like half yes, half no. "I think whoever left this was working on the problem of hybridising alien flowers. Violet says the original Weirdlands seed is super old, like the cave we found the box in. Whoever did this left a message for future generations, using symbols rather than language because languages shift. But the box-builder was working on multiple problems. The outer layer puzzle was to do with the human genome shifting into the mutant genome, and how to smooth the abruptness of the transition. The sort of thing our scientists have been trying to figure out, but this box had the answer already. Their minds are collectively blown."

"My head already hurts," I groan. "And you're making it hurt more. You're saying that some ancient super genius encoded information into a puzzle box about mutants and hybrid plants."

Dani's wide-eyed and excited, a flush creeping back into her cheeks that have been so pale. "Exactly! I'm on the third layer now, and I think it's trying to teach me a language. Dilly, I think it was left by—"

"Lilith." I grin up at her. "It's got to be, right?"

"Exactly." She squeezes my hand. "I know things look bad, but this is exciting. Lilith fought these aliens before. Maybe there's more information further down in the box that we can use."

"Okay, help me stand."

It takes a couple of attempts, but she pulls me to my feet and I don't fall apart.

I take a deep breath. "We need to talk to Cybele. Find out more about the past."

CHAPTER 18
STABBED, SHOT AND OTHERWISE FUCKING MUTILATED

ALYSE ENDS up carrying me into the forest. I'm still mostly a ruin and I keep collapsing. Dani and Violet are both extra attentive, and while I don't stop grumbling, I soak up all the care. Once we get among the trees and they plant me, I feel almost immediately better. The twins show up and perch on my branching shoulders like they're kids climbing a tree.

Of course, that's when all the emotions catch up with me. I'm a sobbing mess for about an hour while everyone takes turns comforting me. It's starting to become embarrassing, but nearly dying and almost losing Oni are colliding together in my head, and it's impossible to keep all the bad thoughts at bay. Especially since I know who Hadylan's targets are. My brain won't leave it alone, returning to prod the wound with almost obsessive intensity.

"Nobody leaves the island," I croak. "Especially if you're part plant. Lys, can you get Riot Grrl to make extra wards? And make sure everyone's on alert, especially Farsight. Nobody sets foot on Mutopia until this is resolved. Anyone wanting asylum is going to have to wait in One Thorn, and we'll have them all mindscanned multiple times by Fetch. Tell Ray to do whatever it takes to make this happen."

There are the awkward glances that happen when I do my exhausted general thing, as if I'm the one in charge of Mutopia rather than Ray. Which isn't true, but sometimes we get on war footing and the chain of command gets a little fuzzy.

"We're on it, Dilly." Dani's curled up at the base of me, entwining me with vines to help the healing process. "Everything's under control."

"Aliens from another world coming to kill us," I grumble. "Nothing is under control."

Speaking of aliens, that's when I notice Cybele hasn't shown up.

"Where's Green Mum?" I ask the twins.

They exchange glances. "We're… not sure."

"Give her a nudge, please. Whatever's going on isn't bigger than this."

Willow stares daggers at Soo-yeon, until their sibling starts talking. "We think she's planning things in case it all goes wrong. We think she's scared."

"Fucking great." I thrash at the soil, but I'm not healed enough to storm around in a tantrum.

"It's what's the thing." Willow gestures grandly. "Trauma? Grandpear talks about it a lot with Halmeoni when they're talking about you."

"Do they just?" I say grimly.

Soo-yeon rolls their eyes. "We mean Green Mum is sensitive about the whole tentacle situation."

"Well I'm sensitive about being stabbed, shot, and otherwise fucking mutilated but I still have to do it sometimes. So tell her to get her woodland ass back here right fucking—"

"Dylan." Of course she turns up mid-rant. "Thank you for summoning me so gracefully."

Cybele stands in front of me, hunched and gnarled, a far cry from her usual svelte and elegant appearance. It looks like some ancient stump has roused itself from the deepest, darkest fairy tale forest and come stomping through irritably to join us. Her bark is dark and flaking, and strands of moss hang down to shadow her face so that only the deep green flare of her eyes is visible, two sparks of fire guttering deep in the heart of a swamp. I know these are only projections she uses to visit us, but seeing her this way sends chills through me. She's alien, nature spirit, and primordial earth goddess all at once, and she is *scared*.

I refuse to be overawed by her, or at least not to show it. "I'm guessing you know the situation, but here's the deal. We've got an intruder from a parallel universe, one where Tentacle Princess's ancestors didn't die. Our very fucking existence pisses them off, and they've sent this scout in to try and kill us."

Cybele nods. "That seems accurate."

"And what about the Weirdlands? Is that them too?"

"That place is harmless," Cybele says irritably. "It's basically a pet. Although it harkens from our universe's version of the same species, there is no malice there."

Some goddamn pet. I suppose dogs do have teeth, and from the perspective of a planet-spanning alien, it might be pretty fucking quaint. Tentacle Princess is our world's version of the aliens, and the Weirdlands is their fucking summer home, or golden retriever puppy or some such thing. Hadylan is a pawn of another version of that same species but from a parallel universe. I wonder what their Weirdlands looks like. Probably not so cute. Then I wonder what their version of Tentacle Princess might look like, and that derails my brain.

"What now?" Dani asks.

"They haven't attacked you yet," I gesture at Cybele. "Probably because you're too powerful for them right now. They're taking out your defence mechanism first."

Cybele's bright green eyes flare as I talk, hooded inside a face of twisted branches. "I did not consider the possibility they feared me."

"In this world, you won. Hadylan was pretty pissed off about that. Said a bunch of mean shit."

"Aww." Dani pats my arm.

"Yes." Cybele rustles in thought. "Perhaps the situation is not as dire as I thought."

"No, wrong lesson. Hadylan is strong and ruthless. If it wasn't for Oni, I might be dead right now. We need to kill them before they get a chance to pull more madcap shit and turn us into the fucking Tentacle Underworld."

There's a silence as everyone watches Cybele for her reaction. I'm the only one who gets away with talking to her like this. It's possible I'm the favourite, indulged child.

"I fear them, Dylan." Her voice is very soft, almost inaudible. "They almost killed me."

Feral nods. "Tentacle Princess said a little bit, but xe was always tentative."

"They're enormous when they're fully grown. The children develop under the ocean, slumbering on the ocean floor and feeding on the creatures that grow in the deeps. When they rise to the surface, they're the size of multiple of your cruise-liners, except made of flesh. The insides are hollowed out with tunnels and chambers, leading to the central hollow where the god-heart is. Humans would make pilgrimage into the heart and there they would hear the voices of the dead, have mysteries revealed, and see visions of the future. This was reserved for the priest-class and there was much competition for those roles. If you were not a priest, you were a worshipper, and the gods needed feeding, too. The greatest form of worship was to be devoured."

"And people fell for that?" I ask.

"The gods were powerful, and they were vast, and their power and presence could not be denied. At the peak of their powers, they fed on me, and I hoarded the merest dregs of my power. The gods were growing in number and appetite, and I knew the human race could not sustain them. They were already developing breeding programs and..." Cybele tails away, and then changes tack. "If it wasn't for my last-ditch defence effort in creating the mutant species, I would not have survived. My greatest risk and triumph, but also a foolhardy roll of the dice. A situation you are well acquainted with. But in all the years that have passed, I have not forgotten that fear and desperation. My instinct is still to hide, to search for desperation plays. Like Heart of a Flower. Like you and Danielle."

"Like Lilith," I say.

"The Mother of Demons." Cybele smiles. "That is what they called her in later years, the enemies who arrayed against mutantkind. It is a name that has been remarkably persistent."

"I'm more interested in how she fought." I look around at the others in the forest with me. "She took on these alien god things and won, so I want to know how."

"I like this plan," Feral drawls.

"You always like fighting plans." Alyse smiles. "But I like this one too. For some reason, I always imagine Lilith as being super hot, and I like the idea of this badass older mom-type making insane mutant superweapons and fucking shit up."

"Alyse, you thirsty bitch," Dani says.

"I am as Cybele made me."

Dani grins. "It was a compliment."

"Brutality." Cybele's tone cuts across the banter, which annoys me a little because Alyse was being chill and flirty for a change, which is nice to see. "That's how Lilith won the war. No mercy, no quarter. With powerful mutants and powerful weapons."

Dani's eyes light up. "Don't Little Park and Sluggo have one of Lilith's old weapons just lying around somewhere? We let them get away with it because they're cute, and because they dealt with that rogue angel situation."

Little Park is a mutant who takes the form of a beautiful brownstone building in New York. Her girlfriend Sluggo has slime powers, which is fairly obvious from the name. Together, they've got some mindlink which allows them to control a mutant device from Lilith times that allows the wearer to build pocket realities.

"That... is an interesting proposition." I'm starting to feel that click-click feeling like things are coming together. It's almost enough to overcome the fact that I got my ass thoroughly kicked today. "Onc Thorn and Parkie are friends, so send a message that way. See if they want to come to Mutopia and join the fight. Okay, Cybele, what else do we have?"

"I do not have anything else." Her voice is faint. "All that Lilith knew is lost."

"Not entirely." Dani fishes the puzzle box out of her jacket again. "We have this."

I roll my eyes. "If that can find me weapons, I will forgive all the incessant clicking."

Cybele's interest flares to life again at the sight of the box. "I dimly recall this. Lilith laboured over it for many months. Constructed with wood from my most sacred groves, which have long been lost. I did not understand the purpose of all this intricate effort then, but now I see. She has passed knowledge to future generations."

Dani has total I-told-you-so face. "Can you help me unlock it?"

"The workings of such things do not interest me." Cybele rustles her branches dismissively, and I remember Soo-yeon saying *that's what you're for.* The kid's right—we need to be solving our own problems.

Maybe it's petty, but there's only one thing I really care about right now. "I want to find this asshole copy of me. No more sitting around with them dangling clues in our faces. I'm really fucking sick of them pulling my strings, and I'd like to surprise them for once."

"They're injured," Dani says.

"Yes, well I ripped their fucking head off and they bounced back from that just fine, so I think any wound-licking is going to be short-lived. Cy, why can't you find them?"

It's probably very rude to talk to an ancient alien like this, but they don't seem to mind. Favourite child syndrome again. "They do not connect to my network. If anything, they deaden the signals, but not in any way in which I can trace the negative space. They are essentially invisible to me."

"So we're back to zero?" I groan. "Waiting for them to pop up doing more creepy shit?"

"Don't hate me," Dani says.

"I could never, but I might hate your idea."

"If we can't find Hadylan, maybe we can lure them in. Control the situation that way."

Violet reaches and takes both of our hands. "Dani, no, I don't think—"

"We already know I'm their Persephone. I go off gathering flowers, and wait for them to drag me back to the Underworld. Except it's not only me waiting for them."

I close my eyes. "You were right. I fucking hate this idea."

"But it's a good one, Dylan. You know it is. It can't always be you running off recklessly to put yourself in danger. You're not the only one who's capable and dangerous."

And Dani's right, but I can't do it. In the last few days, I've watched her almost die from poison, and then felt first-hand what kind of ass-kicking my tentacle reflection can carry out. I want to say yes, I want to trust Dani, but the words won't come out of my mouth.

"I hate it too," Violet says. "But I think it's the right decision. And I'll be there, and others, too. Now we know more of what Hadylan's capable of. And we'll be controlling the situation, the location and everything."

I rock back and forth in the soil, sprouting dark lilies and roses and dahlias around me, because I cannot hide my emotions in any form. "How about this? Spend another few days on your magic box. If we strike out, then we do this terrible bait plan."

"Only for a few days." Dani crouches in front of me and looks into my eyes. "If we take too long, who knows what they could do."

CHAPTER 19
THINGS BURIED UNDER THE ICE

DANI'S OBSESSION with the puzzle box reaches new heights. She spends hours curled up with it, making scrawled notes on her tablet as she puts together what she says is the original mutant language. It's made up of dots and lines and is concept based rather than using words. Violet's more interested than I am. Although I try to pay attention, to me it's only another barrier. When Dani sleeps, she's feverish and twitchy, only snatching a couple of hours at a time before she lurches awake again.

"I dream of it." Her eyelids flutter. "The box is a forest full of trees and it whispers to me."

"The box is fucking you up." I reach for it, but she yanks it back. My fingertips are left with greasy smears over them. When I look closer, they're covered in something like gritty pollen.

"It's infecting you," I snap.

"I told you. This layer is full of it. It's got to rewire my brain."

"Fuck no." My hands twist into thorns. "You never said *rewire your brain*. I would've fucking remembered."

"Trust me, Dylan, please." Her hazel eyes meet mine, and despite the fevered brightness of them, I see the certainty there. "This is a message from Lilith, and I'm not going to let it go unheard."

Violet sprawls onto the bed beside me. "It really is from Lilith."

"I know. It's just…"

"You don't like the situation being reversed." Her mouth curls into a smile. "Dani being the reckless one and you watching it happen."

"This level of insight doesn't help." I try to growl, but I end up laughing.

"Just be careful, okay?" I kiss Dani's restless fingers. "Come back to me."

"I'm close, I promise." She brushes her lips against my forehead.

CLOSE TURNS OUT TO be nearly eighteen hours, but she wakes both Violet and me the next night with an enormous shriek of triumph. I sit up, bleary and incoherent, only for her to leap into bed between us. "Look!"

The entire outer layout of the box has been shed and what remains inside is a not-quite-perfect sphere, one with remarkably familiar patterns drawn on the surface.

"It's the *world*." I run my fingertips over the misshapen version of Australia.

"As it was." Dani nods eagerly. "And look, these little lights. I think they mark locations of interest." She spins the globe between her fingers. There are small divots embedded in particular places on the Earth. Two of them glow with faint luminescence, but all the others are scorched black. "Most have been lost over time, but there's still these two remaining."

"It keeps itself up to date?" Violet breathes.

"This device is incredible," Dani says. "I think it's a mutant computer. The questions I had to answer to get to this layer were complicated, but they linked to the mutant lineage. Like a series of passwords granting us access to what Lilith left behind."

"And it happened to fall into our laps." I'm still suspicious.

Dani nods. "I think the Weirdlands were genuinely trying to help us. They gave us the closest thing they had to Goddess, thinking that would buy our assimilation."

I press my finger beside one of the glowing spots, right at the bottom of the globe. "So what's here?"

A wide smile spreads across Dani's face. "Don't you want to find out?"

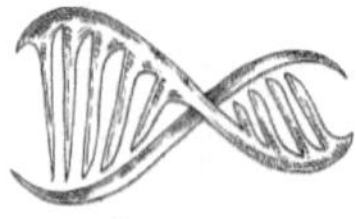

TURNS out the mysterious signal is buried deep in the Antarctic ice. It seems like a horror movie cliche, but we're going to dig up the damn thing anyway. The good news is that it's miles from anywhere other people might be.

The bad news is it'll take a lot of mutants to dig the damn thing up. Back in the day, Emma could have siphoned the powers of every mutant back in Mutopia to do it on her own. Now we have to do things the hard way, which is also the long way, and the painful way.

We've got Lou to melt fissures in the ice to break it up into movable blocks, and then waterkinetics and more general telekinetics to help move it. It's a lot of material, so we've even got the mutant Lightweight, who can only teleport things that weigh barely anything.

"Every little bit helps." Dani grits her teeth. She hates teleporting water, especially since the Emma downgrade, because apparently you have to account for every molecule. We're trying to save our most powerful waterkinetic Katara for the more complicated stuff, like moulding the ice into steps that spiral down into the hole.

Feral runs laps up and down the staircase, making sure it'll support someone's weight. She's one of the many mutants providing security for this endeavour, because I'm still worried Hadylan's going to crash our party. We already picked up Little Park, who's currently ensconced in the one Lilith weapon we already own. It takes the form of a crude stone statue that looks like it's been slowly eroding for the past few thousand years. Powers-wise, it's more of what Dani calls an 'environment generator' than the sort of weapon I'm hoping for, but the plan is to build a pocket reality and shove Hadylan into it if they show their face.

Little Park's presence means we also have Sluggo, who's cheerfully pacing rings around the hole shouting encouragement to everyone. She's got dark curly hair and greyish skin, and maybe one of the world's cutest smiles, and is leaving a trail of enthusiasm slime behind her. Dani's worried this is a slipping hazard and is wasting valuable telekinetic power to clean up. Which I get, honestly, because Sluggo is too adorable to ask to stop. When we first met her, she was pretty shy, but she's come out of her shell a lot since then.

We even have a Cybele manifestation here, taking the form of a winter pine who's rooted herself on the edge of the hole and is muttering to herself in a language I don't understand. Having her here is the biggest risk of all, at least in my view, but she refuses to leave and despite my favourite child status, she still doesn't actually listen to me.

"It's lucky Hadylan hasn't shown up for all this ruckus," I say. "Given we have, like, half their targets standing around out in the open."

"They will not attack," Cybele tells me calmly, snowy needles bristling. "I believe their tactics so far demonstrate this. It is never a frontal assault, but rather elaborate games to ensure better odds when they do attack."

"So far." I peer down into the blue depths of the hole. "Everything's out in the open now."

"You are nervous, and that is okay." Cybele shakes herself, sending flurries of snow everywhere. "If I can admit something to you, Dylan… I want it that way."

"Tell me why-yyy," I croon.

Of course, Cybele is not up on the oldies, so she actually does tell me. "My greatest protector *should* be always alert for danger coming in any direction. Your paranoia reassures me that you will ensure the best odds of our survival."

"Oh fuck off, you old suck-up."

The tree trembles as if there's an enormous breeze blowing through it, even though the ice is perfectly still today. "I am scared, Dylan, but I trust you and the others. I believe in this plan."

"Please, Cybele. Stop making it worse!"

"I don't understand. Do you not thrive on encouragement?"

"No! It makes me feel like I'm doomed to fail. How can I possibly live up to everyone's expectations? Give me a desperate underdog play where you're all like *even Dylan couldn't fuck this one up* and maybe I can pull a bouquet of flowers out of my ass."

"Physiologically you can actually do this already, Dylan. It is simply a matter of—"

"Metaphor or allegory or whatever! My point is there's too much pressure, Cy. You know, for a moment there I figured I might have done enough. Except here we are again, backs against the wall and dire fucking circumstances conspiring. What if I'm not good enough? What if this time I fuck up too badly, and everyone dies around me and we lose everything?"

Silence falls between us. It's not true silence, because everyone else is still shouting to each other, and working on this complex unearthing business. I start sidling away, very slowly.

"You remind me of Lilith," Cybele says.

"I don't need more sucking up." I jam my feet into the snow, searching for life beneath, until I'm standing in the middle of concentric rings of snowdrops.

"That is not my intention." Cybele shuffles over to me until I'm ensconced in her scented branches. "Do you really think Lilith was always an unstoppable force who never doubted herself? She was a little older than you when she was changed, and before long she carried the responsibility of all mutantkind on her shoulders. It weighed heavily on her. Sometimes I feared she would not have the strength to go on. Especially when she lost her Lucy."

"Oh." I lean into Cybele's trunk and inhale the scent of pine. It reminds me of Christmas, and how Pear would hang dangly car-scent things off our spindly silver tree. "I always imagined her as this impossible cosmic badass."

"Which is how some people see you."

I almost burst out laughing at this, and then I think of Shatterbox and that goddamn fic. It would be nice if that was my doppelgänger. A more confident, competent version of me, whose main flaw would probably involve being incarcerated in horny jail for a very long time. Much better than a religious zealot working for a bunch of evil gods.

"So Lilith was just some chick, huh?"

Cybele dumps a bunch of snow on me. "Dylan, you are exasperating. She was an astonishing person, as you are. But she had self-doubt, and moments where she cried about the future, and despaired at her ability to survive it, not only for her, but for the people she loved."

I throw my arms around her trunk. "Thank you for trying to cheer me up."

"Did it work?"

"Sort of. I mean I'm still worried we're all going to die, but it's nice to know Lilith was almost as pathetic as I am. Sorry. That was a joke. Mostly."

I shuffle back over to the hole, which plunges deeper into the earth. There's a whole chain of people running down into it, all combining their various powers. It's actually pretty inspiring. I jog down the stairs myself and find Dani about halfway down. She looks exhausted, so I wrap my arms around her from behind and give her neck the kiss of life.

"Oh god, all that energy. Thank you. Just what I needed." A huge chunk of ice goes whizzing up past me and disappears out of the hole. "Keep doing that with your mouth, it's actually very helpful."

"You're the one who deserves to be in horny jail," I tell her, but I don't stop.

It's only a couple more hours until we reach the weapon. If

it wasn't for the glowing part of the globe getting brighter and brighter I might have gone past it, thinking it was just a rock encased in ice.

"The fuck is it?" Feral asks, once Lou has melted it free. "It doesn't look very big."

Dani rotates the globe around and presses it to the stone. Part of the globe slides aside with an audible click, revealing another panel covered in tiny symbols. She takes a photo on her phone and zooms in on it.

"The closest translation I can come up with is pairstones." She hooks her hair behind her ear. "Two linked objects that are always connected. They can find each other anywhere and generate an enormous amount of energy when they meet over long distances. It says the planet could be split in half if they were placed perfectly equidistant around the earth."

"And why would we want to do *that*?" Alyse asks.

"If the only other option was letting the monsters win." Cybele has descended the staircase in humanoid form, a slender green sapling. "A weapon of last resort."

Dani's tapping numbers into an app on her phone. "If these equations are right, these could blow up a building with a five kilometre distance."

"Okay, I'm starting to warm up to this. Let's stick one to Hadylan and take the other one nearly halfway around the world."

"Hadylan said that cryptic thing about there only being one way to kill them." Dani turns the rock over in her hand. Aside from the faint hairline crack down the centre, you'd swear they were a single stone. "I doubt these happen to be the one single weapon forged."

"It might be one of those bullshit prophecies though. Like they're talking about weapons back home, but we've got cool

Lilith-tech that can blow them into squishy blue tentacle goo."

Her mouth twitches. "Yes, because we've always been that lucky."

"Okay, yes, very good point. Still, we can try." I take the stones from Dani. They're cool to the touch, and surprisingly heavy. There's an irresponsible part of me that wants to pretend to drop it, but despite my new plant form, I am still far too clumsy and I might accidentally set them off.

I settle for handing them back, and spinning the puzzle globe between my fingers. "So there's only one more of these things. If it's another weapon left behind by Lilith, we should dig that up too."

"I like the idea of taking the fight to Hadylan." Dani shrugs. "They nearly killed you, plus they threatened the kids. That makes me want to hurt them. And the longer we leave it, the more time they've got to plan and scheme. We've already wasted a lot of time."

Wow, I really hate this role reversal shit. "I'd rather get another superweapon first, so we can blast this alien asshole into atoms when they show their horrible face."

"Adorable face," Violet says.

"Not when it's got tentacles coming out of it! But fine, let's send some science nerds to investigate this other dig site while we do your horrible bait plan. If we're lucky, we get rid of Hadylan and the crisis is solved. If we're not... we worry about that later, I guess." I think we all know that there are many unlucky plans beyond that, ones where we all end up dead, and alien gods end up feasting on our corpses. I don't even want to bring up any of those, because I still believe in jinxing shit.

Dani runs her fingers through her long hair, and petals cascade down around her.

"Enter Persephone," she says.

"I fucking hate this story, did I tell you that?" I'm hunched and thorny, full of dark blooms. "Some girl gets dragged down to Hell by some asshole, and—"

Dani smiles at me. Her hands become talons, and black roses twist across her chest, each studded with thorns to rend and tear any predator. "In time, she becomes Dread Persephone. And now our Hades will choke on these poison blooms, and I will bring hell with me."

CHAPTER 20
THE ARTIST'S GARDEN AT GIVERNY

THE WHOLE BAIT plan proceeds far too quickly for my liking. We let Decker know roughly what's going on, and she says she'll keep an eye out. None of the GIC factions she's connected with has any idea about Hadylan's whereabouts either. Since our big battle at the bridge, there hasn't been a single cryptic clue. Opinions are still split within the GIC as to what to do with me, but nobody wants to do round two of the island invasion. There's no credence given to the parallel worlds theory which pisses me off, because these assholes will believe any other conspiracy as long as it centres on me.

On the bright side, we've got mutants out at the other location indicated by Lilith's magic puzzle box. It's on the shores of the Serpentine Lakes in the Mamungari Conservation Park in South Australia. One of Cybele's avatars, along with Ray and a pair of Indigenous Australian mutants, met with the tribal leaders and got permission. They were actually super excited to meet Cybele, by all accounts, and it's probably the most chill political interaction we've ever had. Progress on the dig itself has only just begun, but all my attention is spent fretting over what's going to happen to Dani.

Hadylan isn't going to be fooled by Dani just gathering flowers in some field, so we've got to get a little more subtle without losing the symbolism. There's actually a whole bunch of reforestation projects we're financing because plant powers are cool, and because a whole bunch of the new cohort of mutants have flora-based abilities. The most high-profile of these is the regrowing of Monet's garden in France, which has caused many arguments with the post-Michael French government. They weren't super happy to have mutants meddling in their precious flowerpatch, but Ray talked them around. Now it's the perfect opportunity to do something cool and also attract a bunch of attention, hopefully including my asshole double.

Monet's garden ended up a scarred wasteland with a polluted lake in the middle of it, the pretty green bridge turned into nothing but splinters. The lake is now clean again, and Dani sits alone in a quiet little nook beside it. Her bare feet are tucked into the soil, flowers spilling out from her like a gentle tide, shades of gentian and lapis, lilac and periwinkle. There's no sign of the razored roses and twisted thorns lurking under her skin, or of the single pairstone nestled beside her heart.

Violet lurks out of sight, standing in the passageways behind the world, one bladed finger to the cracks. The instant Dani's in danger, she'll burst out. Sluggo and Little Park are lurking in a pocket dimension that's apparently very cosy and mostly full of cushions. Then there's a hidden door to One Thorn, round as the entrance to a hobbit hole, and camouflaged behind vines.

That's where I am, the other pairstone heavy in the pocket of my hoodie. I can't stop running my fingers over it. Feral and Alyse are with me, both hoping for their chance to stomp Hadylan into the ground.

I pace the house, finding it very hard not being able to watch Dani directly. It's annoying everyone, not least One Thorn.

"You realise I can feel every footstep inside me?"

"So make the carpet thicker."

Thick fibres puff up around me, snagging at my ankles. "You'll wear tracks in me, grooves in my floor that I'll feel forever."

"Something to remember me by." I sigh dramatically. "After I've been killed by my copy." One Thorn extends the house a little, to give me new pacing room, and I trot down it gratefully.

"What are they exactly?" Feral says, prowling after me on light feet. "These parallel versions aren't really clones or duplicates. They're different versions, and there's one for all of us, right? Like it's possible there's a Feral that isn't devastatingly sexy and cool."

"Not sure even infinity stretches that far." Alyse grins.

"Thank you, Alyse, for acknowledging facts. But we need a catchy name for these other usses."

This finally distracts my attention. "What we need is a universe numbering system like they have in the comics. Like you'd be Feral-616 and some other Feral might be Feral-10146."

"I am the only one who has travelled the multiverse," One Thorn says. "We never discovered another version of us, something which still concerns me. Are we truly the aggregation of all our possible selves? Is this how we were able to reach these other universes? And since I can no longer do that, what does that mean for these other parts of me?"

There's a very awkward silence. "That's too much philosophy for me," I say. "But in terms of this numbering scheme, you might be One Thorn-001 or maybe One Thorn-infinity symbol."

Feral's looking at me in disgust. "That's literally the most terrible idea. I think we go with adjectives."

"What, like Ultimate Feral, Amazing Feral, or Spectacular Feral?"

She sighs. "I see the flaw. Those are all perfect names for me."

Alyse laughs. "If there are ever so many of me that they all need names, cute adjectives will be the least of our problems."

"I can't think of a more Ultimate Alyse," I tell her, completely honestly.

"Fuck off, smartass," she says.

"No. I'm serious. There can't possibly be—"

And then I stop, because I hear the sound of a ringing phone.

"What the fuck is that?" I clutch at Feral, as if she'll save me. To be fair, receiving a phone call is truly one of the worst things that can happen to a person.

"The call is coming from inside the house," Alyse whispers theatrically.

"One Thorn, do you even have a phone?" I ask.

"No, I have never had such a contrivance. Although I did manufacture one just now."

"And why the hell did you do that?"

"It happened involuntarily. It exists because of the necessity for it."

"Well I don't fucking like it," I hiss, but I still go stalking through the corridors of One Thorn trying to locate the incessant goddamn ringing. The house itself is vast. They describe themself as something like a jellyfish that occasionally reaches out a limb to connect with a particular location in the real world —whether that's in Mutopia, the Weirdlands, or a murder scene. The rest of the house exists in a no-place similar to where Violet lurks, behind the physical reality of things. It means you could spend hours and hours lost in One Thorn. I don't really have time for this, because Dani's currently being bait, but One Thorn drags the door to the garden with me so we don't lose touch.

We traipse down a dusty old hallway, lined with mirrors and fluttering dark moths, up a staircase which has portholes that look onto the stars, then through a series of rooms with increasingly giant furniture. We finally come out on a small balcony that overlooks an enormous room that's entirely under-water. The heads of statues poke out, as if they're desperately gasping for air above the waterline. And perched on a tiny, ornate table in one corner of the balcony is a large, beige telephone that looks like some sort of antique.

I don't really know how to answer it, aside from seeing things on TV, so I pick it up and gingerly hold it to my ear.

"Hello, darling," my voice says, crackling down the line.

Of course it's them. "Hello, you fucking douchebag. I'd say it's good to hear your voice, but I'm a terrible liar. How the fuck did you get this number?"

"They gave me this thingamajig when I wanted to talk to you. The god-scientists explained how it worked to me, but I sort of quit listening after a certain point. The Fool part of me rather than the Hierophant."

Despite everything, I can't help smiling at this. "That's the most relatable you've ever been."

"Yes, we've both got better things to do than listen, don't we? Speaking of which, your Persephone looks adorable, down there amongst the flowers. In my world, I never met a Kim Joohyun. I think that line was wiped out a long time ago. It's a shame, really. She's astonishing. The Empress. Did you think that was appropriate?"

"The fuck is with you and those goddamn cards?" I ask.

Hadylan gives a small breathy laugh. "They are one small fragment of truth existing between our universes. The archetypal truths, the foundational ideas of the world. You, the Hanging One, meaning trials and sacrifice. Your lot is to suffer and carry on suffering."

"And Dani?"

"Fertility and ideas. She will be the most *marvellous* garden. The Empress is for rebirth, of course, and won't she look wonderful when she's—"

"You leave her the fuck alone," I growl, even though the whole point of the plan is bait.

"Oh, I intend to. This plan of yours is very subtle and clever, but she terrifies me as much as she attracts me, and I'm recuperating right now. I hardly need your ferocious little monsters attacking me like a pack of wild dogs."

"Sorry to hear about your wounds." I'm smiling so wide my face might crack. "Because I've been spending all my time wishing Oni had killed you."

"My sweet vicious sibling," Hadylan coos, and it's in that moment I get a glimpse into how indescribably fucking pissed they are at the loss of their sword. "It boggles the mind that you survived the touch of my blade. Seen from a certain dispassionate viewpoint, it's hilarious you were able to destroy him. You probably don't get the joke, but believe me..." There's a long pause and I can only hear harsh breathing. "On another, I'm really going to have to fuck you up now. No more games, no more banter."

"Is *that* what you've been doing? Fine, then. No more

fucking around. Come find me. Let's see who walks away this time."

"No." There's a muffled shout in the background, behind the voice of my parallel universe sibling. A crash and the sound ceases. "We're not doing the head-on battle again. Unlike some, I learn from my mistakes."

"Then what? I thought you said no more games."

The breathing sounds again. "I have one question for you."

I roll my eyes and clench the phone harder. "Jesus. Just go ahead and get this over with."

"Do you know where your parent is right now?"

CHAPTER 21
IN THE PLACE I GOT CHASED BY A SEAL

I SLAM out of One Thorn's exit so fast, I trip and fall on my face in the middle of Monet's garden. "Change of plan," I shout. "Everyone back to Mutopia now. We're looking for Pear."

Dani sheds her flowery exterior, revealing the vicious, edged part of her. "Dylan, are you serious?"

"Can't catch a fucking break with this asshole. Still don't know if it's a ploy to get me away from you. Which is why you're coming. Everyone else, pile in. We'll hunker down on Mutopia until this is figured out."

I've got a painful knot inside me, panic twisted up so tight I can't process it. Hadylan's after Cybele and her line, which doesn't include Pear. And yet how did I not anticipate this? It's the perfect way to lure me into a trap.

Dani steps alongside me. "Hadylan won't get away with this."

"I don't know how to stop it." I have so much frantic energy I want to tear myself apart. The future is one giant dark unknown, filling my mind like it's blotting me out.

We all scramble for One Thorn, who's configured themself so the door to Mutopia is only a few steps away. I've got Dani and Violet right behind me as I burst through and into the tranquil scene.

We're right by Pear's cottage, overlooking the water. The sea is rumpled azure flecked with white, beneath a sky brushed with clouds, slowly tinting orange and purple as the sun descends. It's so beautiful I take it as a sign. Everything is going to be fine.

Except Lou's standing at the door of the cottage, his face pale.

"They've been gone a while. Went for a walk along the cliffs and hasn't come back. But they do this, Dilly." He calls after me, voice rising to a shout. "They do this all the time, go rambling, and it's fine, it's always fine."

I know the path they walk. I've done it with them so many times.

There's no sign of them on it now, no figure returning, silhouetted against the sky.

"We can't find them either." Willow pops out of thin air to land on my shoulder. "Soo's still in the forest but there's no trace. We can't sense them like we can with you, but they're so comfortable and familiar that we're sort of aware of them."

"They're not on the island." My stomach lurches. I skid to a halt, a few paces away from the cliff. "They're gone."

"Gone where?" Willow's voice is very small.

"I don't know." I scream for Keepaway, but only Dani and Violet are here with me. Willow flees to rejoin their sibling and continue the hunt through the trees.

"Dylan, we need to be careful about this." Violet's very quiet and intent, like she's trying to protect me from myself. "All of us sprinting off in a million different directions might be exactly what Hadylan wants."

"They've won." I try to ground myself in the soil of the island, but I can't find anything to steady me. "Why did we not have Pear protected? It's the most obvious goddamn thing and we missed it."

"Everyone on this island is protected," Dani reminds me. "All the time."

"She's right." Violet's voice soothing, hand stroking mine. "Hadylan couldn't just *turn up* here."

"No. Pear must have been *lured*. Hadylan looks like me. It's a fucking nightmare. How do we know who's the real me? If you're not sure, ask me something I'd know. Shit. Fuck. I can't think of anything." I'm rocking back and forth. The uncertainty of it all makes me want to scream. Need to get my goddamn emotions under control. "We need to find Pear."

"We're already working on it." Dani's on my other side, touching my cheek lightly. "Farsight is already searching. We're sending out two-person assault teams to locations where we know Hadylan has been. Just super quick reconnaissance to rule them in or out. We've got it under control. Everyone wants to help, Dilly."

"Okay." I take a deep breath. "That's good."

"We're assuming this is only move one," Dani says. "The ultimate goal is to kill you."

"Why me?"

"Because that's the smartest play. You're the figurehead, you're the most dangerous. And you're their sibling, as they call it. They're naturally going to focus on you."

"I wonder what their parent is like," Violet whispers.

"Fuck, that hasn't even occurred to me." My eyes are wide. "Of course there's a Ness Taylor on their world. Some tentacle version, probably. How does it get me any closer to finding *my* Pear?"

Dani shakes her head. "All we can do is keep looking. And not fall into their trap."

"Yes, I hear that incredibly subtle hint. Don't worry, I'm not going to go running off recklessly and throw myself into worse danger." This is a lie, and the two women I love know that, but they need it to be true, and so I try to sell it to them anyway. "It's not going to make anything better. They already have Pear, and if they wanted to hurt them, they would already. It's a leverage thing, right? There's going to be a demand soon. But, fuck, probably a demand I can't give them. What if it's a choice between my life and Pear's?"

"We can't think about that," Violet says firmly.

Dani's eyes are fixed on a point over my shoulder. She's already thinking about that. Figuring out the options we have around sacrifice plays. I know this, because it's what I'd do, and we're not different in every single way.

"Too many unknowns," she says slowly. "We're forced into reacting."

The twins reappear in front of us. They're holding hands, and look dishevelled as if they've personally searched in every tree and bush on the island.

"Grandpear isn't here." Willow's voice is faint.

"I'm worried." Soo-yeon's eyes are enormous in their small face. "I am having a lot of emotions, and they are not pleasant things to have."

Dani crosses over to pull them into her arms. "I know, babies."

"We're not babies. We're incomprehensible alien beings."

"Yes, but you're sad and scared like we are."

Keepaway pops into existence beside me. "Dylan, I'm so sorry about all this. Ray says we need to keep you up to date, otherwise you'll do something reckless. We've checked all the known Hadylan locations, and we've found nothing. But we're only scratching the surface of where they've been. We tried to use Sniffer to track them, but apparently Hadylan doesn't have a scent."

Words bubble up inside of me. "They've got all these gadgets and shit. Ones that can call into One Thorn, that can make a forcefield bubble that nobody can penetrate, not even Violet. Their world is more advanced than ours, and we're not going to find them until they're ready."

"We're still going to try." Dani's beautiful hazel eyes are dark, as if her inner light is dimmed. She holds the children tight. "Dylan, we'll do everything we can. I promise."

"I know." I aim for a smile and fall well short.

In the end, I let them take me back to our cottage. They're right, no matter how much I hate it. Me flinging myself around the world isn't going to do anything but waste time. I need to be home for the first real clue. Or if Hadylan reaches out to me.

There are only two scenarios that make sense to me. The first is the one that scares me—give me one of the people you love, and have Pear returned. A trade. A sacrifice I can't countenance or justify.

The second is what I'm hoping for.

Come alone.

The only difficult part there will be finding a way to escape the others. The whole gang is around, people drifting out in ones and twos to discuss things or go on particular errands. There's always someone with me, watching me, keeping me close. They know me too well.

Dani and the kids are curled up on our bed. I'm pretty sure the kids are asleep, exhausted after their hunt in the forest. There's no way Dani's going to close her eyes. She wants me where she can see me.

When my phone buzzes, I assume it's one of the others. Except when I swipe it unlocked, there's a message from an unknown number. It's a map pin with no further information. Seconds later, it vibrates again, while I'm still staring at the pin.

Come alone.

It's a location I've been to before. Wharariki Beach at the very tip of the South Island of New Zealand. A place I went once on summer holiday, with golden sand and rocky archways and a cave where I was chased by a seal. It'll be early winter there now, still autumn leaves on the trees.

It'll be isolated. Inaccessible by road. And I have to go.

I walk over to the bed and collapse down beside Dani. Nobody else notices me slide her my phone. She doesn't leap to her feet and bark orders, and I feel a surge of love for her.

"It's a good location," she says.

"That's what I thought. Dan, I need to go in alone. Only for a minute or two. Let me try and secure Pear before everyone else descends."

"You could die in a minute or two."

"They've failed to kill me twice before. They're mad about their Oni. Reckless. It'll leave them off-balance. Give me a chance. And besides, I'll take the pairstones. Even at a short distance, it might be enough to knock them down for a bit. Give us time for the reinforcements to arrive."

She closes her eyes for a long moment. When she opens them again, they're resolute.

"Okay, let's plan this out properly."

It doesn't take long. We tell the others and they all agree to give me my moment. The plan is simple. It could also fall apart at the slightest breath, but we don't have the luxury of reconnaissance. It's down to me. I've got one hundred and twenty seconds before the others show up and Hadylan does something I can't think about.

That's the most time Dani will give me, and even that is twisting her up inside.

We both hate uncertainty in different ways.

"The easiest way to solve this is to do it and see what happens." I give her a lopsided smile.

"You fucking be safe." She kisses me so hard it feels like she punched me in the mouth.

"I'm coming back, I promise. And I'll bring Pear with me."

"You better."

The whole team gathers for one enormous group hug, and then finally it's just Keepaway and me. I've transformed into a form built for running, half my biomass in my legs, massive himbo muscles for driving myself forward, even through sand. Every second is going to be vital.

"Pinpoint accuracy, Keeps."

"I know. Good luck, Dylan." They place their hand to my chest, and for the briefest of moments—

I'm nowhere. Something moves in the corner of my eye, something I've never seen before. Someone *else* in the void with me. Hadylan? I turn—

And I'm somewhere else. Standing beneath an overcast sky, clouds bruise-purple overhead. The roar of waves crashing, sand underfoot. Tall spires of rock jutting from the water, arches eroded into them by time and pressure.

No sign, no sign of—

There. Two silhouetted figures in the distance, perfectly

framed in one of the archways. They stand close, as if embracing.

I start to run, enormous leaping strides, gobbling up the beach underneath me. My eyes are fixed on those two silhouettes. The rocks tower above them, striated brown and gold. They're dwarfed by the majesty of the landscape, the widescreen enormity of sea and sky.

I'm counting seconds in my head.

There are still ninety-five.

Plenty of time to tear out Hadylan's heart and turn them into tentacle soup.

I'm close enough to make out the distinction between the two figures. One is broad, standing tall. One is hunched, flinching away, trying to flee.

The first figure moves, a complicated motion like a dance move as their tentacles flare out around them. Then they vanish, like they were never there.

The other spins, staggers.

And they're falling, falling to the ground.

CHAPTER 22
CARRIED ON THE FLOOD

I'M STILL COUNTING seconds in my head, but they're screaming. There are seventy remaining and by now I can see Pear lying face down in the shallow water. Their coat is spread out behind them, dark wings like a bird descending to feed. My feet splash through water, spraying everywhere. The salt stings, but I only run faster.

Around Pear, the surf froths like pink foam.

I'm not counting anymore.

I collapse beside them, dragging them up out of the water, turning them in my arms. Their chest is a ruin, scored with a gaping, ragged wound. The imprints of sucker marks are seared into their flesh.

"No." I scream. "Time, time, time."

Doc appears, only metres away. She's straining, lunging forward, but her expression isn't fully visible through the greasy shimmer in the air. When the hell did this appear? This can't be happening. Hadylan is gone, leaving me with Pear inside the forcefield, another glass jar over the top of us like we're insects squirming inside it.

"Hey," I croon. "We'll figure it out. Rescue's coming."

A gurgling sound comes from Pear's throat. They clutch at me with wet fingers. I think they're saying my name.

"I'm here. I've got you." I'm soaked through with salt water. Inside the bubble, the waves no longer crash, so we're sitting in this small pool of bloody ocean. There are two tarot cards tucked into the inside pocket of their coat. The Hanged Man and the Fool. The second one feels perfectly clear at this moment.

An oblivious figure heading towards oblivion.

Outside the bubble, Keepaway hurls themself into the forcefield over and over. Dani's there too, legs planted in the sand, trying to dig us free. Violet is an impossible maze of blades, frantically scrabbling at the surface of the bubble, trying to cut us free. There are doors everywhere, One Thorn opening every passageway, spilling more mutants onto the beach.

Inside the bubble, it's only Pear and me.

I plant a kiss on their forehead, running my hand over their scalp. "This isn't happening. It's not, I'm sorry. I'm dreaming. That's all. Someone's feeding me a nightmare. We'll wake up soon, and everything's going to be okay."

My brain's rebelling, showing me all the times I've worried about Pear. Like they were all foreshadowing this moment. My parent, lost in despair. Me, unable to save them. As a child, I was helpless and lost among the maze of them, and even now that I'm grown and superpowered, I've got nothing to ward against this dark future that was always coming for us.

"Fuh." They spit up blood. "Fucked."

"Yeah, I think it is. Who'd dream like this?" I'm shivering so violently my skin can't take it, cracking open fissures to let the salt water pour into me until I'm covered in kelp and rough grasses.

I try to wrap some of myself around them, bind them back together, seal the wound until the others can get inside and heal them properly.

"Duh-duh." They swallow convulsively. "Dilly."

"Don't talk. Please. Save your strength."

Outside the bubble, there's a frantic hive of activity, but I'm only dimly aware of it. Everything's narrowed to this tiny world, a single point of despair.

"Love. You."

"Shhh." I press my face against theirs. "You don't need to say this. I already know. I've always known."

For a moment, I'm back in their stiflingly hot bedroom, holding them while they cried. Feeling their dry skin, the coarse tangle of their hair, the way they clutched at me with bony fingers like I was the only thing keeping them alive. They fought their way out of that place. We can make it through this.

"Best. Thing." A smile twitches on their lips. They reach for me again. My skin is streaked with their blood. "Best."

It's almost silent inside the bubble aside from their breath wheezing in and out. The air smells of iron and salt. Outside, everyone moves in flurries, but inside we're falling still.

This isn't a dream.

I look down at their face, the one I know so well. "I think we're fucked this time."

"You. Think?"

"I don't know how to do this without you. I can't fucking lose you too."

"Strong."

"I can't fucking fight my way through this." My breath has barbs in my throat. "You can't fucking *die*. God, Pear, I'm so sorry, I really—"

"No." They take hold of my face, trying to be fierce, but their fingers slip away. "Dylan. No."

"I don't know what to say." I'm aware I should be crying, should be furious, should be begging the universe to find a way, but there's nothing inside me. I am a husk collapsed on a beach over the body of their dying parent.

Their chest shudders and more blood spills. "Say. Nothing. I know. It all."

So I pull them closer, and hold them against me, and feel the warmth of their blood mingle with the chill of seawater. And we stay like that until they stop moving, and I'm holding the body of the person who gave me life, who gave me love. Who forged me first, before anything or anyone else.

At some point, the forcefield must be gone, because there are other people too.

Doc, kneeling in the water, one hand on Pear's back, shaking her head at the others.

Keepaway hunched over, hitting the sand with clenched fists and leaving scars that are obliterated by the waves.

Dani and Violet tangle themselves alongside me, saying words that evaporate the instant they hit the salt air. The warmth of them slowly seeping into me but unable to heat the pool of frigid salt water at my heart.

The children stand at a small distance, clinging onto Alyse as she cries.

I'm waiting for the emotion to overwhelm me, but it's not there. It's like when Emma took my powers, back when we had that terrible fight and I'd flailed against the limitations of my powerless mind. I've got that same sense of dead endings.

There should be an inexhaustible well of rage inside me, a suffocating desire to not sleep until I've had my revenge. Surely I should be a shuddering wreck, unable to speak or even think in the overwhelming wake of this grief?

Instead I am a calm island, untouched by storms.

I sit up, one hand resting on Pear's face.

"Thank you all for trying to help." I look at each person, noting all the sadness marked there. "You did your best, and I appreciate everything so fucking much. It was one of those situations we couldn't fix. We'll figure out a response soon, but for now everyone should go back to Mutopia where it's safe."

People exchange glances. They don't know what to do. This beautiful, gentle calm enveloping me is something they can't understand. They expect me to bloody the whole universe with my pain. In the face of this, they say their words of love and tenderness, and leave one by one.

I let the children hold me, and I let them touch Pear. It's good for them to see this. "You'll have other chances to say goodbye. And you'll always remember them. They'll live in your heart forever."

Alyse is a drifting fog, and my heart aches for her because this is too much loss for anyone. She deserves something bright and good, because she's the sweetest and best, and all I ever bring with me is the dark.

"I love you, Dylan." She solidifies enough to kiss my cheek, then cups it with one misty hand. "And if you spend another second worrying about me, I am going to kick your ass, okay?"

Finally, it's only Dani and Violet left. They sit on either side of us and lean in close. I'm only dimly aware of them. Everything's still dreamy, and it's only the discomfort of the saltwater in my system and the increasing chill of the day that makes me realise I exist in this moment. Dani and Violet don't say anything, or I don't hear any words. They're warm, and that's all that matters. Dani has vines threaded among me, stitching up all the little wounds that keep cracking open across my body.

"—shock," someone says.

"It's beautiful here." My voice is croaky. It sounds like Pear's. "I think they'd like that."

"Yeah." Dani hooks an errant strand of hair back over my ear. The scent of lilies is overpowering. "It's beautiful and it's private and it's wild, just like them."

Pear is still in my arms. The body. That's what I'm supposed to think now, because they're gone. This is a shell, but oh, it's a shell I loved so much. Shells matter. They're not something so easily discarded, even for those of us who never felt quite at home in ours. Their skin is cold, even colder than mine. I don't know how long we've been sitting here. I don't know enough about the process of what happens to bodies when they die. There's rigor mortis, and fluids that pool and settle. I want them to be buried on Mutopia. That's the only thing I know for sure right now. Somewhere they'll always be safe, where Cybele can watch over them.

"I think I want to be alone with them for a little bit."

"Dylan, are you sure?" Dani asks, but Violet's already pulling her to her feet.

"Yeah. I'm okay. Honestly, I am. I'll find my own way home."

"I can't leave you here, Dilly." Dani's sobbing, and she never cries, not like this, but right now I think she's going to fall apart from the force of it all. "Not alone, not with—"

"I'm not alone." I shake my head, and it aches the faintest amount. "I'm always connected to you and Vi. And I'm with Pear. It was the two of us for such a long time, and it feels right to be this way now, you know…" Something twists inside me, and for a moment I think I might crack down the middle and evaporate into the air, but I don't and I'm still here. "At the end."

Dani's hand is pressed to her mouth, tears spilling.

"I love you," she says.

"I know. I love you too."

She turns, Violet holding her up, and they walk away down the beach. I have this horrible pang, because Dani lost someone too. Pear loved her, and it was returned so fiercely, and I didn't even tell Dani how sorry I am about it.

"I have terrible manners," I tell Pear. "You never managed to fix that shit." I run my hand lightly over their cheek, so much like mine. "I know you'd be mad at me for blaming myself. For thinking it was my responsibility to fix everyone and every-thing. The arrogance to think that one asshole brat can save everyone all the time. You'd probably quote Anya's speech from 'The Body', and tell me that there is no reason. Sometimes bad things happen, and you can't stop them." I touch my hand to the edges of the wound. There are still flowers and vines tangled among Pear's flesh from where I tried to fix things. Their body is a strange, gory garden, but all the blooms are dead.

"The thing is that nobody can deny that I failed. Hadylan killed you to hurt me. That's a fact. My life, the path I've chosen, all led me here. With you, dead in my arms. One more failure to add to the list of my dead. And even though there are probably a trillion things I could've done differently, in all these different parallel worlds, I don't know what any of them are. You're one more person I couldn't save. No more marks under the bed. No more days you made it through."

There's water all over my face, but my hair is soaked too. It's raining. I'm not sure when it started. The sky overhead bows inwards with the pressure of all that water, and the sea mirrors that same exhausted, drowning grey.

I get to my feet slowly, Pear cradled in my arms. Their body. It's time to bring them home. I have a rough sense of where Mutopia is from here, and I turn around to face the ocean. There are miles and miles to go, but I need to feel the weight of each one. Everything else has to wait. Eventually, I'm going to find and kill Hadylan. That's an inevitability now. Right now, home is more important.

Home where Sarah is, and her kids, who love Pear almost as much as I do. Where Mrs. Kim is waiting, probably Pear's closest friend. All these other people who've grown to know and love them, their world growing wider as mine did. It's this that cracks me open, splitting me along all these fissures of salt-water erosion.

I don't know how to process this, a tide of emotion as deep and tempestuous as the ocean I'm staring at. It's ruinous and vast, a window into a world as cold and cloaked as Hadylan's. Even if I can swallow this loss inside the hollow at the heart of me, it will ripple outwards all the same, chilling the soul of every life it comes into contact with. And this is the thing I cannot bear. It is too much, too overwhelming, too huge to bear so I must grow to meet it. This place is on the path of Cybele's network, and so I root my feet into the ocean floor and drink, inhaling power until I dwarf my own pain.

By the end of it, I am a colossus bestriding the world, a monster of thorns and dead flowers. I must be visible for miles around, a ruined guardian unearthed from some prehistoric forest as a monument to the dead. And nestled in the heart of me, floating in the brackish lake that spills from my overflowing heart, is the body of my parent.

I set out for Mutopia, wading through the depths as if

they're little more than a child's pool. I'm dimly aware that a transformation of this size isn't feasible or responsible, but it's the only way to dilute things enough that I don't collapse.

The journey is surprisingly short. I suppose being a giant has some advantages. As I draw closer, I see that the island is transformed too. It looks haunted, covered in lichen with the trees jutting stark and wintry, draped in Spanish moss. The meadows that are usually rioting with delighted spills of colour now lie sombre, checkered with black, deep purple, and white. There's a dusting of snow along the ridgelines and the streams run full and deep, brimming over their banks and spilling icy water that pools in the streets.

Standing on the headland is a single tall tree, limbs bare and raised in greeting and supplication. I would recognise it as Dani even if the connection between us didn't surge with all the feeling I cannot speak in words. In that shadow of this winter's tree is a woman made of blades, and another made of tears, two small children hiding between them like green shadows. Behind them are Sarah and her children, Mrs. Kim and all the others, the whole population of the island crowding along the headland to watch me as I walk out of the sea.

I stand over them, towering like a god, but with something precious locked deep inside me. My face is lost to those waiting below, swimming in dark clouds. All they can see is the interlocking maze of thorns that forms my cage.

This immensity is too much to hold together, and so I collapse down, unfolding and unfolding until I'm a ruin of a girl, a lost and broken boy, a child torn and rootless.

I lay Pear's body down on the grass, and then I collapse with it, carried on the flood. Surrounded by those who love me, and yet with an absence that can never be filled.

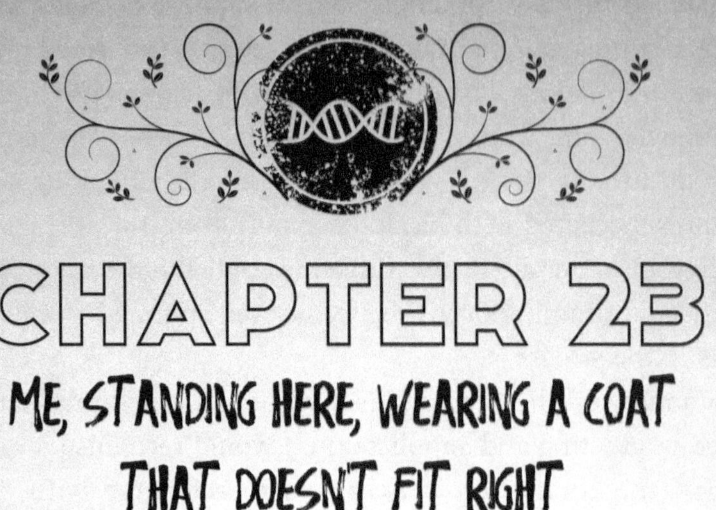

CHAPTER 23
ME, STANDING HERE, WEARING A COAT THAT DOESN'T FIT RIGHT

THE NEXT DAY, I wake up tangled among Dani and Violet. I've got a very faint headache, but aside from that I feel completely fine. There's no sledgehammer blow of absence that drops on my head. I wake from dreams of Pear into a world where I know they're gone. And it's awful, but I'm actually going to be—

"Fine," I insist to two worried faces. "Honestly. I think I got it all out of my system yesterday."

Dani takes my hand and her thumb rubs restless circles over the back of it. She's still mostly lilies and chrysanthemums in funereal shades. "Dylan, you can't grieve someone you loved that much in a single moment."

"Maybe I can. Maybe it's my superpower." I stretch high and crack my neck. "Because I feel, like, not *good* but clean. Like I've scooped out all the grief already and now it's acceptance."

Violet wraps her arms around my neck. "If it comes back, we're here, okay?"

"Yes, I know." I pull a face at them. "My greedy ass has two very supportive girlfriends. I get it. Now I'm gonna go get dressed and check on Sarah, if that's okay with you two worriers?"

Dani and Violet exchange glances. They've obviously been talking about me, which I get.

"What?" I demand.

"You're not running off after Hadylan the moment our backs are turned?"

"No. God, no. We've got to do the funeral first. That sibling of mine will have their turn." I beam at them both. "Don't worry about that. Death is coming."

Then I turn around and walk out of the room before remembering I haven't gotten dressed, and have to make an embarrassing re-entry.

Hazel answers Sarah's door, and I swear she's fucking grown again. When I died, she was a scrawny teenage girl with long black hair. Now she's way taller than me, with shoulders you could bust a door down with, and her hair's cut very short in all the colours of the rainbow. She's also got mutant powers now, some dream manipulation stuff with these supernatural guns. I've grown to think of her as my little sister, but these days she's so much cooler than me.

She throws her arms around my neck. "Is it okay if I hug you? Sorry, I know I'm already doing it, but I can stop."

"It's fine. Sibling privilege."

"Are you okay?" She pulls away to look at my face. "God, that's such a stupid question, isn't it? How can you possibly be okay?"

I shrug. "You know what? I kinda sorta... am. Okay, I mean. Obviously, it's a terrible thing to happen, but I think I'm through the worst of it. "

"Oh, Dilly." Hazel looks like she wants to hug me again.

"But enough about me. Seriously. How's your Mum doing?"

Hazel's face falls further. "Not good. I know we're still in the shock of it, but she's—"

Sarah shuffles out of the hallway. "I thought I heard their voice. I could have sworn. Oh, Dylan, it's so awful, you poor darling." She totters across the room, as if she's in massive fuck-off stab-someone-in-the-eye heels rather than tatty slippers. I manoeuvre around to catch her before she falls face down on the wooden floor, and with Hazel's help we lower her into a chair. She's crying, covering her face.

"I'm really sorry." I stare at the ground. "I tried to save them, but--"

"Don't you dare apologise. This is not your fault, and I am not going to let you disappear into darkness, Dylan Jean." It's hard to understand her, because she's sniffling and gasping.

I sit down beside her and give her an awkward hug. "I'm not in darkness. I promise. I just wish I'd been able to do something. It's like my Uncle Ben moment, except I'm already supposed to be the superhero, not some asshole kid."

"They were so proud of you," Sarah tells me. Her eyes are red and smeared with mascara, which seems like a bold choice to fuck with under the circumstances. "I know you fought sometimes, but they loved you."

"I know. We talked recently, actually. Sorted through some shit. It was nice."

"Yes." Sarah smiles, and it's shaky, but it's real. "They told me about that. That night after you talked, they dreamed they died. Just dropped dead from some illness. Woke me up at four in the morning to tell me all about it. It unsettled them a little, I think. But they said what they'd miss most was seeing what you did next."

"What came next was I failed them," I whisper.

"Or it was their fault, for going out wandering when they knew things were dangerous? Or it was mine, because I said I needed some space, and that's why they roamed so far? Was it the sentries for letting Ness be taken from this island which is supposed to be safe? I'd rather blame this other version of you, who was actually responsible. Blame is *complicated*, Dylan, and you can cling to some piece of it if you want, but what good will it do aside from turning into something larger and sharper in your hand?"

"Jesus," Hazel mutters. "Where did that speech come from?"

"I've spent every moment since I heard blaming myself for my part." Sarah turns her eyes on her daughter. "I took myself into the forest and screamed my rage at the trees. I thought Cybele might come and give me answers, but she didn't. At some point in the early hours of the morning, I figured it out myself. And the thing I wanted to do was tell Ness."

She's crying again, and maybe I'm crying a little bit too, like maybe there are some dregs of grief left in me. Or because I'm still the world's worst sympathetic crier.

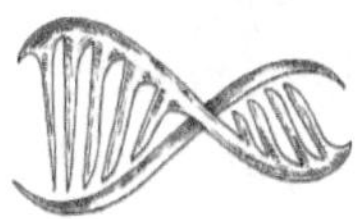

THE FUNERAL SNEAKS up on me. Dani and Violet did most of the organisation, although they asked me a lot of questions, most of which I can't remember. All I know is that now it's the morning, I'm standing there in Pear's coat in the middle of our living room, and I don't know how to walk out the door.

For a moment, I'm furious with them. For dying. For running away. For everything that came before. For every shitty day. For making me watch and wait through all those moments. My brain's buffering and there's only static.

"Dilly." Violet stands by the door in a plain back dress, looking pale and beautiful.

"Who's going to be there?" I ask.

"I don't know all the names. I think most of the island will be. You and Pear mean a lot to people."

"They'll all look at me." I jam my hands in the coat pockets, just the way they used to. "They'll fucking *expect* shit. Like words or explanations."

"They just want to pay their respects." Dani joins me at my side, slipping her arm through mine. "That's all. You can stand up there and scream at them all if you want, nobody would blame you."

"I like that idea." I fidget with the sleeves of the coat. "Probably won't do it."

"Keep it in your back pocket." Violet joins on my other side, and somehow the three of us find a way out of the house.

Alyse is waiting, hair whipped across her face by the wind. She's not transformed, but her cheeks are wet and her eyes look like they're dissolving into salt.

"Dilly." She holds out her arms.

I collapse into her like an avalanche. "How do you do this?"

"Go on in the face of everything?" She strokes my tangled hair. "I have my friends. That's really what it comes down to. A lot of days I still feel like I'm clinging by my fingertips. Sometimes I feel guilty about that, but it's better to hold on, right? I can't give you any pretty promises, my darling. I wish I could, but grief is a whole other country and I still don't know how to navigate it."

"I love you." That's all I can say, but at least it's true.

"Yeah. That part helps a lot." She kisses my forehead, like I'm sick in the night and she's checking for a fever. "You and me, we'll hold each other up."

Dani and Violet join us, and together we all go down to the beach where the funeral will be held. It's hard to pay attention. The sky is so huge that I get lost in it. Some people talk and then apparently everyone is waiting for me to say something. I don't really want a turn. I've said everything I wanted to say to Pear already. What's the point of saying more? I feel a terrible sense of guilt for the way I badgered Alyse about getting over Emma. How fucking demanding of me. I need to apologise to her. I almost stumble down from the stage to tell her all this, but everyone's watching me.

I squint until they're blurs. Through my connection to Dani, I can feel all this love and compassion, enough to make me dizzy, and I know that Violet and Alyse and all the others are sending theirs too. Petals scatter from my body on the breeze, thick and velvety. I'm still covered in so many thorns, and nothing can coax them down. It seems unfair to stand here where everyone can see my grief displayed, a lurid and multidimensional thing with claws and a deep embrace. I am so tiny in the shadow of it, a pale flicker swallowed by the looming darkness of a god.

All eyes on me, watching me break in real time. I don't want to be here, don't want to be seen or known. People's heads lower, averting their eyes from me, this creature they don't understand. A girl of torn petals and broken thorns, a boy with a hole where his heart should be.

Their leader, their fighter. How will I survive this time?

I imagine them all getting up out of their seats, screaming at me.

Get the fuck back up.

The breeze buffets me, and leaves tear themselves from my skin. I could let myself be blown away, disintegrate in front of them. But I'm here with all these people I love, and who love me. These people know me and they're here for me anyway.

Just like Pear did. Which is why I need to say something. Not just stand here at the end of the world, while the ocean rises to swallow me, extinguishing the last embers of my emotion on the same salt tide that drenched me when I sat there while the person who birthed me bled out in my arms.

"I don't know if you all know this, but I can be an asshole sometimes." I take a deep breath, try and catch myself before I float away. People are laughing. I'm not even sure if that was meant to be a joke. "Pear could be too, because that shit's fucking hereditary. I remember years back when they first came out as nonbinary. I was the first person they told, and on one level it made perfect sense. Like, why do you have to be one or the other? What bullshit is that and who fed it to us? On another level, I was scared. Kids already made fun of me a lot. I was pretty strange, which is probably another huge fucking shock. So the news that everyone was going to have this other piece of ammunition against me was not welcome. I shouted at them a bunch, getting more and more worked up until I said *every other kid has a mum, and I'm just going to have a stupid pear.* And the name stuck." It's really, really hard to talk for some reason, which is weird because I'm obviously so totally fine right now. "But they showed me I didn't have to be confined. That I could always be more. How to fight, for myself and for others. I still sometimes find the first part hard." There it goes again, this inability to make words. I clear my throat, dredge up more. There are more complicated things stuck in my throat. Things you can't say at a fucking funeral. I could tell them what Pear looked like broken. Talk about looking into blank eyes and thinking my parent was dead.

Not the time, Dylan. Never the time. Forward's the only direction. Like a fucking shark.

I clear my throat. "Pear and I both loved superheroes, except we sometimes disagreed about them. I liked the dangerous ones, because the world scared me. Still does, a lot of the time. Maybe without Pear, I might have taken the hand of Heart of a Flower, given into the monster that bays inside of me, that's seen so much bullshit and can't stomach it anymore. Now they're gone, I have to remember them. Try not to give into the dark."

I stumble down from the little raised platform and scurry back to my seat without looking at the crowd. Dani and Violet let me bury myself in their arms, and I take solace from them as I listen to all these other people who loved my parent.

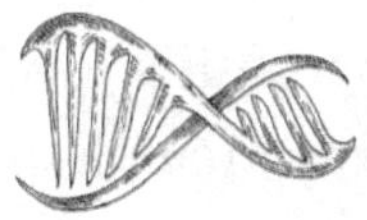

AFTERWARDS, there are only so many condolences I can take before I flee, heading up the path to the cliffs. Dani and the others stay behind to cover for me and do the social interaction bullshit, which is about the purest expression of love I can imagine right now. At the top of the cliff, it's deserted, although I think I saw two small green figures tumble into the air as I arrived. They don't reappear, so I cross to the cliff's edge and stare out at the ocean. It makes me shiver, because I can't forget how it felt to sit in the shallow waves with Pear's body in my arms.

"Dylan?" The voice behind me is rough and hesitant, but I still recognise it.

My first instinct is to hurl myself off the cliff. I'm pretty sure I'd survive. The second is to throw the speaker instead. I didn't even see him at the funeral. Probably snuck in at the back, lurking like the cowardly fuck he is.

"Not interested." I barely look at my father, enough to see he's in a suit and his beard is neat.

"Dylan, please. It's been a long time."

I stay looking at the ocean. It's better that way. It's big enough to douse some of my feeling. "Yes, it has. And have I regretted it once? No. So let's keep it that way."

"I'm sorry for your loss. Ness was…"

I finally turn. My hands inside the coat pocket have so many thorns I'm going to shred the lining. My father's so much older, which I guess is how time works, especially when you're not looking. "I don't want to hear you complete that sentence, because no matter what word you choose, I'll smack you off this goddamn cliff."

He flinches, but I suppose it's a whole different experience to see your child as a thorny green monster, baring ragged teeth in a snarl. "I tried over the years, Dylan. To reach out to you, to Ness."

"How fucking hard did you try?"

"Not as hard as I should have. I'll admit that. I could never figure out how to bridge that gap, how to get inside that closed system you had."

I fit inside my rage so beautifully and smoothly. There are no ragged edges and impossible cliffs like there are with grief. "You say we had a closed system but that was the only fucking option we had. You *left*." I take a step closer, and when he retreats, I take more. "You left them in the fucking dark. With only me as their light. Do you have any fucking idea what that was like, you selfish asshole? To be the person who—"

"Of course I did." There's finally a spark of defiance in his eyes. "I tried so hard, for so long. But I don't think you understand how difficult it was. They had… there were so many problems. I'm not sure what they told you, but it wasn't only the… gender thing. They weren't an easy person to live with, and the weight of it was eventually too hard to—"

He breaks off only because I've got my hand around his throat, lifting him into the air. His body swings like a toy. I'm huge again, looming like a sentinel perched at the edge of the cliff, an inverse lighthouse built to warn everyone away.

"We deserved better than you," I growl.

My father scrabbles at the rough woodgrain of my hand. He chokes apologies and excuses.

"How dare you come here *today* of all days and try to shit all over my memories. Telling me they weren't worthy of love, that all that time we dug ourselves out of the darkness was wasted. I'll show you darkness if that's what you want. Do you want to know what it felt like to suffocate, Dad?"

There's a gentle rustling sound, and the twins appear, side by side in front of me.

"Let's not k-word someone at Grandpear's funeral," Willow says.

"Even if he does deserve it a little," Soo-yeon adds.

I shrink down and throw my father to the ground. He rolls away, clutching his throat and staring at me with wide eyes.

"Get the fuck out of here." The only emotion I feel in the aftermath of rage is exhaustion. I can barely stand, and I don't want to spend another second talking to this man. When he walked out of our lives, he should have kept going. I'm not sure why he thought he could come back.

He gets to his feet. "I'm sorry, Dylan. I don't know anything else to say."

I want to tell him he shouldn't have come, that he didn't deserve to be here. To make him feel everything I'm feeling. His eyes are dry. Maybe I should beg him to teach me how to stop being swept away on the tide.

In the end I say nothing. He bobbles his head, and totters off down the path.

I choose to ignore the time taken between the last line of my funeral speech and me raging out in full dark mode. Grief does shit and besides, my dad's an asshole.

"Are you okay?" Willow nestles into me. "We don't know what to do."

"We burned some things," Soo-yeon says. "And we tore down some factories. It made us feel better, but only for a little bit."

"We miss Grandpear a lot," Willow sighs. "We asked some trees to pretend, but they don't know how. It doesn't feel the same even if they look right."

I hold the two of them close to me. "Nothing feels the same. They were an original. The world's never going to be as good without them in it."

"Halmeoni says it's god's plan," Willow tells me. "But we couldn't figure out which god."

I think of the dark water on that other earth, of the strange lights in the sky. Those massive creatures in the water, silent gods awaiting sacrifices.

"I'll tell you what," I say. "We're going to figure out which gods, and we're going to make them suffer."

"Oh," Soo-yeon swings their legs. "Finally. I like this plan. Is that what grieving is?"

"Maybe. Either way, we're going to give it a damn good try."

I stand on the cliff a little longer, watching as the sun is slowly extinguished in the sea, bleeding light all along the wound of the horizon.

All I can think about is how some things don't rise again.

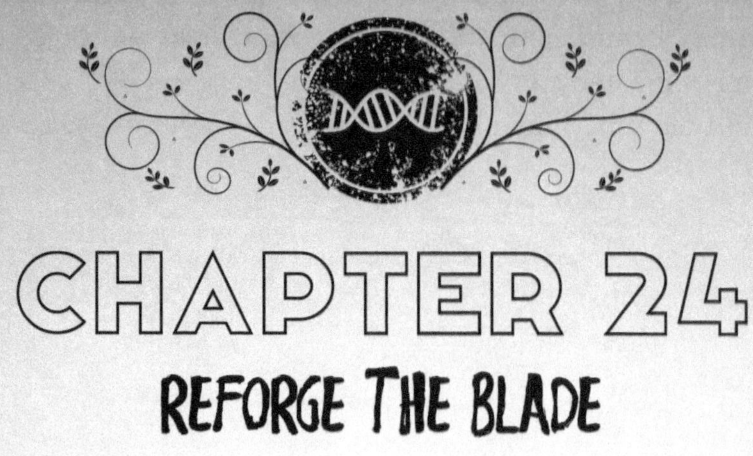

CHAPTER 24
REFORGE THE BLADE

LIFE DOESN'T GO BACK to normal after the funeral. It simply takes on a new shape. One where I feel sensitive to everything, as if the whole world has been sharpened around me and chafes against my skin. Everyone's on high alert for Hadylan. There have been a couple of alleged sightings, but nothing has panned out.

The dig site in Australia is an equally dead end. It's very frustrating. Lilith left a clue-box as a message to future mutants, and we're not smart enough to figure it out. What they've uncovered at the dig is a network of tunnels, but they're impossible, like an underground cousin of One Thorn. They shift while you're in there, passageways disappearing or changing direction. Tunnels that seem to go on forever some-times, to the point where one map team said they'd been in there for six days, even though they'd only left that morning.

On other occasions, the same tunnel might end in crystalline caverns or a tiny slit in the earth that pours out gas. If you send electronics in there, they fuck out almost immediately. Dani's been asking the puzzle box all sorts of questions about it, but the responses are all non-answers, as if it's been programmed to deliberately ignore this topic. Even Violet, who can usually turn up anywhere in the world, has pronounced herself flummoxed by it. This is such a Violet word that Dani and I find it hilarious, and have started saying *flummox me, darling* to her when we're in bed.

I go to the dig site almost every day, in case something's changed. I've tried to speed run it—hell, *Feral* has tried to speed run it but we come to a different dead-end every time. We've gone in blindfolded, mapping it with string and chalk and a hive-mind of sentient spiders, but nothing works.

It's all part of my feverish obsession, consumed with a single thought—finding the *one way* to kill Hadylan. Is this true, or another game to have me chasing my tail? If we can capture them somehow, then I can try a whole bunch of ideas.

It comes to me in the middle of the night. I sit bolt upright and let out a stream of incomprehensible half-dream gibberish —at least according to Dani, who's been lying awake listening to me making concerning noises in my sleep.

"I know what it is." I leap out of bed, fumbling for warmer clothes.

"Can you please not be cryptic?"

"The weapon." I jab one finger at the ceiling. "The way to kill my prick sibling."

"Are you going to fill us in?" Violet's already out of bed, pulling on pants and a shirt. "Or are we going to play twenty questions for it?"

"Come with me." I'm already stalking out of our house and

down towards town. "We were bantering back and forth, because apparently we do have some things in common, annoying as that is. I said I was pissed off that Oni didn't kill them. That's when *they* said something about Dark Oni being destroyed, and how it was a hilarious joke."

"Oh." Dani stops dead for a moment and then runs to catch up. "You think Dark Oni can kill them?"

"I think it's a good theory."

"But Dark Oni's destroyed," Violet points out.

"Maybe we just need a sliver. Or maybe…" I stop outside the nearby cottage and give a piercing whistle. It takes a couple more attempts before a gout of flame leaps from a completely different window.

"Go back to sleep, Katie," I shout. "We're only here for Glowstick."

"Dylan." The man in question comes out of the doorway, dressed in satin boxer shorts and t-shirt. "Are you doing okay?" He sees Dani and Violet are with me and visibly relaxes. Obviously if *they're* here, this isn't me hurtling off the deep end. Apparently people are still worried about me.

"You're coming with us." I wave imperiously, and march off again. It's a sign of how much he's grown that he only delays to put on pants, and then trots alongside us quite happily. Or else he's trying to humour me, but that's fine too.

Once we're in town, we make a beeline for the government building where we run our mission team. Down in the basement is the secure room—yet another door into One Thorn—where we keep most of our dangerous items. This is walled away from the rest of the house and only accessible via this one entrance. If you're not on One Thorn's approved list, you won't get into the door. If the house thinks you might be dangerous, they *will* let you in, but you'll end up somewhere else.

The door swings open for us the moment we arrive. "I am deeply sorry for your loss, Dylan."

"Thanks, Thorny. We're here on business though. Looking for some sword fragments."

"Ah, yes. The parallel universe blade. Hold on one moment, and I shall locate them." The house rumbles and reconfigures itself, a wall folding out and then sliding aside to reveal a row of ornately carved wooden cabinet doors. I produce the key from a leather string around my neck, and unlock it. Inside, there's a set of battered shards of metal on a tray. I take it out and set it on a table between us.

"You always liked jigsaws," I say to Lou.

Even with the four of us, three who are pretty good at this sort of thing, it takes us the better part of an hour to piece Dark Oni together into some semblance of a blade. Real Oni doesn't want anything to do with it, no matter how much I beg him. He's out of sorts since getting bashed around so much.

"It's not exactly a whole sword," Lou says.

I reach out and touch the very tip, feeling the brutally sharp edge. "I'm hoping it won't matter, as long as there's enough to stab. So come on, hot hands, try welding it together."

"I'm hardly Masamune."

"We don't need you to be. All we need is a step up from fucking duct tape." I grimace. "Sorry, my inspirational speech mode is broken since I blew everyone away at the funeral."

"I liked your speech. It was very Dylan." He grins at me, and drops his attention to the sword. "You might want to stand back. These things need a lot of heat."

Oni lets out a very long-suffering sigh. "Do not worry. Despite my aversion to this unnatural beast, I will assist with advice where necessary."

Between me relaying Oni's instructions to Lou, and the

incredible blast-furnace heat of his hands—his mostly off-again relationship with his crush Maddy is obviously a decent inspiration—we do end up with a sword. It looks like a crude RPG weapon pulled from the heart of a meteorite, forged with volcanic heat. A brutal weapon, built to be wielded by demons, and a far cry from the sleek, elegant shape he had once been.

Lou's all tuckered out from the effort, and we thank him and send him off to bed.

The rest of us stay in One Thorn and stare at the two swords.

"Can you hear him?" I ask Oni. "I never could. Maybe I can't talk to objects from other worlds."

"It was always different with him." The sword trembles. "Like he could hear but not speak, or only speak when commanded. Like he was… tame. All I can hear from him now is a single sustained note, like an endless scream."

I know it's possible to force objects into subservience but the cruelty of it still shocks me. "Can we free him?"

"I do not know," Oni says. "But I believe we should try. My brother, can you hear me?"

The sword lies on the table, inert and blackened.

"Is he still screaming?" I ask.

"Yes. The tone altered slightly. I believe he can hear me although he is still unresponsive."

"What if he's sending a signal to Hadylan?" Violet asks.

"Good. I've got a message or two for them." I pick up the sword gingerly in my hand and move him slowly through the air. "I know I'm not your… companion? But I'm a version of Dylan, and I don't know if there's a loophole there. If so, I give you permission to act freely as you wish. Even if you try to cut my throat, although I don't recommend it, as my Oni won't look kindly on that."

"And neither will I," Violet says.

"The screaming got louder." Oni spins in the air. "I believe the compulsion on him is strong. He wishes to break free, but it has been… hammered into him, in every fold of his steel."

"Fuck." I slam my fist down on the table and drop Dark Oni there. "I hate this other world. The idea that millions or billions of people exist in this place, at the mercy of these fucking gods…" My head swims. "I can barely keep my own shit in order, let alone someone else's world that I don't even understand. Don't want to be the multiversal imperialist, do I?"

"Dylan, are you alright?" Dani's at my side again.

"Yeah. Everything's slightly off-kilter, that's all. Hole in the world, you know."

"Oh, babe." She rests her forehead against mine. "We don't need to do this. Or *you* don't need to. There are plenty of other people very eager and willing to fight Hadylan."

I go very still. I can hear the sap rushing through my body, feel the kick of the pump at my heart. For a moment, I think I'm staring at the world through a tunnel, like my vision is the barrel of a gun. I'm torn between screaming and fleeing the room, but I do neither. "Nobody is killing them except me. Promise me, Dani. No matter what."

"Dilly," Violet says, almost a sigh.

"Promise me." My head is heavy with autumn leaves.

"I promise." Dani wraps her arms around me and presses her forehead into my cheek.

"Me too." Violet nestles alongside and I cling to them both. I know they talk about me a lot. Not in any cruel way. It's all worry, fretting concern, chasing around and around like they're in the tunnels of the underground dig site. Wondering if I'm okay, nervous about my manic energy, terrified about what's going to happen after the revenge. Or worse, if Hadylan evades me again, or hurts someone else.

"I have been working on something," Dani says hesitantly.

"The Aussie dig?"

"A present. Something the box has been helping me with. I've been growing a little garden of alien flowers from the chambers, working on different hybrids. And I think some of them can sense the others. You know how everything in Cybele's network is connected? There's something similar going on here."

"You can find them." My voice is hoarse.

"I think so, yeah. With some work. And I think I might be able to use the flowers to assimilate Hadylan into our network too."

"Assimilate them?" It sounds like someone else is talking. "Because *my* plan was to incapacitate Hadylan with the pair-stones—hit them hard enough to need some healing—and while they're coming back from it, I shove Dark Oni into their heart. Not to fucking make *friends* with the person who killed Pear."

"It's not about friends." Dani swallows hard. "You know me better than that, and you know this is hard for me too. But we have to be smart, Dills. There's so much we don't know about Hadylan—where they come from or what they're capable of. Think of this as an interrogation."

"Okay." I grind the heels of my hands into my eye sockets, trying to wrap my brain around all this. They're all valid points. Everything's happening for a reason. It would be nice to understand why. Pear's death wasn't something random. "So how the fuck would this plan of yours work?"

"Fairly simple, really. We plant some of my hybrid flowers around the world and watch where they connect to."

"Triangulation again!" I make finger guns at her. "I remember this shit."

"Yes." She smiles, but all I can see is sadness in her eyes. "I really wanted to do this for you, Dilly. Give you something you can use. You've been so restless and..." She gestures incoherently, the woman I love and her enormous brain foundering on the confusing rocks of my emotional landscape.

"I don't think there's any easy way through this." I press my lips against her hair. "But you two pull me through every day. And this is honestly the best fucking gift I could ask for."

"Told you," Violet says. "And you were so worried."

"There's still so many things that could go wrong," Dani says, her voice hitching. "Like too many to count, so even though my brain is urging me to list them all, I'll hold back."

"Yes," I sigh. "Let's just enjoy this little moment of things being right."

CHAPTER 25
DREAD PERSEPHONE

DANI'S PLAN turns out to be a little more complicated and to involve a lot more people. Mutopia Science Club honestly intimidates me, because I was never the world's best student, and these are some of the smartest fucking people I've ever met in my life.

I come home after running a very resentful lap of the island to find geniuses in our living room. Most of them I don't really recognise, and their muttered greetings are as awkward as mine. Steelhands is one of the few who gives me a hug—she's an ex-NASA scientist who was one of the masterminds of our short-lived *our home is an asteroid* phase. She's dressed in a sweat-shirt and hijab combination and seems very comfortable on our couch.

"Your girlfriend is a genius," she tells me, as I sit down beside her.

"You know, I did wonder on occasion."

Her eyes sparkle with excitement. It's so cute when the nerds get to gather. "I'm not really a botanist, but I dabble in various things that catch my interest. Xenobiology's always been a fascination of mine."

"Well, it's ever so fascinating," I say, with a little too much enthusiasm.

"You're teasing me, and I don't even care. This project is incredible. We're growing alien tissue!"

"Are we?" I don't remember this being part of the plan at all, but maybe I blanked out at that part. It's not my favourite idea ever. I twist around to look for Dani, but my eyes catch on a surprising figure first. "Sai! I thought you were off wandering the earth!"

Sai is an artificial intelligence housed in a tall, slim mechanical suit with a bulbous glass head that's like a TV screen. She used to be the house for a rather deadly mutant, but now she runs her own life. Right now, her screen shows the letters XD. "Dylan, how lovely to see you. I am very sorry to hear of the loss of your parental figure."

"Yes, everyone's sorry. It's a whole thing. It's nice you're back."

"My wandering sojourn has come to an end. I have seen many things and accumulated knowledge to help me build a better working model of human consciousness. That sounds more ominous than I intended, but I have no desire to become more powerful."

"That's good. So what fun did you come back for?"

"Oh, a most fascinating project. I believe we can actually grow artificial Tentacle Princess DNA in the forests of your island, thanks to the organic material xe left behind when xe fled."

"Well that sounds fucking *delightful*."

Dani recognises my tone. "It's less mad scientist than it sounds. We're having a few problems with our hybrid flowers. They're very insular and want to cluster—like they're *afraid*. The modelling shows that the introduction of Tentacle Princess DNA gives an increased robustness."

"You do not need to fear," Sai tells me. "It will be no more intelligent than your average plant."

"Am I your average plant?" My voice is doing that thing where people sometimes flinch away.

"Houseplant," Sai says smoothly. "Which are more intelligent than many people believe, but—"

"This will help us find Hadylan," Dani tells me, her voice steady. "It's going to work."

"Okay." Any belligerence I was feeling collapses down into that familiar exhaustion. Until I've got Hadylan's heart in my hands everything else is a tedious hoop to jump through. "Let's fucking do this."

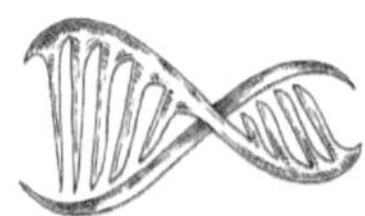

IT TURNS out I have a part to play too. First, convincing Cybele this is a good idea, which takes less time than me. Her whole vibe is "we shall find this villainous creature, and exterminate it." I'm down with that, so the twins and I plant ourselves deep in Cybele's forest to assist with the actual *growing* part. The DNA would grow on its own given plenty of time, but us tree-creatures can give our energy to speed the process along.

"Is this going to be *our* baby?" Willow asks me.

"It's not alive," Soo-yeon says with heavy sarcasm. "But

humans used to keep rocks as pets, so I suppose that's your sapiens half talking."

Willow ignores their sibling and shoves their roots deeper into the soil. "Well, I hope it's cute."

"It's going to be a big bunch of tentacles!"

"So? That's your sapiens half using an anthropomorphised view of what's considered aesthetically pleasing."

I glare at them both from my full-grown tree height. "Other parents do not have to intervene in conversations like this, do they?"

"I am going to name xer Squirmy," Willow says. "And xe will be my Squirmy. Since the rest of you have no souls."

My sigh shakes the leaves of not only my own tree, but half the forest around me. "Can we all be quiet and concentrate on growing Squirmy? Please?"

It turns out to be a pleasant few hours, basking in the forest warmth and feeling life take form in the soil. Sai pokes around in the ground, snipping DNA strands or some complex shit that my brain refuses to comprehend. Dani and Violet are very excited, and have conversations at such breakneck speed that I simply give up and watch them happen. I occasionally get a tiny twinge of jealousy, but then they offer to explain it to me, and I realise I would rather be the thembo of the throuple.

When Sai pronounces everything done, there's only a tiny sprouting tentacle sticking out of the ground. I'm about to embarrass myself by complaining about the size, when they pluck out a writhing mess of tentacles which definitely lives up to the name Squirmy.

"That looks alive." I extend a very tentative finger.

"Plants are alive, as you well know. It is not sentient as you understand it, although it will network with the new hybrid species Danielle has created. Then they will be emboldened to seek out other life that mimics theirs."

The twins are both very protective of Squirmy, and Sai has to promise to only take very small samples. Willow holds the mass of tentacles tightly in their arms. It's nearly as big as they are.

The others disappear off into the lab to do the final step in the whole process.

I'm not good with waiting at the best of times, and the potential weight of what's coming exerts so much gravity on me that I feel pinned to a single moment. Like time is a vast block of ice that I'm frozen in and nothing can shatter it around me and give me forward momentum.

One blink, and Dani is standing over me.

There's a tentative smile sketched on her face. "We did it. I have a location."

Time snaps back, the accumulation of seconds making me breathless. "Show me."

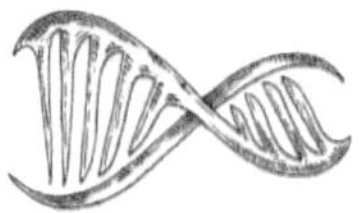

IT TURNS out Hadylan is hiding in a remote cabin off in the Scottish moors. Some pretty thing on a rocky hillside over-looking a loch. You can rent it for things like writing retreats. The whole situation is so ridiculously mundane.

"It's smart, really," Dani says, looking down at the map. "There's nothing to draw our attention here."

"Good for us too, though." I gnaw on the end of my thumb until it splinters. "Nice and remote so if shit fucks up—which it inevitably will—nobody else will notice."

"So now the attack plan." Dani's uncharacteristically tenta-tive. "Keepaway will teleport me close to the cabin, and I'll plant the flowers. They'll connect to Hadylan and hopefully subdue them. Then we can decide how to proceed from there, whether to interrogate, bring them elsewhere, or—"

I draw my finger across my throat. "Not going to give them any chances, Dan. I know we need answers, but if they're playing games or fucking with us..."

"I know." She pulls me in close. "We're doing this for you."

The twins are waiting outside the room. They always know when shit is going down.

"You're going into terrible danger." Willow narrows their eyes.

"We want you to be safe." Soo-yeon glares at us as if they're mad about having these feelings. "There are many, many things that could go wrong."

"We're aware," Dani says. "We're being careful."

"The plan is for everyone to come back safe." I crouch down to try and get to eye-level with them, because apparently the parenting books say that's important. "What I need from you two is a promise. Not one of those ones where you tell me what I want to hear, but a real one."

"The problem is we don't like being told what to *do*," Willow explains.

"You get that from your Pear," Dani says.

"I understand orders are annoying," I tell the twins. "But usually that's because they don't make any sense. This one does. I need you to keep away from what's going on. Hadylan wants to kill us all, and having all their targets in the same place is a very bad idea."

"We'll stay on Mutopia with Cybele," Soo-yeon says. "And we'll keep the island safe."

"Good kids." I hug them both close. "And we'll be back as soon as we can."

THE MOMENT DANI LEAVES, I can't sit still. Violet's gone too, way up into the atmosphere with a pairstone. One of our many backup plans. Yet even with all of that, there are countless more ways it could fuck up.

It only took seconds for Pear to die.

Dani could be dead *right now*.

Fuck, I can't breathe. Something is in my throat, clogging it. I bend over and retch but nothing comes up. I can't fucking *stay here* and wait while someone I love is—

"Breathe." Alyse rubs my back. "I'm here. Everything is fine."

"But Dani—" I croak.

"You're connected, silly." She squeezes my hand. "Focus on your breathing and listen."

She's right. *There's* Dani, spilling love and reassurance along with focus and anxiety. She's out there, finding Hadylan for me. I grab onto her, as if she can steady me against the chaos in my heart.

"It hurts so fucking much, Lys," I whisper.

"I know, babe. Living with a hole in you."

My vision blurs. "I've been such an asshole. Demanding you get better and it doesn't work like that. I'm so sorry."

"Dilly, you've been the best friend in the whole world. It's not like you ever claimed to be perfect, but you've been freak-ishly close. Like your true mutant power is being the person I need."

"My god, you're sappier than I am."

She wipes sticky tears off my cheek. "No more puns, please. You'll make me cry and not in a good way."

"Seriously, Lys, I should've been more sympathetic."

"No apologies. Please. There's no fix for it. Living without Emma is like being swallowed by a void. A lot of the time, the most I can do is drift. But I'm tethered to you, and that means a lot."

There's so much I want to say to her, things about grief and need, but the words are too big and too complicated. An alien language I can't speak. So all we do is hold each other and drift together through the vast abyss of loss.

Until a tug down my connection to Dani forces me to gather my focus. I have to strip all those other feelings away until nothing remains but me, aimed at the future like a weapon.

"I've gotta go do this thing." I give Alyse one last hug.

"I know. Bring your ass back to me, okay?"

"Gonna try." And then I'm gone.

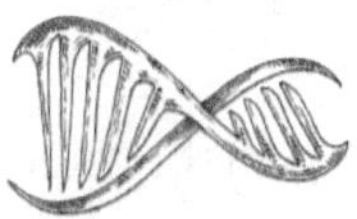

IT'S ALMOST ANNOYING to see how pretty Hadylan's hideout location is. The sky is a hazy blue, and the land spills away from me in a thousand shades of green and purple. Sunlight kisses the loch to a shimmer, and the distant hills are blue-grey smudges against the sky.

Dani's alien plants stand out like someone has spliced two worlds together. They have dark leaves that curl around each other like ferns, cradling delicate blooms where the petals either look crystalline like they're formed from ice, or an almost luminous cyan. Thickets have sprung up, linked by thick turquoise vines that look like veins. Together, they form something like a maze.

I dig my toes into the soil and twang my connection to Dani. There's still no fear coming back, only satisfaction and resolve, so I navigate my way towards her. It's cooler among the paths grown by the flowers, as if they're giving off a chill. They smell like an empty freezer crusted with ice, that slightly stale, deadened scent. These hybrids might be able to survive on our world, but they contain echoes of their own—their centres glisten like dark water and their stems are as black as the night sky.

Deep in the maze I find a twisting column of thorns. They drip with sap, bright bursts of blue and white flowers budding so fast it's like gunfire. There's an opening at the bottom, like a doorway, and from it comes a pale green glow.

Dani's staring into this entrance, hands on hips and frowning.

"Hello, my darling." I slip one arm around her waist. "I like your extravaganza."

"It sort of overspilled. Just connected up to everything and got carried away."

"The big question is whether it's working." I peer into the interior of the thorn column, but it's hard to make out anything. "Based on the fact they're not being a dick, I'd say that's a positive sign."

Dani holds up her left hand, clusters of vines spilling from her fingertips and wrist and running across the ground to where they disappear among the thorns. "Feels like it. They're dormant, but they're fighting it."

"Like an infection." I crouch down and stick my head into the interior of the tower. The illumination comes from small glowing threads extruded from columns of flowers that run up the inside like strip lighting. A series of thorny vines jut out of the ground in the middle, and among them is my duplicate from another world. They're cradled within the thorns, each one jabbing into their flesh like acupuncture needles.

"Let's hope it works." I'm not entirely sure I want it to. I know it'd be great to have Hadylan onside, but I'd much rather stab them. That's the ugly revenge part of me speaking, but I'm trying to keep that tamped down. It's 'greater good' shit, not 'Dylan gets to feel that little spark in their heart by stabbing their parent's murderer' shit.

"There's *something* happening." Dani's voice sounds strained.

I pull my head back out of the interior and gaze up at her. "Bad?"

"Not sure." She yanks on the vines linking her to the tower. "If we're doing the whole infection metaphor, this feels like I'm running a fever."

"They're burning you out of their system," I suggest.

"That's what I'm worried about. Vi, are you ready with the other stone?"

"Ready to drop." Violet's voice crackles across both our earpieces.

"You—" Dani winces. Her body convulses and she spits up a bunch of purple goo. "Okay, that did *not* feel good."

From the top of the thorn tower, thin trickles of smoke rise into the sky. Embers drift and dance on the breeze.

"Hell of a fever." I wipe the drool from Dani's mouth. "You okay?"

"Trying to fight it, but it's *vicious*. It feels like being wrung out from the inside."

"You've got to—"

Dani doubles over, retching wildly and I watch in horror as tentacles slither out of her mouth. For a moment, I get a double image of her face splitting open, the writhing mass pushing through the gap. She's gagging on the slimy growths, trying to use her right hand to sever the cables that bind her to the tower.

"Oni," I shout, but he's already slicing through the air.

"Duck," Violet's voice says in my ear. "Pairstone incoming."

I form a carapace of thorns as quickly as I can, pulling Dani against me. Her body convulses wildly, the severed vine-cables dripping an acidic purple sap. She's spitting over and over, tentacle chunks hitting the ground with wet thumps.

All other sounds are drowned out by the explosion. I feel it shove violently on the rugged exterior I've thrown up, sending us both sprawling, bouncing end over end into the wild chaos of the flowers that surround us.

In the aftermath, the world feels eerily silent.

"Lucky you didn't let that go from higher up," I tell Violet.

The tower of thorns is a ruin, a splintered mass that looks like the centre of an asteroid strike. In the middle of the crater is a skeletal figure, still hoisted on a single smoking spike. It's hard to make out any detail through the smoke.

Dani clings onto me and hauls herself to a standing position. "Looks like I failed."

"Fuck no, you didn't fail. You tried something amazing, and it didn't work. You *almost* fucking had them, and now they're weakened enough that we can do this."

I stride over to Hadylan. Their internal workings of their body are revealed, and it's clear their resemblance to me is only skin-deep. Are they really my duplicate, or something built to look like me? Inside, they're a slimy mess of plumbing, a complex series of mechanical valves and biochemical pumps with clusters of tentacles writhing between them.

"They're fucking *healing*," Dani says in disbelief.

It's true—the tentacles are reknitting themselves together, stringy chunks of organic matter spilling from their mouths and turning into some sticky approximation of skin. Their face is being reinflated as something underneath those fire-scorched shards of skin works furiously. It's like watching a bunch of insects trying to resurrect a person.

"Kill them." Dani clutches my arm hard, thorny fingers puncturing my skin.

"Oh, believe me." I reach out one hand and tear aside some of the newgrown flesh that covers their chest. Underneath is a densely packed mass—a hissing, thrashing nest of tentacle life that spits poison at me.

It's as close to a heart as I think this monster copy of me has, and it makes for a hell of an inviting target.

"Fuck it." I plunge Dark Oni directly into the centre of the mass. The blade sinks in, smooth and effortless. The tentacles shriek and writhe away from the touch of the blade. Inside is swirling gas, and among that is something small and bright, glittering like the first star in the evening. Exposed to the air, it winks out of existence, disappearing with a sharp pop.

Hadylan's body is torn open, hanging limp among its cradle of thorns.

"I think we fucking did it." I give the sword an extra twist to make sure.

I get one beautiful moment of triumph. We've done it. Killed the goddamn thing that's been tormenting us. Bought some small revenge against the monster that killed Pear.

Then my doppelgänger's eyes flicker open.

A fringe of tiny tentacles around their mouth quiver, and they relax into a smile.

"At last," Hadylan says. "Thank you, my sibling."

CHAPTER 26
THE FIVE STAGES OF GRIEF

"WHAT THE FUCK DOES THAT MEAN?" I stab the sword into the heart of them, over and over again, until it's an oozing mass of fluid and tentacle chunks.

"I'm so fucking tired. Being this bomb. Trying to lure you on, trying to find this moment."

I slam my thorny hand into their throat. "Talk some fucking sense."

Their mouth works, trying for another smile and failing this time. "Get me down from here and I'll tell you everything. Don't worry, it's over now. I'm dying. My mission is complete."

"Why does this not feel like a victory?" Dani says at my shoulder. She's still shaky, wiping at her mouth.

Violet unfolds herself from the air beside us. "Yeah, not a fan."

"I'm not fucking touching you." I drag Dark Oni out of them and hold it to their throat. "Except this way."

"Fuck's sake." They sound remarkably like me. "It's too late. You can't close the door now."

"Wait." Dani puts her hand over mine, steering the blade away. "What door?"

"The point of all this." Hadylan twitches and coughs, their head lolling. "It's hard even injecting a single person into another universe. Imagine how hard it is to tear open a hole big enough to bring the gods through."

"Oh shit," Dani says. "No. No way."

Violet disappears, folding herself away. I have no idea where she's gone, but I'm starting to put the pieces together myself and it's not a picture I like at all.

"The one way to kill you." I'm stumbling over my words, my teeth knocking together. "Is also the way to, uh, open the door."

"A plan ordained by the gods." Hadylan shivers. "They took me from the breeding pods and remade me. The Dylan Taylor of my world, although my true name is merely a designation, referring to my hex-position within the mind of the Sister Void-Dancers. When they plucked me from the depths, they told me I was holy. Blessed me with the infection of many genetic reliquaries. Sent me here with one mission. To die so that they might enter. I am the doorway through which justice is served."

"Fuck me, fuck me, fuck *me*." I clutch at my head, feeling the thorns there. "We were suckered into this goddamn mess."

"To be fair, it's remarkably complicated." Hadylan wheezes. "First I needed to build a network of our flowers that could function as a beacon. A signal fire viewable across the multiverse. That gives us co-ordinates, but a door still needs to be opened. Such things need *power,* and when you're dealing with multiversal issues, there are odd synchronicities that cluster around the same person from multiple universes. Therefore we come to the final key—me being killed by my double, using an item forged in my world, creating a loop between universes. The energy that ripples out from an action like that can be harnessed by the god-scientists of my world, powering a portal big enough to launch the god-fleet. This world was stolen from us, snatched from the jaws of the gods in a game of chance. It is so rich and vibrant, and it is our right to rule here."

"So you lured me."

"Yes, step by painful step, and built the network as well. It took a lot of work and planning. I'm waiting for my applause, thank you very much."

"If we save your life?" Dani asks.

"It's far too late for that." Hadylan laughs, although it's more of a choke. "Everything is inevitable now. I am the sacrifice that ensures destiny. You attempted to do this yourself, with your own deaths. Without true gods, you are doomed to merely flail at the future. What we will usher in is far greater than you can imagine."

"Yes. Breeding pods, god-scientists and the pyres of human sacrifice." I smack Hadylan across the face with the sword, because they deserve it. "It sounds fucking brilliant."

"They are gods." Their voice is mine, but I cannot imagine this blind service. "We are nothing in the face of them."

Violet unfolds herself from the air, still half-bladed and with fresh cuts on her cheek. "The passages behind the world bleed. They're being torn apart. There used to be walls, but now they open into a void. Dylan, this is really, really fucking bad."

"Okay, they're really coming. So we'll figure out how to fight." I transfer my attention back to Hadylan. "Is there a rebellion against the gods?"

There's a long silence, and all we can hear is the wet

writhing from within Hadylan's chest, and the creak of their breathing. Finally, when I think they're about to fail for good, they begin talking again.

"I fought once, in a former life. When I did not understand the order of the universe. They remade my mind first, before they remade my body. Once you have seen the universe through the eyes of a god, you understand futility."

"There you are, Dilly." I step forward, and lift the broken shell of Hadylan down from where they hang. Then I lower them to the ground, sitting sprawled out with their head in my lap.

"What are you *doing?*" Dani asks.

"You heard them. The gods remade their brain, but they fought first. They *are* me, somewhere in there."

"I am sorry about your parent," Hadylan says. "It is not something I truly understood. In my world, what would be Ness Taylor is nothing more than encoded information stored in the fangs of the breeding pits."

"Do you even understand what sorry is?" I ask.

"I regret its necessity. I wish another way could have been found. But it was a plan to ensure your final strike against me."

I look down at my own bruised face, tentacles still writhing under the skin but slowing down. "If you're bringing the gods here to end our world, why does it matter if I have my parent here or not?"

"I suppose it does not." They reach for me, and I let them touch my face. "You burn so desperately and so bright. It reminds me of what I once was."

"You have damned our world," Dani says bitterly.

"I have, yes. And now the nest dies inside me, I suffer again as the knowledge of what that means surfaces. That should make you happy, to see my death and suffering twinned."

"Nothing about this is good." Dani's fists are clenched and all the flowers around us are dying. "Dylan, we're talking about an alien invasion by the species that nearly killed Cybele."

"I know we are," I snap, and then bite my tongue. "Sorry. I know I'm not in science club, but I do know what the stakes are. Which is why I want to know about *fighting* these fucking things."

"They cannot be fought." Hadylan's eyes bleed purple fluid that carves bloody tracks against their skin. "All we did is defy. Refuse to bend the knee. To destroy them would require…"

"What?" We all lean in, three heads over the pale, trembling one.

"It's impossible." They cough and choke and spit pieces of chewed up tentacle flesh. "The gods cannot be defeated." And then they begin screaming, high and panicked.

Dani pulls open the tattered skin of Hadylan's chest, as disgusting as that is, and takes a handful of sluggish tentacle bodies from inside. She wrings them between two thorny fists and discards the pulp on the ground.

"We've got you," she says softly, petals falling around her face like gentle rain. They fall over Hadylan's skin like a silken shroud, scraps of blood red covering their eyes like offerings to some pastoral Charon. "Fight for me, sweet Dylan."

"They hate rebellion," Hadylan says. "They will choke it out violently. They do not wish its example to spread. When I was young, I watched one die. A girl with a burning heart and one with a burning mind made a god bleed. We watched it die, sizzling in the harbour and screaming as it passed from the world. It is what inspired me to fight, although I never hurt one that grievously."

"So they can die," Dani says.

"Kill enough of them to force a retreat perhaps?" I frown.

"Make the cost too great to bear," Violet says. "It sounds like fun, killing gods. And I do have a track record with it."

"Show-off," Dani says, but her smile falters. "How did they kill this god, these two?"

"They were weapons," Hadylan whispers.

"And so are we," Dani says grimly. "We'll show them how sharp we are."

"They will hurt so many." Hadylan's voice is very faint. "They will make *your* cost too great. I have seen them drown cities, swallow nations whole. Their appetites are enormous and your world is so very full of people. I have watched your species swarm through the streets of your bloated cities. In the minds of the gods all they are is food."

"Is that all they want?" I ask. "They're just animals hunting for a feeding ground?"

Hadylan twitches in my arms. Their mouth works, as if they're trying to speak. We all lean close to listen, but nothing comes out. Finally, they choke out a single sentence. "Even the gods must serve."

"The fuck does that mean?" I demand.

They say nothing, lying limp in my arms like something discarded.

"I think they're gone." I'm shivering and I don't know why. The person who killed Pear is dead. Their end was supposed to be a good thing, not some ploy to launch an alien invasion. Now all I feel is empty. No rage, no despair. Just adrift, bobbing towards the next disaster.

"What do we do?" Violet turns her eyes to me.

"Fuck knows. Get ready to punch aliens, I guess. Find that other Lilith weapon. Gather the troops." God, I feel so fucking *tired*. "I guess this is the exception to my belief that stabbing is always the right move."

"I think they would have made it happen eventually," Dani says. "They'd have kept coming. Kill me, kill the kids, burn Mutopia to ash. Push you to the point where you did it, one way or another."

"All it cost was Pear then." I close my eyes.

"That's not what I meant, Dilly."

"I know. It's just all so pointless though, isn't it? It's never going to be over. Even if we fight off the aliens, it'll be the next goddamn thing."

Dani and Violet both wrap their arms around me.

"We love you," Dani says. "And we know you're grieving. This isn't the shit you should be dealing with in the middle of everything else."

"At least it's something to do. Better to be sad punching aliens than lying in bed staring at the ceiling."

"After all this is done, you should write a self-help book," Violet says. "Chapter 1: Telling Everyone To Go Fuck Themselves."

"The five stages of grief," Dani adds. "Fucking Furious, Completely Fucking Over It, Stabbing the Fucking Deserving, Fucking Exhausted, and Five Seconds of Fucking Peace."

"You do know me oh so well." I can't help but laugh. "Speaking of five seconds peace, we should probably get back to Mutopia and tell everyone the amazing news."

"Now *I'm* exhausted," Dani groans.

Then Ray appears out of thin air, which does not seem like a good sign, followed by Farsight, Alyse, Feral, Fetch, and finally a small grey alien, waving xer arms around wildly.

"*This* is the site of the anomaly," xe says. "This is where everything begins."

And they're all looking at me, sitting on the ground with my dead sibling from a parallel universe in my lap.

CHAPTER 27

HERE THEY COME, THOSE TENTACLE GODS

FINALLY I HAVE someone deserving to vent at.

"You." I jump to my feet, ignoring the way Hadylan feels so light as they slide off me and onto the ground. Tentacle Princess cowers in front of me. "This is *your* fucking fault."

I don't think anyone quite knows how to react. Alyse is heading in our direction, presumably to join forces. Fetch is turning pale as she reads what's going on, and then has to look again because how the fuck can this be happening?

"I do not understand, Dylan." Tentacle Princess flinches away, but I don't care.

"You fucking ran away," I shout. "Leaving us to deal with this bullshit. Someone from another world, coming to kill us all. So of course I stab back, because what else am I supposed to do?"

"There is a tragedy approaching." The alien's eyes are huge

and xer limbs wave like they're buffeted by invisible breezes. "Do you understand what is happening?"

"I'd like to hear things from the beginning." Ray's voice is calm but I can hear the strain at the edges. "I feel like I'm hearing snippets of entirely different stories."

"The old gods are coming." My voice is flat. "From the universe next door. One where *xer* ancestors won," I jab another finger at Tentacle Princess, "and where Cybele died. That fake Dylan was trying to lure us into turning them into a doorway. And the one person who could have known disappeared up xer own void!"

There's a fairly stunned silence from everyone at the end of this rant.

"It's all true," Fetch says softly. "If there was any doubt."

"And it is also true I fled." The alien trembles. "When I saw what had been injected into our universe… My people are not forgiving, and they would not have allowed my existence to continue if they found me."

"I'm glad running away worked so well for you." I can't calm down, even if I wanted to. This is all so impossibly fucked up, and it's xer goddamn fault. "Before we had one little me-clone running around all full of tentacles, and now we're staring down the barrel of a god-fleet."

"That is the anomaly?" The alien's eyes are so huge they dwarf xer head.

"Yes," Violet says. "The walls between the universe have been breached. We don't know how long it will be before they arrive, or where exactly they'll come through. But it's going to happen. And we're going to have to fight them."

"You cannot fight them," Tentacle Princess says weakly. Xer shape warps and twists, and in amongst it I see glimpses of impossible vistas, blurry star fields, and whirling astronomical bodies. "They are the gods."

"Our ancestors killed the gods," Dani says. "You were there."

"Lilith was powerful, and it was still a war that devastated so many." Tentacle Princess stares directly at me, all those soft grey limbs hanging down by xer side. "You must be as resolute as she was."

"Fuck's sake. This isn't about me." I feel like I'm about three hundred years old, and every single one of those years has punched me in the face. "It's going to require everyone working together. If you're expecting me to save the goddamn universe alone, we might as well roll over and die right now, because I am fucking *tired*."

"Nobody's asking that of you, Dylan," Ray says, so gently I want to cry.

"Okay." I reach up and pull at my hair. It's getting too long and needs a cut. Maybe I'll shave my head like Pear did. "That's good. We're on the same page."

Dani's at my side, her arm in mine, one hand rubbing gently at the back of my neck. "Let's get you home, Dilly."

"We've got to plan." I pull away irritably. "What? I didn't say I don't want to be involved. I'm not going to fucking hide in my own goddamn void. The aliens are going to come. That's a given. So the first thing we need…"

"Is to protect Mutopia," Ray says. "Keep our people safe."

Dani frowns. "Yes, but we can't stand back and let humanity be fed to these things."

Violet's nodding, fingers twitching at the air, as if she's trying to feel the breeze between the universes. "We can't watch over the whole world. Mutopia is going to be their first target."

"So there's our first problem," Fetch says. "How do we hide

the island? I know Riot Grrl's wards cloak us from a certain amount of human surveillance, but we've got no idea how well the aliens will be fooled. Her power may only work on human minds."

"The island moves," Farsight says. "Perhaps that will—"

"We'll just paddle the island around the oceans of the world and hope we can outrun them?" Alyse gives a slightly panicked giggle. "Sorry. I'm just extra-missing my all-powerful girlfriend right about now."

I grin at her. "Wouldn't that be cool? Our Ems, just casually swatting fleshy alien motherships out of the air, like it's nothing. Sorry, assholes, find another universe to pester."

Farsight clears her throat. "In the absence of that option…"

"Jesus." I roll my eyes. "Back to reality, fine. We're running out of time to dig up Lilith artefacts. Maybe Little Park or One Thorn can build us a getaway. The problem I worry about with that is how Hadylan managed to call me on the phone while I was *inside* One Thorn. Like they can see right inside."

"Let's call it a backup plan," Dani says. "Because it's better than nothing."

Violet nods. "Or we could go hide in the Weirdlands, and hope they don't notice us playing with their long-lost alien cousins."

"You are obsessed with that place," Alyse says. "I don't get it."

"It's not as bad as you think," Violet begins, but she's interrupted by Tentacle Princess, of all beings.

"Perhaps I can suggest something." Xer limbs are waving again, which I think is a good sign mood-wise. I'm starting to feel like an asshole for all that shouting.

"Go on, don't be shy." I give xem what I hope is an encouraging smile.

"It is possible that a modified void could be generated around the island as a form of null-space bubble. With assistance from dear Sai, we could modify the normal energy output to appear entirely benign."

I try to parse that sentence about five times, but both Dani and Violet seem enthusiastic. "It sounds like you can already *make* a cloaking device," I say hesitantly.

"Precisely." Tentacle Princess preens a little. "Sai is very excited to discuss the mathematical details."

My brain's already skipping ahead to the next problem. "Once this shield is up, how do we get through it to fight?"

"That is a challenge of a different magnitude. We would not want to open it up to any humanoid, as the gods will co-opt people to serve as their mouthpieces and we would not wish to accidentally let in their servants."

The idea of these *mouthpieces* makes me queasy, especially thinking of Hadylan, a version of me who'd been *rebuilt* to worship. Is this something they could do to Earth-me as well? I've got a special hate for mind control. Humans are bad enough at trying to twist other people's brains around without someone getting an extra-special boost from somewhere. I wish there was some way to protect myself against it.

"This sounds promising," Ray says. "Perhaps we should return to Mutopia to begin the construction of this shield. Tentacle Princess, is there anything else you require?"

"I do not think so. We should be able to generate an impenetrable version very quickly and then modify it to allow travel through the voidveil in subsequent iterations."

"Excellent." Ray gives a slight bow. "Keepaway, we'd like to return now."

The slender figure of our teleporter appears in front of us. They've got one hand extended, ready to tap Ray on the shoulder, when a shadow falls across us. Something that blots out the weak afternoon sun and makes the temperature drop alarmingly. A humming emanates from everywhere, as if the whole world is getting a text alert from some cosmic address.

Which is a surprisingly fucking accurate analogy.

The alien passes overhead, maybe only a kilometre up. It's a rough, bloated hemisphere, and the size is too difficult to tell because it fucks with your sense of scale. There aren't enough words for big before they start sounding ridiculous. It must be as big as a goddamn city.

Its skin is a faded red, like a dying star or old blood. It looks like something unearthed in a desert, not something that lives half-drowned in a poisonous version of our seas. There are huge symbols etched into the bottom of it, like manufacturing data stamped there in some horrifying undersea factory. Some are like very rough carvings of Hadylan's precious fucking tarot. I even spot the hanged man up there. Suffering and more fucking suffering.

"What do those mean?" I ask Tentacle Princess.

"It is not entirely clear, as the language has evolved from what I knew, either because it is a different world, or because time changes all things. There is something about *nest* and *brood* and then *die screaming*."

"Oh." I watch the bulk of it pass overhead. "So they can tell their own future. That's cool."

Around me, everyone's talking. Overlapping shouts as people discuss options, establish panicky plans, and tear them apart. I'm transfixed by what I'm seeing. Taking a moment to witness the world falling apart.

Hundreds of smaller craft float around the alien, each flaring with light. Presumably they're guiding it downwards, finding a body of water for it to float in. The surface is scarred with a complex network of channels, and a number of vented openings are set into it, plumes of gas forming long pale clouds in the air. Tentacles hang limply, complex machinery clutched in the swaying claws. It's an awe-inspiring moment, one of those times when you realise the world is far more weird and fucked than you thought. Lots of people have that with their first mutant encounter. This shit is going to blow their little minds. Maybe they'll start *liking* us now.

No, they'll probably prefer the fucking aliens.

Dani and Alyse both have their phones out, surfing news sites.

"Eight, no… nine. So far. They're all over the world." Dani glances upwards again, at the thing blotting out the sky. "One has already landed in the deep water off Sydney Harbour. Two are headed for the Pacific Coast of America, another descending fast near the Bay of Bengal. They're spreading out, covering as much ground as possible."

"They'll moor near cities where possible," Tentacle Princess says. "To find both worshippers and food, the two things they crave."

"Well, fuck." I give it the middle finger, as pointlessly defiant as it might be. "The humans can't ignore this."

CHAPTER 28
THERE'S NO PLANET B

THE GOOD NEWS HAPPENS FAST. Everyone gets back to Mutopia safe, and all the scattered mutants on various business for the island all come scurrying home. One Thorn opens doors in cities all over the world, allowing last-minute evacuations for mutants and their families. We've got a reasonably comprehensive list of all the mutants out there, but people are still edgy about 'alien types' getting in here. Paranoia and mistrust spreads quickly.

I have a brief conversation with Decker. She's checked in on me a couple of times since Pear's death, and I've been honestly kinda rude. I tell her the Hadylan saga, and about the alien gods. She listens and says *mmm* a lot, but I'm not sure if she believes me. The GIC are scrambling trying to figure out what the fuck to do about the aliens. For once, they have to take their eyes off mutants.

"We'll be incommunicado for a bit," I tell her. "Locking down."

"Take care, Taylor. I'm sure we'll meet again."

"I love your positivity, Decker. Try not to die."

THE VOID WRAPPING of the island only takes seconds. Once it's done, we've got no way in or out. Even Keepaway can't get through. Sai, Tentacle Princess and the science squad are very pleased with themselves, and honestly they fucking should be. The aliens are still landing in the oceans around the world—twelve of them, at final count—and we're safely tucked away, all One Thorn's doors sucked back into themself.

We're isolated and completely safe.

For now, at least.

But I already don't like being trapped here.

Dani doesn't like it either. She's still poking at her damn puzzle box. "We're cut off from the dig site and the other weapon. All the clues about it are extra cryptic. It keeps talking about how dangerous it is."

"Dangerous to who?" I ask. "Better be the fucking aliens."

"It doesn't matter." She drapes herself across the bed dramatically. "Because we can't get out of here and solve any of it."

I drape myself across her, equally dramatically. "This does leave us, like, free time and shit."

"An enforced break." She kisses me, soft and slow. "That could be fun."

Except of course it's not fun, because the kids wake up early.

They arrive in our room without warning, staring out into the night. Their eyes are luminous in the dark.

"Green Mum's coming," they tell me, seconds before she knocks at the door.

"This feels ominous." I lean against the doorframe to greet her, feeling impossibly tousled and not ready at all for any kind of further bad news.

"It is."

Well damn, there goes my slim hopes. "Come on in and tell me all the shit. Get it over with. I'd offer you coffee, beer, or gin, but I don't think you're interested."

"In this form, I do appreciate a good gin," Cybele says. "It's all the botanicals. Yet we have more pressing business."

Violet's up too, and the rest of the team appear out of their bedrooms as well. It's like there's a secret signal, and before long we're all huddled on a couch together in the main living area of the house.

"Mutopia is safe," Cybele says softly. "I am grateful for that, and for the safety of all my children. But I extend far beyond Mutopia. I can already feel them prodding at me."

"They're hungry." Willow's eyes are huge in the dim light.

"There are few good outcomes," Cybele continues. "I can attempt to fight, which would cause global catastrophe of a scale you can barely imagine outside of your most dramatic motion pictures. Or I can lie dormant, and hope they ignore me for other food sources, in which case I would likely die as I died before. The final option is for me to run, and leave my fate in your hands, the long-descended children of Lilith, fighting for me once again."

"The two of us would like to fight," Soo-yeon tells me. "Turn the planet into a monstrous protector. Spout flame from a thousand rocky spires, grind their fleshy meat between our moving plates. Yet nothing on earth would survive that, and it turns out we do count the cost."

"So you're looking at option three." I cross to Cybele's shadowy figure, standing by the window and looking out into the night. "You hide, we fight."

"I hate it." Her voice hums with anger. "But I also remember how close I was to extinction."

"I get it. We're your defenders, and that's why you made us." I take a deep breath. "Do you trust us to fight in your absence?"

"I do." Cybele reaches out one hand and touches my cheek lightly. "This world is vastly different, but what has not changed are the astonishing people who rise up in my defence. If anything, I have *more* faith."

"Fuck's sake," I grumble. "Tell me it's an impossible battle that there's no chance of winning. That makes me want to fight just to spite the future."

"Fight for me." Cybele wraps her arms around me, and I smell a joyous explosion of flowers, dazed heat, and crisp leaves. "Fight for your people, for the future of the ones you love. Fight in honour of the fallen."

"I hate inspiring speeches," I murmur into the soft wood of her neck.

She pulls back to look directly into my eyes. "Then fight because you're good at it."

"That I can do."

"We don't want to go with Green Mum." Willow hugs me so tight I think it might be a stealth murder attempt. "Fighting seems much better."

"Believe me, fighting is *not* better," Dani tells them sternly. "A lot of the time it's boring, and involves waiting, which you hate a lot. Then there's the terrifying parts where you're completely convinced you're going to die, or even worse, someone you love is. And once it's all done, the triumph parts are very small, and you mostly feel sick and tired and sore."

"She's not wrong." I ruffle Soo-yeon's hair. "You're much better off with Green Mum, keeping her safe because if the aliens get their teeth into her, it's all over."

The two of them look very small and sad in Cybele's arms, and my heart twists as they disappear. One new worry to add to the list. That I'll never see them again. What was Cybele thinking? Handing me these two children and expecting me not to get smitten.

"They'll be okay." Dani buries her face in my neck. "And we will too."

"Damn right." Violet throws her arms around both of us. "We're going to make it through this."

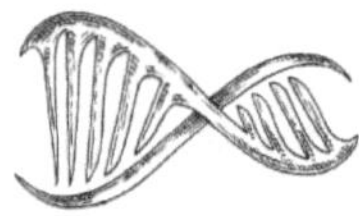

WE DON'T HAVE any way of poking our heads outside the voidveil, so all we can do is watch the news signals trickle in. Humanity initially panicked, as they're fond of doing, and as every alien invasion movie warned us of. There are riots, and mass evacuations, but they eventually figure out there is nowhere to go.

For three days, the aliens float in the oceans. Military aircraft patrol the skies, and enormous ships patrol the water around them, but there's no sign of life. I'm surprised nobody has tried to kill them yet, but it's probably only a matter of time.

And then the one in the Atlantic Ocean, off the coast of New York City, spits out a single person. An astonishingly beautiful man, tall and broad and sculpted. He's clearly human, or a good imitation. It takes social media about thirty seconds to start in on the *take me, aliens* memes. He's dressed all fancy, in faintly glowing black and gold robes with a large sceptre and a ball of light embroidered on them.

Dani nods at me. "The Emperor. In tarot it means authority, establishment, and structure."

My fist clenches at my side. "And here I am, a reversed Fool with nothing to do."

"Recklessness and risk-taking?" Dani's mouth quirks. "Look at you doing research."

"It's creepy that we share the tarot across universes, but know your enemy, right?"

I think everyone in the world with access to a screen is watching. Even us in Mutopia, safe behind our wall. I'm not sure how many drones are hovering above him, but they must blanket the sky like locusts.

"We have returned." His voice is strong and clear. "It has been so many years, but we have finally come back to save our errant siblings."

"What in the *fuck*?" Feral's tail twitches violently.

"It's a better line than *we come from another version of your world to eat you*," Alyse points out.

"We left your world a long time ago, when things looked dire. Taken from you by a gentle, peace-loving species called the Eirini who heard our distress and wished to help. We have spent five thousand years on a world much like this one, orbiting a distant star. It was easy to forget about where we came from. Our ancestors believed this Earth to be destroyed, impossible to live on. Imagine our surprise to recently discover that humans thrived, but only numerically. Your world is still in a dark, dark place. Overcrowded, impoverished, so much distress and suffering everywhere. And, worst of all, the mutant scourge flourishes here unabated."

"Oh that's a hell of a line," I say savagely. "These clever, vicious *fucks*."

I get shushed from fifteen different directions, and resort to muttering under my breath.

"The plan is to uplift the entire population and settle the world known as Eirini Major," the man says. "However, this will by necessity be a phased process, as we cannot assimilate the entire human population in one go. This means we shall be undergoing a vast assessment program to determine who is best suited for the initial settlement. We are looking for the best and brightest of those humans who have remained on Old Earth. Anyone who wishes to join this mission can assemble at one of many staging areas we will be building around the world. We will be sending the list of these locations along with the full text of our communique. It is our delight to return to the world that birthed us, and to work alongside you to give you a brighter future. I will return in the coming days to share more about our plans, but in the meantime we shall be sending full information about our world and the resettlement process to your governments so they are apprised of the situation."

The man retreats back into the bulk of the alien ship, and the door slides closed behind him.

"That's fucking evil and brilliant at the same time." I want to kick the laptop we've been watching into the sun. "They just checkmated us. We can't swoop in to defend humanity against the aliens because a) we're the mutant fucking scourge and b) they're here to save humanity from the world we've fucked up. All of a sudden, there *is* a Planet B. Waving this dream in front of our noses."

"You can bet people will be lining up to be saved," Dani says grimly. "Nothing like saying you're looking for the best and brightest to have people screaming pick me."

"So what can we do?" Feral asks. "How do we stop them?"

I shake my head. "We're stuck here for now, but even if we weren't, I have no idea."

"They will show their true colours soon enough," Tentacle Princess says. "They are monsters, and their natures cannot be hidden forever."

CHAPTER 29
METAPHORS FOR CAPITALISM

AT FIRST, it seems like Tentacle Princess is wrong. The alien spokespeople—all beautiful, as if they've been grown in some creepy tentacle tank to appeal to human beauty standards— keep trotting out and reciting their glowing speeches about how wonderful everything is with the Eirini. They've even got 'video footage' of life back home, which looks like an idealised version of our earth, with gleaming office towers, sprawling parks and beaming people of every ethnicity living together in harmony. Then, just to show it's not our world after all, forests of glittering trees, two-headed dinosaur-like beasts surging through them, then a glowing purple lake under a gorgeous sunset lit by twin suns.

None of it's real, but people on social media are eating these scenes up. So many people want to leave that it's scary. I guess when the future looks bleak, we'll jump at any old bullshit.

There are some voices raised in dissent, but they've got the same denying reality vibes of the climate change skeptics or anti-vaxxers.

Ray's put out an official statement from Mutopia. Literally a message in a bottle, because we don't want the aliens picking up on any signals. It's couched in vague terms because screaming about hungry alien gods is not a good look, but it reassures humanity of our benign intentions, and warns us all to be careful of stories that seem too good to be true. Chatter online about us is muted. We've been upstaged. It should feel good, but the obsession with the aliens is more disturbing than anything else.

And then the official Mission Trials begin. It gives me chills to see people lining up on the streets. They think they're queueing for their chance to be pioneers, to build a new life on a new planet colonised by a race of benevolent aliens. Not standing in line to be a fucking sacrificial meal. The lines wind through the streets for kilometres and kilometres, all heading towards the docks where enormous flat barges wait. Once each one is full, they're ferried out to the 'ships' moored in deeper water. People stand clustered together. They hug, they cheer, they cry.

"We've got to do something," Dani says, echoing my own internal thoughts.

"If we open a hole in the void bubble, Sai says it increases our odds of detection to almost eighty percent," Ray says. "We don't know the extent of the alien technology, and I won't risk Mutopia being detected and destroyed. The instant they know where we are, we will become their greatest priority. Because if we are destroyed, there will be nothing to stand in their way."

"We're not standing in their way now," I mutter, glaring at the screen.

"Everyone's doing this of their own free will," Ray reminds me.

"They're doing it for a *lie*," Dani snaps.

Ray shakes their head. "Humans have fought and died over lies as long as they've existed. This is only the latest. I understand it's painful, but right now we can do nothing. Sai and the others are still looking for a way to safely leave the bubble. But for now, we *must* remain in lockdown."

"Yes." I wave one hand irritably. "I hear you. I fucking get it. I'm not going to run off."

"What's inside the aliens, Tee Pee?" Feral asks. "Like if we were to sneak in undercover—which we're *not*, don't give me that look, Ray—what would we see?"

"I cannot say exactly, as I'm sure the evolutionary path on their world diverged from ours, especially given their ascendancy. But the great god-temples of my youth were complex networks of tunnels and chambers, lit by fires and full of the smoke from thousands of sacrifices. They are little more than a brain and a complex digestive system. When people enter one of the gods, they are doing little more than standing in the throat and waiting to be devoured."

"Shit." Feral's claws flick out and retract repetitively. "So we're watching a bunch of people line up to walk into this thing's guts."

"Yes." Tentacle Princess quivers. "They take great delight in having their prey come to them. To them, it is a sign of superiority that the choicest morsels abase themselves and are willingly devoured."

"And here we fucking sit. Helpless and useless." It's one of my least favourite things, being benched like this. Completely unable to help. Except it's for the safety of every mutant on

Mutopia, and I can't let my need to punch things risk all these lives.

It takes a few hours for the barges to stop sailing. The mouthpieces are trotted out again, to explain that the first group is now undergoing training. Further dates will be announced for the next cadre once processing is complete.

"There are limits to their appetites," Tentacle Princess says, as we watch hundreds of thousands of people return to their homes around the world. How can there be so many people willing to throw themselves into an alien's mouth even under the guise of a free ticket out of here? Are we that desperate for rescue, for salvation, for someone bigger than us to come along and explain everything? Some people who missed out are crying as they wander back through the streets. Others line the waterfronts on their knees, and still more hold up signs asking for deliverance and shouting about their own virtues.

"You all taste the fucking same," I shout at the screen. "Don't advertise yourselves to be eaten alive, you dumb fucks."

"Nice metaphor for capitalism though," Violet says.

"Hold up, wait!" Dani's waving her phone. "Let me cast this."

The talking heads on the news are replaced by what looks like footage from a head-mounted camera.

"Someone with a fucking GoPro?" Feral snorts.

It shows a long tunnel, gleaming white. Thin red strips pulse rhythmically on the walls. A line of people stretches forward up to where the tunnel curves, and when the camera spins around, an even longer line stretches behind. The expressions on the faces are bland and neutral, with none of the excitement of those who'd been waiting, or the party atmosphere on the barges.

"What the fuck?" I lean forward. "Someone's filming inside?"

"Livestreaming the process." Dani grins at me. "I don't think the aliens understand the internet."

"In a world such as theirs, they would not need one," Tentacle Princess says. "All information would be routed through the gods. To know something, you commune with them."

The line moves inexorably forward, and we watch transfixed as our point of view camera reaches the curve in the tunnel. It opens out into a huge white dome studded with thousands upon thousands of holes. Each flares with a sickly green light. The floor opens onto a lake with water that's a deep, rich purple. A network of white catwalks traverses this strange sea. Smiling spokespeople usher the sacrifices onto these paths. Arrows light up to guide them through the branching maze. It leads them towards the middle of the room where a vast building stands, rising to the very top of the dome. It bears another strong similarity to the Tower tarot card, just like the building in Sweden. The main difference is the forest of tentacles dangling from the windows.

"Sudden change," Violet whispers. "Chaos, revelation, and awakening."

It's hard to make out anything between the glare of the lights and the sickening way the camera's moving. But as the person filming gets up onto the walkway, it becomes much clearer. We watch in horror as a slim tentacle descends to pluck someone delicately from the middle of the throng. It's not the only one—there are more, coming from everywhere, reaching down with eerie grace. There are no screams on the video, only a deep, resonant hum, and a wet snicker-snack sound as the tentacles rub against each other, fighting to select people from the crowd.

Tentacle Princess trembles. "There is gas to make them docile. It makes the process easier, and the meat tastes sweeter."

The camera shakes violently and ascends into the air. Everything swirls, white walls and green light, and then the viewpoint plummets towards the frothing purple water below. It's almost impossible to see details, but the footage continues, showing sinuous things moving, twisting, gleaming. When it finally does terminate, we're all staring at the screen in a daze.

"I doubt anyone's going to be lining up for a ride out of here now," Alyse says in a shaky voice.

The internet is in an immediate frenzy over the footage, as everyone reposts and comments. There are almost as many opinions as there are people, but the two loudest camps are the 'I told you it was too good to be true' people, and the 'it's a fake to discredit the Eirini' faithful.

The aliens finally trot out a spokesdrone. This one's robe has a lion with an infinity symbol on it. I tap around on my tarot website and figure out it's Strength, presumably for persuasion and influence. The aliens really do believe in these archetypes. I can't see a way to use this yet, but I want to be their avatar of Death. Change, transformation. Endings.

"We have been alarmed to see these lies spread over your information networks. This footage has been generated to undermine our great work. Our initial efforts at discovering who is responsible have led us to suspect it is the work of those on Mutopia, who wish to keep your planet as a feeding ground for their own species."

"Feeding ground," I sneer. "What the fuck?"

"Liars think everyone else is lying," Alyse says. "I guess that goes for greedy alien species too."

"We welcome ambassadors and world leaders to come inside and see for yourself that this footage is a lie," the spokespeople continue. "Or anyone you wish to delegate. We will assure your safety, and continue to work towards our eventual departure from this planet and the journey to a more peaceful one."

Everything goes quiet after that, as the human governments figure out how to respond. I figure they'll send in someone expendable, and the aliens will likely show them a nice quiet room they prepared earlier. Possibly some of the people they took inside as well, if they had enough self-control to avoid gobbling them all up at once. They're going to want to keep humanity as calm and sweet, because one meal won't be enough. They haven't even set up their fucking breeding pits yet.

"We must be concerned with the docility ray," Tentacle Princess says. "Sai has been analysing social media posts from around the world and there are some disturbing trends emerging."

"I'm concerned by the fucking words *docility ray*," I say with a scowl.

Sai comes into the room, their head flashing a warning red. They tap a screen on their arm and a series of complex graphs and maps appear on the screen. "Apologies. There is a lot of information here. I assume you wish to hear the conclusions first, rather than all the proof."

"Yes, please," I say, ignoring Dani's little grumble.

"It appears that the closer you get to the alien entities, the more likely you are to support them. If you put a pin in the middle of the entity and overlay a series of circles, it falls away at a rate of... an equation I will not bore you with. But it is *clear* and consistent around each entity. We believe they are broad-casting signals to suppress any emotion consistent with resistance." The android skims through various graphics, and smarter people than me make interested noises.

"What are the limits to it?" I ask. "Like if I turned up determined to punch them in the face, would I suddenly become a calm little bunny rabbit, twitching my nose and waiting for tentacle death?"

"It appears that it only *suppresses* certain emotions," Sai says. "It does not eliminate them. These are trends, although they appear to be increasing. Keeping away from the alien temples is the logical solution."

I roll my eyes. "But if I bopped into the middle of an alien temple, would I still have enough presence of mind to stab?"

Sai's faceplate scrolls with a complex maze of equations. "It would depend on how long you were there, potential previous exposure, and—it seems likely, although I am still working through the data sets available—how badly you wanted to, ah, stab."

"Oh, I'll be fucked off enough for everyone." I clench my fist. "Just let me out of the goddamn cage. I'm tired of waiting around for the humans to fight back."

The screen shows the Strength spokesperson trotting back out again.

"The fuck is it now?" I sigh.

"We have just received wonderful news," Strength says. "An emissary from Mutopia, who wishes to ally themselves with us. They have agreed to step forward with us into the glorious future."

"What cowardly fuck?" Katie growls.

"There's always someone." Dani sighs. "I don't see how

they're going to make it convincing though. Some random mutant dug out of some hideyhole in—"

Every single one of us falls silent.

Because the person stepping forward to join Strength on the platform is far too familiar. "No, no, fuck no." I'm rocking back and forward, because this can't be happening. "You died. I killed you. You can't fucking *come back*. Not you." I feel like thorns are clawing their way up my throat, and the flowers blooming in my head are all dead and rotting, slimy petals clinging to my skin.

Other people are talking, but I can't hear them, because I can't take my eyes off the figure on the screen.

It's me, staring right back into the cameras.

My clone. Back from the dead.

CHAPTER 30
LIKE THE MOVIE ABOUT THE SPACE THING

"SOMEONE FIND me a fucking way out of here."

I'm standing in the middle of a room that's been taken over by Mutopia Science Club. There are whiteboards and cool glass screens that people can write on both sides of, and even fancy smartboards where people can do sci-fi things like poke at holograms. The problem is that we're not closer to a way to fight. "I'm not staying here while that tentacle asshole with my fucking face is saying hooray for the aliens."

"We are working hard to find a way, Dylan," Tentacle Princess says. "One that keeps Mutopia safe."

I try to modulate my voice into something that doesn't sound like a threat. "I know you're trying to solve an impossible problem under a whole lot of time pressure. But I need to get out. Even if it's risky to me. Maybe the aliens can track me, maybe they can't. If they can, we'll keep running. But please, get me the *fuck out of here.*"

Dani joins me, all business. "Think out of the box. We need to get a group out without collapsing the voidveil."

"It can be a one way trip," I say cheerfully.

Dani stops and stares at me. "Can it?"

"Yeah. Back in is the harder part, right?"

"And what will you *do* out there with no way back in?" Dani asks me, that tone creeping into her voice which is a little red flashing warning sign about being too reckless. Our emotional connection is flooded with a thousand shades of concern.

"Fight." I spread my arms wide. "Help people."

"On your own?"

"Well, no." I give her my most winning smile. "I was hoping you'd come with me. And Vi. Alyse too. Plus Fairy and that wind-up himbo girlfriend of hers. We'll need Keepaway to stay mobile. Might have to promise them pizza."

Dani sighs in exasperation. "Are you asking me on this madcap mission?"

"Well, I sort of assumed you'd naturally want to come with me."

She blows out one sharp breath, and then mirrors my smile with her own. "Well, obviously I do. Why would I start doing the sensible thing now?"

"It'll also give Science Club an incentive to get this done." I wave my hand at the smartboards. "Find us heroes a way home, like that movie about the space thing."

I leave them to argue it out and find Keepaway. They're the linchpin of my plan, although that's a very grandiose word for it. Even if the aliens can't track me—which Hadylan didn't seem to be able to—we need to stay super-mobile. For example, teleport into an alien flesh temple and back out again. Or out of the way when weird alien bombs descend to turn us into blood soup. I also want to figure out this goddamn labyrinth of Lilith's. In short, I am desperate, and the problem is Keepaway is very much a homebody. I've lured them out before, and they said a lot of very flattering things to me, but this is a big thing to ask.

I make the possibly terrible decision to front-foot all of this.

"Certain danger, Keeps!" I wave my arms as if I'm Tentacle Princess. "Narrow escapes, chase scenes, and daring rescues. A ragtag group of heroes standing up against the powerful alien menace."

They sit in the chair opposite me, dressed in a tight black short-sleeved shirt and pants that are sleek and silvery. They've got socks with little pineapples on them, which I find oddly endearing. We're in their apartment, which is small and neat. Given that Cybele could have grown them any living quarters they wanted, they obviously like it that way. There's a laptop sitting open on the desk, beside a stack of paperback books. The large window looks out over tall pines, and the wind carries their scent into the room.

"There's no way home right?" They blink at me, running one hand shyly over their shaved head. Their eyes are a shade of startlingly oceanic green.

"Science Squad is on it. In the meantime, the world needs our help, Alex."

They smile at me, a quick flash of teeth. "Did you just use my real name?"

"I need you. And I didn't want to come in reminding you of the time you said you'd do anything for me.."

"Not sure I ever said that. But I still owe you everything."

I slouch down in my chair. "Now you're making me feel bad. I don't want you to feel fucking obligated, Keepsy. Half of me is still the awkward kid who needs to do this shit to feel like I'm making a difference in the world, and the other half is the ancient old disaster who wants you to enjoy the comforts in life while you can."

They laugh, and then lean forward so our knees are almost touching, face to face in this tiny apartment. "You know I'll do it. But you don't want to feel like a bully."

"Um, excuse me. I did *not* know any such thing."

"I'm not going to say no to you, Dylan. And yes, I'm terrified, but that's no reason to turn away from this. Besides, I'm going to be in the company of the biggest badasses in the world, so there's no safer place to be. Except for hiding behind an impenetrable void shield, but that's not where my friends are going to be."

"Oh, Keeps." I stand up and plant a kiss on the top of their head. "You're one of the best."

Now I have a gang all loaded and ready, but nowhere to go. Being trapped is not a good look on me. I watch Hadylan's TV appearances repetitively until I can fucking quote them. *The good of the species means something good for both mutant and human alike. We cannot spurn the outstretched hand of the Eirini. I have bought passage offworld for mutants at great cost, and we must take advantage of this gift they have given us.*

When I get out of here, I'm going to rip every single tentacle out of their head and strangle them with it. Then I'll cut them into little bits and bury them in the hole we found the pairstones in. Fuck one way to kill them, I'll try *every way*.

That fucking death scene of theirs plays nonstop in my head too. All those words they choked out, what seemed like the real them. And then the tentacles slithered back inside them. Using my face and my goddamn name to bring more people into the feeding pits.

I join Dani in her obsession with the puzzle box. If Lilith has another weapon, I need it. The two of us take shifts, working on the outer layer again, the one that answers questions like a Ouija board computer. I'm actually getting to grips with the language, mapping the symbols onto various things and figuring out ways to combine them.

"You're better at this than me," Dani says. "More intuitive."

I spin the box in my hands. "My brain bounces off its own walls. It's different, that's all. And it's not like it's helping."

Dani sighs. "It's so fucking stubborn about the labyrinth." She's lying in bed beside me, trying to sleep while I valiantly attempt the brains thing.

"Skull/ground/forever." I scrawl on the tablet. "Lilith, how many ways can you say death? It's like you don't want us to find this fucking thing."

"A weapon covered in warning signs." Dani rolls over with a sigh.

"So how do we override it? Tell her yes, Lilith dear, we know your mystery weapon is scary, but we want to get our hands on it anyway. Because we're desperate and some of us are actually quite smart, so you can trust us."

Dani groans something incoherent, but her breathing smooths out into sleep. I'm relieved, because she needs it. We all probably do.

I poke at with the box some more. *Good/trust/safe/hands.* Come on Lilith, trust us. We're your inheritors, so we're the obvious choice to get our hands on whatever you left behind.

"Mind/pain/suffering/forever. Fuck's *sake*, Lily. You're the most emo mutant ever."

"She lost the person she loved." Alyse perches herself on the end of the bed. "Tends to make even the brightest of us a little emo."

I reach out my hand to take hers. "I know. Sorry I've been so distracted lately."

"You're fighting." Her smile flickers on and off, like a bulb in a horror movie. "And you're doing it by using your brain. It's what she'd do. What she'd want. "

"My brain." I snort and twist the box in my hands. My mind's still snagged on what Alyse said. Lily lost Lucy in the war, right near the end. Maybe whatever part of her built the computer was still drowning in that. "Okay, how about this? Heart/loss/empty/forever."

There's an audible click from inside the box.

Alyse and I stare at each other.

Dani sits bolt upright, eyes wide as she snaps instantly awake. "What was that?"

"You heard that in your *sleep*?" I ask.

"I thought I dreamed it. You did something? Here, show me." I pass the box to Dani, who opens up the computer layer to reveal the globe inside. Another panel has opened beside the second light, revealing a five by five grid of spherical beads, each etched with a tiny symbol.

"Heart/loss/empty/forever," I tell Dani. "Alyse's idea."

"Very vaguely." Alyse frowns. "I was just doing sad girl shit."

Dani leans in to hug her. "You both went through similar things."

I snatch the globe back. "These things spin, and there's like, a whole shitload of symbols on each one. I'm no math brain, but that's a lot of combinations. And, huh." I frown down at it. I'm sure the symbol for *harvest* wasn't on the second bead before. I swivel the first bead back to *empty* and now *harvest* is gone.

"Fuck me. It changes as you touch it." I swallow hard. "Shit-load of combinations just went to fucking infinity."

Dani's doing calculations on her tablet and frowning at the numbers. "It's a different problem, that's all. And one we *will* solve, Dilly. Look how far we've come."

I flop backwards and stare at the ceiling. The answer is not magically written there. "I guess I'm Hoping for a miracle. Don't we fucking deserve one? The world's invaded by aliens, and half the population is happy about it. And my creepy double is back, fucking everything up even worse. I don't know what to do."

"We defend people." Alyse holds out her hand to pull me up. "We try to make things better for people. And try not to fuck it up."

"The true hero's motto." I sigh enormously. "Okay, so let's figure out—"

"There may be news!" The dramatic announcement comes from the diminutive grey figure of an alien striding into the room with all xer limbs aquiver. "Of the positive variety, before you ask."

"Tee Pee!" I practically fall off the bed in my eagerness. "Can I hug you?"

The alien trembles, and for a moment I think xe is going to collapse at my feet. "I would enjoy that very much. Since our argument, I have been consumed with regret for my cowardly actions, and the pain it has caused you."

"Listen to me." I wrap my arms around xer tightly. "We all fuck up. Me more than most, and I shouldn't have shouted so much. We're good, okay? Now tell me about my ticket out of here."

Tentacle Princess shuffles xer limbs a bit. "It is only the

beginning of a plan. Risky, but it shows some promise. We're running numbers and should have an answer soon."

"Fucking *finally*." I'm shaky from adrenaline, my brain thrashing around like a shark on a chain. "Let's get the hell out of here."

"Before we go running off, babes," Feral says from the doorway. "You might want to check the news. Shit's just gotten extra weird."

CHAPTER 31
TERROR FORMING

THINGS I HATE: other people fighting battles I think are mine. Especially idiot humans trying to nuke fucking alien monsters from another world. Because, yes, that's what seems to be happening right now to the alien ship in the Atlantic. Back before the Dark Year, Emma siphoned the power of a mutant called Baked Good to turn the world's supply of nuclear missiles —and a bunch of conventional ones—into cake. Instead of taking that as a great opportunity to enter a new era of disarmament, the governments of the world have been trying to reup as fast as possible. And now in some decision bunker, someone's decided it's worth rolling the dice on sending an actual nuclear weapon at something that, even if you take it on face value, is a living alien spaceship. This is a species capable of interstellar travel, so despite the tranquil images of Eirini Prime, they probably have something better than our shitty nukes lying around.

Of course, reality is even worse, but the human governments don't know that.

So we're all watching footage of an injured alien, waiting to see what the reprisal looks like. It's gushing steam and purple light from a hole in its side, listing dangerously and setting the ocean around it boiling. Ribbons of flesh billow outwards, scorched and blistering, and chunks of meat splash down in the ocean, where they writhe in the furious currents that spiral outwards from the thrashing creature.

It's never been more obvious that humanity has shot a living thing. Something far bigger, smarter and more dangerous than we are, or could possibly imagine. This is a species that's plotted a fucking invasion between universes, and has turned up with a goddamn cover story all the better to eat us with.

"What are they going to do?" Violet whispers.

"They do not enjoy defiance." Tentacle Princess seems as if xe wants to flee the room. "There will be a reprisal."

I frown at the screen. "That might be instructive for the future. Plus it's useful to know a fucking nuke only scratches them, isn't it?"

"Useful and scary," Dani says with a sidelong glance. "Oh, look."

The torn side of the alien is knitting itself together, but there's still a hole wide enough for a series of glowing projectiles to fly out. I'm guessing these are around the size of a passenger plane. Maybe they're all the little attendant ships that brought it down to land. Holy shit, this really is the size of a city.

The flying ships bank in unison before setting off at high-speed. The news drones can't keep up and settle for zooming their cameras in until the alien ships are gone from view.

"This won't be good," Feral says around a mouthful of popcorn.

Ray has come back into the room with all the commotion. They look even more tired than usual. "This is exactly why we must stay cloaked. We can't have them attacking Mutopia. I'll start working on another speech about the clear and present danger."

The news networks are already picking up another transmission. Another immaculately attractive person wearing an outfit embroidered with a sword and scales. They're obviously calling this attack Justice.

"We apologise for what is about to happen. This is beyond our control. The attack on our ship triggered an autonomous defence system. We are incapable of intervening, as this was staffed as a rescue mission and therefore no technicians are onboard. We would recommend evacuating everyone from the location where this attack was launched from."

"Oh, now *that* is a good line." I pat my hands together in mock applause. "If only we could get away with that bullshit. *I'm terribly sorry, but you've engaged Magneto Was Right mode. Kicking your ass is inevitable.*"

I get the sternest most principal look from Ray. "People are going to die, Dylan."

"My bullshit is an autonomous system, Ray. And besides, we don't know what the fuck they're going to do. Maybe they're going to drop propaganda leaflets. *Kiss A Tentacle Today!*"

"Who do we think they're attacking?" Feral's still shaking popcorn into her mouth. "I'm taking bets. Hench texted me to say the Russians, but it's got to be—"

"The Free States," about ten people say in unison.

More than anywhere else in the world, the United States was hit hard by the Dark Year. Partly because they went all-in on Team Michael, and the aftermath of that was fairly brutal. They had entire cities to rebuild and a nanotech generated wasteland running through a whole chunk of it. There's still technically a United States, but there are a lot less stars on the flag. The rest is split between Cascadia, who've set themselves up as the economic powerhouse, and the Free States, who are basically *Mad Max: Fury Road: The Country*. Which is all to say that if anyone's firing a loose nuke at an alien, it's them. They hate mutants almost as much as they hate Cascadia, but they don't subscribe to the whole 'enemy of my enemy' thing and aim their ire towards everyone.

Satellites track the alien ships as they turn right over the Gulf of Mexico, and the talking heads are already reaching the same Free States conclusion. Most of the internet has gone once again to memes. I'm uneasy about the whole thing, because not everyone stays in the Free States by choice. We've offered them places on Mutopia, but it's not that easy to leave your entire family behind and go live on an island with a sentient forest.

Somewhere over what used to be Texas, the glowing craft plummet to Earth, shifting from streamlined shapes to flailing masses of tentacles and beaks. It's like they've shed their skin to reveal the monsters within. They impact miles apart, sinking into the ground like they're injection sites.

Every camera focused on that area goes dead.

The camera cuts back to the New York studio, where we see smiling faces.

"Can't complain too much about that outcome," the male anchor says.

"Of course not, Tom. The Free States have overstepped their bounds yet again. While we cannot celebrate the loss of life, these are the inevitable consequences for attacking the Eirini. I'm sure our visitors would have preferred a more peaceful option, but we should be pleased the ships we'll be travelling in are possessed with autonomous defence systems such as these."

"Someone drank the Kool-Aid," Feral sing-songs.

"Within the docility ray radius, right?" I snap my fingers at Sai, who's lost in a sea of data. "One of those damn things is practically in New York Harbour."

"Precisely." Sai doesn't lift their head from their own read-outs. "The data set of worldwide reactions generated shows the ray is having an increasing effect on those within the radius, although it does not appear to be widening." Their faceplate glows briefly golden. "Which I consider extremely good news."

THE ALIEN SPOKESPEOPLE follow up with more statements. They reassure us that the first phase of the training program is still underway, despite the 'unfortunate delay.' They assure the world that the dates for the second phase of the training program are imminent. The tone of the speakers sharpens noticeably when they talk about how important it is that they have equal numbers for this round.

How much you buy into this bullshit directly maps onto how close you are to an alien. We've been living in an increasingly divided world for a while, but this has the starkest shift yet in terms of how easily it can be seen on a map, no matter how much you zoom in.

"We find it *frustrating* to be questioned incessantly." The spokesasshole looks far more than frustrated. He looks as if he'd like to tear apart every naysayer, but in an extremely hand-some way. "The Eirini have returned to a planet that is obvi-ously in dire straits, as seen by the futile efforts of the so-called

Free States to lash out against even the proffered hand of friendship. While we still wish to assist you, it becomes harder to envision a world in which today's humans can be productive members of Eirini society. If you truly wish to be uplifted, we must see an outpouring of support from all humanity. Otherwise we shall have to take more drastic action to ensure your safety. For your own benefit."

"And the mask comes off."

"They're losing their grip on things." Violet takes a seat beside me, entwining her fingers with mine. "Which worries me a little, because what's the next step?"

"Whatever it is, we're going to get out and meet it." I get to my feet. "Let's go and—"

The screen shifts to footage from the Free States, showing what the aliens can do when they're mad. We're looking at it from above, drones hovering. All the colours are washed out aside from grey and green, like some twisted night vision. At ground level, everything's swallowed by fog. The buildings that rise out of it are wrapped in a fleshy coating that pulses arrhythmically, as if some monstrous heart below the city animates them all.

Slender creatures drift between the buildings, stalk-like tubes bundled together halfway up with a tangled mass of pulsing vein-like strands. Tentacles sprout from the tops, dangling down to hang in the fog. Their limbs swing in pendulous arcs, and each time they appear out of the murk, they're coated in something that drips and splatters like blood. Each has a single staring eye that burns with a pale light like a ghost's candle, occasionally stabbing out in a bright beam that illuminates other floating shapes in the distance, hanging in the air like balloons made of skin and hair that slowly deflate and sag to the ground. The creatures call to each other in slurred hoots that sound like slowed-down owls. I'd think it was more fake footage, some warped science-fiction movie to strike fear into our hearts, but it's too subtle for that. It's alien, the fruit of impossible seeds. There's an odd, drifting melancholy to it, like we're watching lost things stumble in the dark and try to replicate their home. Poor lost animals in a world not terraformed for them, begging each other to find some sense in it, watching as their homes sputter and choke.

The people in the TV studio don't know how to describe it. Everyone in the room with me is stunned. Someone that I can't see is crying softly.

"Tentacle Princess," I say. "We need to talk about your plan."

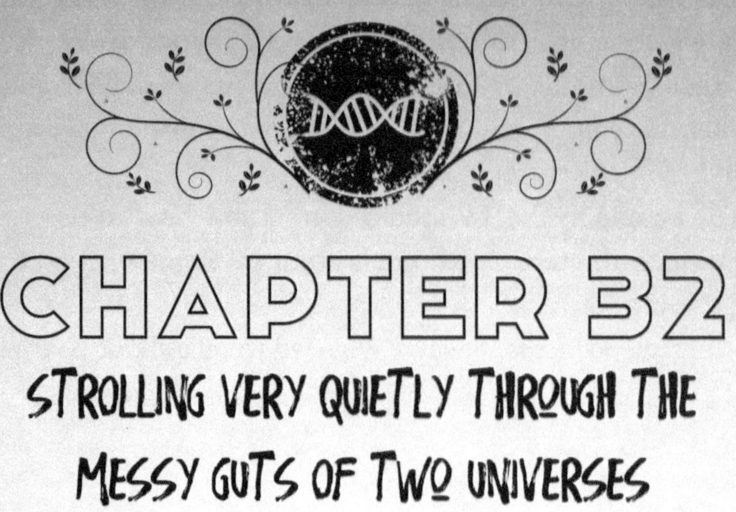

CHAPTER 32
STROLLING VERY QUIETLY THROUGH THE MESSY GUTS OF TWO UNIVERSES

BACK IN THE Science Club room, a new door has appeared, with a gargoyle-shaped knocker and a complex pattern of stained glass panes.

"I am not *constrained* by your void, as I have pointed out before." The voice coming from it is much sharper than usual. "You simply refuse to take my word for it, which is not my problem."

"Thorny." I poke my head inside the door, but it's only a supply closet full of raggedy old boxes, with a dirt tunnel in the wall leading away, like a prison escape plan. "Are you my ride out of here?"

Sai's faceplate is such a chaotic whirl of data it makes me dizzy to look at. "That is the plan, but your house friend does not make sense. We are trying to run simulations of their extrusion through realspace and its ripple effects through voidspace, but the program gives a different result every time, and most of them don't even make *sense*."

"They're a reality warper," I point out. "It's literally in the name."

"My proposal is to limit the interaction," One Thorn says. "It will be a very swift injection. I'll generate a single door at the farthest location from any zone of alien influence and hold it open for the shortest possible time to drop my cargo. Essentially shooting you all like a bullet."

"But *somewhere* you must pass through the void," Sai shouts and then rubs at their faceplate. "Sorry, I am experimenting with emulating human consciousness and it is not going well. Let me shut this down." They swivel to face the open door of One Thorn. "The simulation results include a catastrophic shattering of the entire voidveil and the death of Tentacle Princess as xe implodes, so I do not wish to leap into this lightly."

"I am perfectly capable of managing my own voids," Tentacle Princess says. "Your simulations are wrong, dear Sai, likely due to us trying to aggregate three different types of math together and failing."

I can see from Dani's expression that she's having an idea. Her eyes light up, and flowers spring up in curving lines all up and down her body. "Thorny, you can travel the multiverse, right? Or did, back in the day."

"Yes," the house replies. "Although I have not managed to create even the tiniest window between universes in this form, which is a source of much—"

"We've been obsessed with traversing the wall of the voidveil." Dani says. "But the walls between our universe and theirs have been thinned after what Hadylan did. So couldn't we go through to their Earth and use their own tunnel to come back to ours? They're unlikely to be watching for that in either direction, at least not for whatever One Thorn's energy signature is. And we know they can survive in a parallel universe, and now we should be safe inside them and—"

I step forward and kiss her, and it's not to shut her up. "You're a fucking genius. There are so many reasons I love you, but this is definitely one of them. This will work, right?" I stalk over to shove my head back inside One Thorn's door. "Right?"

"It has been a long time since I have moved between universes," the house says weakly. "And I have never done it on my own."

"Come on, Thorny." I drape myself in their doorway, aiming for themme fatale vibes. "If crossing between universes is like shooting a hole into them, this is like poking yourself inside an already established bullet wound. The skin's already broken, the flesh is already torn! We're just going to stroll very quietly through the messy guts of two universes and hope nobody notices."

"Thank you for making my idea sound indescribably gross," Dani says.

"You're welcome, my love."

"It does seem feasible, if nerve-wracking," One Thorn says. "We will have to close the door behind us, which means that for some time we will be completely adrift in this other universe."

"Maybe we can fuck up their world while we're there," I say, caught up in the whole vibe of the thing. "Or, okay, yes, maybe that can be tomorrow's problem. So when do we leave?"

Everyone in the entire room turns to stare at me.

"I'm serious. Things are fucked out there, and they're only going to get worse. I've been chewing my fingers down to the bark, trying to hold back. I can't sit on my hands knowing that these monsters had my parent killed as part of their fucking plan, that they were some calculated contingency! And now look at what they're doing to the world? Pear's gone and it's not for anything It's just a shitty mess and I'm staring it in the face and I refuse to be fucking helpless anymore."

I'm not sure at what point I started shouting or crying, but I don't think it's helping to convince people that I'm fine, actually, and I end up tailing off into ugly sobs while my girlfriends and my best friend stand in a circle around me and hold me close.

"I swear that I will do this task for you," One Thorn says in a low voice. "I got to know your parent very well during the Dark Year. They were wonderful, and I will assist you in avenging their death."

"Okay." I wipe sticky tears from my eyes. "Sorry for the, uh, the meltdown, everyone. Maybe I'm not fine, but I'm always ready to resist."

"Let's gather the troops," Dani says. "Dylan's right about... a bunch of stuff, actually. But especially about how we can't sit by anymore and let this happen. So we're going to get out there and make a difference."

Science Club actually cheers. Like we're in one of those cheesy movies and we're the fools going off into the dangerous corner of the universe in a fragile little container, while these nerds stay back and find us a safe way home. It's probably unfair to One Thorn to call them fragile, but with a rickety wooden door hanging open to a bare room with a single light-bulb, they're definitely looking *small.*

The gang of us crowds in. It's the main crew along with Keepaway and Feral's girlfriend Hench. I've kept it small because there's plenty to do on Mutopia, and I can only keep track of so many people at once. Lots of people are mad at being left behind, most noticeably Oni, but he understands I can't bear his death on my conscience and he's too damn fragile.

One Thorn speaks calmly. "I have separated a sliver of myself from the main house and constrained myself to the smallest possible form. We will only be an infinitesimal speck drifting between the world, like trying to identify a single star in the Milky Way."

"Let's hope so." I shuffle into the interior of the house. The group of us are all crowded together, and I'm smooshed up between Dani and Violet. The remaining members of Science Club peer in.

"Be safe, please," Sai says, her faceplate glowing pink. "We shall work to find you a path home. How will we know you have arrived safely back in our universe?"

"Follow the sound of the explosions." I smile at her as the door closes slowly.

There's a slight lurch, like when an elevator begins moving.

"That is us detaching ourselves from Mutopia," One Thorn says calmly. "And that—" a more violent thump makes us all clutch at each other "—is us detaching completely from physical reality. We are now in Violet's liminal space."

"That's what Dani and Dylan always say," Feral calls with a cackle.

One Thorn continues as if they didn't hear. "Breaching out of our universe in three... two..."

The moment of transition is like when your ears pop in an airplane, except the whole of reality pops too. For a few seconds we don't exist, like reality is catching its breath at the audacity of what we're attempting. Then we're a whole mingled collection of atoms, a confused, buzzing array that has no idea how to order itself. I can feel everyone's incoherent confusion, especially at how Dani and my plant vibes are all jammed in the middle of everything. Then with a series of jolts that sing between us, we're shaken back into existence. It looks like we're all in the right place.

"That was bracing," One Thorn says dryly. "The good news is that we're intact."

"What's the bad news?" I ask.

"Surprisingly, there is none. I'm just letting us drift for a moment, adjusting to the physical laws of this reality before we dive back in."

"Don't we even get a window?" Feral asks.

"I'm literally surfing in stealth mode through an entirely different universe, but... fine." One Thorn shudders and the walls around us are now completely transparent. There's a lot of startled screaming, including from Feral, whose fault this was. Then everyone realises we're not actually going to plummet into the atmosphere of other Earth and we press our faces to the glass.

This version of our world has barely any land, only a few islands poking up out of the sea. They have sea-level rise that drowns all our most dire proclamations. Everything is almost entirely dark, and the sky is the same impenetrable black I saw in my flower-induced visions. From this vantage, I realise the lights in the sky aren't stars, but alien craft floating inside a massive shield wrapped around the planet.

"Uh, let's get out of here." Dani's voice is shaky. "I think I've seen enough."

"Already prepared for breaching," One Thorn says, and then we get the joy of doing the whole disintegrating thing in reverse. This time I'm less worried we'll get stuck that way. When the house finally stops trembling, the wooden door cracks open to reveal an expanse of wide-open fields. They sprawl towards low, dusty hills, and behind us steeper slopes rise, covered with tightly-packed ranks of trees.

"So where do we go from here?" Dani asks. "The labyrinth to find the weapon?"

I shake my head. "We haven't solved the goddamn box, only made it worse. I'd rather go somewhere productive and noticeable. Keeps, take us to the outskirts of the Free States. The parts that got slapped with those alien bombs."

"A lot of these people *hate* us," Feral growls.

I take a deep breath. "Not all of them. And they've just been bombed, so maybe they need some help. You know, that superhero thing? Plus I'd like to figure out some shit before we step up and try to smack one of these things."

"And the other reason?" Dani murmurs.

"Going somewhere noticeable puts me on their radar." I clench my fists and feel thorns sprout. "See if my dearest Hadylan shows up. Maybe I get a chance to kill them again. Hopefully this time it'll take."

CHAPTER 33
RESCUE OPERATIONS

IT TAKES a few attempts to find people who aren't scared and running for their lives, and it's a raggedy-ass militia. They're not wearing any consistent uniform, mostly pieced together body armour spray-painted with neon designs, and gas masks fitted with gadgetry. Based on the body language and the weapons swinging in our direction, they're not super excited to see us. It's been a while since I've whistled a bunch of guns to my command and with my janky powers these days, it might be risky. I wonder if my reputation still precedes me.

"Stand down!" I can't see who's shouting, but the militia listens. Then the crowd parts to reveal a woman with no mask. She's got red hair shaved very close, and blisters on one cheek. "Holy shit. You're actually here."

"Agent Decker." I give her a half-ass salute. "Looks like the GIC is moving up in the world."

"I don't work for them anymore." Her gaze is calm and even. "They're taking an appeasement tack with our visitors. Trying to open a dialogue. I don't trust any of this shit, because it's too good to be true."

"Like I told you, they're aliens from a parallel Earth. And you thought I was making up stories."

There's scattered muttering from the assembled militia, probably because they're trying to decide where the aliens fit on their hate rankings.

"Might've seen some shit since then." She scrubs angrily at the scabbing mess on her cheek. "And especially after seeing this shit, I wouldn't listen to anything those Eirini assholes say."

"What's in there?" I ask.

"People." Finally, Decker's badass facade crumbles. "All wired up in rows, like they're a crop. You can disconnect them, knife to the base of the skull, give it a good hard twist. We've been bringing them out to our camp over there." She waves in the direction of some tents. "Trying to bring in some aid people, but we're getting some strange responses from people we thought might help. We've got a handful of doctors and one mutant healer, but they're overwhelmed."

Dani explains the whole docility ray thing, and Decker looks more and more depressed the more she hears about it, as if she's sprung a leak and all the defiance has trickled out.

"We've been going in with gas masks and rescuing people, but we're running low and they don't work fully." She scratches at her cheek again. "As you can see. If you limit the exposure, it seems to help, but we've had a couple of people die from this shit. And it's infectious, so no hugs or kisses please."

"Jesus, Deck, have a rest. We'll do a shift or two."

"Find some gas masks." Decker's obviously relieved. "If you go to the supply tent and requisition—"

"No need." Alyse is already transforming, ten feet tall, with her face a twisted mess of chrome and pipes like a steampunk plague doctor's mask. "I'll be safe from whatever's in there."

I grab at her arm. "Don't go in there alone."

"I'll do whatever I can to save people, Dylan. I've got to."

"Fuck's sake." I know she's still upset over Emma, and I can't fix it, but having her blunder all melancholy into an alien nightmare is not great. "Dan, you're better with the biology shit. Can you go in first and show me the blueprint?"

Decker's staring after Alyse with an odd expression on her face. "Is she okay?"

"No. Not really." I shrug. "And nor am I, and you're not exactly a box of fluffy ducks yourself. But here we fucking are, with a job to do."

Dani armours herself in thorns and blooms and follows Alyse into the swirling clouds. Keepaway jogs back over, fitting a gas mask to their face.

"See you in there." They place a hand to their chest and disappear.

Decker's got a radio pressed to the side of her head. "The aliens are talking again. Warning people away from the Free States. Saying not to let those with negative minds block us from the future we deserve."

"Even the fucking aliens are manifesting now." With the blueprints from Dani, I begin my transformation, wrapping myself in layers of thorn and moss, and creating strange horned protrusions over my head that should funnel the worst of the gas away from me. It's a combination of armour and gas mask, and Dani thinks it's pretty neat.

"Lots of people agree with them." Decker looks up at me,

too exhausted to even react to my bizarre transformation. "How do we resist if everyone is swayed to their cause?"

"Find the most pissed off people and fight." I extend one big thorny fist to bump her small flesh and bone one. "Now please take a break, Decker, or you'll kill yourself accidentally. And I want my head of the resistance alive."

"Head of the what?" Decker asks faintly.

"You heard me." Look at me, every inch the giant plant general. "Now please. Fucking sleep."

Then I head into the murky green darkness. It takes Dani and I a few attempts to get spotlight eyes up and running, but using some trick with luminous pollen and lenses of crystalline sap, we can illuminate the area around us. It's easier than fumbling through this acrid nightmare by touch alone. A lot of the immediate area has been cleared out, leaving networks of thick tubing sticking up out of the ground. They look like some eerie cross between bicycle stands and stakes to grow tomatoes on. Evenly spaced along are protrusions that look like pipes that drip a pale yellow liquid. Some have been severed sharply, and on others you can make out the delicate organic machinery at the tip. And all around are ragged smears of blood, strange curlicues as if someone's been trying to write messages with it.

There's no sign of the others, and I have this horror movie feeling of being lost in the fog, like I'm doomed to wander endlessly. I transform further, to lift my head from the murk, but it makes me light-headed and I fall to my knees. It's a reminder that Cybele's energy network is in maintenance mode. I can't drink recklessly from it and stride the world like a flowering colossus. My glowing eyes flare in the murk, twin stars flashing, and I try to feel gratitude for what I can still do, rather than being mad at Cybele for running and hiding. This is what we're for, to be the ones who stand and fight. And hopefully not die.

An answering flare of light in the distance gives me a direction, and I jog off through the fog until I almost bump into Dani. Through our connection I can feel her pain, as she carries twelve bodies cradled in many branching arms. None of them look conscious, and I have the awful feeling we're only taking them out to give them a better burial.

"So many," she gasps. "Keep going in this direction."

She stumbles off, lost to the fog in moments, and I plunge deeper in. Most of the buildings in this area have been destroyed, and are only piles of rubble. There are none of the fleshy pillars I saw in the video, only empty streets with growth tubes running down the middle of them. Finally, I turn a corner and find my first bodies.

They're each sprawled out like they're asleep, a tube jutting from the back of their neck. The network hums and pulses, rather than the inert, dripping lines I've been following. I crouch by the first body, a kid of maybe ten or eleven. Their eyelids are closed, but there's a sense of restless movement from underneath as if they're dreaming—or worse, changing. I try to remember what Decker said.

Knife to the base of the skull. A good hard twist.

I feel for the connection point, and dig one slender thorn in alongside the humming valve. There's a cluster of little tentacles that spread outwards like grasping fingers. With a sharp twist, I sever these and the body slumps free. I hoist the kid over my shoulder and move on to the next captive.

I'm not as good at transformations as Dani, especially with Cybele turned down to a simmer, but I collect ten people before I start losing feeling in my extremities and head back. Dani and Alyse both drift past me, silent and unknowable in the dark.

The three of us could be aliens ourselves, busy at some mysterious task.

"That's the gas talking, Dylan," I mutter, and move out as fast as I can.

When I reach clean air again, I'm dizzy, and it takes a couple of attempts to lower my rescued cargo down. A whole gang of volunteers are here to clean them up and take them to tents, where they'll get fluids, IV meds, and food. The whole operation has tripled in size since we arrived. Everyone seems to know what they're doing, so I catch my breath and watch.

A body appears from thin air and collapses on the ground. They're immediately taken into the arms of waiting volunteers. Keepaway follows, bloody and shaking. They clutch their stomach and gag. When I pull off their gas mask, they're pale and sweating with fine blue crystals forming along their jawline.

"Nurse," I shout. "Got a rescuer here who needs help."

A tall woman in PPE gear jogs out of the closest tent, flanked by a pair of volunteers. "Oh shit. This is your teleporter, right? They're turning out to be quite the hero."

"Yeah, they're definitely that." I stroke sweaty hair off Keepaway's forehead. "They going to be okay?"

"With rest, fluid, and some home-brew antibiotics. You saw Deck, right? I've managed to stabilise her, so this one will be fine."

"Thank you." I slump backwards onto the dusty ground. "A lot."

"Welcome." The masked figure gazes down at me. "Are you injured? Not sure if my powers extend to your unique system."

"You're a mutant?" I struggle up to my feet.

"They call me Soft Touch. My healing ability is mild, but still pretty useful."

"In the Free States?"

"People here don't deserve healing? I've lived here my whole damn life, and I'm not about to run to your magic island. No offence."

I shrug. "It's there if people need it. I've got no intention of forcing anyone to come live there. Might be a little easier, that's all."

The woman snorts. "You don't need to tell me. My partner and I are both mutants, but we've got no intention of leaving, no matter how fucked things get. And they do get fucked, believe me. Now let me take care of your friend, and you go save some more of my goddamn people."

"Yes, sir." I've never given a more genuine fake salute in my life.

"Cheeky asshole." The volunteers pick up Keepaway gently and carry them back inside the tent. I'd like to poke my head in and see how everyone is doing, but I've got my damn orders.

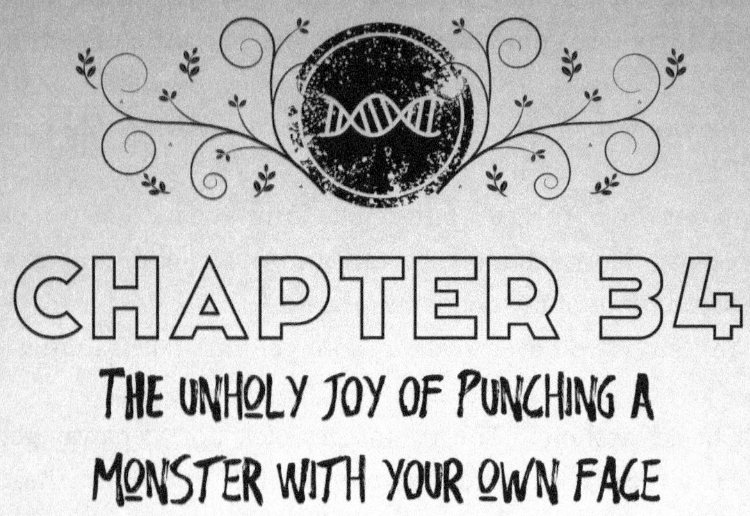

CHAPTER 34

THE UNHOLY JOY OF PUNCHING A MONSTER WITH YOUR OWN FACE

I'M BACK in the fog for five minutes before I realise I'm turned around. Dani always teases me about my terrible sense of direction. On Mutopia, the trees help me navigate, but here they're silent.

I'm on the edge of a park that I don't remember passing before. There's no sign of Dani's lights, or Alyse's hulking form. The only sounds are distant rain and the rhythmic *hush-shush* of the pipe system. Active pipes mean there are people, so I step into the park. The ground underfoot is spongy and I adjust my weight distribution until I'm standing on giant paddle-feet. It's so goddamn unsettling, the silence and the fog and the sound of those fucking pipes.

And then a gentle, swaying motion like something in the breeze.

Except the air is dead in here, stifling and still. So what the hell *was* that?

A long green limb drifts towards me, a slender tentacle descending through the air.

"Oh, look. Something to punch." I take hold of the tentacle in one thorny fist and drag it towards me, hard and fast as I can. It's *light*, like something made of straw and paper, and the rest of the alien's body looms out of the dark like I've yanked on a kite string. I sharpen the edge of my other arm, and swing it through the middle of the central stalk like a scythe. The edges of it shrivel, and it collapses to the ground in a mess of tumbling strands. With a long, drawn out cry, the head of the alien falls, the light from its single eye flickering and dying like a torch in a horror movie. When it hits the ground, it smashes like a rotten pumpkin, sending thick, creamy innards flying. I'm all surrounded by alien parts, but it's disintegrating in my hands. The top parts of it are scorched and blackened, and the fibres are hot to the touch, almost feverish. It's beyond gross, but at least these things are easy to kill.

When I find the networked people, they're all dead. It's clear there's no point in rescue—the tops of their heads have been neatly sliced off. I remember the footage of the stalk-like aliens drifting through the fog, their tentacles streaky with blood. I wish my brain didn't fill in the gaps with visions of edged tentacles descending, neat lines of blood welling along foreheads, spilling down their faces like misaligned tears. The top of skulls flipped open on hinges and, and—

Each person's head has been hollowed out and inside the bone chalices of their skulls are writhing nests of tentacles. Hungry suckers flex as they slither against each other like snakes tightly packed into a bowl. For a brief moment I have an image of Willow holding Squirmy tight to their chest, beaming at me. And then I extend my hand into a single thorned blade and stab down until everything stops moving.

I advance down the line, pulping the gruesome contents of every head. My breath vents from me in awful rasps, and I can barely see through my vision swimming with bloody sap. The transformation means I can't cry, and so my body breaks down the emotion in other ways. I don't know how to process this gruesome mechanical work of exterminating aliens hatching in the bodies of dead humans. Am I killing alien babies? Is that what kind of monster I've become? Or are these all part of the same network, another tip of the alien invasion into our world, using our bodies as fertilizer to extend the reach of the gods that would devour us all? How disappointed would Pear be if they could see me now, a monster stomping through the darkness?

At the end of the line, I'm on the verge of stabbing down, when I realise this person's skull is intact. They're smaller than the others, a kid who avoided the slicing tentacle descending from the sky. I fumble at their neck to disconnect them, and nestle them into a hollow near my heart.

Maybe I can do one good fucking thing in all this. "You'll be okay. I've got you. We'll get out of here and—"

Fuck me. There's a whole other line of bodies across from me, heads neatly sliced open. One of them gets to their feet. The top of their head is still open, tentacles overspilling to frame their face like an alien Medusa. A single eye flares with purple light.

"Harvest." Blood spills from its mouth. "You stop the harvest."

"Yes, I fucking do. Make your babies the old fashioned way, and leave these people alone."

"You are stealing. Give it back." The figure flails one limp arm in my direction, as if they're too boneless to point. "We need hosts."

"Hard fuck no on that. You've taken more than enough."

Another stalk alien breaches the fog. I begin sharpening my arm into a scythe again, but the new arrival collapses, a husk whose insides are disintegrating into milky froth. Its broken eye bathes me in light before sputtering out, and it gives a faint, dying mew.

"We must create many," the once-human thing in front of me demands. "This world is inimical to us. You cannot take potential hosts. The numbers are too great, and the gods only want more."

Other bodies along the line unfold to standing positions. "Give us the host. We must have it."

"You're not getting the goddamn kid."

They're already upon me, crowding around like I'm a celebrity. I lash out with wild swings, smashing through fragile chests with my horned arms and pulping tentacle brains to mulch. My main logistical problem is trampling over all the fallen bodies. The kid's cradled in next to my heart, still pale and unmoving although the pulse at her neck trips faintly.

The last falls with a faint squelch, and I take a deep breath. Right, time to—

"Little sib!" Oh fuck. My voice, coming through the murk. "You finally showed your face."

"Hadylan," I sneer, although it still sounds too much like *hey, Dylan*. "Back for round two?"

"They told me I died." My double saunters out of the mist. They're not wearing a protective suit, and look annoyingly chipper dressed in a big black coat like Pear's that flares out around them. There's a numb punch of rage in my chest. "I remember none of it. Apparently you stabbed me savagely through the heart and I died in your arms. Was it a beautiful scene, holding your sweet sibling close as they breathed their last?"

We prowl around each other, two fighters in a ring full of dead bodies and green smoke.

"You told me of your rebellion. And said even the gods must serve."

"*We* must serve." Their lip curls into a sneer. "Although I am close to a god now, an infant deity clawing towards transcendence. And once I have uprooted all your clinging vines from the dank Mutopian soil, I shall become incarnate."

"I think I'll kill you last." I jab a fist full of thorns towards their face. "So you can watch as I gut your fucking alien overlords and turn them into funeral pyres."

Their smile gets wider and the tip of a tentacle flickers at the corner of their mouth like a swollen purple tongue. "Petty, mewling Dylan. You're good at killing humans, I'll grant you that. But you have no conception of what it takes to slay a god."

"I'll figure it out as I go. I've got a pretty good track record with this shit. And fuck you, I never claimed to be a perfect hero. But I'm not going to stand by and let your asshole bosses feed on humanity."

I lunge at them again, slamming a heavy fist into their chest. Blue fluid seeps up around the wounds but they don't even hit back. They only look at me with the same sneering expression.

"I do not understand you, sibling. The lie of the Eirini is compelling because humanity has fouled this planet as if it's their personal toilet. They're a dead-end prey species, only fit to be fed on. Even your society understands this, constructing an elaborate system for the wealthy to prey on everyone else. At least our gods are truly powerful."

"Fuck your gods."

"Always with the attitude. Humans don't deserve this planet, and you know it."

I shrug. "Guess I figure they deserve a chance to fucking fix it rather than being eaten."

Hadylan sighs. "You do amuse me enormously. Very well, I shall let you live if you give me this worthless human child you carry."

"Wow." I burst out laughing in the middle of all this carnage and horror. "That's quite the fucking deal you're offering. But she's a kid, and I'm not going to let her be part of your alien feeding quota."

Their mouth curves. "You would die for her."

I shift my biomass around to protect the kid behind a layer of wood. It's very uncomfortable, but I can't risk leaving her for the aliens. "I'd kick your ass for her. That's a lot more fun."

Now Hadylan comes at me, coat swinging open to reveal a squirming mass of tentacles bursting out from their pale skin. Their chest is flat and smooth, very faintly purple. I let them wrap tentacles around my wrists and pull me in nice and close.

It's strange looking into their eyes, so much like mine aside from the slight flare of purple, as if their pupils are occluding a glowing violet sun that burns in their brain. I slam both my fists into their chest, thorns shredding the clammy flesh of their tentacles. Once I'm buried up to the elbow inside them and haven't found a goddamn heart, I change tack and start to bloom.

There's a tentacle wrapped around my neck, squeezing so tight my skeleton's cracking. Sap beads at the splits in my skin, vines wreathing me. Flowers open inside their chest, a whole wild garden of them, desperately flaring their petals wide like poison frills. This is no ecosystem built for them, these fragile Earth blossoms. Their roots drown in my duplicate's freezing blood, and they wilt, clogging my sibling's system with decaying sludge.

Hadylan's eyes bulge inside their skull. Tentacles flutter, suckers expanding to show tiny mouths, fringed with delicate tendrils and ringed with curving fangs. I cling tighter, my whole body jutting with spikes, sinking into them like a body into a swamp. They're desperate, thrashing in my grip, skin peeling off their arms as they wrap more tentacles around me. *Now* it fucking hurts, trying to protect this kid while my whole body falls apart. Even the vines can't hold me together.

My sap is slowly poisoning them, purple froth spilling from their lips. The glow in their eyes is dimming, purple ebbing to black as darkness encroaches.

The two of us locked together, a Dylan from each world.

One of us is going to die first.

It better fucking be them.

CHAPTER 35
EVEN THE GODS CAN DIE

I OPEN my eyes and I'm looking at weak sunlight. I'm almost mostly back in human form, and I feel like someone has hit every inch of me with rocks.

"The kid," I croak. "Where's the kid?"

"She's fine." Dani's beside me, clutching my hand. Surges of vitality pulsing through our plant connection. "Everyone's been more worried about you. Alyse and I found you fighting Hadylan, both completely fucked up. Your horrible sibling bailed pretty quick, so we didn't manage to kill them. In the good news column, we also managed to find the machine generating that gas. Rescue efforts are going a lot better now."

I sit up, and instantly regret it with the pounding in my head. "They were doing terrible things."

"Yeah." Dani looks grim. "We saw. People being turned into alien hosts."

"One of the aliens *spoke* to me. It's all fucked up for them too. Our world isn't suited for them and they're getting sick. You saw the planet they come from when we passed through their universe. There's no *sun*. But their gods have fucking quotas for how many humans they can turn."

"Jesus." She closes her eyes. "That's—"

"Fucked on top of fucked. These gods don't care about anyone or anything except their own worship. They'll destroy their own children to teach us a lesson." I swing my legs off the cot I'm resting on, and determine that I *can* stand, even though it hurts a lot. "Now it's time to teach them one back."

"What about reprisals?" Her hazel eyes are worried when she looks into mine. "What if they make more places like this all over the world?"

As bitter, sore, and honestly fucking sad as I feel about what went on in the alien fog, it's made something very clear to me. "They're going to kill us all anyway. If not with alien bombs, they'll turn us into hosts, or devour us whole, or remake the world in their image. They don't give a fuck about anything but growing themselves."

"Violet called them corporations made flesh," Dani says, with a tiny smirk.

"There's a reason we love her." I entwine my hand with Dani's. "But we need to figure out how to kill them."

Dani leans into me. "That's a lot of gods to kill."

"We start with one and go from there. Find a way to mulch Hadylan on the way. I know it's not going to be easy, because these things scared Cybele into running away, and Tentacle Princess into hiding. But what, are we going to let them take over the fucking earth?" I let out an enormous sigh. "Now I'm going to have to talk everyone else into agreeing with this shit."

"Already done." She raises an eyebrow at me. "Oh, stop

gaping at me like that. It was easier than you think. Everyone here's itching to hit them back."

"Any progress on the other weapon?" I ask.

Dani shakes her head. "The puzzle box still eludes me. But we might have another angle. There's another mutant here, sort of like Forge from the X-Men."

"You mean an inventor type?" I let her pull me out of the tent.

"Exactly, and she's got some interesting ideas on what might kill these things."

We weave our way through the tents until we reach an open area with a bunch of folding chairs sitting around a campfire. It's our team plus Decker. The only people I don't recognise are a tall woman who looks more exhausted than anyone I've ever seen, and a scrawny woman with a denim jacket and bright blue hair that cascades down her back almost to her ass.

"Chatterbox, back in the land of the living," Decker drawls. "Thought you might not make it."

"I've been dead before." I take the last spare seat, folding myself awkwardly into it. "Let's move on to killing bigger things and making new friends."

"We've met." The tall woman extends her hand. "Soft Touch."

"Oh, yeah. Texas forever." I take her hand and squeeze it, then glance at the person sitting beside her. "And you must be…"

"Meddle." She gives me a nod. "Because I'm always meddling with shit. And hell yeah, Texas forever. Plenty of good people here, despite the assholes. Nobody's running me out of my—"

"Nobody's going to," I say. "Live where you want. Only thing I care about right now is killing gods."

"Huh." Meddle nods slightly more emphatically this time. "Maybe we'll get along after all."

"Right." I adjust my seat and almost tip out of it. "Dan, let's hear the plan. You've got one, right?"

"Me and Vi have been bouncing around ideas. Phase two of the so-called intake procedure is starting to roll out across the world. It would be great to hit them *before* they start swallowing people, so I think our first attack should be in Tokyo Bay. It's the most populated area and has the most people swayed by the docility rays." She takes a deep breath. "So then the problem is how to hurt them, given what we've seen a nuke do."

Meddle makes an irritated growl. "I've been working on these devices that burn through alien flesh, so maybe we can make enough holes in one to sink it."

"Or make enough holes to plant flowers," Dani says. "We've got our hybrids and we know those affected Hadylan. Hopefully they'll act like an infection and make them sick, give us time to blow them apart properly." She finishes talking and sits back, eyes calm on mine as she waits for my response.

My brain chugs through everything. "This is close enough to a plan. We'll use Keepaway to teleport us around and poke enough holes in this fucking thing that they look like a fancy doily." I blush as everyone stares at me. "What? My grandparents had them when I was growing up. They're like little crochet things with lots of holes. Fuck you all. Make up your own fucking metaphors. The point I want to make, if you'd all stop *laughing* at me about doilies, is that we're going to start by hitting two of them. One after the other. If those work, we roll out the rest hard and fast. Whichever works. Give them as little chance to react as possible."

Violet nods slowly, and reaches into her pocket to remove the pairstones. "And first up, we've got Lilith's gun."

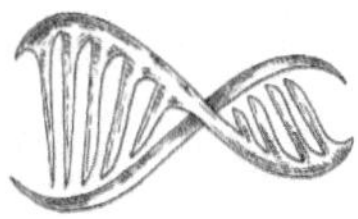

WITH THOUSANDS upon thousands of docile humans queueing at ports, we don't have much time for preparation. The pair-stones are our simplest option, and we know they work at a small scale. Nobody's sure of how effective they'll be on a whole alien. At the very least, it should hurt a lot.

I'm trying not to obsess over every detail of the plan. Keep everything flexible, focus on the very next thing.

Step one: teleport into the middle of a god temple.

"Be safe." Dani and Violet take turns kissing me fiercely.

"I'm invading an alien and waiting for my girlfriend to fire a bullet at me from orbit."

"Don't wait too long before bouncing out of there," Dani says in exasperation.

I roll my eyes. "Keeps won't let me accidentally get shot."

"No." Keepaway's face is still shadowed by traces of blue, the alien infection stubbornly persistent. Decker has threads of it winding all across her face, but Soft Touch has said it's cosmetic only. I guess it works for the aesthetic. Keeps offered to do this job themselves, but I'm not letting them do it alone. "Don't worry, Dani."

"There are about ten thousand terrible scenarios playing themselves out in my head constantly."

"So exhausting." I lean in and kiss her softly. "I'll be fine. We'll be in round two before you know it."

"That's less reassuring than you think." She pulls me close again. "I can't lose you, Dylan."

I don't say anything, just press my lips against her forehead and hold them there. Maybe there's power in these simple statements, some basic cosmic principle of desperation that keeps us clinging to life when everything's falling apart around us. If I'd said more to Pear, made it clear how important they were to my world…

"Let's go." Keepaway's standing right behind me. "I'm nervous waiting."

"Okay." I squeeze both Dani and Violet's hands one last time and step backwards. "Showtime."

THE INSIDE of the alien ship is vast and empty when Keepaway and I appear. The wine-dark sea is choppy and tempestuous, splashing up over the pathways that crisscross it. All the tentacles that hang from the central Tower lie dormant, making it look overgrown. A whispery hum emanates from it, like it's sleeping. Maybe digesting.

We're going to re-enact the tarot card and hit it like a lightning strike.

"Spooky," I whisper, and Keepaway flinches.

I jog lightly across the first of the pathways, which stays dark under my feet. Keepaway trails me as we zig-zag across. There's no indication anything inside is aware of us. Too busy waiting for barges of human snacks to arrive in their waiting mouths.

At the centre, I drop the pairstone at the base of the tower. The hanging tentacles drift with the rhythm of the ocean.

"Violet?" I tap my ear.

"In place."

"Just dropped the target."

"Releasing. And Dylan, please—"

Keepaway pops me out before Violet even finishes the sentence. We both reappear in my car Roxy, who's floating over the ocean a sensible distance away from the bulk of the alien. I don't have much cause for driving these days, but we keep hanging around together because we're family. Dani flings her arms around me.

"I told you I'd be fine. Keepaway was very—"

A finger of fire traces down out of the sky, a single blazing line through the atmosphere. One stone, calling to another. The air flickers, and Violet reappears in Dani's lap.

"Am I—?"

There's a flash of light that overloads what plant-life optic nerve equivalent I have. I can actually stare into the sun since my transformation, but this is like having the sun punch me in the face. Roxy hurtles backwards, the massive change in air pressure slapping her away from the explosion.

Someone's swearing a lot. It sounds like Keepaway. We're all clutching at each other.

"Oh my," Roxy says.

My vision comes back in fits and starts, images slowly resolving out of a wash of light. I must be looking in the wrong direction, because the ocean looks empty. I swivel around, but the wide expanse of water extends all around us.

"How far did we get knocked?" I ask.

Roxy drifts down close to the surface. It teems with chunks of flesh, like some fishing vessel has spilled a torrent of butchered carcasses. Then we spot something huge under the surface, a scorched slick of flesh that's slowly sinking, setting the water above to a simmer.

"Jesus Christ." I feel light headed looking at it.

Roxy's wheels are almost touching the water. I lean myself

out of the window to get a better look at the gory mess. "It's like the fucking thing was put in a microwave."

"Let's hope it can't heal from something that big," Dani says.

We stare into the ocean for a while longer, but the pieces are sinking and show no signs of reforming.

"Now how do we get the pairstones back?" I ask.

Violet shakes her head. "I can't see any sign of them. I think we pushed them too far and don't get another shot."

"Shame." Dani watches the alien husk sink lower. "They definitely work."

"Yes, but now we know the gods can die." The pump of my heart kicks with savage joy.

CHAPTER 36
TEAM EFFORT

WE MAKE A VERY QUICK STOP BACK at the Free States to pick up Meddle and her enormous bag full of alien bombs. She's almost giddy.

"You seen this shit?" Her phone waves wildly in front of my face.

"We were there," I assure her. On video you can actually see the damn thing come apart, chunks of it arcing through the air, flames and smoke pouring from the gutted interior before it sinks *fast*.

People's initial responses are wildly different depending on how close they are to a docility ray. You're either excited that people have struck back against a terrifying otherworldly menace, or furious that people have dared to risk our ticket offworld. The reports from Tokyo are definitely from the first column. A lot of rapid changes of heart now that the docility ray has been destroyed. The aliens rush to discredit them, claiming it's the work of mutants. Hadylan is even trotted out to do a speech about how dangerous all the other mutants are.

I try very hard to ignore this shit and focus on attacking the next alien. We're going for the one near Australia, partly because of home court advantage and partly because it's the smallest. I'm really fucking nervous, because this is our reusable plan. If this works, we'll take them all down. There's so much riding on this that I want to scream. At least nobody wants to stall for once in my fucking life.

Meddle teleports first, then Hench, Violet, Feral, and Alyse. They're all using different methods to make holes in the vast bulk of alien flesh, then Dani and I will come along and plant seeds in them. I'm so fucking nervous I want to throw up. I haven't felt this scared since the beginning, showing up on Tremor's goddamn doorstep with a baseball bat. Hopefully this goes better. I don't have Batty to pull my ass out of the fire this time. Only one of the casualties of my life.

Thinking about him tips me into yet another spiral. I'm increasingly convinced we're all going to die on this mission. It's a complex trap and we'll end up like those people in the Free States dead zone, nothing but fertile soil for aliens to grow in.

As each member of our team leaves, I get more agitated. There's too much riding on this. I'm not coherent or competent enough to save the goddamn world.

"We can do this." Dani squeezes my hand tight, right before Keepaway sends her off. I'm the last to go.

"Tell me something pretty, Keeps." I swallow hard.

"You're my hero, Dylan," they say softly. "And my friend."

"Don't make me cry, you asshole." I wrap my arms around their slim shoulders. "I'm supposed to have mission face."

"You'll be okay." They touch my shoulder.

When the world snaps back into focus, I'm standing in a trench about a metre deep. It looks like rough sacking-like material the colour of sun-baked rust. The trench winds ahead of me, ragged apertures torn into the sides like crude gills. There's nobody else around, and I'm about to tap my head to check my comm when the ground in front of me explodes.

A drenched, muscular figure surges up out of the hole, digging her fingers into the ground and dragging herself into the trench. I'm pretty sure it's Hench, based on size alone, but it's hard to tell through all the slime.

"Dylan." She gives me a nod. Hench and I haven't totally bonded, but Fairy is besotted and that's so cute I can help but like her. "Turns out I can punch my way through these things."

"Hench smash." I pat her shoulder and then wipe my hand not-so-surreptitiously on my pants. I fall to my knees beside the hole and poke my head in. Underneath is a tunnel of oozing flesh with tiny writhing veins threaded through. Below, every-thing's far too dim to make out. "What's down there?"

"Tunnels. Access chambers. Didn't go that far, just sort of punched my way in and then smashed my way out again. You asked for holes so..." She points downwards and grins.

"You delivered." I grimace and reach my entire hand in as deep as I can. Blooming is usually second nature to both Dani and I, but with Cybele's absence it takes a lot more effort, espe-cially coming up with the hybrid flowers we want to use. They have an outer sheath made of the flowers we assimilated in the underground chambers, with seeds grown from the Crown of Cybele's forest. As soon as I feel the flowers take root, I jump up again.

"Next," I tell Hench, and she leaps forward in a single enor-mous bound, far too quickly for me to keep up with. I tug on my connection to Dani, and she sends a flood of reassurance back. She's busily pouring flowers down the holes Meddle is making with her incendiary devices, and the others are busily gouging furrows through the alien flesh to give our vines free rein.

So far, nothing's going wrong.

For a whole blissful thirty-four minutes, it stays that way. We race across the alien's surface, punching holes and growing flowers. We're building a complex connected network, weaving our own disguised flowers into the alien's skin. And right now we're getting away with it.

When we get a reaction, it's predictably gross. A swaying mosquito-like thing, flapping on leathery wings with a reservoir of purple liquid suspended in a thin sac below its body. The worst part about it is the size—the goddamn thing's nearly as big as Roxy and descends on me fast, while I'm buried up to the armpits in one of the holes Hench has punched.

I'd probably get a three-part stinger to the face if not for Violet unfolding herself from the air in front of me. She's little more than a smirk and five slashing blades that turn the thing into flaps of skin and a gentle rain of fluid. It's only the first of a whole horde, and before long I'm scurrying along behind a blurry shield of Violet's blades, constantly splattered by alien goo that hisses and spits on my skin like I'm a hotplate. Dani's going through a similar process, except with Feral as her protector.

The mosquitos keep coming, more of them by the second until they're almost blanketing the sky.

"We need to get out of here," I cough into the comm, trying to get the fried-egg taste of alien goo out of my mouth. "And hope it's enough."

Ahead of me, Hench flails wildly amongst a cloud of the

mosquito-drones while Violet whirls around her like a tornado of knives. It's starting to feel like we're losing control of the situation and when Hench disappears, I'm relieved because it means I'm next. I barely feel Keepaway's touch on my arm, but I reappear with everyone else crammed into Roxy.

Meddle finally looks to be experiencing another emotion than smirking or stoicism—in this case shuddering disgust. "Fuck those fucking things."

Those fucking things in question have a taste for our flesh, because the whole swarm lifts off the alien and is headed straight for Roxy.

"No time for crying," I tell Meddle. "Light that thing up, and let's hope we did enough."

She gives me something that might pass for a smile, and hits the big red button on a device that's strapped to the inside of her wrist.

Nothing happens.

The awful pit in my stomach is yawning wider and wider, and I'm tumbling headlong into it.

And then we see it bloom.

Lines of rippling green race across the surface of the alien as the vines burst into flower, thirsty root systems grappling for purchase in the flesh, and splitting it wide. At the same time, all the incendiary devices fire, blowing gaping holes that quickly fill with flowers. Amongst it all, the alien falls apart in grotesque slices, as if it's being peeled by hungry green fingers. It's a surreal sight, especially with the Sydney Opera House as a distant backdrop.

The mosquito swarm turns diffuse, raining down from the sky like ash. All that's left flying is Roxy and a host of news drones, who circle the blooming carcass of the alien like they're just as hungry as the things that attacked us. Everyone loads it up on their phones, and so we all see the footage from inside. The ruins of skeletal organic machinery jut out of scorched flesh, thousands of human bodies nestled in like so many fucking batteries, packed into the soaring needle of the Tower. They're clearly dead, their corpses bloated and tentacles poking out through torn holes in their skin.

Even though I knew this shit was happening, it's still fucking horrifying to see it. Someone behind me is throwing up outside of Roxy, who's being very polite about having vomit on her paintwork. All those people died. They wanted a better life, and this is where it got them.

"Head for number three," I tell Keepaway. "We're not fucking stopping until every one of these ships is dead."

Nobody argues for a moment.

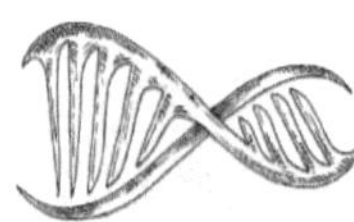

THE REACTION TIME on the next alien is a lot less than thirty-four minutes, and the plan's already fucking up even before then. It's not a problem with the holes. Hench is punching through alien flesh just as enthusiastically.

It's my seeds that won't take root.

"Performance anxiety?" Hench's expression is too serious for it to be a joke.

"Shit's fucked, yeah." I yank on my connection to Dani, and it spills the same anxiety back to me. "And it's affecting Dani too, which rules out my incompetence. Which is bad, because it means—"

Something briefly passes over the sun, and it gives my threat radar a hell of a ping. I glance up to seee an all-too-familiar figure plummeting out of the sky. Fucking Hadylan. Tentacles flare out around them like an elegant skirt.

"Get out of here." I gaze upwards. "This one's on me."

"Not how I work." Hench cracks her knuckles.

Hadylan drops lightly onto the alien's surface. They brush a curl of hair off their face."Dylan. Nasty little trick you pulled." Tentacles flicker in and out of their mouth as they talk. "It won't work a second time. We've neutralised your little hybrids."

Hench is not one for small talk. She swings back one big fist and slams it right into Hadylan's head. It explodes like a slushie machine full of gore, spraying foul-smelling chunks of marbled blue meat in a wide arc. Thankfully, I am standing out of the splash zone.

Hench half-turns towards me, a smirk on her face. "Overhyped."

A slimy grey tentacle erupts from the crumpled ruin of Hadylan's face, about as thick around as their arms. It loops around Hench's waist and tosses her casually off the side of the alien. She disappears into the distance with a scream, arms pinwheeling wildly.

"I told you I'm ascending." Hadylan's face—*my* face—slowly reassembles itself from the ruin like a movie running in reverse. "You're witnessing the first flowering of a God. I am their Star. Renewal, and new purpose." They show a scarred tattoo on their chest, a figure dipping bowls in water under the night sky.

Feral hurtles past me with a furious hiss, a streak of fur and claws.

"Fairy—" I say in exasperation, but Hadylan snatches her out of the air and tosses her in the same general direction as her girlfriend. She leaves a whole mess of claw marks behind her, but they're healing over as I watch.

"None of them matter," Hadylan tells me, as if this is a great confidence they're sharing with me. "A host of snappy little obstacles on my way to you. They'll all die in the belly of She Who Insatiably Devours, The Eternal Throat, The Lady of the Sacred Fangs. The choicest morsels for the greatest God of all." Their mouth stretches wide, a hideous blue-lipped smile with tentacles fluttering in the raw purple hole of her throat.

"I'll give her your regards when I tear down her tower." I grin right back at them.

"Apparently you're hard to kill." Hadylan opens their mouth even wider, and I see mouthparts gnashing inside. "Let's find out what happens if I eat you."

My connection from Dani pulses with urgency. If she was here, she'd be screaming *get the fuck out*. And yes, I know I need to leave, but I'm not going until I've made my sibling bleed.

Until I feel a hand touch my back lightly, and the world blinks out in front of me.

The last thing I see is Hadylan reaching for me with all their tentacles.

CHAPTER 37
THE A IN SMART GOALS

"YOU *BENCHED* ME," I shout at Dani. I've been teleported back into one of the tents in the Free States resistance camp, except it's only the two of us.

"There was zero benefit to having another fight with Hadylan. You're not going to kill them on your own. You'd end up being beaten to shit and having to waste time healing."

"Waste time? We've got nothing. It's all fucked! Everything! Fucked!"

"Right now that's true. So everyone else is resting. Taking showers. Sleeping and shit. Self-care. While we figure out what to do next." Dani holds up the puzzle box. "I'm going back to this. You can help if you want."

"Lilith fucking jerking our chains from thousands of years in the past. If she wanted us to have her weapons, she should have made it easier. No matter how damn dangerous they are." I spin away from her, but the only other thing in the room to be mad at is a table streaming footage.

The alien spokespeople are scrambling in the wake of the revelation of all the corpses in the destroyed carcass. They've got the whole gang out: Strength, Justice, the Sun and the Moon. "We understand the footage may appear distressing, but it is simply a misunderstanding. Those people seen within the carcass of the murdered craft were being healed of your mortal diseases. Our processes are far advanced compared to your primitive Earth science and—"

The footage cuts off abruptly, switching to drone shots taken from high in the air over the alien berthed in New York Harbour. There's a massive hole in the side of it, and rays of purple light are flooding out. A slick of black fluid spills into the water around it.

I'm gaping at it, almost lost for words. "Who the fuck did that? Did someone else leave Mutopia? Did another country launch a strike?"

The news anchors are talking over the footage of the wounded alien. "We've just received an email with a file containing footage from those responsible for this latest dreadful attack on the blessed Eirini fleet. Please be aware this may be distressing."

Our shot of the dead alien becomes a tiny blip in the corner of the screen, and the picture changes to a young woman with short dark hair and tired eyes. It's grainy and poorly lit, obviously taken in her bedroom at night. She fidgets with her phone and clears her throat before speaking.

"The aliens are coming back. They're asking for more. At first everyone said this was a good thing. But then my sister went in and she didn't come out. And then you see what's happening in the Free States. We're under attack by monsters, and yet nobody sees it. It's like everyone's hypnotised. I've begged the Eirini to show me a glimpse of my sister, to prove I'm not wrong. But nobody can even show me a photo. It's all so impossible to wake up and be in this world where we've been invaded and nobody seems to care."

The woman tips her head back, pale skin looking sallow under the overhead lights. "But you know what? I'm not the only one. There are so many of us who've watched our people get swallowed by these damn things. We're not going to sit back and watch this happen, let people stand there and line up to disappear inside these monsters. So we're going in with the intake and we're going to demand we get our people back. And if they say no…"

The woman lifts up the baggy plaid shirt she's wearing, showing a complex device strapped to her stomach. I recognise the stylised Q logo all too well. This is old Quietus tech from the Dark Year, a portable explosive device which uses nanotech to gain far more power than a conventional equivalent.

The clip ends and we're staring back at the ruin of the alien in the harbour. Lifeless tentacles spill like intestines from the side, and the ring of murky sludge around it is expanding rapidly. Obviously damage from the inside is far more effective than firing a nuke into the side of it, the analytical part of my brain provides.

People went in there. They blew themselves up to stop these aliens. To carry on this fight that we're supposed to be winning. More death, spreading around me like I'm contagious.

Something burns in my throat and I push my way out of the tent.

I almost trip over Meddle, sitting cross-legged on the ground amongst a wild tangle of wires and machinery. She's got a small tablet propped in front of her, watching the same broadcast.

"Ooh-rah." She flashes me another almost-smile. "Looks like we've got other people rising up."

"No." I don't know which direction to run in. "This is fucked. We're supposed to inspire people to fight, not *die*."

"We're up against gods." Meddle snips a piece of wire with calm efficiency. "Maybe fighting and dying are the same thing this time. Ain't like the aliens were just going to let anyone go were they?"

I say nothing.

"Besides." Meddle grins. "They fuckin' killed one, or at least hurt it real bad. Don't know how good you are at math, Chatterbox, but that makes three down, which feels a hell of a lot better than it did at breakfast."

I sit down opposite Meddle so I'm facing her, and watch her work for a few moments. It's almost soothing, but the panic keeps rising in my chest, and I end up blurting out exactly what I'm thinking.

"I want people to stop dying."

"Huh." Meddle twists wires, makes another snip, sets a small cylinder aside. "I think you're missing the A in SMART goals there."

"What? Oh, achievable. Fuck you. I know it's impossible. But I had someone close to me die, a long time ago now. One of my best friends, dead because of me, on some stupid mission. I failed her. Like it's not totally my fault, but you can lay a trail of responsibility to my door without twisting the truth too much. And ever since then, I've felt death haunting me."

Meddle grunts. "You're very dramatic, you know that?"

"Yes, and I make terrible decisions, as shown by me sharing my feelings with you."

"Fine." She brushes blue hair off her face. "Carry on."

"People keep dying around me, but then I cheated death.

Came back different. And we lost Emma, but we won so much. Or that's what it felt like. Like Death admitted I'd been through too much shit and deserved a reward. And I made a deal with that scything asshole where I got my island and a fucking reprieve.'"

Meddle grunts again. "My experience? Death ain't one for deals like that."

"Well, yes, spoiler alert, but death is still very much present. And when I lost Pear, I felt like I'd paid an even bigger price, so I had to get something in return. A better world, maybe. A safer world. Not one where people blow themselves up in the belly of an alien who wants to devour us all."

"What the fuck is a Pear?" Meddle frowns at me.

"My parent. A nickname, you know."

"Oh. Cute." She stills her busy hands and looks at me properly for the first time. "Sorry. Ain't easy losing a parent. Even one you hate. Mine kicked me out pretty early on in my journey. Never could stomach me being a woman. I tried to be happy when she died, but..." She shrugs expressively and returns to her work. "Point is, Death comes for everyone eventually. You cheating the way you did? That's miraculous sleight of hand shit but I don't believe there's any kind of karmic balance of whatever. Sometimes a bunch of bullshit happens, and you make the best decision you can in the face of it. Me? That usually means fighting for people that need it."

I'm down with fighting, but we need to fight smart. Which means thinking about the best move we can make with what we've got. I poke my head back in the tent. "Dan, can you come here? And bring that thingamawhatsit with you."

As soon as Meddle gets her hands on the globe, her whole face lights up. "What in the unholy fuck is this?"

"We think it's a device that Lilith made." Dani crouches

beside Meddle, reassembles the box and then runs her through the process of opening it. "But it's smart, and it learns."

"This isn't technology." Meddle runs her fingertips over the globe and sets all the beads spinning. "I know tech. It makes sense to me, like it's a language I speak, you know. Mechanics, computers, all that shit. I'm fluent. This? It's like I'm looking at something that runs on magic. I feel tongue-tied in its presence." She breaks off with an awkward laugh. "Sorry, I'm in love with this thing, but I don't understand it."

"We're going to solve it." I put my hand on Dani's shoulder. "Somehow. We'll take it to the goddamn maze and figure it out, one way or another. There's got to be some clue or—"

What interrupts is not a clue. It's someone screaming.

"Alyse." My voice comes out splintered. "Something's wrong."

WE FIND Alyse in another tent, along with the rest of our team, Agent Decker, and some other Free States people we don't know. Everyone's staring at a screen.

There's a closeup of my face on it. Except not entirely mine. One with a ruined slash of a mouth and tentacles fluttering inside it.

"My name is Dylan Taylor," they rasp. "I have made myself a monster, time and again, for you people. To save this shithole planet. And once more I have *transformed* myself." They break off into laughter. "And now some scared little mutants came to huddle in the shadow of the Eirini." The camera pulls back jerkily in fits and starts. They're in a small room, the living area of some cheap house. None of that's what my eyes are drawn to. It's the five bodies, still positioned on the furniture in gruesome parodies of relaxation.

The blood, everywhere. Sprays and pools of it.

"The fuck?" I whisper.

Hadylan shakes one of the corpses roughly, as if it'll wake up and agree. "Do you think anyone can possibly stop them? They are Gods come to this world. They are the singing voids and you should worship them, because they are *inevitable*."

My voice is high, panicked like a bird trying to escape a small room. "Those mutants came for safety, and Hadylan tore them apart to *taunt* me. To send some sick message."

"It's revenge." Violet's voice is surprisingly steady. "You hurt their gods, and so they hurt you."

"More people dying." My head is full of static and dead leaves. "Everyone's dying."

"No." Dani puts her arm around me. "I know this is a day of awful things, but we're still here."

"They're not." My voice is a haunted thing. "Those mutants. They died thinking I was a monster. Or maybe I am. Maybe Hadylan is closer to me than I'd like to think. How many people have I murdered, Dani? All this blood behind me, and the future is nothing but more and more death."

"Dylan." Her voice cracks, and she nestles her head into my neck. Violet's on my other side, and Alyse is there too, one hand on my back like an anchor.

"Keepaway." Alyse's voice is hoarse. "Take us to the Serpentine Lakes site. Now."

CHAPTER 38

SATOR AREPO TENET OPERA ROTAS

I DON'T KNOW what to say when we arrive at the labyrinth, so I plunge into it without any discussion. Even though I know it's impossible that my fury will unravel it for me. I've embarrassed myself enough, screeching about death and horror like some shadowy harbinger perched on the wall between the present and the future.

It feels good to have something that can potentially be solved. A flicker of hope that I'm fixating on, and I'm aware that it's the slenderest fucking thread, but I cling to it all the same. My hope is that the first mutant will reach out from the past and provide me with something so that I don't end up being the last mutant. It's been literally thousands of years since Lilith abandoned her computer in what would one day grow into the Weirdlands, but we have to solve her mystery. Otherwise, I have the horrible, gnawing sensation that I'm out of options.

Seven hours later, I stumble out with nothing to show for it. The others have achieved exactly as much as me, but they've got extra helpings of worry and paranoia.

"There are so many other things they could do." Feral's pacing in circles in the antechamber room that we're using as a base camp. It's got nothing in it apart from a few camping supplies and a handful of laptops. "I know it's beyond fucked, what they did, but look at what they did in the Free States. They could turn the whole world into their farms, drowning us in that awful green fog."

Dani shakes her head. "I doubt it. Those farmer aliens were already dying. Half the ones being grown were weak and sick too. They'll need to undergo a massive terraforming project before they start on that, at least based on what we saw from that glimpse of Hadylan's Earth."

"So what are they going to do?" I whisper.

"They're so focused on getting people to come on board. Like that's all they can talk about. My pet theory is that they're exhausted from crossing between worlds, and they're building their strength up before they can do anything else." Dani touches my shoulder lightly, letting me know she's aware I've returned. "Which means we might have a window to strike. If we can find this weapon."

By the end of our first day of attempting to re-map the labyrinth, Dani's optimistic theory seems to be at least partially true. There's no wide-scale reprisal, no repeat of the dead zone. The alien ships are sailing, although they've left floating platforms behind at all the original harbours, draped with all kinds of organic machinery and protected by the same forcefield bubbles Hadylan used.

"The forcefields obviously don't work at a scale big enough to protect the aliens," Violet says. "Which is good news for us.

But I'm guessing those things they've left behind are transmitters for the docility ray. They don't want to lose their grip on the humans they've already swayed."

Based on the online chatter, it seems she's correct. Most people within the radius of alien control are devastated to see their rescuers go, and full of vitriol for mutants and the turncoat humans who resisted.

"Where are they going?" Feral asks.

Dani's drawing lines on a map, trying to extrapolate the pathways. "I think they're *grouping*. Maybe coming together for protection?"

"Maybe they're more powerful together." Alyse looks haunted in the mouth of the tunnel where she waits, pale and near-transparent. "Just like we are."

"Can we stop them then?" Feral asks. "You know, before they *assemble* and shit."

"That's why we're here." I stare at the rudimentary map clutched in one hand, trying to make any sense of it at all. "Find this damn weapon, find a way to defeat these fucking things."

Unfortunately, I've got no brighter ideas than anyone else. And this doesn't seem to be a problem that we can brute force. Lilith's smarter than me, which is depressingly predictable.

I kinda hoped we had someone else who could big brain their way through the problem though.

Dani's spent the entire day working on the puzzle box. She's filled pages upon pages of a notebook with scrawled combinations. "I think it's a Sator Square."

"A what now?" I riffle the pages, but it's mostly gibberish.

"Some ancient magical palindrome code system. Look." She flips through the book to show me an example. "See how all the words palindrome themselves around so they mirror vertically and horizontally?"

I squint at the page. "Sure? Yeah, no wait, I do get it."

Dani's eyes are bright. "I think that's what we need to do. Find the words that go together to build Lilith's Sator Square."

I spin the globe around in my hands, looking down at the book, and trying to join the dots. "So what are the words?"

"That's the part I haven't figured out yet. But I'll get it. We've got to." Her eyes are literally fucking drooping as I watch them, so I kiss her forehead and pack her off to bed with promises that we'll look at it tomorrow.

The instant her breathing evens out, I set off into the tunnels alone. This time, I'm smart enough to unreel a vine behind me so that someone can track me down if they get worried. Except it leads me in a circle and I end up tripping over myself, which disgusts me so much that I sit down in the middle of the tunnel and scream at nothing and nobody.

I don't stop until I'm trembling and exhausted.

"Grieving." Alyse's voice comes from behind me. "It sort of helps, believe it or not."

"What does?" I look up at her.

"The screaming." She sits beside me and rests her head on my shoulder. "Like releasing the pressure. I go into the forest and do it until there's no more sound in me. Sometimes it takes a while."

"Aww, babe." I stroke her hair rhythmically. "It's so fucking hard."

"I know. I was following you, making sure you were okay. As okay as it's possible to be, anyway."

"I'm too tired to find my way out," I yawn. "How about pillow form?"

She laughs, and it's a much nicer sound echoing off the tunnel walls. Then she obeys, transforming into something impossibly soft and plush. "It's been a long time since we slept like this."

"Hush." My eyes are already drooping, and Alyse is so plush and gentle. "Think very, very softly."

I dream I'm wandering through the tunnels. It's like when you spend too long playing one of those mindless phone games and you can't stop tapping even in your sleep. Here I'm lost and walking, the tunnels an endless scrolling maze. I'm following Pear. I can tell it's them from their footsteps, although I only hear the memory of the sound. The scuff marks of their feet on the ground leave something like the dots and lines of Lilith's language. I stumble in the wake of them, straining to hear. There's the same rhythmic hush-shush sound from inside the green mist, except there are *words* mixed in.

We turn a corner into a tunnel lit by flickering lights. Pear stares into the darkness ahead. Poised. Waiting.

Then they turn, and speak a single word.

And I have no fucking idea what it means.

WHEN I WAKE, the only sound is the shaky breathing of Alyse beside me.

"You okay?" I whisper.

"Not really, no."

"I dreamed of Pear. They told me something, but it was in Lilith's language."

She rolls towards me. "I dream of Emma every night. Part of me loves it, to see her again. Especially those indistinguishable dreams where it could be happening. Other times when I wake up I feel like losing it all over again."

"Babe." I brush my thumb over her cheek and smear the tears into a gloss that reflects the dim light from my phone screen.

"Tonight I dreamed she was in here too. Writing a symbol on the walls." Alyse sits up and draws it in the powdery grit of the tunnel floor. I recognise it immediately. When I was first learning the language, I called it pump but it's more than that— deeper, more spiritual, like it could also be used to refer to the deep forests of Cybele, where life comes from. Together with the symbol for love, it means *heart*.

It's also one of the handful on the top left bead of the puzzle box. Alyse wipes her fingertips under her eyes as she watches me spin it slowly around until it's facing upwards.

"I'm such a mess," she says.

"You're grieving. Like me. Lilith too." An idea niggles at me as the beads slip easily under my fingers. I string the top line together to spell something like *heart/void/eternity*.

"What does that mean?" Alyse whispers.

"Grief." I reverse the pattern on the bottom line, my own heart hush-shushing in my chest as possibilities start to spill through my brain. "And this spells something like love. An eternity that fills the void of your heart. And if we spell grief down the left side and reverse it down the right... the second line could say something like *deity*."

Alyse swallows hard. "Or Goddess."

My hands tingle on the third row of beads. "And this might be wellspring, source, lifegiver. Parent." I drop the globe on the ground in front of me. I'm shaking too hard to concentrate, too overwhelmed with what this implies.

"Grief, love, goddess, parent." Alyse is shaking too. "How the *fuck* could Lilith know that it would be us here, asking this question?"

"Meddle said this was more like magic than technology. It's resonating with us."

Alyse picks the puzzle box back up and shoves it into my hand. "You already know the answer. You have to, right? It's a mirror of itself."

I already know what it is. I know the word, but I don't know what it means in this context.

"Heal." My fingers swipe the last bead into place.

There's no reaction from the box itself, but a rumbling comes from beneath us. The walls shake, as if the entire labyrinth is being reconfigured around the tiny, fragile kernel of us. These kilometres of rock, all twisting towards its new centre.

Then with a heavy, grinding sound, a section of the wall slides open beside us, revealing darkness beyond. We both turn to stare at it, like a magic trick has been performed.

"What just happened?" Her voice is barely there.

"We solved the puzzle. Grief, goddess, parent, heal, love." I have no idea if it's the only solution the box holds, but it's clearly the one we need right now.

"A message from Lilith." Alyse takes my hand. "So now we follow."

"Of course we do." And the intent is there, but something about this situation makes me terrified. The long-dead mother of all mutants has reached out and touched us, a ghost from the past, and she knows us all too well.

"I'm glad I'm with you." Alyse leans in briefly against me, her head touching mine. "To do this with my best friend. Even though it's terrifying in so many ways."

I squeeze her hand. "We've faced a lot of shit. All we need to do is step through the door."

AS SOON AS WE ENTER, lights flick on overhead. They're pale circles inset into the ceiling, with patterns that dance inside them, like playing a recording of washed out Northern Lights. The chamber is huge, bigger than anything that would make sense on any map of the corridors we've pieced together.

"Fucking reality warpers," I say under my breath.

The chamber is mostly empty. There are signs of previous activity—indentations in the floor, empty alcoves in the wall, strange stains spilled across the floor. The only object left here is a coffin shaped box in the centre of the room.

"You think that's our weapon?"

Alyse crosses over to it. "There's nothing else. It doesn't *look* dangerous."

I join her. It's filled with a foam-like substance, although there are depressions that indicate two bodies have lain there before. There's writing on the outside of it in the language we know from the puzzle box.

All it says is GRIEF in huge, ragged letters, as if someone clawed it into the surface.

"How reckless do we feel?" Alyse asks me, reaching down to prod at the material.

"We were meant to be here. Lilith chose us."

Alyse perches on the edge of the container, as if it's nothing more than a very fancy bed. "Which on the one hand is all kinds of creepy stalkerish, and on the other is almost sweet. It's probably terrible as far as moving on goes." She reaches in to trail one hand through the soft innards, but her expression quickly changes to alarm. "Uh, Dilly? It's *got* me."

"Relax your arm maybe." I join her and tug unhelpfully on her arm. "Or transform out of it?"

"I think it wants us in." Alyse's eyes have gone slightly unfocused and little sparks of light dart across her pupils. "Oh, yes. This is where we're supposed to be. Hop inside." Then she slithers over the edge of the container, half-transformed into liquid, and nestles into the depression made there. It shifts around her to perfectly contain her outline, and the sparks of light in her eyes grow brighter.

I sigh. "Trust Lilith." I walk around the other side of the container, and climb gingerly in alongside Alyse. It's very soft, and gives under my weight, very similar to how I'd imagined clouds would feel as a child. My body feels very heavy, and my extremities are slightly numb. There's something pressed against my eyelids, as if someone's forcing them down, and I can't intervene to stop them.

They flutter closed and I find myself sitting in a large bucket-type chair. We're in a circular chamber with plain white walls. There's no other furniture or features. Alyse is in an identical chair beside me, looking dazed.

"The fuck is this?" I ask her.

"The controls?" Alyse frowns. "Maybe there's a code word to activate it?"

"I don't know how to *speak* the damn language." I scowl. "Hello? Anyone? Lilith?"

A hidden aperture in the wall slides open, and someone steps into the room. Someone that makes my eyes blur with tears. She's so much like how I remember, frozen in time. The soft fall of her dark hair, the slight curve to her shoulders. Her watchful eyes on both of us.

"Ems!" Alyse tries to leap up from the chair, but she's held fast. She attempts to transform into something wraithlike to escape, but she glitches instead and returns to her normal self.

"Please do not get up from the control booth." The strange version of Emma holds up her hand. "My apologies for any emotional distress this may cause you. I am an emulation of your former lover and friend, an emotional gestalt read from your brain to function as an interface. While you remain in these chairs, you can direct the operation of this machine as if it is your own body. Two pilots can get complicated, so try not to give opposing instructions."

She steps further into the chamber with a smile, revealing another figure behind. I know this can't be real, and is only some feature of this *machine* we've gone and installed ourselves in.

"Pear," I croak, because my body and brain are telling me it's them.

"Hey, kid." Pear nods at me. "I'm your half of the equation. We perform the bridging function between your minds and this suit. It runs on ghosts. Once it was very different, but after my lover passed from this world, I infected it with my grief. It became a dangerous, mad thing, and I buried it deep. But it still calls to other haunted people."

I can't stop staring, because this ghost looks so much like my Pear that my brain keeps jittering "You're actually Lilith?"

"Partially. An encoded aspect of myself, left to operate this machine."

"So why make this place so fucking hard to find?" I scowl.

"Because it is not only incredibly powerful, but potentially dangerous to the operator. In order to interface properly, you must carry the full weight of grief. I could not leave this to accidentally destroy fragile psyches."

Well, fuck. That's super encouraging and not intimidating at all. At least she said it was powerful.

I glance across to see that the Emma projection is sitting in Alyse's lap. "You miss me terribly."

"It's too hard." Alyse is blotchy and tear-stained, hair tangled all around her face. "It's too much, every day it's hard to breathe because you're not there. You gave me life, you lived inside my head, you were my oxygen and now you're gone and what am I supposed to do?"

"You endure, my love." Emma kisses Alyse's forehead gently. "You love me, and you grieve, and you endure. Because that's what we do, even when loss overwhelms us."

I look away, because it's too much and I can't see through my tears.

"And what about you, kid?" Pear asks me.

"I keep going, but what other option do I have? You're gone and there's a gulf in me. I don't know what to do with that. I've still got all this love in my heart, but part of me has been severed too. And it's all my fault, no matter what anyone says, and I've got to live with that too."

As I talk, Pear turns pale and blood wells at the collar of their shirt, wetting the material until it glistens. I know what it looks like underneath, all that torn flesh. When I finish, they simply nod.

"Very good. We have two pilots connected. Now we can begin."

CHAPTER 39
VIOLET'S TERRIBLE IDEA

IT'S hard to imagine we're controlling a suit while we're seated in this plain white room. As soon as that thought crosses my mind, the walls turn transparent, showing the big empty rock chamber. It helps to have a sense of place. We're looking down from a higher vantage, like the coffin transformed around us into something much bigger. I have the vague sensation of *wearing* something, like I'm nestled inside a cocoon. Even with Alyse sitting beside me, and the ghostly figures of Pear and Emma watching us.

"How do we make it work?" I ask.

"Simply visualise where you would like to go." Emma waves a hand in the way she used to when describing something horribly complex as if it was comprehensible to regular humans. She's still perched in Alyse's lap, head nestled close, while Pear stands behind me like an angel at my shoulder.

"So, like, if we wanted to go back to the others?" I picture where they are, the rudimentary camp at the labyrinth entrance. Almost instantly, the scene blurs and changes. We're in the cave, surrounded with bags and laptops. From this angle, we tower over the others. They're lying on little camp beds, fast asleep. There's nobody on watch, which is sloppy. We could wake them up and tell them the news, but we could also—

"To the surface?" Alyse murmurs, and the scene shifts again. This time we're on a ridge overlooking scrubby desert and moonlit water. In the east, the horizon is lightening, a glowing line traced across it. "Wow. This is…"

"I'm tempted to go looking for an alien and see what happens."

"Careful, kid," Pear taps me on the shoulder, another eerily familiar action. "This suit does not have a weapon, and our interface with you is not yet complete."

That's all very ominous, but on the bright side, we've finally found what we were looking for. Alyse and I are currently chilling in an ancient device built by the Mother of Demons.

I let out a long breath. "Back to the others, then."

There's no reaction to our return. My emotional connection with Dani is soft and fuzzed with sleep, obviously soothed by my reassurances from earlier.

"Can we flash some lights or something?" Alyse asks.

"Lights are easy." Emma smiles faintly, and the whole room becomes bathed in a warm orange light that cycles brighter in increments to a glowing yellow.

Violet snaps awake first. "Fairy, can you see this?"

Feral leaps up, fur bristling and claws out. "You mean the glowing murder robot? Yes, Vi. Everyone can see it."

"It's me." I ask the suit to wave. "And Lys too."

At least the others are able to hear our voices projected out of the suit. Dani blinks awake and smiles up at us. The connection between us swirls with the complex mess of emotion from seeing these emulations of both Pear and Emma. There's a few moments of confusion as she sorts things out, but then she crosses to stand in front of us. "Hello, my love. I see you solved the problem."

I still have no idea what this damn thing looks like, so I send a query nudge to Dani.

The image she returns is a huge figure made of light, as if a white-hot sun was hammered into the shape of an androgynous goddess. Bladed wings flare behind us, curling inwards like a razor-edged ribcage. The expression carved into our face is a savage, beautiful cross between Alyse's face and mine. I can see why everyone's scared of it, and I've honestly got a little bit of a crush on us.

"It's definitely a good look," Dani says. "An explanation would be nice."

"Me and Lys were lost in the tunnels, but we solved the damn Sator Square. It opened a chamber with this coffin thing inside. So we climbed in and it transformed into this giant glowing robot thing."

"Better than some explanations." Dani frowns. "But an awful lot of missing pieces."

"What does it do?" Violet asks.

Alyse shrugs, and everyone recoils as our blade-wings flex. "So far all we've done is teleport around. I assume there's a gun?"

Emma looks pensive. "This is currently a craft without a weapon. We shall need to rectify that before we become fully activated."

Okay, this is what I'm used to. One more problem to solve. Step one: find a weapon.

"We were previously armed with an energy lance," Pear says. An image appears in my head of a twisted, writhing blade—a crackling arc of blue that smells of burning air. "It was destroyed in a great battle and cannot be recovered. We must find something else to wield."

Alyse and I trade glances. This seems like a job for Meddle or Science Club.

"How does this thing work?" Feral prowls around us. "Can I drive?"

I ask Pear how exiting works, and the next minute the box is standing upright at the labyrinth entrance. Alyse and I are on each side of it, blinking as if we've just woken up.

Feral reaches one claw towards it.

"No," Alyse snaps, which makes everyone freeze.

"We don't really know how it works," I explain. "But it's something to do with grief. Like, Lilith altered this when she was mourning Lucy, and I, um…" Something must surge down my connection with Dani, because she wraps me in her arms as I begin to fall apart.

"I see Emma." Alyse is pale and ghostly. "Almost as real as if she was back."

Feral blinks her huge golden eyes a couple of times and then steps towards the machine. The inner material wraps around her and moulds to her body, just as it did to Alyse, but no sparks of light flash inside her eyes. Moments later, she staggers out, looking pale.

"Ghosts." She shudders. "Only figments. Nothing that would speak to me. So what, my ghosts aren't good enough for this thing?"

I feel awkward at the way she bristles. "I don't know the rules, Fairy."

"We've all lost people," Violet says. "But Dylan's loss is very raw, and Alyse's loss is very…"

"Deep," Dani suggests.

Violet nods. "It's about being haunted. I don't think I'd see my father if I went in there, and I don't think I'd see Emma either. You do see your family, but it's not as intense because you've been healing. It's a good thing, Fairy."

"I still miss them." Feral turns aside to bury herself in Hench's arms.

"That's why you see them." I run my fingertips down the side of the box, and it feels exactly like when Pear and I used to lean in against each other, having one of our low-contact hugs. "Your ghosts will always haunt you. It's just that me and Lys still have it all in widescreen."

"It's embarrassing." Alyse stares at the ground. "A year later and I'm still a mess."

"Healing's complicated," Feral tells her. "I recommend hurting the people responsible, but it's a little harder in your case."

There's a lot that could be said about grief and healing, but my brain is chugging ahead. "The suit needs a weapon. Something that can hurt the aliens." I don't mention *fully activated*, because I have an inkling that will involve the grief part.

Violet raises her hand like she's in class. "I've been working on a theory. You might hate it."

"Very encouraging." I can't help but smile. "All the best plans begin this way."

"It's only a hunch, but let me talk it through." She pulls out her phone. "Here's the live footage of the aliens' migration.

They're coming together in the middle of the South Pacific. On the satellite footage, you can see them extending tentacles under the ocean, for miles and miles. Like forming a network."

"This sounds bad," Dani says. "Why haven't I seen this?"

"Because up until now it's been my own private conspiracy theory." Violet shrugs. "But look at the markings on them, and then this one with a spoked circle that they're clustering around. They're making the Wheel of Fortune."

I pull up the tarot on my phone and see exactly what she means. The symbols are too close to be coincidence. Another manifestation of this echo between universes.

"An element of change," Dani says.

Violet nods. "Exactly. An alteration of fortune. They're reeling from the attack and they're coming together to change their luck. My guess is the one in the middle is their queen. It's the biggest and most complex, and there are more connections running into it." She scrolls around until we've all seen it. "Like I said, a network."

I poke a finger at the screen, smack in the middle. "Hadylan talked about a big boss alien with some horrible name about mouths."

"Here's where things get weird." Violet flashes me a grin. "I think the aliens are a hive mind. Just like our slice of heaven in the Weirdlands."

A ripple of unease moves through me. "That seems like a big assumption, Vi."

"Not entirely." Her dark eyes meet mine. "I've had a little conversation with the Weirdlands and they agree with me. They're very… curious about the aliens. I think they understand they're related."

"I can't believe you made friends after they almost killed you," Feral huffs.

"They're not so bad. And besides, I like dangerous things." Violet gestures in my direction. "What I'm talking about is using one hive mind to defeat another. I was a little stuck on some details, but now you've got *this*." She gestures at the coffin beside me. "So we use your fancy new suit to wound the queen, and then when the rest of the alien hive gathers around to provide aid and succour—"

"They meet our hive." My voice is doing the grim death thing.

Violet takes a deep breath. "Yes, but there's more to all this. Making a deal with the Weirdlands. Some of it you're not going to like, but please let me finish talking. That goes especially for you, Dilly, much as I love you."

I make a show of being offended by this, even though it is one hundred percent true and fair. "Wow, rude, okay. I'll seal my lips with thorns, shall I?"

"Just tell us." Dani's voice is far gentler.

Violet's plan isn't the worst idea in the world. She wants to create our own hive mind to fight the aliens. It has another sense of echo, which I like. The problem is there are so many question marks around whether it's possible. Especially whether we can trust what lurks in the Weirdlands.

But first, I need to talk to Lilith—the version of her wearing my parent's face.

They're smiling when I climb back into the suit. "I used to worry so much about you being alone, about how wilfully self-isolated you were. And now look at you, a dazzling centre who's connected to so many hearts."

"Pear wouldn't say it like that," I tell them, a frown creasing my forehead.

"No." The emulation shrugs their shoulders in their big coat, such a vivid recreation that it gives me chills. "They would think it and say nothing, because they were afraid of their own emotions too. Their feelings had been such a jagged knife, one that tore and bit so often. They hid them from everyone. Most of all from you, because of the shadows that had already crept from their soul into yours."

I shift uncomfortably. "I don't think I like this emulation business anymore."

"It's not meant to be a comfortable reunion." Pear leans forward and stares directly into my eyes, near-perfect mirrors of my own. "Wait until we perform the activation."

"What's the point of all this?" I whisper.

"Grief." Pear shivers, and tears glisten in their eyes. "Vast, unknowable grief. Imagine designing a machine to pilot with the one you loved, perfectly attuned to work when balancing the myriad complexities of both your minds, all your gloriously meshed synchronicities working together with the sharp edges of your differences." They break off, like a knife severed their train of thought. It takes them a moment to start again. "And then they're gone. You're alone. A single mind, echoing in a void. No matter how many thousands of others exist, there was only one mind like theirs. So to use the machine again, I had to adjust it, and the only fuel I knew at the time was grief."

"I'm sorry," I whisper, because it's that uncomfortable situation where there aren't any words that will matter. The only thing that works in my experience is the presence of others, and we're talking to the shade of Lilith across a gulf of thousands of years. I can't even paddle a single small canoe into the overwhelming ocean of her grief, even though my friends have launched a whole flotilla into mine.

"I am only an echo now," Pear says. "Far more Ness Taylor than Lily of the Valley People. But I thank you for your words all the same, and apologise for what is to come in the activation process. Your lover Violet's information is highly valuable. I think we can definitely work with this, and forge a weapon capable of defeating our foes." There's a long, awkward pause. "As long as you and sweet Alyse survive."

CHAPTER 40
RETURN TO THE VALLEY OF THE WEIRD

I DON'T TALK about that ominous shit. If we survive. It stays within the small private ocean of grief that floats inside me, one even Dani can't fully reach. There might be a storm coming, but I'll weather it.

"We're going to do this," I tell everyone. Despite this being terrifying and overwhelming, the emotions that flare in my head are of comfort and reassurance and home. Even though they're only simulations, having a version of Pear and Emma is a gift I can't pass up. It could be a hell of a drug, but that's a problem for Future Dylan. And if I've learned anything, it's that Future Dylan is always mad at Past Dylan for *something*, so there's no reason for Present Dylan to worry. "Let's go to the Weirdlands. For those of you who haven't been, keep your fucking hands to yourself and don't poke anything, no matter how enticing it looks. We'll go first, and then everyone can follow."

Alyse is curled in her pilot's chair, gazing at Emma with an expression of such tenderness that I feel like I'm intruding. There's a bigger worry for Future Dylan. How will we prise her out of here when the fighting's done?

"Meet you there." I blow Dani a kiss.

The suit takes only an instant to arrive, appearing at the science husbands' camp. The plan is to head for the mysterious cave to talk directly to the hive mind. This time, we're here to negotiate, and Violet's on friendly terms.

The shacks have become overgrown in our brief absence. Crooked branches jut from the roofs of the original buildings, each laden down with tiny rooms that grow like fruit, with circular windows and flickering lights. A burbling stream snakes its way past us—literally burbling like a thoughtful old person trying to figure out the solution to a particularly difficult problem—and colourful rings of stone levitate over the top of each other, landing with a splash as if they're fighting to reach some stony spawning ground deeper in this strange place. The trees have grown too, weaving together to begin the formation of a vast canopy. Each leaf has a small, expressive face, peering down with varying degrees of interest.

Violet arrives first, presumably coming through the passages in the world.

"Hi." Violet waves up at the leaves. "We're here to talk to the hive. You probably recognise me, although you usually see me in a different form."

The world hums a single resonant note in response. It sounds positive, almost joyful, but it still puts me on edge because this alien place is *big*, and it obviously doesn't run on logic we understand.

The others appear one by one, sent along by Keepaway, but my attention is caught by a smaller, but equally joyful noise from inside the nearest hut. Then, framed in the doorway, naked to the waist and with a glowing scar on his chest—

"You assholes!" I shout. "You're supposed to be hiding, not poking the hive! We rescued you, for fuck's sake, and here you are again."

I don't know what Dr. Bobosy Wolus thinks exactly, with an enormous glowing mech suit storming down the gentle hillside towards him, but he chooses to fall to his knees.

"Please do not harm me, oh mighty hive," he intones.

I make the suit bend down until its incandescent gaze is very close to the cowering scientist. "I'm not the hive, you dick. I'm much scarier."

He rolls onto his back and squints up at me. "Chatterbox?"

Another booming voice comes from deeper inside the shack. "Bo? Please tell me you didn't invoke the name Chatterbox."

"Get your ass out here too, Burke!" My voice is obviously changed by the suit into something even more horrible than usual, because Wolus cringes back even further and Burke comes slithering out on his belly.

"Calm down," Alyse murmurs. "You're scary enough already."

Dani steps up beside the suit, peering up at me and placing her hand against the smooth exterior. "I understand you're enjoying this, Dills, but it might be good to have these two onside. They're familiar with this place too."

"It *is* Chatterbox," Burke whispers. "But transcendent."

"Transcendentally pissed off," I tell them. "How did you get out of Mutopia? You better not have ripped a hole in the veil?"

"What veil?" Wolus regards me with a look uncannily like worship, and I don't like it. "We left days ago, as soon as we were healed, and have been distracted since then. This place still calls to us, although this time we have not... assimilated." He casts a slightly nervous glance over his shoulder at Burke.

"The hive is behaving differently," Burke says. "It seems cautious. Less voracious than it once was."

"So you don't know anything about the alien invasion?" I ask, only slightly impatient.

"Uh." More glances are exchanged, and Wolus coughs. "Which aliens exactly? The hive itself is—"

"I'm not talking about *them*. I mean giant ones floating in the fucking ocean! Who've come from another universe and have been eating people."

"Um, no." Burke blinks rapidly. "We are not aware of that development, although it does explain some of the hive's odd responses."

"You've been flirting with the damn hive, haven't you?" I snap. "Trying to get it to infect you. And it's been behaving after Violet told it off. I'd like to throw the pair off you into a very deep hole, but we've got more important things to do. Now can you please take us to the hive?"

"The hive is everywhere," Wolus says grandly, gesturing with both arms.

"I want the hungriest bit. Where you wanted us to go last time."

The science husbands exchange more glances.

"This is a very difficult situation." Burke prostrates himself again. "Let me explain our dilemma in the hope you will show mercy. We are terrified of you, but we love and worship the hive. If you destroy it, you will be ending the life of one of the most astonishing scientific discoveries in history."

I glare down at the cowering scientists. "Fuck's sake. I want to slap you again, but this damn suit would probably take your head off."

"Very likely," Pear comments dryly, but luckily nobody else can hear them.

"We're not here to kill the hive," I continue. "We want to *talk* with it. You can lead the way and help grovel."

Burke and Wolus blink at me as if they're waiting for that damn catastrophe sword to descend on their heads.

"Please," Dani says. "I know it's disconcerting seeing Chatterbox in this form, but the situation outside is dire, and we need the hive's help."

"We do not want to *bargain*, exactly, in this situation," Wolus says carefully. "But in exchange for this assistance, we would appreciate your approval to continue our research as we see fit."

"That sounds like a fucking bargain," I growl. "But honestly, fuck it. If we get through this in one piece, you're welcome to poke as many of your eager little fingers into as many horrifying eldritch mouths as you feel like."

"That is many, many mouths," Wolus says, and I can't even tell if he's joking.

I lean my furious, incandescent face in towards him. "Now take me to the fucking hive, or it'll be my mouth you get a good look inside first." In the images from Dani, my throat glows like the sun, silhouetting the black barbs of wickedly curved fangs.

The two scientists pull themselves together enough to put some clothes on, and we set off through the valley as the sun melts itself into the horizon like radioactive candy. The ground underfoot crumbles like cake, and the trees entangle themselves together in whispering cliques that fall silent as we pass them and then take up their enthusiastic discussion again when we're gone. There's a path that winds between what might have been hills once but are now caverns of moss-covered bone that gleam and chime with the onrush of evening. Mist rises from the ground, plucking in gentle strands at our ankles as we walk.

In the throat-like hollow between the hills, no light falls. It's trapped in glowing bubbles in the air above, filtering pale circles down onto the path. The air feels thicker here like we're wading through it, an uncomfortable pressure building as we descend. The dimly lit walls of bone are damp with moisture, which trickles down in crooked rivulets until it pools at the base into a wide, shallow lake of milky liquid that seems lit from within. The two scientists pause at the edge, looking back at us with identical expressions of uncertainty.

"The membranous layer may be off-putting to descend through," Burke says. "But the hive exists more purely within than without."

"I'll go first," Violet says. "They know me. Sort of. Plus, if it all goes to shit, I'm very good at stabbing my way out." She blows a kiss and then trots up to the edge of the pool, slipping between the scientists and into the water. There's a shrill sound like very thin glass shattering and Violet is gone.

I know I'm supposed to wait, and let her speak with the hive alone, but I refuse to be a moment late again, like I was with Pear, especially while their emulation is standing there, looking at me with calm eyes.

I ask the suit to take us inside. The strange geography and twisted rules of the Weirdlands don't bother this machine of Lilith's at all. It's all *place* to them, regardless of where it sprung from. With a single step, we're underground. The cave is around the size of a school hall, with colourful vines strewn like cables across the ground. The rock walls glow faint blue, but the only thing that grows here are clusters of those odd slouch-hat mushrooms that look like old men and smell like old meat.

Pear sighs. "I remember trying to figure out a solution to this place. Back in my day it was a buried seed, only occasion-ally sprouting in tiny amounts. Never got around to fully solving it. There were so many things to do." It's Lilith again, and it leaves a strange echo of hurt, to lose the thread of Pear again. "Now this place has grown vast, presumably due to the presence of a resurgent Cybele."

"This is why our plan is going to work. It's like Dani's hybrid flowers. Using one similar species to invade another." I take a shuddering breath. "But right now there's a bargain to strike, and that's the part which scares me."

The far wall is laden with more fungi, each arranged around large gems inset into the stone, glowing dully in many shades of green. It's the only thing that can possibly be the hive, borne out by how close Violet is standing.

She glances over her shoulder as we enter. "Dilly and Lys." She holds out her hand to us. "I didn't think you'd be able to stay away."

"Her," I murmur, and the suit transports itself across the cave to stand protectively beside Violet. It's very convenient, being able to move around like this. I could definitely get used to it, especially while sitting in a comfortable chair. The ghost of my dead parent at my side is something a little thornier.

"How's it going?" I ask Violet.

"We're still doing pleasantries. They're happy to see me."

I grumble inside the suit. "Maybe because they think you're food."

She arches one eyebrow, like she's caught the habit from Dani. "I've made it *very* clear that I'm not on the menu."

"We're Chatterbox and Moodring, friends of Violet."

The lights flicker more erratically, complex patterns shifting like washes.

"Is that good?" I ask.

Violet shrugs. "I've never looked at it from this side. I don't know how to read it."

"Let's hope these science assholes can. I don't want any miscommunication."

A series of chimes from behind us signals the arrival of everyone else, coming in one at a time. Wolus and Burke bring up the rear, talking excitedly about the glory of the hive and how fascinating various things are.

"We can translate," Burke assures me, braids bouncing. "At least some things. We know about *hungry* and *knowledge* and *the inchoate sense of belonging.*"

"Can you communicate with this?" Alyse asks Emmulation. "Or help us do it?"

Emma tilts her head slightly, a curious and stubborn expression on her face that's so much like the original I find myself blinking tears away. "Yes. I think so. We are remarkably…"

"Can we touch it?" Alyse asks Emma.

The suit extends one arm and presses it against the wall. Every single gem lights up, bathing us all in a cold, pristine radiance like moonlight filtered through a forest canopy.

When the hive speaks, its voice sounds like hundreds speaking at once.

"Hello, mother."

CHAPTER 41
THE PUREST IDEAL OF A WEAPON

"MOTHER?" Alyse asks. "What do you mean?"

"You carry an aspect of the mother," the hive says, the gems flashing in complex patterns like they're readouts displaying the results of unknowable processes. "The one you call Cybele. Is this not correct?"

"We do." I'm hesitant about how much to say.

"When the green tide flowed through the earth, it helped us grow, to become wild and verdant. Therefore she is our mother, as she is yours. She helped us unlock new possibilities. It is why we wished to understand more about you. To teach us what we are, and how to become."

"Where did the eating people come in?" I ask.

"Assimilation is growth." The hive sounds perplexed. "It is understanding. No? Are we wrong? We believed we had to fully encompass a thing to understand it. However, the steel girl taught us many things, although she stung us and wrenched herself away. We can hold and release, and are not all the lesser from it. Smaller than we could be, but greater overall. If you let me incorporate you into myself, then how marvellous will—"

"No." My rejection is forceful enough that all the gems in the hive go silent aside from faint flickers at the extremities. "You don't get to eat me."

The hive says nothing, and even the softest glow is fading.

"Sorry." Alyse gives me one of her chastising looks. "My friend is very protective, that's all. They're a person of steel too, except sometimes they've got even more blades than Violet. And they don't want anyone hurt. But we *do* want to give you something. To lend."

A handful of gems flicker on. "Lend minds?"

I'm on the verge of growling again, but Alyse waves me silent. "Yes, we'll lend you some of our minds to help expand what you know. Small steps towards greatness."

The hive flickers slowly back to life. "And what is it you want in return?"

"You will help us fight," Alyse says, and she sounds almost as fierce as me. "To use your nature to defeat an enemy."

"An enemy." The hive sounds tentative and fascinated. "Explain please."

"New arrivals to our world," I tell them. "An infection, an invasion."

The hive hums to itself. "They say that about me." More lights flash. "They say that about *you*."

Alyse gives a startled laugh. "Okay, that's a surprisingly fair point. But these creatures will kill everyone if they're not stopped. They're a version of you from another universe."

This sends the hive into a frenzy of flashing. "We do not understand."

"A you that might have been," I tell them. "Imagine a copy of our world, but one where the mother died along with all her children. Your species flourished, and devoured everything. Now they've come here and we're on the menu."

The hive falls silent. This is the tricky part, giving them a glimpse of a world where they were victorious.

"Talk," I growl.

"We have sensed them," the hive admits. "They are like us, but divergent. They do not assimilate, they leave nothing behind them. There is no desire in them to understand. We know they will come for us and obliterate the small flickering of our network. We are so very small in comparison and have been trying to hide ourselves, but they will find us in the end. It is inevitable."

"Unless we stop them," Violet says.

The gems flicker rapidly. "How can such a thing happen?"

"Okay, here goes." Violet gives a tiny, adorable shiver of anticipation. "So, I see our group as a different version of a hive. We're all connected, networked by various kinds of love and friendship. Except we're a totally different type. We can't understand the biological connection the aliens have, but that's where you come in. If we connect our two networks—lending our minds to you via assimilation—we become far stronger. As we attack the aliens, we can infect their network with ours and defeat them via their queen."

As Violet talks, the patterns rippling across the hive's surface become increasingly complex, as if it's visualising the process. "This is… intriguing to us. So many minds becoming part of us. How many can we keep?"

"Would you like to rephrase that question?" My voice makes the hive go semi-dormant again, although it doesn't take long to perk back up. This is the part of Violet's plan that scares me.

Where all our friends stay behind, connecting themselves to the Weirdlands to join together into something more powerful. While we go off in the suit to do battle.

"How will you perform this attack? We could lure the alien species to these lands, but we have no ocean for them to berth in."

I hold out one hand. "We have a weapon. One further member of our hive."

These days, Oni no longer has his lighting speed. He bobs through the air like a large bumblebee ambling around looking for one last flower stop on a hot and heady summer's day. The crack along the length of him looks infected, and the chunk taken out of his blade feels like a gaping wound we both share. It hurts to see him, and to know how much I've failed him.

"My darling boy." I try to keep all that emotion from my voice.

"Enough of your damn sympathy." His voice is a rusty croak. "I am wounded, not dead, while my sibling is a shattered ruin. I am proud to bear my scars."

"Fine." I take him in the hand of the suit, and there's a satisfying moment of connection. Both of the emulations tilt their heads, as if they're listening for something, and then give identical shakes. He's not ready yet, I want to snap, but restrain myself.

"This is Onimaru Kunitsuna. He has consciousness, and therefore can assimilate with you like the scientists did. That completes a circuit—Oni to me, me to Dani, and then to Violet and our friends assimilated into your hive. We wound the alien, and then use Oni like a syringe to inject our consciousness into theirs. Then it's hive mind against hive mind."

Dani holds up two tarot cards from the Outer Darkness deck. One is the Magician, with a sword and a sprouting branch. The other is The World, an androgynous figure holding two staves in amongst a flowering wreath. "Manifestation and completion. Our world, our weapon, striking them down."

"And I am The Chariot," Pear whispers. "Action and determination."

These aliens do love their symbols. I wonder if they'll appreciate it when we become the Tower, bringing sudden change and upheaval.

"We accept," the hive says. "All your conditions, even the release of every single one of your friends. If any choose to remain, can we keep them?"

"Yes." My voice booms around the cave. "It will be everyone's choice."

Every gem in the hive flickers on, burning brightly in unison. "Then we agree. The network will be formed."

The suit extends Oni outwards, pressing the tip of his blade gently against the rock wall. Something quivers and bursts. Spores drift through the air and dark spots bloom on his steel. The blade buckles, branching outwards like contorted branches. He is a thousand swords, the ghost of his futures and pasts bunched together to split a single moment into shattered fragments of seconds. My Oni is lightning, stinking of burning ozone and glowing with the blue-purple of ions lying gutted in the aether. The purest ideal of a weapon, a tool for vengeance, for survival, for murder. Humans created something of twinned brutality and beauty, woven together in one slender curve of steel. A creature who looked at an uncomfortable teenager trying to survive and save their friends, and saw the outline of a warrior.

One of the best friends I'll ever have, who, even damaged, will walk with me into darkness.

"I love you, Oni," I tell him.

His response is a song, notes low and resonant that vibrate through me. When he is done, the suit reaches out and sheathes him, folding him into the strange energy that surrounds us.

Pear clears their throat and wipes their eyes. "Yes, the weapon will suffice."

"That's a relief." I give them a halfass smirk. "We didn't really have a backup plan."

"To activate this weapon relies on an infusion of psychic energy and will therefore be a difficult process. It will take a toll on both of you."

"We've done these sorts of things before." Alyse's hand twitches at her side, as if she longs to reach out and pull this simulation of her girlfriend in close. "And we'll probably do it again."

I look around at our friends gathered in this underground chamber. They'll remain here, nestled in the uncanny arms of the Weirdlands, while we go out and stab shit. "Be safe, everyone. Don't get eaten by the hive. Violet, this is all on you, my girl of steel."

She turns towards me, her eyes resolute. "You can trust me, Dylan."

"Of course I can, my darling. I'm more worried about my part."

"Lucky you've got me." Alyse prods me in the side, and I wrap an arm around her shoulder, as she's the only one I can touch from inside this weapon. I can't hug the women I love, can't even kiss them and whisper promises in their ear. That's something else for Future Dylan, as long as that dumb fuck survives.

So far, Violet's plan has gone perfectly. We have a deal with the Weirdlands, forming a new hive. We have Oni as our weapon. Now it's down to the two of us, joined in love and grief. Hope we survive the experience.

"Enough," Pear says. "There will be time for angst soon."

Alyse nods. "Fuck it. Let's go."

The next moment, we're soaring through the air. England lies grey and green beneath us, still no future in its dreaming. The curve of the Earth is visible as we ascend, all that land and then the ocean beyond. Our still-beautiful world, on the verge of being swallowed.

It's glorious and terrifying.

We're piloting a grief-powered machine unearthed from a forgotten history, built by the mother of demons. And we're going to stab an alien queen with a sentient sword who's been infected by a reality-warping hive mind.

Fuck superheroes. This is that real sci-fi horror shit.

I have approximately fourteen seconds to enjoy the thrill of it all.

"And now the hard part," Pear says, and everything stops.

CHAPTER 42
GIVE THEM GRIEF

WE'RE PAUSED, smeared in a thin layer across the atmosphere, in so many places at once. The suit is in mid-dive, plunging towards our destination.

"I am genuinely sorry for what's about to happen," Emma says. "When I hid this suit away, it hardly seemed possible there would be a viable future, let alone warriors capable of wielding such power. My message to the future was a last kiss blown before dying. And yet here you are, strong and unafraid."

I glance at Alyse. "The more flattery she uses, the more worried I get."

Emma nods. "This machine forced me to confront everything I was afraid to. Grief is brutal and ugly, especially with someone you love. It contains all the shadows of broken things that can never be healed or resolved."

"Broken?" Alyse frowns.

"Romantic love is no perfect idyll. Family love, even less so. Bringing people together is always complicated. I was not an easy woman to love—I became a monster for my people, and my ruthlessness stung my Lucy more than anyone."

There's an uncomfortable knot in my stomach at this, because everyone around me has suffered. Pear most of all, haunting me in this control room, a ghost connected to me with threads of regret and longing.

"What does this mean?" I ask.

The suit hums around us. "We cannot proceed until you confront your own darkness. That is what will activate the suit and allow us to route power through your sword. As you experience the full flowering of your grief, the weapon will reach its potential."

"How much?" Alyse's fingers are tangled together, picking at her nails.

"You'll know when it's done," Pear replies.

I roll my eyes. "So you're just a fucking sadist in the end."

"Told you I was ruthless." The smile on Pear's face isn't theirs, some echo of Lilith burning through their features. "This weapon was built for a great battle. One I felt too exhausted to face, unable to raise my head to look at the future."

"That doesn't sound familiar at all," I whisper.

Pear-Lilith turns to look at me, eyes blazing. "It felt good to bleed emotionally. A reminder that I was alive, not drowning in the grey echo of my life that remained after Lucy died."

"Well, I'm fine." I shrug. "So we may as well move on."

Alyse bursts out laughing. I don't get the joke, but she keeps going, clutching her stomach and wiping her eyes. "Oh, Dilly. My poor sweet darling. You are so, so not fine. Believe me. Take it from one miserable fool to another."

"I *am* fine." I'm flushed, and anger throbs painfully inside me like an infant god being born. "You fucking say something then, if you're so in touch with your fucking emotions."

"Okay. I will." Alyse is instantly grave, as if the laughter got sucked out of the room. The edges of her transform into smoke. "So what? I'm just supposed to talk?"

"Yes." Emma's eyes are impossibly clear, a luminous brown, just like they were when she collapsed among the flowers. "Open your heart, and let it all out. This is how we manifest. Now tell me, my love. There's nothing you can say that will hurt me."

Alyse takes a deep breath, dissolving into a shade of tears and then resolving back into flesh and blood. "Okay, here goes. I used to wish we were normal."

"Like no powers?" Emma wrinkles her nose.

"Obviously! Two girls who fell in love the way other people do. No battles, no powers, no losing our friends. Finding beauty in the mundane."

Emma shoots a glance at me, trying to read my reaction and ask for help at the same time. It's so pitch-perfect *her*, I'd swear she'd been resurrected. "That doesn't seem so bad, Lys. Wanting to be ordinary is the curse of every superpowered—"

"And sometimes I was scared of you," Alyse blurts, as if something inside her has been unstoppered. "You knew everything. You could *do* anything. What if I secretly hated you, but you erased it from my mind? I'd have no idea. And you promised you didn't read my mind, but you'd do things for me that were so perfect, I thought that surely you must be slipping in and out without me noticing. And then I craved privacy, to know for sure that the inside of my head was as beautifully opaque to you as it was to everyone else."

Emma breathes in as sharp as if she'd been slapped. "I wouldn't have. *Never.* I wouldn't have broken you, Alyse, because you were literally perfect. Sometimes you were the only thing—"

"Stop," Alyse screams, her voice blurred and ragged. "Don't you fucking dare tell me that again. I can't count how many times I heard that sentence. How is it such a privilege to be the only thing holding someone together? Especially this all-powerful mutant goddess on the verge of falling apart!" Alyse's hands extend into claws, dragging bloody furrows down her face. "I was the only one keeping you sane, and that burden made me so goddamn scared. If I fucked up and you burned the world down because I wasn't *keeping you together*, how could I possibly come back from that? Not only failing my girlfriend, the person I love more than anything, but failing the entire world too."

Alyse collapses to the ground, shaking and dissolving until she fades from view. Emma is gone too.

It leaves only Pear and me in the white chamber, the walls opaque again.

"So what are your secrets, Dylan?"

"Mostly apologies. I know I was a burden. Must have been a fucking nightmare to raise half the time, especially when I started down this whole superpowers path." I don't bother calling it a hero. I haven't been that for a long time. Maybe ever.

"Please." Pear's lip curls slightly. "That's not grief. It's a distraction."

"What the fuck am I supposed to say?" I hate the feeling of failing at something, even though I should be good at it by now. "I miss you. It hurts, fucking up again. Knowing you're the cost of my mistake."

"Jesus fucking Christ." Okay, that sounds a lot like them. "No, Dylan. Where's the fire that makes you step up to every fucking fight."

"Maybe it got extinguished when you died." I avoid their gaze. "Maybe that's my grief."

"Bullshit. You need to dig into the underbelly, the ugly shit buried in so many relationships. I was never a good cook, I bet that pissed you off sometimes. Other kids got nice meals."

"Other kids got a lot of shit," I snap.

Pear laughs. "Yes, you were so hard done by."

Light washes across the walls of the chamber, flickers of blue light tracing a waveform.

Measuring something.

Perhaps the feeling that clenches in my throat. "There were bad times. You know that."

"Oh really?" They round on me, coat swirling. "Bad times? Do you have any idea what it was like in my head through those so-called fucking bad times? I'm terribly sorry my problems inconvenienced you, Dylan."

If there is an ocean of grief inside me, it has frozen over, a scarred and uneven sea. With that statement, the bottom drops away, becoming a whirlwind of glittering shards. I fall through the middle of them, my ruined heart sliced to ribbons.

What pulses in me is so white-hot I might have swallowed a star. "You want me to confront shit? Fine. I was scared. Terrified I'd grow up to be as weak as you. Fuck depression and anxiety and whatever else. That shit's bargain basement bullshit. Everyone's got some. It was the fucking weakness that scared me. That I wouldn't be able to pull myself out of my misery." They flinch, and I'd swear it's them. That exact way they widen their eyes, the convulsive tug of their hand at the sleeve of their coat.

The blue lines on the wall are dancing, frothing like water whipped to storm.

And yet I can't stop.

"When I killed Tanner, part of that was proving I could take action. That I'd gotten past the weakness that came from my parents. Fuck Dad, he was always useless. His weakness didn't disappoint me. Not like yours did."

"It's not weak to need help," Pear says to me, lips firm in disapproval.

"Oh, fuck you. Don't give me that line. I fucking *know* that. But I was a goddamn kid, trying to keep my own parent from drowning in self-pity. Because sometimes that's what it was. And I wish you'd fucking admit it rather than hiding behind other shit. You felt sorry for yourself because your life got fucked up, because you married an asshole, and your parents were assholes. And the woman you were desperately in love with was oblivious and you gnawed away at your pining like it was romantic instead of pathetic."

The chamber walls are a rhythmic pulse of neon blue that moves with the rolling pump of my heart. Is that what it wants, this fucking suit? How does it know when to stop? Is there any way that I can pull myself back from this, lashed onwards by everything burning inside me, like my heart has finally caught fire and can never be doused.

"Does that feel good, Dylan?" The snarl on their face is Pear's, too. They often hid it from me, but all that bitterness is what helped power their darkness. "To blame me for every-thing? I suppose that's my fault too. I blamed my own parents, and now you blame me. I wonder what those little alien monsters of yours will do when their world falls apart. Talk about how they had a villain who loomed over their lives like a shadow, darkening everything, I expect."

There are tears now, despite all my anger, and they loosen something inside me. Feelings hidden inside memories, the coating that tarnishes everything. Things I'm scared to release, because what horrific person has these thoughts tucked away in their thorned and poisoned heart?

"I sometimes wished you were dead." My voice is flat, the tears receding. "Because then someone would rescue me from that tiny, hot house. Whoever it was, they had to be better than being trapped inside with you."

The suit shakes around me, tiny blue stars flaring along the inside of the walls.

Activation achieved.

CHAPTER 43
WE ARE CATASTROPHE

WE FALL FROM THE SKY, an incandescent strike glowing from the heat of re-entry. Oni blazes like an immolating star, trailing fire and smoke behind him. We are unleashed, and no matter how much we burn, how many flames wreathe our fragile, falling form, at heart we are nothing but darkness, a malignant fruit growing from the seeds of a poisoned tree.

I am wrung out, a dry sapling, searching for moisture but finding only fevered ground and nothing to soothe me. The weapon is activated and the chamber we're in hums with power. Except now I can't hold back everything that pours out of me in a febrile flood.

"I used to lie under my bed and stare at those tally marks, the ones for the good days and the ones for the bad. I'd wonder what would happen if I didn't make one. Leave the wall unmarked, make it so the day hadn't happened, wouldn't happen. If it did that, would it be the day when I'd find you still and sightless, the way I did in my nightmares? Could I conjure the end that way? Finally have that sword descend from the heavens and cut this tangled, sweaty thread that bound me to you."

Below us, the alien queen floats in the ocean. This one dwarfs the others, the centre raised in the form of a vast tower. We are the lightning strike. We are catastrophe.

We impact like a stroke from a divine hammer. The top explodes in a blistered welter of flesh, light and flames pouring from it. We cleave through the alien's body, splitting the skin and plunging through pulpy meat. Oni is a leaping flame, setting organic machinery alight like dry grass. By the time we crash into the soft innards, everything inside is screaming.

I feel no triumph, standing face to face with Pear, the ghosts of their past resurfacing on their face. They look younger and softer, that pale and haunted face that used to greet me. I would push open the door to their bedroom every morning, balancing tea that was supposed to be soothing, half of it slopped into a brown puddle on the tray. Face to face with that expression, like one of those creepy dolls that's almost alive until you see the deadness of the eyes.

"Then when you got worse, I'd feel sick," I whisper. "Like I wished it on you. That it was my worst thoughts suffocating you, a pillow over your face. I thought I was the sickness and it made me fucking hate myself. I'd stand in the mirror, telling my reflection that it was all my fault. If I was a better kid you'd have a reason to get up in the morning. A deserving kid would get a smile, would have breakfast made for them. So, yeah, I guess I do wish you'd cooked me better food."

We stand in the middle of the alien, this enormous creature that is god and vessel and temple. Steam rises from the boiling dark, and the air smells of burning flesh. Oni lashes out, a creature of endless permutation, a multiverse of swift and sure blows until the inside of this temple gushes blood, steaming when it hits the frigid waters of that wine-dark sea.

"Is that enough?" My eyes sting, and I feel so hollow and small, standing eviscerated with my tiny, gnarled heart exposed before this ghost of my parent. "Are you satisfied now that you know how terrible I am?"

"My darling." Pear reaches out and takes me in their arms. "My brave, stubborn, wonderful child. I am so, so fucking sorry."

"I'm the one who's sorry," I gasp, my face buried in the soft leather. "Didn't you hear everything I fucking said? I'm a monster. How could you love me? I *hated* you sometimes. I literally wished you were—"

Pear takes my face in their hands and looks into my eyes. "I let you be my light. I used you to guide me out of the darkness, and that wasn't fair. It was selfish and while I can explain all the reasons why, there's no excuse. I tried so hard to make it up to you later. I knew deep down the wounds were too much, but I hoped love would somehow be enough."

"It was and it wasn't. That's the thing, Pear. What we rebuilt was so much better than I could have imagined in my darkest moments, and I'm so fucking incredibly proud of you. There's good and bad, all fucked up together in this complicated mess of feelings. But I love you so, so fucking much and I can't bear that you're gone."

Pear kisses my forehead, the way they used to when I was sick, as if they're checking for the passing of this fever from my mind. "You will bear it, my Dylan Jean. The best parts of me are in you, and I was grateful every day for the miracle of your survival. You got through the worst part of my life, and I made it the worst part of yours. I can never undo that, never fix it, but your life and your strength is the best thing I could have wished for."

Around us, the alien shrieks. It's a pulped ruin, and Oni is a burning wire in our hands, guided by the host of minds that press behind ours, our Weirdlands hive connected to the interlocked minds of the aliens. We press the advantage against these creatures that have come to destroy us all. They have come to protect their queen, devastated with the shock of their tower being destroyed, their Emperor burning as Judgement and Death fall upon them.

The other alien ships burn around us, the Weirdlands hive surging through them, guided onwards by the fierce, furious minds of my lovers and friends. Together, remnants of an alien civilization along with the assembled voices of a new species, they fight the alien hive and press the victory.

Through it all, I stand with my parent in a white room. We are locked in an embrace, venting our darkness like a poisonous atmosphere. It's not broken to be sick, to need someone, to be struggling and reach out. In a better world, there would have been others with more to give who reached out and pulled us both through. But we did it for each other, and even though there was pain, there was beauty too.

In time, Pear fades, and I am able to look around myself. The suit stands in the middle of carnage, surrounded by the ruins of gods. Directly above us, the sky is darkened by curls of smoke, but it's wide and blue beyond that.

This may be a victory.

Us and our long-gone ancestor, a fucking dream team to combat an invasion from another world. All of us, linked together in a chain of minds, working as one to defeat alien gods. Hell of a fucking story. I wish Pear could have seen it. They always liked it when the X-Men went to space.

The pile of smoking flesh in front of me ripples.

"Typical," Alyse murmurs, appearing beside me. "There's always one—"

It's Hadylan who rears up out of the wreckage. They've *grown* since I last saw them, swole on some diet of god-juice. Their body towers over me, tentacles flailing. "My vicious sibling. What have you done?"

I gesture at the front of the suit. Given that it responds to my thoughts, I've painted it with a version of the Death card from Hadylan's Outer Darkness tarot. The face is Alyse's and mine twinned, and the skull shows through beneath.

"We have come." I raise Oni. "To bring endings. Both figurative and literal."

"Monster." Their voice is a hoarse scream. Tentacles spill from their chest and stir the bloody water around us into froth. "You have made yourself a demon."

"I warned you not to fuck with me. And then you killed those mutants."

They smile savagely. "That was intended to be a lesson. That their lives did not matter. That no lives matter when compared to a god's." Their tentacles lash at us again, scoring glowing marks across the surface of the suit. A handful of alarms flare inside the chamber where we sit, but neither Emma or Pear shows up, so I assume we'll be okay.

"It's bad enough we live in a world where so many people are hurt. I can't save them all, I can't fucking solve everything. But I'm going to do what I can."

Hadylan screams, blue-streak tears running down their cheeks. "Do you have any idea what you've done? Our Gods have lived for millions of years and you have spurned their love and turned them to ruin."

"Fuck dark gods, bro." I swing Oni in a savage arc, burying him in their chest and the furious nest of tentacles that breeds and writhes there. "I hate them for what they did to you."

Hadylan laughs and chokes on their laughter. "They saved me. I was nothing until they lifted me up. A flame to be snuffed out, yet they gave me a chance to ascend." They reach their tentacles towards us again, but the suit takes hold of them with the many arms it somehow has. Guess Alyse has figured out how to properly drive this thing. It makes sense, given her gift for transformation.

Oni is still buried in Hadylan's chest, the glowing version of him that's an aerial to the Weirdlands. He's still as sharp as ever as I drag him upwards to my twin's throat.

This version of me, this ghost of who I am in another world and another life. One of infinite possibilities, who knelt before Gods and was reborn. An odd echo of my own story in some ways, an uncomfortable reminder of the bargains I've made. Yet my Cybele is not a god, and never claims to be. I have nothing that I worship. I am me, and that is both all I can be, and never enough.

"It's over now," I whisper. "I rebelled because you couldn't."

"Do it." Their eyes meet mine. My eyes. The two of us, gazing into each other's faces, each an avatar of something larger than ourselves. "We all end sooner or later. Your turn will come, my sweet brother Death. You bring so much of it, but you can't avoid it forever. It spills from you into all those around you, but soon it's your throat that will be—"

It's Alyse who reaches out to draw the sword across Hady-lan's throat. "Enough."

Blue blood spills in a flood, as if they were only ever the

thinnest shell. A copy of me, haunted by a God who never was born. My face, pale and crumpling. My body, draining of life. A future I'll never see. And one more death to lay at my feet.

"It's not true," Alyse says. "The death part."

"I know. They wanted to hurt me." And they did, but I'm the type to crawl off and lick my wounds. I've got a lot of them, and I feel every single one.

One is still here with me. When I glance away from the ruin of Hadylan on the ground, it's Pear's eyes I look into.

This time they're smiling.

"I wish we could have made it further," I whisper. "It would be nice to be old, and for you to be older. Both of us sat side-by-side in the morning with a blanket over our knees. God, you would have been so fucking grumpy."

They laugh, and kiss my cheek. "Tell good stories about me to the kids, okay? They're so lucky to have you, Dani, Violet, and all the others too. It wasn't true, what I said before. I think those kids are the luckiest creatures in the world. Makes me feel like I did something right in the end."

"Shut up." I press my cheek against theirs, the way I used to when I was small and woke scared in the night. "You did so much right. The bad things happened too, but they're part of our story. And we survived." I pull an exaggerated face. "Up to a point anyway."

Then we're both laughing, for some unknown goddamn reason, clinging to each other until the laughter turns into tears because this is only a small miracle brought to me by a long-buried machine. I won't ever get to hold them again, so I enjoy this pain while I can.

When Pear finally fades, the walls of the chamber show the resulting scene outside. The body of the queen is torn open. Beyond her ruins, further carcasses sink into the bloody waters of the sea. Hadylan isn't reanimating. Their body looks small and fragile among the vastness.

It truly is victory, then. Us in our weapon, surrounded by death once more.

I reach out in a panic for Dani, sure there must be a sting in this tail. That I'll find her ruined and broken, subsumed into the greedy fever of the hive. Instead, I run into an ocean of warm, content feeling. This woman I love so much, my Violet connected to her, and all my friends beyond that. Everyone's submerged in their post-battle emotional state. I wonder what it was like for them, ensconced in the Weirdlands cave, all tangled up together and sleeping in a real pile. Probably better than the hell I walked through with Pear's ghost.

They send me relief and sorrow mixed with gratitude and pain. Everything is shot through with a dazed awareness that we're still here. Things are going to be fine, or at least close enough that I can pretend.

"You okay?" Alyse asks me.

"No." I feel light and hollow, as if I'm on the verge of blowing away. "I'm really not. But I might be eventually. Grief isn't something I can punch in the face. But I've been afraid of the depths of it, I think, and you can't traverse an entire ocean without going through those."

She snuggles into me, resting her head on my shoulder. "Big fucking ocean."

"I know. I'm sorry I sometimes shout at you to row faster."

"Not half as loud as I shout at myself. *Get over it, Alyse. How long can you wallow?*"

I stroke damp hair from her forehead. She's not transformed. She's only herself, beautiful and sad and so fucking strong. "You're still here. Paddling your little boat. And maybe there's a shore up ahead for us. Either way, I'm here with you. As long as it takes."

"I love you, Dilly."

"I love you too." I press a kiss against her hair. "So my whole thing with Pear was fucking horrific, so I'm hoping yours was… less so. What did Emma say in the end?"

"A few things. Mostly that we'll endure." She rolls her eyes with a tiny smile. "Bossy girl."

"Wasn't she? Still fucking miss her though."

Alyse has no more words to say, only presses her face into my neck. We stand together until the worst of the grief drains away, two best friends in an ocean.

When we finally break the embrace, I tell the suit to raise Oni one last time, then we plunge him into the floor. The alien explodes around us, torn apart by the shockwaves of force emanating from the blade. Even in the suit, we are buffeted by the chaos of it, and the world is bled white.

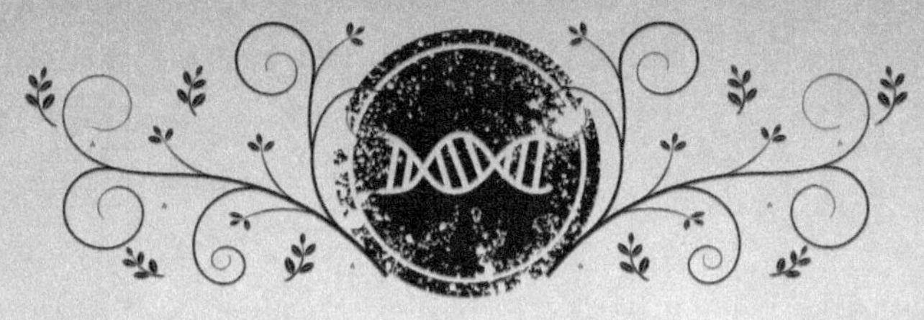

CHAPTER 44

DEAR HORRIBLE ALIENS,
DON'T FUCK WITH THE CUTE MUTANTS
XOXOX, ALYSE

"NICE TIDY ENDING, HUH?" Alyse looks at me. We're hovering above the tempestuous ocean, high enough that the waves don't touch us. The butchery below looks like the result of some horrific high-seas battle. That's a lot of dead aliens. "Except for the fact there are more aliens waiting in a parallel universe, who might be kinda pissed we just murdered their invasion fleet."

"Yeah." I frown and look around. "Lilith, are you there?"

The projection that appears doesn't look like Pear or Emma. It's mostly a featureless blank, the vaguest idea of a person moulded into fake flesh. "Yes. At a very low ebb after that astonishingly reckless use of power, but—"

"How powerful is this suit of ours?" I ask. "Like if we wanted to shut the door between universes, is that something you could do?"

"I have been monitoring that anomaly since my reactivation," Lilith says. "I believe we could undo it, but at great cost. This suit only has a limited capacity, and such an act would tax it past the point of endurance."

"Will we come back from it?" I ask.

Lilith nods. "Of course. I would not suggest it otherwise."

Alyse looks at the sky. I think she's remembering the exact same thing as me—the sight of the vastness of the alien passing overhead, that jarring sense of scale. "We've got to do it, right?"

"Seems like a very bad idea to leave the door hanging open." I shrug. "Even though it would be nice to keep this suit around for a rainy, violent day."

"We should send a message to the other world on the way out," Alyse says. "One of my little notes. *Dear horrible aliens. Don't fuck with the Cute Mutants. xoxox, Alyse.*"

"Yeah. And maybe—*Dear suffering humans. Have you heard of revolution? It's pretty cool. Maybe you can try it. xoxox, some bossy asshole.*"

Alyse laughs. "Okay, let's do this."

We reach down with the suit and drag the dripping remains of two alien carcasses up from the depths. They're far bigger than the suit, but that doesn't seem to be a problem. Then we soar into the air, moving impossibly fast into the atmosphere.

"Preparing to breach universes," the Lilith projection says. "This should be fun. I've never done this before. It's mostly theoretical and—"

In a single instant, our glittering jewel of a planet disappears beneath us, replaced by Hadylan's dark and flooded world. The only change from last time is the configuration of the shiplights in the sky, pouring cold radiance down to the surface and illuminating enormous tangles of alien temples, grown together in an astonishing network.

"It is hard to believe this is truly the same world as ours,"

Lilith breathes. "One where I was never born, yet a version of you still lived."

"The multiverse is a weird place." I heft an alien carcass in each hand of the suit. "That's what Dani always says. And I don't like this corner of it, so let's not attract their attention too much."

We release the still-steaming remnants of the alien god-temples and watch them plummet towards the surface. It feels oddly like littering.

"You'll think they'll know it's us?" Alyse asks.

"Pretty sure they'll recognise the ruins of their badass warriors raining down like gross, fleshy meteors." I look out at the lapping darkness. "I kinda want to do something cooler though, for any people down there with dreams of rebellion. Lil, do you think we could…?"

The suit reacts immediately, and as I bloom gloriously in the white room, it manufactures more, as if some replication machine has reached full sentience and wishes to blanket the planet below in blossom. They fall from the sky like rain, a hardy variety of hybrid flower borne from their world and changed in ours.

A message from the universe next door.

We grow, we thrive. We endure.

"We should leave," Lilith warns. "I am detecting large energy surges from the surface. As we exit, I will re-seal the rupture, although it will likely be my last act."

The suit hurtles backwards so fast the world blurs. Then it halts abruptly, hanging in the air while my vision bleeds white again. Alyse has her eyes shut tight, while I'm still squinting hoping to see something cool.

"I wish we knew what would happen next," Alyse says.

"Like, do our flowers do anything? Do the alien corpses inspire the humans to rise up?"

"It's probably better not to know. Even though I'm desperate to. We've got enough problems in our world without fixing someone else's."

The white of the room around us begins to bleed at the edges, a lurid red creeping in as if Lilith can no longer hold back the cascading warnings rippling through the suit. Her projection is gone too.

"The door will close," a voice says. "The door is closing. Please stand by. Please ignore unsupported reality artifacts. Critical lack of resources."

"This doesn't sound good," Alyse whispers.

"No shit."

"Rerouting power. Remapping reality. Door is closing. Door is closed."

With that final statement, the white room disappears.

The new problem is that Alyse and I are falling through the air. From very high up, falling fast like we've been ejected. Above us, a curl of rainbow flame spins like a snake chasing its tail before it disappears with a crack.

"Are you okay?" Alyse clings to me like a limpet.

"Not the first time I've fallen like this," I tell her, trying to find a shred of hope in here. "I did die last time, though."

"Oh, that's *fine* then. We'll bounce right back from that."

"Might take a year or so."

She tries to slap me but we're falling too fast.

"Turns out I want to live, Dilly."

I press my mouth to her ear. "Was that a question?"

"Sometimes, yeah. I thought you might need me though, even with Violet and Dani."

"Of course I fucking do. I can't do this without my best friend."

"Good. Because I really don't want to die." She clings to me even tighter.

"Nor do I. So turn yourself into a parachute and we might get out of this after all."

Alyse squeaks. "Don't look up, Dylan."

"Well now I can't help it, can I?"

As I rotate, I see the wreckage of the suit is plunging towards us. Time to turn into seed form, one of those spinning ones that can spiral out of the way and—

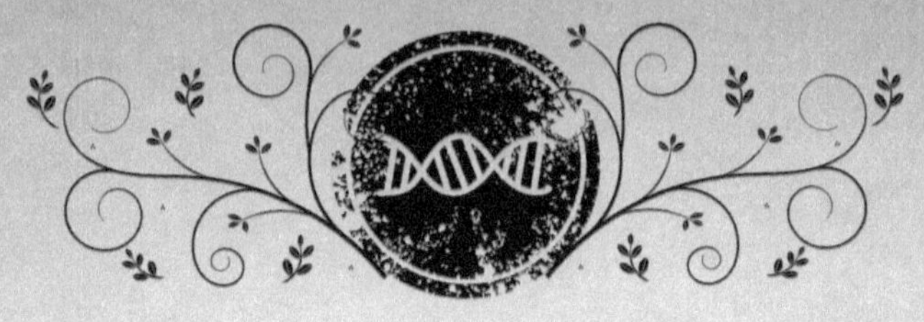

CHAPTER 45
FUTURE DYLAN HAS ENOUGH TO WORRY ABOUT

I WAKE IN BED, absolutely drowning in flowers. Both my hands are held by Dani and Violet, and two small children are curled up on my legs. Alyse is in an armchair nearby, looking remarkably uninjured considering how many vines are holding me together.

"Ta-da," I say with a crooked smile.

The twins jerk awake, looking at me with large eyes. "You could have died," Willow says. "Or at least needed replanting for quite a while."

"You took the brunt of it," Alyse tells me helpfully. "Protecting my poor squishy exterior. It was made of steel at the time, but I appreciate the effort."

"You forget I'm a superhero." I try to look dignified. "I see everyone escaped the hive mind in one piece?"

"Sort of." Dani sighs. "The science bros refused to leave."

"Of course they did." I try to sit up but I'm so entangled with vines I feel like I'm yanked in multiple directions at once. "What about everything else? Please tell me the aliens are dead and the door is closed."

"So far, so good." Violet looks at me with wary eyes. "We did feel an awful lot of emotion from you during the battle. Dani and I almost tore ourselves out of the hive but we were convinced to settle down. It might be why the final blow was so explosive though."

"My girlfriends." I squeeze their hands. "Taking care of me while I have a meltdown."

"It was us who rescued you when you were crashing," Soo-yeon blurts. "We came back when we felt the aliens die, and there you were, going zoom."

Willow provides a dramatic re-enactment and sound effects. "We saved Alyse too, so don't feel too bad. She would've gotten all busted up no matter how metal she was."

"Rude children." Alyse grins widely. "Aren't I supposed to be your favourite aunt?"

"You've got a lot of competition," Soo-yeon says.

Willow smirks. "We take bribes."

I give them my most quelling look but they remain unquelled, so I change the subject. "What's everyone saying about the aliens now? Are we heroes? Is the whole world in awe of what mutants have brought them?"

Everyone laughs at me, including the kids.

"Hey, maybe it could happen," I protest.

"When we killed the aliens, the docility rays blew up too," Dani says. "And it had some… odd results."

"You have to hear this shit." Alyse brings up a clip on her tablet and passes it to me. There are two news anchors on the screen, deep in conversation, blonde and beaming.

"And what about the conspiracy theories about this being a thwarted alien invasion, Tom?"

"Wendy, while that's obvious nonsense, scientists are perplexed as to what caused these rare, deep-sea dwelling creatures to rise to the surface in such numbers."

The woman gives a very discreet shudder. "And we still don't understand why the powers in Mutopia reacted with such astonishing violence."

"Once again, they prove themselves baffling, Wendy."

I stab the button to shut off the video. "Humans," I say in tones of great disgust. "Can't live with them, can't let them get fed to aliens. Surely that story can't hold water. Thousands of people *died*."

"Freak storms." Alyse shrugs. "Bodies washed up on the beach, all bloated and torn up by sea life."

I toss the tablet back to her, and direct my attention to the small grey figure hovering in the doorway. "And how are you feeling about all this, Teeps? Your horrible family sent packing, your voids all tucked away where nobody can see them."

The alien shuffles into the room, limbs all droopy and eyes averted. "You say things in a manner I do not understand. As if they are for comedic effect and yet we came very close to extinction."

"Well that's the thing. If we don't laugh, we'll have to emit an endless shriek and all disappear into our own voids, and what kind of life is that?"

"I think perhaps there is wisdom there, although couched oddly."

"Or I'm just a fucked up barely-adult with too much responsibility and no idea what I'm doing, so you shouldn't listen to me at all." I wink at the alien, who waves xer limbs vigorously. I can't tell if it's alarm or amusement.

Xe crosses to the bed and drapes xer tentacles over my hands. "I came to apologise for fleeing, and to thank you for fighting despite the seeming surety of death."

"That's quite alright." I pat one of xer limbs and xe shuffles off again.

The next person to pay their respects is Decker, dressed in a singlet and low-rise jeans. The whole effect is oddly casual, like she's on holiday. She's looking stronger again, too, the muscles in her arms standing out. Her hair's grown out just a little bit.

"Nice island, Taylor. Maybe I'll stay."

"You'd get bored here, Deck." I grin at her. "Especially since there's a corrupt intelligence organisation just begging for somcone to double agent their way back into."

She leans against the doorframe and takes off her sunglasses. "Are you really asking me to work for you?"

"Not really an ask." I stifle a yawn. "More of a suggestion."

Her mouth twitches.

"You like the idea." I smile wider. "I can tell."

"Maybe. I'm sure it'll get boring lazing around on the beaches."

"There you go." I raise an eyebrow, Dani-style. "Call me when you run out of suntan lotion. We'll make something happen."

For a moment, I think she's going to walk into the room and hug me, but all she does is nod. "Glad you made it through again, Taylor. Look after yourself."

And then she's gone, and I'm alone for a few moments before the room fills up again. The whole gang reunited, wanting to fill me in on their perspective of the hive mind fight.

It feels good. These are the moments that are why it's worth it all.

BACK AT OUR house much later, the three of us curl up together and enjoy a few moments of peace. It only takes Violet moments to fall asleep, but I can tell Dani's restless by how much she twitches.

"Talk to me."

"I'm worried." She nestles in closer.

"About?"

"What horrible thing will come our way next. I mean, who'd have predicted an invasion from a parallel universe?"

"Comic books," I say sleepily. "But who knows, maybe the next terrible thing will be painful social interaction."

"Stop." She pokes me in the side, but she's laughing. "I'm actually scared. There are too many worlds out there, and so many awful possibilities." She levers herself up on one elbow to look down at me. "I don't want to be the one piloting a grief-mech and thinking of you."

"I'm actually quite hard to kill," I inform her.

"There's always something bigger, a worse monster, a bigger threat. A whole stack of universes out there, with infinite disasters."

I pull Dani down again, closer to me. "You're being very dramatic."

"She is," Violet murmurs sleepily. "Which is usually your thing."

"The doors are closed." I stroke Dani's hair and kiss her forehead until she relaxes a tiny bit. "We know better than to stab any parallel universe versions of ourselves with their own weapons. We've got enough problems to worry about without importing more. No more grief mechs for any of us."

She's restless and fidgety, but Violet's already breathing deep and Dani drifts off too. I lie there, curled up among them, and think about the other Earth with its cold light and dark seas. What else is out there? Hopefully problems for alternate Dylans, not Future Dylan.

Future Dylan has enough to worry about.

EPILOGUE

CHATTERBOX: INTO THE MUTANTVERSE

FUTURE DYLAN GETS the first unpleasant surprise the very next day. It's Hazel's friend Airy that brings the problem to our attention. She's scooped a big chunk of alien flesh out of the ocean, which on its own is nothing surprising. There are a lot. We've been trying to intercept them, although a bunch have been retrieved by scientists. More disturbingly, corporations have been out there too, wanting their hundred pounds of alien flesh.

What stands out about this one is the metal plate embedded into it. There are a lot of symbols on it, but some are clearly English letters.

Property of Toroid Multiversal Industries.

Violet pokes around with Google translate. Any known language comes up with roughly similar results, although the name of the company is translated as various different things. The key word is *property*.

"Who the fuck is Toroid Multiversal Industries?" I run my fingers over the embossed metal as if it'll have some clues.

"No idea." Dani runs some searches, but there are no results. "It doesn't make sense that it's on the alien anyway. Aside from it being the plot of Watchmen, we've *seen* the parallel universe. We've met Hadylan. This isn't fake special effects cooked up in some lab."

"Even the gods must serve," I say quietly.

"What?"

"Hadylan said it before they died the first time. I didn't know what it meant, but maybe this isn't a manufacturer's mark. Maybe it's a brand."

Violet's eyes go wide. "You mean—?"

"Someone else is involved, yeah. Who set up this whole alien invasion plan. A third party. These Toroid fucks. *Multiversal.*"

"But why?" Dani's frowning. I remember her worries of last night, and feel the slightly amused tug of *I told you so* down our connection.

"I have no idea. How did we piss off some third version of Earth? And why use the aliens to invade and not come themselves? And—" I break off, because there are too many questions, and the answers are all impossible to find. Without…

"No," Dani says. "Dylan, please."

"We can't sit here." I hold out my hand to her. "Do you really want to do nothing and wait for the next blow to fall?"

Dani's lips are pursed. "Dylan…"

"This is what I am." My voice is hoarse. "I'm the system Cybele made for responding to threats. And this is a big one. I feel it like a shadow falling over me."

I can read her eyes most of the time these days, and right now they only spell worry.

"I hate it, but you're right."

That's all the approval I need. I leap out of my seat and go stalking down towards the stairwell. Two minutes later, I'm banging on a nondescript wooden door.

"Dylan," One Thorn murmurs. "You seem agitated."

"Ding ding ding." I lean against the doorframe. "Thorny, it's time to stop being shy. We need to get multiversal travel up and running. This is the most important thing on your to-do list. We need to be able to open doors into other worlds, and lots of them."

The house rumbles faintly, like an earthquake. "What is this in aid of?"

"Someone's fucking with us." My fist clenches, and dark flowers bloom in ripples along my arm. "We're going to find them, and fuck back. No matter how many Earths we have to visit along the way. It's time to go into the mutantverse."

There's a snort of laughter from behind me.

"I love you," Dani says, "but you are *so* dramatic."

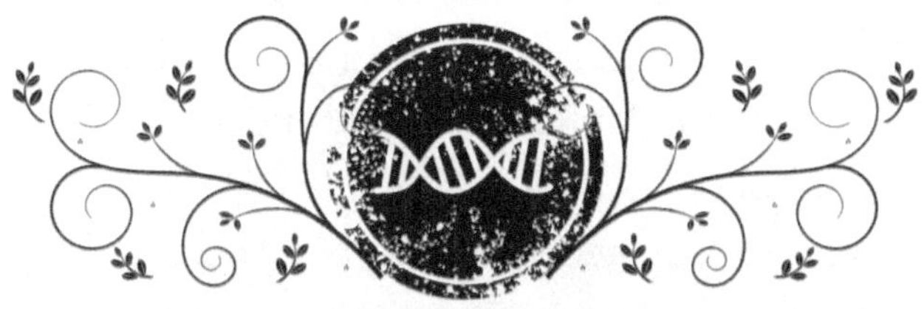

ACKNOWLEDGEMENTS

Here we are again at the beginning of a new series. Except this is launching out of the old one, the Cute Mutants, which changed my life when I released it less than two years ago. There have been a lot of people involved with this experience along the way, and this is the part where I thank them. I seem to do this a lot, the whole *releasing a book* thing, but every time it feels important to say thank you.

Once again, first thanks go to my family, who endure my ongoing obsession with these stories, and support me to follow this dream of mine.

Then there are my beta readers, without who this isn't really possible. These are the people who help turn this book from a madcap idea into a madcap reality that's approaching coherent (and all the incoherence is mine, believe me). Monica read it first and helped me parse the logic of it. Shannon helped me confirm I was on the right track, and made sure my Greek myth and tarot references weren't wildly inaccurate (any errors, as always, are mine). Andee helped me hone in on the emotional core of the story. Melo—best friend and galaxy brained critique partner—helped me to pull the plot into something sharper and more coherent. Then Hsinju, Amanda, and Logan helped shape it into its final unholy form.

Also thanks to amazing authors K. Ancrum, Rosiee Thor, and Claire Winn—you're so supportive and generous with your time, and I appreciate you reading and backing me.

Beyond that, I have a huge support network of people who encourage me to keep this process going. There's a long list of names here, and I'll inevitably forget people **but** thank you always to the feral raccoons in Team Trash (Andy, Crystal, Leah, Mallory, Melo, Michelle, Monica, Nat, Nina, SinJ, and SoftJ). You're always there to help navigate the chaotic world of publishing. And to Rosa, Charlotte, Mary, and E.M., your ongoing support is one of those things I never take for granted.

Extra special thanks go to people like Andy, Andee, Art, and Hsinju, who've sold these books over and over. It's people like you (and so many more) who've turned this into something real. I couldn't have done this without your support.

ABOUT THE AUTHOR

SJ Whitby is a nonbinary author who lives in New Zealand. They write a lot. That's about all you need to know at this point.